Billionaire's Mistress

Complete Series

Table of Contents

Billionaire's Mistress

Book 1

Chapter 1

Allie

Coffee.

There was nothing on earth quite like it. Leaning back against the counter, I focused on the few seconds I had to myself. My step-father was down in the laundry room, probably looking for a clean shirt, and I could hear the shower running upstairs, which meant my mom was running a bit late. The usual banging noises came from my brother's room that told me he was up, which was a miracle. A quick look at the clock told me that if he wasn't down there soon, I'd have to go hurry him along, but for now...coffee.

Humming with appreciation, I savored another sip and sighed.

Few things in life matched a good cup of a strong brew, but coffee was even better in solitude. At least in my opinion. Privacy was in short supply in this house, though, so I had to take it whenever and wherever it offered itself.

At twenty-one, I still lived at home, and while the house wasn't small, it certainly wasn't the kind of place where I could wander around braless in a tank top and panties if I got the munchies in the middle of the night. My parents let me come and go as I wanted, but I still felt more like a child than I did an adult. I couldn't even bring myself to bring guys home even though I could've probably gotten them in and out without anyone noticing. Hell, I could barely allow myself the freedom to get myself off even though I was certain no one would hear me.

One of the reasons for my lack of alone time barged through the door, dragging his backpack in one hand and hitching up his jeans with the other.

TJ, my little brother. Tyson McCormack, Jr. Twelve years-old and thought he could conquer the world.

He signed, "*good morning,*" and I smiled back at him, waggling my fingers in greeting but not forming actual words. Not yet. Right now, coffee was king.

He buried himself in the fridge, most likely looking for the most sugar-filled breakfast he could find. He ate a leftover donut while I finished my coffee. Once I was done and had the appropriate amount of caffeine running through me, I started with the same questions I asked every school day.

"*Are you ready? Books? Homework?*"

He rolled his eyes at me and signed with fluent sarcasm, "*Yes, mother.*"

Making a face at him, I grabbed my coat and pulled it on. He was almost out the door when I caught the back of his shirt and yanked him back. I shoved his coat at him, raising my eyebrow. It was early March, and although that might've meant spring in some places, it wasn't in Philadelphia. The sun was deceptive, and I knew that the wind would be brutal. TJ gave me that look kids his age perfected, but he put the coat on without complaint.

The ten-minute walk to his school would do as much to wake me up as the coffee, although not quite so pleasantly. The moment I stepped outside, I grimaced. I didn't mind the cold in general, but I hated wind like this. I shoved my hands into my pockets and hunched my shoulders, trying to get my coat to warm me up.

TJ tugged a worn baseball out of his pocket and started to toss it up, catch it, and repeat. It was a nervous habit, one he'd inherited from our dad. Well, technically, Tyson was my step-father, but he'd been in my life for fourteen years, and he'd always treated me like his daughter. We weren't close, but I always knew that I could go to him with anything I needed.

After TJ tossed the ball once more, I caught it before he could, waiting for him to look at me. "*Are you okay?*" I asked,

4

signing the words.

He jerked a shoulder in a typical moody response. Without offering anything else, he held up a hand for the ball. Teenagers.

Sighing, I handed it to him, signing again. *"They won't bother you today, TJ,"* I told him, guessing what was on his mind.

He'd been dealing with some bullies at his school, and last week, it'd reached the boiling point when they'd chased him halfway home. Somebody had seen him running and interfered, so he hadn't been hurt, but it'd been enough to make my parents and me worry. It hadn't happened on school grounds so the school's hands were tied, of course. They hadn't bothered to respond to TJ's claims that no one had done anything about the stuff that *had* happened on school grounds. Since they weren't going to do much, we knew we had to handle things ourselves. And by *we*, I meant *me*. Protecting my little brother had always been my self-imposed responsibility.

I continued, *"I'm walking you to school and picking you up. You've got friends sitting with you at lunch, and you don't see them between classes. Pretty soon, those assholes will get tired and give up."*

TJ didn't even crack a smile at the cuss word. It almost always made him laugh. Mom hated it when I cussed around him. TJ heaved out a sigh and started walking again, tossing the ball into the air. I caught up with him and hooked an arm around his neck, hugging him. He hunched a shoulder and made a face, but I caught the faint smile before he elbowed me in the side.

"It could be worse," I signed my words automatically. My mom had started to have hearing issues when I was younger than TJ. By now, it was instinct to sign when I spoke. I had to force myself to remember not to do it with hearing people. *"You could have Mom walking you to school. She'd give you a big sloppy kiss right in front of your friends, and if she saw the kids who've been hassling you, she'd let them have it."*

He clapped a hand to his forehead, and I laughed at his expression. He knew I was right. We both loved our mother, but she was notorious for embarrassing us with physical affection, as well as her overprotective streak. I knew I was the reason she bristled at the smallest implied slight, so I never asked her to back off. TJ didn't know the whole story, so it bothered him more. I knew we'd have to tell him someday, but that was Mom's decision

5

to make, not mine.

He threw the ball at me, and I tossed it back.

It bounced off his fingers, and I swore as it went into the road. TJ went after it, and I swore again, lunging after him as I heard horns honk. Brakes screeched as my baby brother bent over to pick up the ball. I grabbed his arm and yanked him back as the car skidded to a stop. TJ spun around, glaring at me, still unaware of the car that almost hit him.

I started to sign at him, but at the sound of a car door slamming and a raised voice, I stopped. TJ and I were on the side of the road, in between two parallel parked cars and the driver who'd just barely stopped in time was coming toward us, his lined, weary face red with anger – and probably some fear.

"You idiot kid, are you trying to get hit?!" he shouted, his eyes locked on TJ.

I rested a protective hand on my brother's shoulder. I'd been about ready to ask TJ the same question – and I still planned on letting him have it as soon as we were back on the sidewalk – but TJ was my brother. I could call him an idiot. No one else could.

"Hey!" the man shouted again as he came closer. "Are you deaf or something?"

"Actually, yes, he is," I snapped as my temper flared. "So please, keep on shouting. It won't do you much good, though."

The man stopped, embarrassment washing away some of the anger. "Uh…"

"Trust me, I'll make sure he gets yelled at." I signed the words this time, wanting TJ to know that he wasn't getting out of this without any sort of consequence.

TJ looked at me, then swung his head around to look at the driver. People behind the now-parked car were honking their horns, some even shouting obscenities. He signed something at me, but I only caught part of it out of the corner of my eye. My attention was still on the driver. I didn't trust him not to do something stupid.

"I'll talk to him," I said firmly. "I apologize for what happened. He can be careless."

The guy still looked pissed, but he just gave a short nod and stomped back over to his car. I gave TJ a dark look and signed, *"Come on."*

The rest of the walk to school was spent with me lecturing

him. I knew it wasn't going to help him get off to a good start, but he'd almost made himself into a pancake, and I was as much shaken as I was angry. *"You've got to start paying attention,"* I said as we came to a halt right in front of the school.

He didn't respond, and I wondered how much of what I'd been signing had even gotten through to him. His eyes scanned the exterior of the old brick building. I could see the anxiety as clearly as if it was written on his face. My stomach clenched, love and empathy overpowering the negative feelings I had. I knew all too well how it felt to be bullied.

"It's okay, buddy," I told him. *"I'll be back here at the end of the day to get you. You'll be okay."*

He nodded and started forward. As he passed by, he bumped his shoulder against me. The closest I'd get to goodbye. I wanted to say something else, but I knew there wasn't anything I could do to make things better for him. TJ refused to give us the names of the boys so we could speak with their parents. The most I could hope for was that someone who cared would finally see something at school and get involved.

He was almost in the building when I saw a couple of boys nudging each other and pointing toward him. Before they did anything else, a teacher stopped TJ to ask him a question, and the two boys disappeared into a sea of students.

"Bastards," I muttered, shaking my head.

They'd done everything short of shoving him in a locker. Chasing him home had been the final straw, but it never should have gotten that far. The "accidental" bumps in the cafeteria that sent him to the floor, the textbooks that had ended up on the bottom of the gym's swimming pool, his locker vandalized, the word *retard* written on it in big, ugly black letters. The principal had assured me on more than one occasion that they'd tried to find the culprits, but that no one would give names. The last time she'd said it, I'd less-than-politely suggested that maybe the faculty could pay a little more attention and that might give them some idea of who the bullies were.

I was pretty sure the principal wouldn't want to talk to me any time soon.

Blowing out a breath, I turned away from the school and started down the sidewalk. I had about twenty minutes now to get to work. My nose and cheeks were already numb, and I could barely feel my fingers – definitely one of the drawbacks to having to sign when it was cold. Not for the first time, I wished I had a bit of extra money so I could grab a taxi instead of walking.

"I'm so ready for summer," I grumbled.

As I strode down the sidewalk, shoulders hunched against the cold, I thought through the appointments I had for the day. A couple of regulars and a couple of empty slots that I knew would be filled by walk-ins.

Once I was done, I'd be back here to pick my brother up, but tonight I was thinking about going out. I needed something more than just a few minutes alone in the kitchen, enjoying my coffee or a few minutes of freezing my ass off as I hurried to work. It'd been nearly two weeks since I'd been anywhere but work and home, unless I counted my little detour to take TJ to school, and I didn't.

Maybe I'd luck out and get a new client who'd slap me with a sweet tip, and I could splurge on something fun.

That would be nice.

And it was about as unlikely as snow in summer. I might work at one of the most exclusive salons in town, but one thing I'd learned about rich people as a rule: they were some of the most tight-fisted, greedy creatures ever created.

Chapter 2

Jal

"It's a cold one this morning, Mr. Lindstrom."

"It won't kill you to call me Jal," I told Thomas, although I knew I was wasting my breath. I'd had this conversation in one form or another dozens of times over the years. It always went the same way.

"Of course, sir."

Grimacing at my driver, I shoved my hands deep into the pockets of my coat, wishing for a pair of jeans, a sweater, and the battered leather jacket that hung in the back of my closet, safe from the greedy hands of those who might try to donate it to the less fortunate. I didn't have anything against the general idea of donating itself. In fact, I'd given away hundreds of items of clothing over the years. What bothered me was the fact that anything deemed less than satisfactory for a Lindstrom was often relegated to the donation box, and my mother had suggested more than once that my favorite jacket was less than suitable.

As much as I preferred comfort over style, today wasn't the day for it. As I settled in the back of the Bentley, Thomas shut the door, but I didn't get even a moment of peace. My phone buzzed, indicating I missed another call.

Blowing out a breath, I tugged the cell from my pocket.

Mom. Again.

Even though I was more than capable of handling everything I had to get done in the next day or so, my mother kept insisting we meet and go over everything. I was tempted to ignore her, but I knew what would happen if I did. She'd call again, and I could ignore those calls too, then she'd be in a lousy mood at lunch.

I'd just as soon skip lunch as well, but that wasn't going to happen. Overbearing as my mother was, I loved her, and sometimes it was easier to play along with her games.

So we'd go have lunch.

She'd grill me and fuss and hover.

Then I'd go on and do things my way.

We'd both be more or less satisfied.

And my morning would be more peaceful if I got the call out of the way now. At least when I reached my destination, I'd be able to tell her I had to go and be honest about it.

So I called her back.

Her phone only rang twice before she answered. "Hello, Jal," she said, her voice cool and cultured. Everything about my mother was cool and cultured, even when she spoke to me, her only son.

I could play the part too. Harold Lindstrom, Jr. had to be cool and cultured, or at least the world had to see that aspect of him. But my full name was like a suit I put on and took off at will. It was just a mask I wore. It wasn't a part of me. I'd christened myself with a new nickname by the time I was twelve, and refused to answer to anything else. It'd taken my mother almost a year to give in.

She didn't particularly like that I didn't fit into the perfect little WASP boy she'd always wanted. Oh, I had the blond hair so pale it was the color of corn silk. Light blue eyes. Tanned skin. I was tall – six and a half feet – and athletic. Smart. Good looking.

But I still wasn't the child she truly wanted.

She loved me. I didn't doubt that. But love and approval were two totally different things. I doubted I'd ever get the latter from her.

"Are we still on for lunch?" Mom asked, interrupting my maudlin thoughts.

"Of course." I couldn't help but shake my head. It didn't matter that we'd just made the plans twelve hours ago. Ginnifer Lindstrom was a control freak, in the fullest sense of the word. If my dad wasn't so laid back, the two of them probably would have filed for a nasty divorce or killed each other years ago. Instead, he simply gave in and let her do things her own way.

"Excellent." Affection underscored her words as she asked, "Are you nervous?"

Nervous. I thought about it, trying to decide if that was the right word to describe how I felt. I couldn't exactly say I was nervous. Resigned? I guess that was more like it. Nervous implied that I was excited, or that I had doubts about how things might go. I wasn't, and I didn't. I knew exactly what was about to happen. I could almost write out a script for how everything would play out.

I doubted, however, she wanted to hear that I was resigned.

"Perhaps a little," I lied.

"Everything will be fine," she told me in a soothing coo.

"I'm certain it will."

We spoke for a few more minutes, chatting about things that mattered very little to me, but always seem to hold so much importance for her. The latest charity dinner, who was going to be there, why I should attend. If I did, what I should wear, and who I should talk to. The way she made it sound, I was some awkward teenager who was likely to screw up a business deal by smarting off to the wrong person. Not that I had done so well with my trust fund after graduation that Dad had put me in charge of the family money.

When the car slowed, I glanced up and smiled. Thomas had gotten to know my habits after working for me for the past decade, which meant I hadn't needed to tell him to stop at my favorite little coffee shop. He didn't even need me to tell him what my drink of choice was. Once I was alone in the car, I stretched my legs and cracked my neck.

Mom, as if sensing my boredom, shifted topics away from the dinner. "What will you be doing today?"

"Taking a beautiful woman to lunch." I deleted an email from somebody I had no desire to do business with, then shot one to my assistant and told her to make sure he got the message. "Before that, I'm going to stop and get a haircut."

And coffee, although I didn't mention that. I'd been coming to this coffee shop for almost two years, and it'd all started because I'd met the owner at a club and we'd shared a few hot nights twisting up the sheets. That brief flirtation had ended amicably, and she'd moved on to greener – and more interested – pastures. She was the marrying kind. But I liked the atmosphere and the coffee, not to mention the scones and Danishes she made by hand. Plus, she was just fun to talk to. She hadn't treated me differently because of who I was, and I couldn't say that about a lot of my relationships with women. Including my current one. It was satisfying sexually and socially acceptable, but fun?

Hell, no.

I'd never been able to find someone who both intrigued me and met my mother's approval. I'd given up on ever finding that kind of woman, so I was resigned to that too. Resigned to pretty much everything in my life at the moment.

While my mother prattled on, I brooded about that. Spying Thomas from the corner of my eye, I said, "I'll have to cut the call short, Mom. I need to take care of some business this morning. Talk to you soon?"

She said goodbye, and I ended the call, but not because I had to make any more. I just didn't want to listen to any more dull shit about a charity dinner or a party coming up that I really should attend. I loved my parents, and I couldn't lie and say I didn't love having money, but I didn't love the social obligations that came with our family name.

The door opened, and Thomas handed me a cup. I saw that he had one of his own and flashed him a grin. "Finally decided to try the place out for yourself, didn't you?"

He handed me a small bag, smiling – a real smile, not that polite, professional one I usually saw on his face. "I did. I made my wife very happy with the cookies."

"Make sure you try the pie sometime. The woman in there can cook like nothing else."

"I'll do that." He went back around to his side and settled back into the driver's seat, tucking his coffee carefully into place. I'd been nagging him to try the coffee at Sinclair's since I'd discovered it. He'd finally cracked. At least enough to get a cup. No scones, but I wasn't surprised. I'd never had a driver who had relaxed enough to share a scone and coffee.

I'd rather he focused on driving than eating anyway.

"Thomas?"

He started the car, but at the sound of his name, his eyes came to meet mine in the rear view mirror. "Sir?"

"You're a married man."

"Yes, sir. Five years." He looked confused. We'd talked about his wife a bit, but nothing so specific.

"Are you happy?"

He looked a little surprised by the personal question, but he answered easily enough. "Yes, sir. Couldn't imagine not having her in my life."

I shifted my attention to the window but still kept talking. "How long have you known her, your wife? Did you...I guess you knew how you felt when you asked her to marry you, but did you know before that?"

"We've known each other since high school." His voice had softened, and the affection in his voice was clear. I didn't even have to look at him. "I knew the minute I saw her that I wanted to marry her. It just took me a while to convince her." He chuckled fondly. "Like eight years."

I imagined he loved her, or at least he thought he did. Love wasn't something I put much stock in. Not romantic love. Familial, sure. That I understood. I just wasn't sold on the idea of that sort of love. My parents got along well enough, but were they in love? I had no idea. I couldn't see it, my controlling mother and my easy, laid-back father. Affection. Companionship. Lust. Those I all got. The other thing? Not so much.

"Come on, Thomas," I said, shifting gears. "I need to get the haircut taken care of, and I still have some business to deal with before I meet my mother for lunch."

By the time I finished my coffee, Thomas had pulled up in front of the salon a friend had recommended. It was a little fussier than I preferred, one that catered to both men and women, but I'd yet to find one I liked.

Besides, even though the place was nice, it still wasn't exclusive enough for my mother, which meant it was perfect for me.

Chapter 3

Allie

Humming under my breath, I swept up the remnants of hair on the floor from my last haircut. Daisy Caldwell was one of my regulars and one of my favorites. Seventy years old and a transplant from Mississippi, the widow loved jazz, good looking men thirty years her junior, and she had a bawdy sense of humor that matched her sharp tongue.

She also lived to shock her children.

I adored her.

She'd announced that she wanted something that would give her son a heart attack when he descended upon her that weekend. I'd told her she could always get a nose ring, and she'd laughed herself silly. We'd decided on dying the tips of her snow-white hair hot pink. She'd been delighted, and I'd ended up with a thirty-dollar tip.

As I swept the remaining hair into a pile, I tried to picture Daisy's son. I'd met him once when he'd come to pick her up. He was a stiff, cross piece of work, and he thought she spent too much money on her girl time. The arrogance pissed me off. It was Daisy's money. I figured she could have her hair tipped with gold leaf, and it wasn't any of his concern.

My boss, Alistair Hopkins, came bustling over. He was tall and rail thin, bald as a cue ball and his long, thin hands were never still. He made a Pomeranian puppy seem calm.

"You've got an opening?" he asked, his voice low. His soft,

mellow voice didn't suit his thin, stretched out appearance or his overall twitchy personality.

It did suit his secret passion though. He loved to sing, and when we occasionally managed to nag him into going out with us, after a drink or two, we sometimes talked him into karaoke. I looked at paying for his drinks as an investment. When he let off steam, he was relaxed at work for a few days, which made things easier on all of us. Plus, we got to listen to him sing.

He was that good.

"Yes." Shooting him a sly smile, I finished dealing with the last of the hair and leaned on my broom. "You have some new song you want to wow me with? I'm your captive audience."

He flushed and looked around. "Hush, Allie. No, we have a client. Very important. If you do a good job, we might be able to convince him to become a regular patron."

Wow. That sounded good, especially if the guy committed to the same stylist every time. I could use another good regular.

Sliding my eyes to the front door, I saw a man standing there and actually recognized him. I'd seen him a few minutes ago as I'd walked Daisy to the door. He'd climbed out of a sleek, shiny car that was worth more than I made in several years. He was...well, hot seemed like an understatement. Beautiful and sleek and sexy, a perfect match to the car. And he was loaded. Even guys who had nice six-figure jobs didn't ride around Philly in the back of a car like that. That was treatment reserved for the ultra-rich.

I glanced back at my boss and tried to pretend that the man at the door wasn't the sexiest guy I'd seen in years. "Let me finish straightening up. Can you stall maybe five minutes?"

"Just hurry." He made shooing motions with his hands, and I rolled my eyes, as I turned away, moving to the small closet where I kept the dustpan. By the time I had my station straightened, Alistair had the man seated up front, a cup of coffee in hand, along with one of the buttery croissants we had delivered every morning from a bakery a friend of mine owned. As I adjusted the black tunic I wore as part of my uniform, I gave myself a moment to admire my new customer one last time since once I approached him, it would be all professional.

He looked like something out of Norse Mythology, tall and blond and perfect, from the flawless hair to the dent in his chin.

Strong shoulders lay underneath a sport coat that fit him to perfection. That kind of fit only came from an excellent tailor. Damn. He was pretty.

But nobody knew better than I did just how little a pretty surface meant.

A pretty surface usually hid a vapid, arrogant soul, and that was one road I had no interest in traveling. Men with money held no appeal for me.

Reminding myself of that made it easier to walk up to the sitting area, a polite smile on my face. I addressed my boss first, "Alistair." I turned to the stranger next. "I'm ready for you, Mr...?"

As I turned my eyes to his, the man came to his feet, a smile crinkling up the corner of his eyes. Blue. As in a perfect shade of light blue that I suspected could turn into a million different shades based on his emotions. It figured. He was like the living, breathing embodiment of what so many saw as the perfect, all-American dreamboat. If that kind of thing appealed. As the smile deepened, I felt my heart kick up a few beats. Apparently, I found that kind of thing appealing.

"Lindstrom. Jal Lindstrom." He held out a hand. "Call me Jal, please."

I smiled politely and stepped aside, gesturing to my station in lieu of shaking his hand. "Nice to meet you, Mr. Lindstrom. If you'll just follow me?"

I didn't see it as a rebuff. I preferred to keep certain barriers in place and that's just all there was to it. He either didn't notice or he didn't seem to mind, moving forward to walk with me to my station.

"Why don't I take your overcoat and sports coat?" I asked as I stopped next to the chair.

"Anything else you'd like me to take off?" The flirtatious lilt in his voice was playful, nothing I hadn't heard before.

I was pretty, and I knew it, a nice mix of DNA from a black mother and white biological father, my skin a warm, soft brown that complimented my dark brown hair and pale green eyes. I had a rack that had been a pain in the butt ever since middle school, and a figure that required I stay active if I didn't want it to go from curvy to plump. I walked a lot and loved to swim, so that was never an issue.

In short, I was used to men flirting with me, and I knew how to sidestep it. "I think that will do the job, Mr. Lindstrom."

"Jal," he said, lifting a brow. "Mr. Lindstrom is my father."

It was an odd name, but I didn't ask about it. Instead, I just gave him a smile that was neither assent nor dissent. I'd avoid a name altogether.

After he turned over the coat and sport coat, I hung them up on the ornate – and ugly – coat tree next to my station. At least, I thought it was ugly. FOCUS, the salon/spa where I worked had been designed in what Alistair called minimalism, so most of the fixture was little more than sticks with pegs sticking out of chrome so shiny I could see my face. When I'd first started working here, it had been art deco, which I thought was much prettier than this stark white and silver. Once I turned back to Jal Lindstrom, I had my smile firmly in place and gestured for him to follow me once more.

Services here were top notch. All shampoos came with a head massage along with manicures and pedicures with hand and feet massages. I had a flash of this man requesting a manicure like plenty of other men did. None of the guys I hung out with would, but they were a world away from the clients that came through these doors. My mind did a weird little stutter as I thought about holding this man's hands in mine, rubbing his fingers and palms...

A familiar sort of tension settled in my gut, and I shoved the image away, indicating for him to sit down.

"Far be it from me to argue with a lady," he murmured as I folded a towel around his neck, covering it with a black protective cape. His skin was warm when I fastened it at the nape of his neck. I pulled my hands away and told him to close his eyes and relax.

He really was a flirt. Now that his eyes were closed, I let myself look a little, my gaze lingering on the lowered fringe of his lashes before slipping down to study his straight nose, his mouth. Perfect lips. Not too thick or too thin. He'd be a good kisser, I bet. Very good.

Hot water pumped into the sink as I began to soap his hair. "Is the temperature fine?"

"Perfect." The low pulse of his voice had me glancing down, half expecting to find him staring at my chest. He wouldn't be the first guy to take advantage of the situation.

But his eyes were still closed. I had to admit, it impressed me. Relaxing a little more, I set about washing his hair. By the time I'd started the massage, I'd settled into a rhythm. It helped that he hadn't made any more pseudo-flirtatious comments. With the sound of the water, the familiar smell of the salon shampoo, I was able to slip into the rhythm of the way my hands always moved through hair, strong and sure, no hesitation.

"If you could keep that up for the next two hours, I'd be just fine with that."

His voice was even lower now. Sliding my eyes down, I saw that he'd opened his. And he was staring straight up at me. At me, not my chest.

"I'm afraid a two-hour head massage isn't on the menu." I gave him a tight smile, thankful that I managed to keep my voice even and polite.

His eyes closed once more as I moved to a conditioning treatment, then wrapped a warm towel around his head.

"You've got magic hands," he said, following me this time as I led him to the chair.

"So I've been told." I kept my tone easy as I looked up at him. Damn, he was tall. After I had him sitting down, I removed the wet towel and snapped a dry cape around him. "What are we doing today, Mr. Lindstrom?"

"I take it I'm not going to get you to call me Jal." There was amusement in his eyes as he met my gaze in the mirror.

"How about you worry less about that and tell me what you want for your haircut. I heard that you were in a time crunch." Lifting my eyebrow, I dragged my fingers through his thick hair and watched it fall back into place. "You've got good hair. Healthy. What do you do with it?"

"Comb it." The short, succinct answer made me smile.

"So no styling products? Does that mean you just want to keep something similar to the style you have now?" I met his eyes for a moment. "Do you just want a trim, and maybe shape it up a bit?"

"You're the professional…Allie, right? I'm in your capable…magic hands."

His eyes stayed on me as he settled into the chair, and I had to fight the urge not to squirm. I was used to flirtation, but not this sort of intense scrutiny. I'd heard the sentiment of someone's gaze

18

feeling like a caress, but I'd never experienced it until now.

Forcing myself to focus on the job at hand, I reached for my shears and a comb. "Well, let's just see what we can come up with, since you're putting yourself in my hands."

He smiled, and my stomach twisted a bit.

Dammit.

Chapter 4

Jal

Her eyes were nothing short of amazing.

Almost as amazing as her hands. I hadn't been kidding when I told her I would have been perfectly happy if she'd just kept on doing what she'd been doing for another couple of hours. It had been relaxing. Not that kind of relaxing that made me want to sleep, just…relaxing. Like all of my worries had simply melted away.

But now that I was sitting in the chair and her hands were no longer working away tension I hadn't known I'd been carrying, my brain was back to working overtime.

Her eyes.

That mouth.

Yeah…that mouth, distracting in oh, so many ways. Not only was it just about perfect, lush and wide and soft, but she hadn't given me any of the simpering deference I was used to. She wasn't impressed with me. I dealt with it a little too often to not know when somebody was trying to suck up.

I had to admit, it was nice. While she was sticking with the usual Sir and Mr. Lindstrom, something told me that if she wasn't here at work, if she'd met me out on the street, she wouldn't have had a problem using only my first name.

I had a feeling the easy way she'd brushed away my teasing would've gone out the window too. She seemed like the sort of woman who would've told me to go fuck myself but said it with a smile.

The scissors moved around my head, and I closed my eyes as they came toward them.

"How long have you worked here?" I asked. I didn't so much as care about the answer, but I wanted to hear her voice. It was on the low end for a woman, but the sort of tone that felt like something warm and sweet coating my skin.

My fingers twitched, and I willed myself not to get hard.

"A few years."

"Do you like it?" Her hands brushed across my forehead, and I wondered what it would feel like to feel her hands sliding lower, cupping my cheeks as I kissed her.

It was a dumb thought. Really stupid. I was...involved, and this girl wasn't like the women I took to bed for random flings.

"It's a good job," she was saying, reminding me that I'd asked her a question. About her job. Because I liked hearing her talk.

"I guess you meet some interesting people."

The smirk that crossed her face was gone so fast, if I hadn't opened my eyes just then, I would have missed it. Her face folded back into that polite, professional mask. She wore one too. I wondered if she put hers off and on as easily as I did. And why. That curiosity right there made me want to talk to her more, ask her more questions, of a different sort. Nothing that had to do with inane bullshit like whether or not she found her job stimulating, either. But real questions. Ones that would tell me more about the type of woman she was.

My phone buzzed in my back pocket, reminding me of who I was, what I was. I had business to attend to, and none of it had anything to do with a pretty little hairdresser.

The urge to ask her to join me for coffee was stronger than I liked, so I lapsed into silence, and she didn't try to coax me out of it. One thing most stylists had a knack for was knowing when to talk and when not to. She didn't speak until she finished and pulled off the cloth covering me.

"Sonya can give you my card if you decide you'd like to come back. I'm here nine to two-thirty Mondays through Fridays and on Saturdays from nine until noon." She walked over to where she'd hung my things and picked them up.

"And where are you the rest of the time? With your

boyfriend? Husband?" I slid her a look as I accepted the coat and overcoat. I put my jacket on but hung my coat over my arm as I pulled out my wallet.

Light glinted in her eyes, amusement mixed with minor annoyance. A look I didn't get too often. It made me want to jab at her again, just to draw it out. See if I could get her to let down her guard. As I offered my card to the woman behind the counter, I glanced down at my overcoat. I had something tucked inside the pocket that I couldn't leave behind. It needed to go with me to New York later.

"I'm doing the sort of things a woman typically does when she isn't working, Mr. Lindstrom." Her lips curved and once more, I found myself thinking about kissing that pretty mouth.

Licking at the seam, pushing my way past the barrier of her lips, tasting her. She'd be sweet and hot, and she wouldn't wait for me to guide her, either. I knew it instinctively. She was too cocky, too confident. I was willing to bet she could actually be my match.

Moving a little closer, I said, "I have to admit, I'm curious about just what those things are, Allie."

I held out a hand, wondering if she'd accept it this time.

She did. Her grip was firm and warm, but it didn't linger.

"Thanks for the haircut, Allie."

I took my card back from Sonya and dipped my head a little closer to Allie's, close enough that I could smell a different scent of shampoo. "Have a good day."

Without waiting for a response, I turned and strode out the door.

It was bitterly cold, even more so without my overcoat, but if I hadn't left it on the chair inside, I wouldn't have a reason to get back in touch with her again.

"Sir, your coat?" Thomas said, glancing back to the storefront of the salon. "Would you like me to go get it?"

"It's fine, Thomas. Let's go."

The tension that had melted away under Allie's hands was back full strength and then some. Mom had already called. Again. She'd been the one to call while I was getting my hair cut, and I knew she wouldn't be happy that I hadn't called her back.

I didn't plan to either. Whatever it was could wait until she had me trapped in front of her for however long our meal took. I really did love my mom – I reminded myself of that several times a day – but my patience with her need to micromanage my life was getting thin. I was already doing a shitload of stuff I didn't want just to please her and my dad. Mostly her. She didn't need to take over every minute.

"How long will it take to get to the restaurant, Thomas?" I rubbed my temples, then remembered what it had felt like to have other fingers on me, and I stopped.

"About thirty minutes, sir. Traffic is pretty light."

"Good. We've got an hour yet. Let's go down to the river." I was going to freeze my ass off, but I needed to clear my head again.

The weather worked.

The cold wind blowing off the water cleared my head and froze my blood. I was almost positive that my balls had pretty much retreated all the way up inside my body and might take an entire month to thaw out. The sun shone down bright and clear, but didn't offer much heat. Still, I didn't retreat back into the car.

Thomas stood next to me, his hands tucked into the pockets of a serviceable green overcoat, part of the uniform, a pair of sunglasses shielding his eyes.

"You don't have to stand out here and freeze with me," I told him.

"I like the river myself, Mr. Lindstrom." He lifted a shoulder in a half-shrug.

We both lapsed back into silence, and I didn't do much of anything but brood. First, over seeing my mother, then the flight to New York...and what would happen after that.

"What time is it?" Thomas told me and I blew out a sigh, my breath frosting the air. "I guess we need to go, or I'll be late. Heaven forbid." The last came out in a sardonic drawl.

I had a feeling that Thomas wanted to smirk, but he didn't. He was far too professional for that.

I sighed. "All right. Let's get this over with. It's going to be a long couple days, and I just want to get it all over with."

As far as I was concerned, the lunch with my mom would be a nightmare, but I knew if I tried to put it off, she'd do something crazy like show up in New York. Just the thought of that made me shiver.

Chapter 5

Allie

"Man, he's hot." Sonya leaned against the counter, staring after my client as he walked out the door.

I had a few minutes to spare before I had to get back to work, so it didn't surprise me that my co-worker wanted to chat. My next appointment was currently finishing up her facial and would be done shortly, ready for the haircut and style she absolutely had to get done today, thanks to a last minute invitation to a very important social event. I always found it amusing that she always had these "very important" last minute invitations.

Thanks to the empty lobby, Alistair joined us to put in his own two cents. "Oh, yes. Very hot. And straight."

Sonya and I snickered at the annoyance in the last two words. Giving my boss a sober look, I said, "Yeah. All the good looking ones are straight or taken."

"It's not funny." He sniffed imperiously. "The good gay ones are taken, or they just aren't ready to commit. You'd think it was a dirty word."

"For some, it is." I shrugged. He wasn't telling me anything I didn't know. Personally, I thought love was overrated. My mother had loved my biological father, and he'd broken her heart over and over. It'd taken her years to find a happy place with Tyson. I was just fine keeping my relationships light and easy.

I started to push a few loose strands of hair back from my face and saw the bills in my hand. Alistair frowned over us counting our tips in the public area of the salon, so I shoved the money into my pocket along with the tip from Daisy, then went around the counter to double-check my schedule.

"Don't tell us you didn't think he was hot." Sonya gave me a skeptical look.

"Oh, he was plenty hot." I shrugged as I studied the monitor. My next appointment and then after that, another haircut. Then I was done. I wouldn't even have to rush to get to school in time to get TJ. That was good. Despite the chill, I could appreciate a nice slow walk.

The door opened and Alistair snapped to attention, all business and ass-kissing now. I couldn't really make fun of him for it. He was good at it. I nodded at Sonya and moved back to my station in time to see one of the other stylists coming in from the back.

Time to get back to work…

At the end of the day, I was so done. My last appointment had been one that usually went to Sandy, another of my co-workers, but she was off today, and Alistair had put the Philadelphia high society princess with me. It was probably because he knew she was likely to end up going off, and I was the one employee most likely to keep my temper.

And she did go off.

The woman had been impossible to please, and she'd practically shrieked when a four-inch lock of hair had fallen into her lap.

She'd given me a picture of a hairstyle, which required losing some length, I'd explained. She'd insisted I knew nothing about hair, and then Alistair had stepped in to soothe her, promising I was one of his best stylists, that I'd make her shine even more than she already did.

He really knew how to lay it on thick when he had to.

Her hair turned out perfect, even better than the picture, but

26

she'd still sniffed disdainfully and gave me a, "It will do."

Then she'd left a dollar bill on the counter.

I'd picked it up and given a little curtsey. "Oh, thank you. I can buy a soda pop now."

My sardonic humor had been lost on her, but not Alistair. He'd stood in his position in the back, shaking his head, his mouth tight.

I'd get it for that one, no doubt, but I hadn't minded. It'd been worth it.

Sure enough, right before I walked out, he reminded me in polite but firm terms that he had the best salon/spa in the city and paid his employees accordingly. That meant we sometimes had to put up with the eccentricities of our patrons. In other words, we had to deal with their rudeness and bullshit. With a smile.

I'd nodded, agreed, and left.

We both knew it would happen again, and unless it was really blatant, he wouldn't fire me. I was too good at my job. Also, I was smart enough to save my sharp tongue for those who were too vapid to pick up on the sly insults. I pretended to be contrite, and we were both happy enough with it as I headed out the door. I was one of his best, and I was the most unflappable person in there. The insults hurled by the snottier patrons wouldn't put me in tears, and if I was given a one-dollar tip by some snide piece of work, I knew I'd make up for it with somebody else, like Daisy.

It was a workable arrangement, but today, it all put me back on edge.

I had to pick up TJ, and by the time I left, my head was pounding. I might've had enough self-control to keep my temper, but it didn't mean the things people did and said to me didn't affect me. Sometimes I wondered if I really did want a job, but I never let myself push it past that wondering phase. It wasn't like a hundred jobs were lying around that paid this well or offered the flexible hours I needed.

In other words, just like all other aspects of my life, I was stuck.

And that was the thought that bounced in my head the entire way to my brother's school. Over and over it played, all the ways I could never get out of the life I was in. Most of the time, I didn't even think it. I loved my family. I more or less liked my job. But there were times when certain things hit me. This was one of those times.

TJ was just coming out the door when I got to his school. I smiled at him and asked how his day was.

His only response was a shrug. It was hard to tell if that was a good thing or a bad one, but I remembered what it was like to be in middle school. It'd kind of sucked for me, and the bullies I'd had to deal with had been nothing compared to the assholes who went after TJ.

As we started down the sidewalk, I caught sight of some familiar faces. One of them opened his mouth before he saw me. He snapped it shut, shifting his features into a casual smile. Not buying it, pal. Giving him a narrow-eyed glare, I lifted my chin and stared him down. His face flushed a dull red, and he jabbed his friend in the side. They both turned, slinking away.

Cowards. I didn't care that they were only kids. They were old enough to know better, and that was what mattered.

"They take one look at you and take off," TJ signed, shaking his head. *"You gotta show me how to do that."*

"TJ, my man, it won't work," I said. *"That's a special trick unique to women, especially effective on the bullying type and the small-minded. But you don't have the equipment to do it, even if you did have the right temperament."*

He snorted when he laughed like he always did, and it was enough to make me smile. Like always. I gave his head a playful shove. He was nine years younger than me, but we were close. We didn't really look anything alike since he looked more like his father with his darker skin and similar features. I was more of a combination of my mom and asshole sperm donor, which meant TJ and I shared very little in the way of a physical resemblance. None of that mattered to us though. Our relationship had never been awkward or weird. It was easy. Sure, we got on each other's nerves sometimes, but it was never for long.

"Okay, man. Let's get you back home. I want some ice cream."

His face lit up as if I had said the magic words. I guess in a way I had. He didn't have much of a sweet tooth, but he did like his ice cream.

It took another hour and a half for me to get any time to myself. Mom and Tyson were at home when we got in. Naturally, they asked how school had gone and TJ had launched into a description of how I'd made the two ringleaders of the bullies take off with their tales tucked between their legs.

That resulted in me being questioned since, of course, I was supposed to take the high road and ignore them. I was only supposed to walk with TJ and make sure nobody bothered him. Since I'd engaged with the bullies, I ended up getting a twenty-minute lecture that made me wish I'd really done something worth it.

Naturally, neither of them were mad at me. They were just concerned that this might result in the bullies further antagonizing TJ.

I disagreed. When they had to turn tail and run from a girl, it'd taken some the wind out of their sails, given TJ a little more confidence. But I didn't say any of that. What the hell did I know about raising a teenager? I had been one only a few years ago.

Since nothing they said would change my opinion and nothing I said would change theirs, there was no point in arguing. Not even if I was getting taken to task like I was fourteen years old and they'd caught me sneaking out the window of my bedroom, but still...

When they finally finished, I headed up to my room. Halfway up the stairs, the house phone started to ring. I'd hesitated for a minute before continuing on up to my room. The light would flash if it was a TTY call. If it was for me, they could call my cell phone.

I just didn't feel like talking to anyone else today, and I knew that's what would happen if I answered that call. After all, my parents couldn't hear who was on the regular phone, and I would have to explain that to a stranger, and I was just tired of doing it. Sometimes, I felt like I was suffocating.

Once inside my room, I fell face first down on the bed, arms spread out. I was itchy under my shirt. I should have gone straight into the shower to get off all the stray hair that managed to work its way into my clothes, but I was too tired to move.

There was a knock at my door, and a second later, it opened. That one knock was all the warning I'd get since I hadn't remembered to lock it. That'd always been the way with my mom and me. Flopping onto my back, I opened one eye. Mom stood there, studying me.

"Are you okay?"

I smiled back at her. *"I'm fine."* Unlike Tyson and TJ, Mom had lost her hearing gradually, but since marrying Tyson, she'd stopped speaking out loud to me and only signed.

"Really?"

I sighed. *"I had a long day, Mom. I just want to have some time to myself, some time to relax."*

There was no response at first, then she finally nodded and asked if she could come in. With a shrug, I nodded and patted my bed.

"We appreciate what you're doing for TJ. You know that, don't you?"

"Of course I do. He's my little brother, and I love him. It pisses me off that some boys are teasing him."

Now guilt chewed at me. She thought I was sulking over walking my little brother to school. It had nothing to do with TJ. But how could I explain to my mother that I was just…the thought withered away and died before I finished forming it. Again, guilt. I didn't blame my family for any of my choices. They'd never pressured me into anything. I was good at doing that to myself.

Mom looked like she wanted to say more, but there was a reluctance to her features.

"Spill it, Mom."

She laughed softly. The sound managed to bring a smile to my lips, reminding me of the times when we'd still talked to each other. I missed hearing her voice. Once she and Tyson had started dating, she'd found a world where she felt more comfortable. I didn't blame her for that.

I knew what it felt like to not fit in, so I couldn't begrudge her that.

Guilt seemed to chase after me these days.

Averting my gaze, I focused on a framed print of the river at night. Mom moved to sit by me, brushing my hair back.

"I love you," she said, her voice soft. It was as if she'd known I needed to hear her voice. That voice, still so beautiful after all these years.

"I love you too." I didn't sign it this time. She could read lips, and she'd know what I said anyway. Leaning in, I hugged her.

She left a moment later and this time, I locked the door. I told myself I was going to shower and maybe read. Something. Anything to get out of my head. As I reached down to pull off my tunic, I felt something in my pocket. I frowned as I tugged out the tips I'd gotten that day.

The money from Daisy, the whopping one-dollar bill from the snooty princess and then there was whatever Jal had given me. I hadn't bothered to count any of it. I started to unfold that bill, expecting to find a five or ten, maybe twenty. He'd gotten a simple haircut, and I rarely got anything staggering for something so simple.

The hundred-dollar bill fell from my numb fingers, and I could only gape at it.

One hundred dollars. For tip on a haircut. "Son of a bitch."

What the hell had he been thinking?

Four hours later, I was laying on my back, staring up at the ceiling while my best friend fastened a pair of leopard-print handcuffs to his headboard.

There was nothing that cleared my head and settled me quicker than hard, fast sex. Since I wasn't involved with anybody, my options for sex were narrowed down to a one-night stand or Tao Maki, who'd graduated from the friendzone to friend-with-benefits when we were eighteen. It worked well for both of us. We were great as friends, but wanted different things from romantic relationships, so we knew we'd never fall in love. We cared about each other but didn't have the petty jealousies that would keep us from remaining friends when either one of us found true love.

Or, more accurately, when Tao found true love.

I didn't believe in it.

When I'd called Tao and told him I needed to clear my head, he'd only asked, "What do you have in mind."

I'd smiled into the phone. "Anything you want."

He laughed. "Anything? So the sky's the limit?"

I'd had to give him some boundary lines there.

Tao was a kinky bastard, and while normally that played in my favor, there were some things I wasn't into. The handcuffs he was currently using to keep my arms stretched above my head were something I did enjoy.

"You know, if you really want to get down and dirty, I can call a friend," he said as his hand cupped one of my breasts, teased my nipple into a hard point with his talented fingers.

I glared at him.

Or, rather, I attempted to look like I was annoyed when, in reality, I was struggling not to moan as he lowered his head to take my nipple into his mouth.

While sex with Tao was hot and fun, I had no interest in making it a threesome. It was funny that the person who believed in true love wasn't so sure about monogamy, while I wasn't into anything that wasn't one-on-one, but I didn't factor love into the equation.

"In your dreams, you pervert," I managed to gasp out.

Tao raised his head. "In his dreams too, baby doll. See, this friend. We used to hook up…and he is hung, let me tell you."

Tao was bi, or more accurately, over the past couple years, he identified himself as pansexual and polyamorous. Basically, monogamy and sticking with one gender wasn't his thing. I was fine with it, always had been, but that didn't mean I was going to join him in it. He knew it, but he still liked teasing me.

And I couldn't deny that hearing about it sometimes made me hot.

"You wish."

He sighed lustily as his fingers slid up my legs to my hips. "Guilty as charged. He's seen us around, and he just wants to play." His sapphire eyes ran down my body and back up again. "I mean, can you blame him?"

I gave him my own once-over. Tao had the jet-black hair and golden skin he'd inherited from his half-Chinese mother, combined with a tall, lean body, and those brilliant eyes courtesy of his Scandinavian grandmother, and whatever ethnicity his father had been. He was gorgeous, and had the confidence to pull it off.

Sometimes I wished the two of us could fall in love. It would've made things so much easier.

"Then you two have fun, baby doll," I said. "Later. Right now, I just want to get off."

Tao chuckled as he swung one leg over my waist, putting his impressive cock right into my line of sight. I licked my lips, the action practically involuntary. I liked giving head, liked the feel of him sliding across my tongue. Most of all, I loved the sight and sound of him losing control and knowing it was because of me.

He moved down my body, letting his cock brush across my skin as he settled himself between my legs. I made an impatient sound and he laughed again. Tao could make things last, take things slow, but we rarely did that. We weren't about making love.

We fucked.

That didn't, however, mean that he skipped the foreplay.

I closed my eyes as the tip of one long finger brushed over my clit, then further down between my folds. I spread my legs wider, and he took the hint. I shivered as he slid his finger inside me. After two strokes, he added a second one, twisting and curling them as he moved them in and out. His thumb moved over my clit in the way he knew I liked, and I raised my hips, wanting more.

My eyes flew open when I felt another finger moving between my cheeks. His eyes locked with mine as the tip of his index finger rubbed over my anus. We didn't do anal sex, but Tao did sometimes use his fingers on me. I wasn't at the point where I asked him to do it, but I couldn't deny that it did sometimes make things more intense.

And considering that what I wanted more than anything at the moment was to not think, intense was what I needed. I nodded, then gasped as his finger breached the tight ring of muscle. He kept it in only up to the first knuckle, twisting it as his other hand drove me into my first climax of the night.

"Yes," I hissed as I came. I let the pleasure wash over me as Tao put on a condom.

"Turn over."

I rolled, letting the handcuffs twist so that my wrists were crossed, limiting my movement even more. Tao's hands moved under my hips, pulling my ass up, and then he was pushing into me. I moaned, moving back against him so that he filled me with one thrust. He wrapped one hand in my hair, giving it a little tug as he steadied himself.

I closed my eyes and gave myself over to the sensations running through my body. The little darts of pain at my scalp. The full, then empty feelings that alternated with every thrust of his cock. The way the thick shaft stretched me, rubbed against me. My clit throbbed, desperate for attention, but all I could do was curl my hands into fists and let him ride me, trusting him to get me where I needed to go.

The build-up was fast and hot, a tight coiling in my stomach that released the moment he pushed his thumb into my ass.

Relief flooded me along with the pleasure, melting away the tension and everything else along with it.

Exactly what I'd needed.

Twenty minutes later, I was cleaned up, my hands free, and Tao was wrapped around me from behind. I snuggled in closer, sighing with satisfaction.

I loved my home, but there were times that Tao's little apartment was a wonderful escape. Sometimes I felt like we shared those two parts of our lives. He sometimes shared his place with me when I needed some time away...and some stress relief. And I shared my family with him.

He'd come out as bisexual when he was fifteen and wanted to go on a date with a boy in our class. His devout Jehovah Witness parents' had given him a choice: aversion therapy or being disowned.

He'd walked out of the house and knocked on my door that same night. He'd lived with us for the next three years, working any odd job he could find to earn enough money to rent his own apartment once he'd turned eighteen.

He turned his face into my hair and nuzzled me, his breath hot against my ear. "Wanna spend the night?"

"Man, do I ever..." I groaned, wishing I could. Tao knew better than anyone how to make me forget all of the things I had on my mind. "But I've gotta walk TJ to school, and if I stay, I'll have to get up that much earlier."

"He still got those kids messing with him?" Tao's usually friendly expression hardened.

He'd always been likable in school, but when he'd held his first boyfriend's hand in the hallway, he'd put up with his fair share of shit. Until one of his soccer teammates had knocked the teeth out of some homophobic bastard and threatened the health of anyone else who dared to come after Tao or anyone else again. It'd worked.

"You oughta teach him some of that Kung Fu bullshit." I poked him in his side as I teased.

"Yeah. Like I know Kung Fu from lo mein."

Drawing my head back, I gave him a look of mock disappointment. "Man, what good are you?"

Tao flipped me over onto my back, his eyes dark. He scraped his teeth over my nipple, his fingers pinching the other one so that I whimpered. Then, in one hard thrust, he buried his cock inside me. "How about I show you one of the many things I'm good for?"

My eyes rolled back in my head as he set a brutal pace, each thrust hard enough to drive the air from my lungs. I dug my nails into his shoulders and held on for the ride. I would be sore in the morning – hell, I'd be sore on the way home – but right now, he was doing exactly what I needed.

Fucking me into the mindless oblivion I craved.

Chapter 6

Allie

Irritated with myself, I stood at my station and rearranged all my tools. Again. The first person I'd thought about when I got into work was Jal.

Actually, he'd been the first person I'd thought about that morning.

The last person I'd thought about last night, despite Tao's skills. I'd come four times but still hadn't been able to get Jal out of my head.

I wanted to think it was because of that ludicrous tip, but I knew better. Those blue eyes and that sexy smile, even his silly flirtation, all of it had gotten to me.

He's a rich, arrogant white man. I knew I should be smarter than that.

And really, my brain was smarter. It was my libido that wasn't. I'd ended up dreaming about him, the kind of dreams I really shouldn't have had after twisting up the sheets with Tao for a couple of hours. All of that lust should've been sated by now, but just the thought of Jal was enough to make my stomach tighten and arousal flare hot and bright inside me.

"Allie!" Alistair's voice tugged me out of my reverie, and I came to a stop, turning to face him. He came rushing up to me, his face tight, eyes bright, almost wild.

For one frightening moment, I thought something had happened to someone in my family. My mind flashed to TJ being chased by those bullies.

"What is it?"

He caught my hands. "Is there anybody who can pick your brother up for you after school? This is an emergency!"

Relief flooded through me. Not my family. Anything else was minor.

Rolling my eyes, I tugged my hands free and shrugged. "If it's a real emergency, sure. But your idea of an emergency and my idea of an emergency are two very different things, Alistair. I consider an emergency something that has to do with life, death, bodily harm, evisceration, a friend's family member in the hospital..." I waved a hand in the air. "You? Your idea of an emergency is some Philly princess whining because she chipped a nail, and she might carry on at her next soiree that you did a subpar job."

"Oh, hush." He glared at me. "I wouldn't consider that an emergency. A pain in the ass, yes. And she might consider it an emergency." He shook his head. "Not the point. Look, I'd do it myself, but he specifically requested you, and when I tried to explain you had commitments...well, you know how some of our clients are..." He flapped his hands uselessly in the air, looking distraught.

Sighing, I propped my fist on my hip as he came around to face me. "Just what is the emergency and what's in it for me?"

"Money," he blurted out. "Of course. For both of us. And word-of-mouth if we're lucky. He's offered a thousand-dollar cash bonus for you, and he's told me he'll be switching his services here, which is all the incentive I need."

Did he say one thousand dollars?

"Okay," I said, after clearing my throat so I could talk, "that explains why you're so eager for me to do whatever this is, but what's the emergency?" I narrowed my eyes, already suspicious that I knew who we were talking about.

"It was your walk-in from yesterday. Jal Lindstrom."

"Oh, no." Shaking my head, I lifted my hands. I had a feeling that guy had been up to something. So intent on not doing whatever it was that Jal had up his sleeve, I didn't even see the box until Alistair shoved it under my nose.

"He left it. He has to have it – *this weekend*."

At the half-mad look in Alistair's eyes, I slowly reached up and took the jewelry box, flipping it open. I couldn't help the gasp that spilled out of me even though I'd already known what was in the box. Light hit the stone, fracturing out as the diamond reflected it back in a million sparkling splinters. "Wow. That's some rock," I said. "Where was it?"

Alistair took the box back, like he wouldn't trust me until he knew I'd do it. "He left it in his overcoat, then left the coat here by accident. He was on his way to the airport when he realized it. He's proposing to her *this* weekend – everything is set up, and he forgot the ring."

Something tugged in my heart. I told myself it was pity for some poor girl who didn't merit enough attention from her soon-to-be fiancé for him to keep up with her ring. Especially since I knew he'd been holding his coat when he was at the cash register.

It couldn't have been any other reason.

"He must really be into her for him to leave the ring here," I muttered. Turning away from Alistair, I moved to my station. "What does any of this have to do with me?"

"He wants you to take it to him. He's already booked a flight, first class."

Gaping, I turned to stare at him. "He what? He can't do that."

"He did. I guess money talks. There's a ride on the way, and a ticket waiting for you." Alistair did that nervous thing with his hands again. "Please, Allie...I can't call one of the richest, most influential men in the city and tell him that we can't help him out on this. It could ruin me. One bad word from him..."

Well, shit.

Here came the guilt again.

Sighing, I rubbed at my forehead. Yet again, that weird feeling of being trapped and pushed and forced in directions I didn't want to go crowded in on me.

Stop it. It's your own doing, I told myself. I didn't have to stay home. I chose to. I didn't have to do this favor. If I did, it was because I wanted the money...

Not because I wanted to see him again.

"Fine. I'll do it. As long as Tao can pick up TJ." I held out my hand. "Give me the damn ring."

Naturally, Tao was happy to help. I was actually a little annoyed that he couldn't be difficult for once in our relationship and say no when I asked him for a favor. I could've told Alistair to let Mr. Lindstrom know that I had a younger brother to look after, and it would've been the truth. I wouldn't have had to feel guilty for sending someone else in my place to deliver the ring. I was sure Sonya would've been only too happy to fly to New York.

But no.

Tao had to be his usual agreeable self and tell me to enjoy a day off where I'd earn far more than I ever could if I stayed at the salon.

And that was how I found myself being escorted to an airplane by airline personnel as if I was some celebrity, or some rich man's wife.

Or maybe his dirty little secret.

The thought that people might think I was some big-shot's mistress irked me more than anything else that'd happened. I wasn't that woman. I'd never let some man keep me hidden away like something to be ashamed of, and I'd sure as hell not fool around with a married man. Okay, so the engagement ring said Jal wasn't actually married yet, but it was the perception of things that had my stomach churning.

By the time I boarded the plane, I was in a dark mood, tucking myself into the first class seat I'd been assigned. When the airline attendant offered me wine, I asked how much, managing not to gape when she told me it was free. I asked for rum and coke instead. It was too early to drink, but right then, I didn't care.

Jal Lindstrom hadn't struck me as the kind of guy who'd leave an engagement ring behind by accident. He didn't look like a man who ever did anything by accident. I was sure his life was carefully planned and controlled, down to the last detail.

Once we were in the air and I could retrieve my purse from where I'd tucked it between my feet, I pulled out the box, wanting to study the ring a little more closely. Heaven knew I'd never get this close to something like this again.

It was big and sparkly, beautiful and elegant without being ostentatious. Not surprising, really. Jal had struck me as the sort of guy who wouldn't worry about showy displays to impress others. He simply did it by existing. By that slow smile and the way he walked, the way he held himself. Everything about him breathed money. Money he'd been born into as well as earned.

I knew the type.

I avoided the type.

And now I was flying in luxury on a ticket he paid for to return a ring to him…so he could propose to the sort of woman who would look at this ring as being no less than what she deserved.

Snapping the box closed, I started to put it away, but the attendant appeared at my side, drink in hand.

"Thank you." I smiled at her and settled back, still holding the box.

I clutched it tighter as I sipped at my drink and stared out the window. After I called Tao earlier, I'd called my mother's work and had one of the women there take a message since the company didn't have a TTY machine. In a way, it'd been a relief not having to deal with her reaction right away. I knew I'd be in for an interrogation once I got home, but as long as she knew TJ was taken care of, she wouldn't be too mad.

I closed my eyes and rubbed my forehead. I was starting to get a headache. Even though she trusted Tao with TJ, I knew Mom wouldn't be happy that I'd gone off to New York, even if it wasn't some fun little trip rather than business.

And it was business. Strictly business.

I wasn't going there for a tryst with Jal, no matter how much I'd enjoyed his flirtations. Or his eyes. Or his smile. Or his long fingers.

Stop it!

Mentally kicking myself for even thinking about a customer that way, I lifted the glass to my lips, took another sip. Just business. I'd get a nice, fat bonus for doing nothing but relaxing in first class. I'd been assured I'd have a hotel room available if I chose not to fly straight back tonight, and my meals would all be covered. I planned on flying straight back, but basically, I was getting paid to be a gopher, and getting paid well.

It could've been worse.

It was a short flight, but that didn't keep me from ordering a second rum and coke, or enjoying the excellent snacks they offered first class passengers. The brownie brittle was something I could get addicted to. When I told the attendant, she rolled her eyes and said, "Tell me about it. Sometimes, it's all I can do not to eat five or six bags."

After she left, I absently flipped open the jewelry box I still hadn't put away.

I didn't know what drove me to do it, but I found myself sliding the ring onto my finger. Just to see what it looked like.

The lights hit it, flashing up at me. "It's a miracle people don't go blind wearing bling like this," I muttered. Someone with a real job couldn't wear something like this. It'd be a safety hazard for sure.

Still, I wondered what it would be like, having a man go down on bended knee and offer me a ring like this. To have a man love me that much.

"Wow. I didn't see that earlier. Congratulations."

I blinked, looking up at the attendant.

"I take it you're still getting used to it?"

Oh, shit…she thought the ring was mine.

Well, no shit, moron! You're wearing it!

My face flamed. "Um, yeah. Very much so." I gave her a nervous smile. "I had no idea it was coming, you know? Just surprised the hell out of me."

"That's so sweet."

The genuine smile on her face made me feel even worse than I already did, and I hurriedly passed her my trash, relieved when a voice announced that we were beginning our initial descent. Soon we wouldn't be able to chat, and I could put this all behind me.

I waited until everybody was told to put their tables up and the attendant was off to make sure everyone complied before I went to take the ring off. I didn't want her to see.

Tugging at the ring, I told myself I deserved to feel bad for being so juvenile. What sort of woman tried on another woman's engagement ring?

And it wasn't budging.

Oh, shit!

Shit!

All throughout the descent and the slow, tedious trip up to the gate, I tugged and twisted on the ring. Tears burned my eyelids, and I only kept them back by telling myself that if I made a scene, people would know how incredibly stupid I'd been. Finally, I made myself stop. My finger was swollen, getting sore now and the more I kept it up, the harder it would be.

What would my mother do?

Smack me for being so stupid. That made me smile a little, and that helped me start to calm down. I needed to think instead of panicking. If my finger was swelling, I needed to get the swelling down. Having an active and accident-prone little brother had taught me that cold brought down swelling. I didn't have access to ice or anything like that – unless I wanted to ask an attendant if there was any I could have – so I needed to figure out the next-best thing.

Water. That might help ease the ring off too.

Having a plan in mind helped me settle down, and I disembarked with a placid smile for the airline attendant, then made a beeline for the nearest bathroom, ignoring the sign with my name plastered on it. At least I wouldn't have to try to explain needing a bathroom after getting off a plane.

Inside the restroom, I held my hand under the water, making it as cold as I could get it.

"Getting cold feet, huh?"

Looking over, I saw a cute brunette with pink hair eying me. "Ah…yeah. Damn straight."

"Try using soap. It'll work better than just water."

"Thanks." I reached for some soap and slicked it over my finger and the ring. When it came off with ridiculous ease, I breathed a sigh of relief. I turned to thank her again, but she was already gone.

I dried the ring off, examining it closely to make sure there wasn't any soap residue on the shiny surfaces. Then I returned it to the box and secured it in my purse. I took a deep breath, gave myself a look in the mirror to ensure I didn't look as frazzled as I felt, then exited the restroom.

I adjusted Jal's coat over my arm and walked straight toward the man holding the sign with my name. "Hello. I'm Allie Dodds."

Chapter 7

Jal

It was past noon.

I'd heard back from the owner of the salon earlier that morning. Allie had agreed to bring me the ring, he'd said. There had been an unusual amount of relief in his voice, so much so that it made me think he'd doubted if she'd do it at all.

Had he doubted?

I hadn't.

Maybe I should have.

Regardless, she was on her way. My driver had texted me right before he left the airport to let me know they were en route. He also mentioned that she'd asked if he could bring me the ring so she could catch a return flight right away. He'd told her that those hadn't been his instructions, so she'd relented.

I had to admit, I was puzzled that she'd asked. What woman turned down a free trip to New York? All expenses paid, including a hotel room where she could stay the night. All of that, plus a hefty sum for the trouble.

While it should've made me annoyed that I couldn't figure her out, I found myself intrigued instead.

The business lunch I'd just finished had gone as well as I could expect, but it wasn't over yet. The company I was dealing with was going to require some hardball. That was fine with me. People tended to look at me and either think I'd be as laid back as my father was, or that I was too young to really be much threat. They were wrong on both counts. The meeting had also served to keep me from thinking about Allie too much, but now that it was over, I couldn't keep her off my mind.

My phone rang.

"Hello?"

"The young lady is here and is on her way, sir." It was the concierge.

"Excellent. And the food?"

"Already on the way." Even as he said it, the doors in the back swung open, and two men dressed all in black save for spotless white aprons emerged, bearing dishes. They were followed by more men who cleared away the steaming trays leftover by the lunch that had been enjoyed, or picked over, depending on the mood of those in the meeting.

My table was cleared in moments, and two new place settings were put down. I hadn't eaten anything during my meeting. I rarely did anyway, and I'd planned on sharing a meal with Allie. Just as the last server swept out of the room, the doors at the front of the small, intimate dining room opened.

Allie stood there, one hand resting on the door, the other in front of her, holding my coat. I'd actually forgotten that I'd left it too, even though the ring had been in the pocket.

I got to my feet, the gesture so ingrained in me it was automatic.

Her eyes sought me out, and she inclined her head. "Hello, Mr. Lindstrom."

There was no smile on her face.

I didn't smile at her either. I was too busy trying to catch my breath.

She really was that beautiful.

Smooth dusky skin, the color of coffee with just the right amount of creamer. Pale green eyes that all but glowed, and a full mouth that had me hungering for things I had no business wanting at all.

She glanced around, the look on her face full of cool disdain. She wasn't impressed by her surroundings or the lengths I'd taken to see her again.

It was that look that goaded me into moving. Taking a step forward, I said, "Thank you for bringing my coat."

"And the engagement ring," she added in a taciturn voice.

"Of course." I stepped aside and gestured to the table. "I was about to have some lunch. Business meetings have tied me up most of the morning. I imagine the flight ate up most of yours. Are you hungry?"

"You imagine the flight took up most of my morning?" She tucked her tongue against her cheek, looking like she wanted to add something else, but good manners kept her from doing so. "Sure. I could eat. The snacks they offer on first class might satisfy the sweet tooth, but they aren't filling."

She came toward me, still holding the coat and when she stopped in front of me, I stayed where I was, a little uncertain what it was she wanted.

Finally, a faint smile cracked her face. "You're standing in front of both seats."

"Oh. Of course." I held out my hand for my overcoat, wondering just what in the hell was wrong with me. This woman did weird things to my head.

Once she'd passed the coat over, I stepped aside, carelessly slinging the coat she'd so meticulously folded over the back of a chair at a nearby table. She'd already sat by the time I'd turned, ready to pull her chair out for her. She was studying the food in front of her critically, and just as I was about ready to tell her I could call the chef and have him make her something else, she used the fork to cut into the light, flaky fish and popped a bite in her mouth.

"Hmmm." She made a humming noise in the back of her throat as she chewed. After she'd swallowed, she shot me a smile. "Not as good as what my mom makes, but it'll do. Have you tried yours?"

As I hadn't even sat down, it was pretty obvious I hadn't, but I took the not-so-subtle hint to quit towering over her. By the time I'd spread my napkin in my lap and taken the first bite, she was already through half the fish and had tried the potatoes and broccoli.

"It's over-cooked," she said with a shrug. "But overall, the food is pretty decent."

I was about to call her on the broccoli – there was no way a place like this didn't serve perfection.

Except the broccoli *was* a little overcooked.

My mouth tightened, but she caught sight of me and laughed. "It's just broccoli."

I could have pointed out that I'd ordered a meal expecting it to be perfect, but it seemed a little idiotic to make a fuss when she was sitting there laughing about it. I didn't want her to think I was petty. It was already pretty clear that she didn't think much of the elaborate display.

"I suppose it could have been worse." I scooped up a bite of the fish. It was succulent, cooked to perfection. That made me wonder just how good her mom's cooking was. "It could have been bad fish."

"Oh, puh-leeze." She nipped up the last bite of potatoes. "Don't even joke about that."

Leaning back in her chair, Allie studied me, and I found myself at a loss for words. Talking to women was easy for me. Or at least, it usually was, but I couldn't think of a thing to say to her. All of the usual smooth talk I used, the flattery and charm, none of it seemed right.

She leaned forward, one elbow braced on the table. "Can I ask you something, Mr. Lindstrom?"

I wished she'd call me Jal.

"Absolutely." She was closer now, and I thought about reaching over, stroking my fingers down her arm. Her skin looked incredibly soft. Just like her hair. I wanted to see it spread out on my pillow, see her spread out under me–

"Why did you leave the engagement ring behind?"

"What?" The question caught me off-guard, especially considering I was wondering just how lush those curves were under her jeans and simple blouse.

"Your ring." She propped her chin on her hand, her eyes dancing with something I couldn't name. "You left that ring in the salon, and I can't help but think you did it on purpose."

I tried to summon up some sort of argument, but my mind was blank.

She didn't even seem to notice as she eased back and settled into her chair, that faint smile still curving her lips.

"See, you just strike me as the kind of man who has all his ducks lined up. I bet you packed for this trip of yours several days ago, and you knew exactly which shirt you'd wear today and with which pair of pants. You've already planned what you'll wear for tomorrow and probably the next day too. Your drawers and your socks all matched up just so. There's nothing extra in your

47

suitcase." She paused, shook her head, and then continued, "No. Not a suitcase. A carry-on. It's just a quick trip, I'm thinking, and you don't want to waste time with luggage, so the carry-on was enough. You have only what you need." Allie's eyebrow rose, and she asked, "How close am I?"

Damn. I stared at her. "Just about spot on."

"Okay, then. Why'd you leave the ring?"

Now it was my turn to lean forward. "What makes you so sure I did? Just because I plan doesn't mean I'm not forgetful."

"Because a man like you isn't the kind of man who'd leave an expensive and hopefully important engagement ring behind. Especially when it was in a coat he'd have missed as soon as he stepped outside." She gave me a hard look. "Unless, of course, he had some ulterior motive."

She bent down and reached into her purse, pulling out the box that carried the ring. She placed it on the table. "So, what reason did you have for leaving it behind?"

Instead of answering her, I picked it up and flipped it open, studying it. I'd only looked at it twice, once when it had been shown to me by my assistant after she'd bought it, and once yesterday morning, right before I left the house. I almost asked her what she thought of it. But when I opened my mouth, the question that came out was something entirely different.

"Did you try it on?"

I expected another flippant reply, something snarky.

Instead, her gaze slid away. "Excuse me?"

Hmmm…interesting. I'd been waiting to get some sort of reaction from her since the moment she walked in, and now I had.

"You heard me." Smiling now, more comfortable that she wasn't in control of the conversation, I leaned toward her. "Did you try it on?"

"Oh, please." She rolled her eyes and reached for her water. Her pretty mouth was damp when she lowered the glass, and I wanted to lick away the bead of moisture lingering on her lower lip, but she beat me to it.

Damn if that didn't send my blood rushing straight south.

"I can always have it checked for prints." I studied the ring and flicked her another look.

"If you so choose." She gave me a droll look. "If you're done with me, your highness, I've got a life to get back to."

Before she could stand up, I reached out a hand and covered hers with mine. "In such a hurry to be off? You've got the whole day off – with a nice bonus."

She tilted her head to the side, studying me. "The whole day off. Is that how you see it, Mr. Lindstrom?"

"Well, you're in New York...and you're not working."

"No. I'm not working." She made a deliberate show of tugging her phone from her purse and studying the time before looking at me. "It's well after one. I'd be coming up on the end of my shift if I was at home." After she put the phone back, she looked at me again. "I don't suppose it occurred to you that maybe I might have responsibilities that don't particularly...coincide with the plans you had for me when you set this little deal up."

Shooting for a grin, I shrugged. "I just needed the ring back, Allie. If you didn't want the bonus..."

"You made it more than clear that I was the one you wanted to bring it back." She looked mildly annoyed now. "Which meant you didn't even stop to think about how any of this would affect me."

I'd gone and fucked up, and I hadn't even realized it.

As she crossed one leg over the other, I thought back to the call I'd made to the salon. Had I been *that* guy? The one who talked over what anyone else had to say because I was so sure what I wanted was the most important thing?

She continued, "See, my boss is a great guy – a little nervous, sure, but a great guy. Regardless, it was made clear enough that you wanted me personally to bring the ring back. Once I did that, you'd bring your not-so-insignificant patronage to his establishment. Alistair is a worrier. He would have made excuses for me because he knows I do have responsibilities, but he asked if I could make arrangements. All it would take is a few wrong words from you and his salon would have suffered for it. So I figured it out for him. Not for you."

"Now wait a minute," I snapped.

She arched her eyebrow and folded her arms under her generous cleavage. "Did you make it clear that he'd do well if he helped convince me to trot up here like a good little girl?"

Son of a bitch. "I made it clear that I'd appreciate it." But maybe I hadn't made it clear that it was no harm, no foul if she

49

couldn't. Carefully, I took a deep breath. "Maybe I wasn't clear enough that regardless of what you chose to do, it was my fault the ring had been left behind, and I was the only one who'd bear the blame for it. I...apologize." The word almost stuck in my throat. It wasn't one I used very often.

"Apologize to him. He's the one worrying himself sick that you're going to ruin him." She lifted a shoulder. "Unless that's just not the kind of thing you do."

She had a smirk of a smile on her face. I couldn't decide if I wanted to kiss it off or just...no, I wanted to kiss it off.

I tried changing the subject, both so I could stop thinking about kissing her and so I could learn more about her. "You said you had responsibilities. Are you taking classes? Is there a second job?"

"I have a younger brother," she said flatly. "I'm responsible for him after work."

Well, shit. Now I really felt like an asshat.

Chapter 8

Jal

It was too easy to stick my foot in my mouth around her, too easy to feel awkward.

And on the flip-side, it was too easy to feel...easy. Not like sleazy, but there was no other way to describe how it was. Then, while I sat there feeling like a piece of shit for my behavior, Allie gave me a look and shook her head slightly, like she'd caught me doing something I shouldn't have.

"You look the same way my little brother did when I caught him peeking over the fence at our next door neighbor."

I wasn't entirely sure how to feel about that comparison.

Allie continued, "She likes to sunbathe in the nude, but then she freaks if she thinks somebody is peeking at her, although that's exactly why she does it."

I was shocked enough by her statement that I couldn't stop myself from asking the most inane question that came into my head. "Why do you think she does it just to get peeked at?"

She grinned at me. "Because she also answers the door and walks outside with her robe hanging open, and then acts all frazzled if somebody looks." Allie lifted a shoulder. "I personally don't care if she wants to let her tits hang out, but if she's going to let them hang out, she needs to be aware that guys – especially twelve-year-old boys – will look. Trust me, guys look even if they aren't hanging out."

She gestured absently toward her chest, and I couldn't stop myself.

I kept it to a quick glance, my blood heating as I imagined cupping those ripe curves in my hands, taking her nipples into my mouth, teasing them with my fingers. Did she like it light? Hard? Teeth or no teeth?

The thoughts continued to rush through my head even after I slid my gaze back to hers. I doubted she even noticed.

"So you think she intentionally wanders around half-dressed, wanting people to look, but then complaining when they do?" I asked, keeping my tone dry through sheer will alone. I'd never had such a blunt conversation with a woman. Hell, I didn't think I'd had this sort of conversation with a man before.

"Well, yes." Leaning forward, she said in a low voice, "See, Trudy just got divorced from her husband about two years ago. She caught him cheating with her best friend. Bad timing for him, because Trudy's mother had just died and Trudy came out of it very, very well. Trudy used to be a bit…" Allie wiggled her head from side to side, weighing her words. "Voluptuous. Pretty, absolutely, but she'd put on some weight over the last year of their marriage, and she always complained that it went to her butt and hips, but never to her boobs. Her best friend was rail thin, but had a decent rack."

She carried on blithely, and I tried to imagine any of the women I'd ever known talking like this. The women I'd dated. The one I was going to propose to. My mother. I almost choked on my coffee at that image.

No way in hell.

And the best thing about this conversation was that Allie wasn't trying to use it to turn me on, to hit on me. She was just telling a story.

"So Trudy files for divorce, wins, and her now ex-husband knows nothing about the fortune coming her way because it's all still in probate. Trudy knew, but she kept it all quiet, carrying on as always, running like a beast and losing weight while her former BFF marries her former ex. Then the BFF ends up pregnant and plump. The BFF came to see her, planning to break it to her gently…the same day Trudy's inheritance was made free and clear. She ended up getting almost half a million, and for a woman living where I do, that's a decent amount of cash," she pointed out as if I thought it was nickels.

I didn't need somebody to tell me that five hundred thousand was a fair amount of money for most people, but I didn't say anything. Her storytelling was fascinating me.

"She'd already had the first consultation for the boob job – she was getting double D's. Apparently, her ex had always wanted them, and now she wanted them…just to spite him." Allie lifted a shoulder and reached for her water. "So she tells her former BFF not to worry her little ol' head – Trudy's from Georgia. I was standing out there talking to my mother, and I heard it all and almost died trying not to laugh. *Oh, honey, I'm just fine.*"

Here, she started to mimic a Georgian accent, getting all into it. Batting her eyelashes, her hand pressed to her chest. Her voice took on a breathy, dulcet tone that brought to mind some attention-seeking southern debutante. I'd met more than a few – slept with several of them too.

She kept going. *"You heard about my mama, right? Well, it turns out that she was sitting on some money left to her by her daddy, and now it's all mine, and I don't have to worry about sharing it with Jeff! I'm going to pay off the house and get me a car and a boob job, and I've already turned in my notice at work, and I'm starting college in the fall!"*

I was laughing by the time she finished, my sides hurting.

She grinned at me. "I kid you not. That's how it went." Her face darkened. "Sorry. Sometimes when I start telling a story, it just all comes out."

I shook my head. "Don't apologize. I love a good story. Especially one told so well."

"I had to recite it for my mom, then her friends." She pursed her lips again then added softly, "It's not quite as much fun when you can't do the accent."

"Why didn't you do the accent for them?"

"Oh." She lifted a shoulder, looking away. "I could. But it wouldn't matter. My mom's deaf. Brother and step-dad too."

"Oh. Did…" Frowning and feeling awkward again, I smoothed my hands down the front of my slacks, as if there were imaginary wrinkles. "Inherited?"

"It can be." She looked over at me. She started to rise,

53

looking around. "I should probably get going."

"Are you that eager to get back?" I didn't know where the question came from.

Actually, I did, but I didn't know why I'd let myself ask it. It was obvious that she wasn't thrilled to be spending time with me. I thought she'd enjoyed herself, but I doubted she'd ever want to see me again.

This was a woman with *complications* written all over her. Not that it mattered. Even if I had the time and the inclination, I wasn't free.

You always make the time…and you are inclined.

Dammit. That sly little voice in my head was going to get me in trouble.

Except I was counting on Allie to shoot me down.

She still hadn't answered my question though. And she hadn't walked away.

I seized the opportunity.

"Come on. Take a walk with me. I'll make sure you get back to Philadelphia today."

We headed down the sidewalk in silence for several minutes before she broke it. "So…you're about to get engaged."

"Brilliant deduction, my dear Watson." I glanced over at her as we slowly made our way around the Central Park Castle, one of my favorite parts of the city. She was staring at everything with a faint smile on her face and part of me wished I could show her everything. But we didn't have time for everything. Barely had time for this. I just had to make the most of it.

"What's she like?"

I opened my mouth, then closed it, uncertain how to describe my…relationship. I liked Paisley. I supposed I did anyway. I was physically attracted to her. But now I wasn't entirely sure I could describe her.

"She's…" I floundered, searching for the right word and the only one that came to mind was… "suitable."

"Wow." It was delivered in a dry tone and the smile on Allie's face was so full of sardonic, sharp-edged humor, it practically cut. "Suitable. I'll tell you what, Mr. Lindstrom. That's probably the most insulting description of a woman I've ever heard in my life."

"Hey…"

She stopped and turned, facing me. Hands tucked into the pockets of her puffy down jacket, she shrugged. "Don't look at me like that. You're the one who said it. *Suitable*. Like a...I don't know. A suit. A suit is suitable. For like a wedding. A funeral. A job interview. Not that you've probably had to attend many of those. But the woman you're going to spend the rest of your life with? *Suitable*?"

The words hit a mark, but the bad thing was, Paisley *was* suitable. Nothing else fit. We had no burning, torrid passion, but the sex was fine. We had similar interests in life, and many of the things that appealed to her appealed to me. We knew the same people and our families were friends.

We suited.

And proposing to her meant getting my mom off my ass about settling down.

"And what are you looking for in a marriage?" I asked, feeling defensive without understanding why.

"I'm not," Allie replied easily. "But if I ever were to be looking to hook up with a guy on a permanent basis, and he described me as *suitable*, I'd kick his ass. I don't want a guy because I *suit* him. I want a guy to want me, to need me...and I'd want to feel the same way about him. Anything else...we'd be short-changing each other."

She turned and started to walk.

"I guess your parents are the kind who took one look and fell madly in love, so you believe in all that fairy tale kind of thing."

She shot me a look. "I don't believe in love. Not the kind that sticks around forever anyway. My parents said they were in love, but my dad broke her heart. My step-dad and mom...them, I can maybe believe have what could be called love." She looked away. "But I don't ever want to be the person someone settled on because I *suited* them."

When she'd first started talking, I'd regretted my word choice. Now, I didn't. I could see her a bit more clearly now.

My fingers wrapped around the ring box in my pocket. "Sometimes you don't have a choice between something you want and something you don't. Sometimes, the only choice you have is between two things that are both unappealing, and you have to pick the one you can live with."

She gave me a look that said maybe I'd just revealed a little

55

too much about myself.

Later that night, as I sipped from a glass of bourbon in my room, I stared out the window, thinking about how the day had gone.

Allie had been fun.

I couldn't remember the last time I'd walked around the city and just talked with anyone, let alone Paisley.

Paisley.

My soon to be wife.

When I was with her, we did talk. Or rather, she talked and I pretended to listen. Kind of like I did with my mother...

Those words had just drifted through my mind when the phone rang.

Glancing down, I saw Paisley's name flash across the screen. I ignored the desire to not answer and picked it up.

"Hello, Paisley."

"Jal..." Her voice was a warm purr, and I closed my eyes, tried to focus on her. "How are you?"

"Well. And you?"

"Missing you, baby. What are you doing right now?"

I swirled the twenty-five years scotch in my glass. "Having a drink before I turn in."

"Why don't you lay down on the bed? I'm in mine...we could maybe chat."

I doubted chatting was what she had in mind, but I went to the bed and laid down anyway. I'd enjoyed today, but there was some tension that had only increased being around Allie. A familiar, heavy tension that I knew would have only one release.

As she talked about how she'd like to wrap her mouth around my cock, I closed my eyes and put the scotch down. I palmed myself through my pants, then opened them, let my mind drift. But it wasn't Paisley who came to mind when I wrapped my hand around my cock. I heard her talking, let the responses automatically fall from my lips, but I was thinking about another set of lips sucking me off, another pair of strong fingers cupping my balls, stroking me.

And it was another name I had to bite back when I came.

Chapter 9

Allie

"So. Two questions…was it worth it? And not because of the money. I know how you are about that." Tao studied me over a plate of bacon and eggs.

I rolled my eyes. "That's only one question, genius." Sipping from a cup of coffee, I thought about it a moment and then shrugged. "I got a thousand dollars out of it. He's a nice guy. A nice, rich, white guy…who'd engaged. The money was the only thing *to* get out of it. Well, that and a nice meal, a headache from spending a ridiculous amount of time flying in such a short time." I paused for a second and then added, "And sore feet."

"Sore feet?" Tao gave me a puzzled look.

"Yeah. I was walking all over the airport, then New York City, and then the airport again. I was only prepared to work at the salon for five hours." With a glum sigh, I leaned back in my chair. "I flew all that way, and I didn't even get any pizza."

"Poor baby." He snapped a bite of bacon off before pointing a finger in my direction. "So question two…how badly are you kicking yourself over being hot for this guy?"

"What?" Heat flooded my cheeks, and I ducked my head, pretending to root through my purse for something – anything. I snatched a tissue out and wiped at my nose needlessly. "I'm not."

Tao wasn't fooled. Best friends rarely were, and he and I were closer than most. "Come on, Allie, how hot is he?"

Puffing up my cheeks, I blew out a breath. Shit. I knew better than to try to lie to him. "Jal is…wow. I think that sums it up."

"And if he wasn't rich?" Tao asked. "I mean, there's nothing we can do about him being white, but if he wasn't rich, then what would you do?"

Him.

The thought leaped into my mind so fast I couldn't stop it. The filter didn't activate in time, and judging by the way Tao started to grin, he knew just what direction my mind had gone.

Grabbing the napkin from the table, I balled it up and threw it at him. He batted it aside, chuckling.

"Hey, sweetie. It's not my fault your mind is going down that dirty, dirty path."

I stuck out my tongue. Childish, maybe, but Tao sometimes brought that out in me. "Look, there's no point in discussing it anyway. He's about to get engaged. I took him his engagement ring, Tao. Besides, you know, how I am with guys like him."

"Guys like him." Tao rested his chin on one fist. "It's kind of–"

"Don't. We've had this fight before, okay?" I stole the last piece of bacon off his plate. I'd told the waitress not to bring me any, and I hadn't intended to eat anything except the omelet on my plate, but my appetite got the better of me. Not an uncommon occurrence for me, especially when Tao's food was involved. He smacked my hand, but I knew he'd asked for the large order of bacon for a reason. He knew I'd steal some.

"So what are you up to this weekend?" I asked, changing the subject away from me.

"Met this guy. We're getting together for lunch tomorrow." He dragged a piece of toast through the yolk on his plate before biting into it.

I shuddered. "How can you do that?"

"Cuz it's delicious." He smacked his lips. "So...anyway. You think you can keep your phone handy in case I need you?"

"Think you will?" I glanced around the diner, the breakfast crowd already mostly gone, the mid-morning crowd yet to arrive. There were only a few others in there besides Tao and me. It was one of our favorite places to hang out.

"Maybe. Maybe not." Tao shrugged. "I like the guy. We hit it off the few times we talked, but this is the first date. He's full-on gay. Doesn't seem to care that I'm bi, but you know how that goes." Tao lifted a shoulder. "Not to mention the fact that sometimes you meet a guy, and he's just an ass."

"Or a girl who's just a diva." I fluffed my hair.

"Well, yeah, but I love you anyway." He winked at me. "What about you? Anybody on the horizon other the pretty, rich white boy?"

"Like I've had so much time to go looking." I hooked my hands behind my neck and rolled my head from side to side. I'd slept on it funny, and now it was a bit stiff. "Maybe I need to stop sleeping with you on my free time and actually go out."

"Hey…let's not get crazy." He glanced over as somebody came in, his mouth turning down into a hard straight line.

Once I looked over, I saw why. Richard Bloom, Tao's ex, and the biggest dick I'd ever met, had just strolled in. And that wasn't "biggest dick" in any sort of positive way. I'd been tempted more than once to kick him in the nuts until he cried like a little girl.

He caught sight of us and gave a stiff smile, taking the table farthest away and indicating to the waitress that he needed two cups of coffee.

I once more felt that familiar kick-in-the-nuts urge.

"We can go if you want," I said.

"No. He'll be convinced I'm leaving because of him. I'm over it…mostly." Tao smiled at me, a real smile. "The worst thing was not seeing what he was doing – feeling like a fool."

"Nobody likes to feel like a fool." I reached over and caught his hand, linking our fingers. "I hear love tends to do that to us – make us all into fools. Makes me wonder why in the hell anybody would wanna mess with it."

"Because when it's good, it's worth it."

We hung around another ten minutes, deliberately taking our time with our coffee, and I made sure to hook my arm through his, leaning against him as we sauntered to the door. Rick the Dick had never liked me, and when he found out that Tao and I sometimes shared a bed when we weren't otherwise involved…well, it hadn't made him like me any more. He was one of those men who thought there was only straight and gay, and he hadn't liked it when Tao insisted he really did like both. I waggled my fingers at him and chirped out a greeting as we passed by his table.

60

"You're such a mean little bitch," Tao said, grinning at me as we passed through the door.

I smiled back. "I know."

I didn't need some false sort of romantic nonsense or fantasies about someone I could never have. I had my family. I had Tao. I didn't need anything or anyone else.

Chapter 10

Allie

The park near the river was one of TJ's favorite places, which was why we were there. If I had my way, we'd be at the pub, digging into some fish and chips while Tao and I had some beer and listened to music. TJ liked it there too. Since they often had live music, TJ could feel the bass and the drums, and sometimes he'd ask me and Tao to try to describe the music.

Tyson didn't like us going there, though. He said it made TJ self-conscious. I thought he was wrong, but I was the sister, not the parent. Once a month, we did a family thing, and everybody took a turn picking where we'd go, and this was TJ's month. Next month was Mom's, then mine. I'd be shot down if I suggested the pub even then, so I needed to come up with an alternative.

"You look glum, sweetie." Tao nudged my shoulder just as a ball came flying our way.

We both ducked and covered our heads. When we raised them, TJ was running up, laughing and pointing at us. I stuck my tongue out at him while Tao signed that maybe he couldn't catch a ball, but he could pick TJ up and duck him in the river. Tao's grandmother was deaf so even before he'd moved in with us, he'd known more about sign language and deaf culture than most hearing people. I knew that was one of the reasons my parents had accepted him. Now, he was almost as fluent as I was.

"You don't scare me," TJ signed.

Tao scowled and started to get up. I laughingly hauled him back down as TJ whooped and took off, running back to Tyson.

Tao trying to be angry or scary never failed to make me laugh.

"Want a refill?" I picked up our cups and shoved to my feet.

"You going to brave the match-making attempts?" He gave me a teasing leer.

Mom had already been at it, telling me, then him, that we really should stop trying to pretend we were just friends. Tao had playfully told her he was waiting for her to wise up and leave Tyson. I'd been more blunt, telling her I was just using Tao for sex. She thought I was joking, but after a lifetime of getting comments that became less subtle with every turn, I was fed up with trying to explain us.

"I'll just tell her you met the love of your life," I quipped. "You're meeting him tomorrow to start making wedding plans."

"Don't." Tao looked at me, eyes going wide as he tried to figure out if I was serious. If Mom pushed me hard enough, I might do it, just to get some peace. I'd done crazier things.

"Hey, for all you know, he could be the love of your life." Ruffling Tao's hair, I turned away and walked off while he shouted threats after me.

"Yeah, yeah. I'm shaking in my shoes." I was laughing when I came to a stop by the picnic table where my mom was sitting, watching Tyson and TJ throwing around a football. She caught sight of my smile and arched a brow.

"You look happy."

"I'm amused," I signed as I spoke so she could read my hands and lips. "With that idiot, Tao."

Her gaze slid to him, and I saw the speculation there, could see the thoughts forming.

I frowned. "Don't start, Mom. Not again."

"I just want you happy...both of you. You're so good together."

"Because we're friends." Anger tried to rise, but I pushed it down. "Can't we go one day without you trying to force this? He and I are never going to fall in love."

I didn't even want to try to explain how I wasn't looking for love anyway. That would lead to me having to tell her why, and that wasn't a discussion I wanted to have. We avoided all mention of my biological father unless absolutely necessary.

Looking away from her was petty, but I didn't want to get into this debate again. I took the bottle of pop from the table and refilled my drink, then Tao's. I looked up as he sat down next to where I was standing, and prepared myself for a volley of comments meant for both of us.

To my surprise, he looked over at her without looking at me. *"Did Allie tell you I'm meeting a new guy tomorrow? I'm kind of nervous about it. I like him a lot. That usually means things will go straight to hell."*

Mom looked from me to him, not saying anything for a moment. When she finally responded, it wasn't with words. She reached over and covered his hands with hers and squeezed. No matter how frustrated I could get with her for trying to push Tao and me together, for the usual mother-daughter issues, I knew I was loved, and that she loved Tao too. That made everything else seem insignificant.

A moment later, TJ collided into me, his arms going around my waist in a tight hug. *"Can you and Tao go around the park with me? Dad's too tired."*

"Sure." I smiled at him and glanced over at Tao. Up for a walk?

"She'll get the point, sweetie." Tao and I watched as TJ bent over the railing, staring down in the churning waters of the river. "Sooner or later."

"You think?" With a dry laugh, I shook my head. "I'm starting to doubt it. She's been at this since we were teens. And she's getting worse."

"It's because she wants to see her baby settled down and happy, producing cute little babies that she could cuddle and spoil." He wrapped his arm around me and hugged me. "That's all. And you know we'd make adorable babies."

"I know she wants what she thinks is best for me." I crossed my arms over my chest as a sharp wind came blowing off the river, threatening to cut right through me. I snuggled back closer

64

to Tao. He was always warm. "I bet if TJ was my age, she wouldn't nag him like this."

"Daughters are different, I think."

With a glum sigh, I said, "Maybe. Doesn't mean I have to like it. She still pops her head into my room when I'm getting ready to go out, you know that?"

A bright laugh bounced out of him.

"So glad to know I amuse you." I tried to free myself from his embrace.

He tightened his arms around me and kissed the top of my head before releasing me. I stomped away, unable to figure out why my mood was so dark.

"It could be worse, Allie," he said as he followed me.

"Yeah? I guess. She could try to put me on curfew."

"No." His voice was serious enough that I stopped and looked at him. "She could be like my parents. Just write you out of her life because you didn't fit the image she had in her head."

"Well, damn." I sighed as I hooked my arm through his and tugged him along with me. "You have to go and make me look and feel like a bitch."

"You're not a bitch. Well, you are, but you're my kind of bitch." He kissed the top of my head again before disengaging our arms. We moved to bracket TJ as he continued to lean over the railing and stare down at the ducks that had come over to beg for food. "You're just feeling stifled. You've got a right to it. I know you want to stay and help out, but at some point, you need to look at moving out on your own. They'll do okay on their own, you know."

"It's not that I don't think they can do okay without me. I just feel like…"

I paused to answer TJ's question. "*Sure, you can feed the ducks.*"

I pushed a dollar's worth of coins into his hand and listened as he fed them into the machine behind us. I continued my conversation with Tao. "I know they can do fine without me, but it's not like I'd be leaving to go off and actually do something. It'd be different if it was school or moving in with a boyfriend. Explaining to my mother that I just want to go…it makes me sound like an ungrateful brat. She sacrificed so much for me."

"She didn't sacrifice anything, Allie. She loves you. That's what moms are supposed to do. She wants you happy. I think if you told her you wanted to find your own place, she'd surprise you."

TJ joined us again, duck feed spilling out between his fingers. He'd fed all the quarters into the machine, and instead of taking his time, he wound up like a world-class batter and let it all go flying. As it went everywhere – including in my hair – his laugh bubbled out, and I grinned.

"Yeah, maybe. But really, Tao. Why would I give this up?"

Chapter 11

Jal

The town car came to a stop, and I told the driver I'd get Paisley. He nodded and waited by the car to open the door for us when we returned.

The steps to the grand, elegant stone building seemed a little longer, a little steeper than normal. I had more dread inside me than I'd expected – actually, I hadn't expected to have *any* dread. My parents expected this of me, and I'd resigned myself to the fact years ago that I'd eventually marry someone like the woman on the other side of this door.

The Hedges were wealthy, moved in the right social circles. They had a home in one of the most prestigious sections of Philadelphia as well as a place in the Hamptons. This house in New York had been a more recent purchase, and Paisley's parents had hinted more than once that they planned to make it a wedding present. They were friends of the family so there wouldn't be any animosity between the in-laws.

It was a good match.

We *suited*.

Suited.

Allie's words echoed in the back of my mind as the door was answered, and I was ushered inside. The butler led me to a sitting room, and again, I waited.

It was pretty much a rule with Paisley. She liked to keep people waiting because that was the best way to make an impressive entrance. And Paisley definitely liked to be impressive.

"Jal, my boy. Good to see you." Kendrick Hedges was younger than my father, his sandy hair still free of gray. He poured me a drink without asking what I wanted.

While I sipped the scotch, Kendrick droned on about how wonderful it was to see me again, and how much he'd enjoyed getting to know me over the past few years.

It was a bunch of bullshit.

Kendrick had known me since I was a kid, and he hadn't exactly spent any time getting to know me over the past few years. He always had his head locked up in his business. I saw his wife more than I saw him. Not that I liked her much better. They were typical of the people who were friends with my parents. They chatted at charity events, occasionally had fancy dinners out together. Before Paisley and I started dating, our families had never been to each other's homes. Since then, we'd only had family get-togethers twice. I doubted much of that would change, even after the wedding.

"Ah, there's my girl," Kendrick said, his light green eyes lighting up.

Rising, I turned.

Paisley stood framed in the doorway, a faint smile on her mouth. Her light gray eyes met mine. She didn't look much like her father at all. With her short mahogany hair and delicate features, she resembled her mother the most. Only Paisley's height came from Kendrick.

"Hello, Paisley."

She came toward me then, that smile widening ever so slightly. "Jal, darling."

She turned her head for me to kiss her cheek – no kissing the mouth until later. Couldn't mess up the makeup before the important date. Her skin was cool under my lips as I grazed it for a moment.

When I lifted my head, I murmured softly, "You look lovely, Paisley."

"Thank you." She edged around me to go to her father while I turned to the next person who'd come into the sitting room.

"Hello, Diamond," I said politely. Russet-colored curls, ash gray eyes, Diamond's coloring clearly marked her as Paisley's mother. Despite the fact that Diamond was barely over five feet tall, she always carried herself like she was the biggest person in the room.

"Jal. Wonderful to see you. I take it your business dealings have been successful?" She held out her hand, and I accepted, squeezing it lightly before letting it go. One didn't shake Diamond Hedge's hand.

She patted my cheek before moving to join Kendrick on the couch, smiling at her daughter with what looked like complete satisfaction. Paisley slid me a look, and I had the uncomfortable feeling of being sized up by some sort of predator. A mother-daughter pair intent on eating me alive.

I was starting to regret having watched that nature documentary the night before.

Although we still had time yet to get to the restaurant, I put my scotch down and held a hand out to Paisley. "Are you ready?"

"Somebody is eager," Diamond murmured to Kendrick as Paisley came to me.

Eager?

I wasn't sure if that was the word. I just wanted to get this done so I could move on with my life.

It looked like something out of one of those tear-jerker romances that Paisley always made me watch. The ones where the couple always had huge obstacles to get over, usually when they learned something important about themselves, but no matter how much they grew, they generally lost each other in the end.

Music played softly in the background. Across from me, light danced on Paisley's delicate ivory skin. She sipped from a glass of sparkling water while I enjoyed two fingers of forty-year scotch.

No expenses spared tonight. She'd be telling this story over and over, and I knew I needed to make it a good one.

"What have you been up to this week?"

Paisley smiled at me over the rim of her glass. "Well. I went shopping with your mother last weekend. This dreadful cold kept it from being as much fun as I'd have liked, but I picked up some of the cutest shoes, so it wasn't a total loss."

Shoes. I offered a smile because something was expected in response, but I found myself thinking of the sly smile Allie had given me when I'd asked her what she liked to do for fun.

It hadn't included shopping for shoes.

The servers had already cleared dinner and dessert. Paisley had taken exactly two bites of her insanely expensive chocolate torte. Again, I found myself thinking of Allie. She'd laughed when I offered to buy her some chocolates from a store we'd passed.

"I don't think so. For what they charge, you could feed a hungry family for a day. Why don't you spend the money on that instead?"

Her words had lingered, and I couldn't put them out of my head, especially since I knew that dessert here had cost double what the chocolates would have been. It would have fed a hungry family for two days. This meal? Probably for a month. And Paisley hadn't finished any of it or asked to have it wrapped up to take home.

"You look so grim, baby..."

Paisley's fingers stroked down my hand, and I looked up, offering a smile that I didn't feel. I didn't know where this mood had come from, but I couldn't push it aside, so I needed to change how Paisley was seeing it. I couldn't ruin tonight. My mother would never forgive me.

"I'm not grim." I took her hand in mine and lifted it to my lips. "I'm intent. Have I told you how beautiful you look?"

"Not recently." Her lashes fell low, a demure smile curling her lips as she made it clear she'd be happy to hear it. Again. Not just now, but in five minutes, and then another five minutes after that. As far as Paisley was concerned, she could hear it from multiple people, multiple times a day, and she still wasn't getting her due.

"You look...magnificent. Ethereal." I kissed the tips of her fingers, then turned her hand upward and brushed another kiss on her palm. It was nothing less than the truth, and I had no problem giving her the words she needed to hear. "You're lovely, Paisley."

"Thank you." She looked satisfied, like she was simply accepting my words as fact.

She did look lovely. The dress she wore was all smoke and ice, a dark gray that highlighted her skin, and small stones set in the fabric reflected the light back, drawing the eye her way. More than a few people had looked at us when we came in, were even still looking now. Not that Paisley would ever point such a thing out, but for her, it was all about being *noticed*.

And of course she noticed others. Not in the nicest way most of the time either, I had to admit. She'd made a cutting remark earlier as we came inside about how one of the ladies was wearing a pair of shoes that had been *last* year's design. Another was shamefully sporting a knock-off designer dress. How déclassé. None of it was said loud enough for anybody but me to overhear, save for the few times she'd made a disappointing noise under her breath about how a certain family was so coming down in the world, or how that woman was going to have to marry up if she wanted to keep moving in the same social circles.

She tugged her hand back, and her eyes slid past me, a cat's smile curling her lips. "I do believe that's Rebecca Stirling. Rumor has it that her little affair with Benjamin Westmore, Jr. completely destroyed his marriage, but she's already moved on to another man."

"Paisley." I took her hand once more, cradling it between mine. "Believe it or not, I didn't come here to chat about Rebecca's affairs or who is or isn't wearing the latest fashions."

"Oh?" Something cool flickered in Paisley's eyes.

I saw the warning but ignored it. She knew what was coming tonight, even though I knew she'd act surprised. Lifting her hand to my lips, I pressed a kiss to the inside of it. "We're here on a date. A *special* one."

"How silly of me," Paisley murmured, leaning closer. "I'm rambling on and on. I must be boring you terribly."

I doubted she'd appreciate it if I told her yes. Not that I'd ever do that, but it was an entertaining thought.

"Boring isn't the word for you, Paisley." Nuzzling her palm, I looked into her eyes. "We've been leading up to this point for a long while, don't you think?"

The scent of her filled my head, and it was enough to keep

my mind on the task at hand.

"More than." She leaned closer, but rather than sound excited, she came off as…predatory.

Thinking about my soon-to-be fiancée as a predator twice in the same night didn't exactly bode well for the relationship, but I wasn't going to back down now.

I reached into my pocket with my free hand and pulled out the ring. As I slid it onto her finger, I asked, "Paisley, will you marry me?"

"Oh…" She batted her lashes, the look on her face that of a stunned, dewy eyed girl startled by the proposal. She was a great actress. Slowly, she tugged her hand away and stared at the ring as she held her hand up high enough for any interested parties in the restaurant to see. "Jal, I don't know what to say."

That was my cue to beg her to say yes, but I waited instead. I already knew her answer.

I knew she wanted things to play out like a script to one of her favorite movies, and I couldn't help but marvel at the coldness of it. Then again, this was Paisley. She was staring at the ring, and I knew the lowered lashes and speechlessness were part of her character. She was examining the ring far more clinically than emotionally. I had no doubt that if the ring didn't pass muster, she'd take it off, and claim she needed time to think. But I wasn't the sort of man who'd buy a less than flawless ring, so I knew I didn't have to worry about that.

Seconds passed – seconds of silence that were weighted, ticking away.

I waited.

She waited.

I'd be damned if she was going to get a plea out of me. We both knew this was going to happen, and while I was prepared to be her husband, no way in hell would I play the fool for her. People in love did that, and I didn't believe in love.

"Jal, I'd love to marry you." She came to me then, wrapping her arms around my neck as she sat on my lap.

From the corner of my eye, I saw somebody moving, kneeling in front of us. I supposed it was possible the photographer's presence was a coincidence, but I knew it was more likely that one of our parents had set it up. Hell, I wouldn't have put it past Paisley herself. I didn't care though. That's what this was all about anyway. Appearances. How it all looked.

Paisley snuggled closer and kissed my neck. A moment later, she whispered something that would have made me instantly hard just a few days ago. Now, it just made me tired.

Something had changed.

Chapter 12

Allie

The park down by the river was a different place this early in the morning. Like TJ, I loved it down here, but for different reasons...and at different times.

It was quieter, calmer. Save for the people who were crazy enough to be out here running, it was empty. I should know. I was one of the ones crazy enough to be out here running. I didn't really like running – any woman with a build like mine understood why – but on days when swimming wasn't an option, this was what I did to keep in shape.

The sound of my feet slapping against the pavement was rhythmic, lulling my brain into that easy state where I just let thoughts come and go as they pleased. Except this morning, my mind drifted to places probably better left alone.

I kept thinking about Jal.

Once we'd gotten out of the hotel and had started to walk, he'd loosened up and was actually...well, almost easy to talk to. Easy, for a guy who pretty much topped the social echelon. Who had more money in his bank account than I'd ever see in my *lifetime*.

For a guy who was about to get engaged.

If he wasn't already. He said he needed the ring for this weekend, which meant that was probably when he planned on popping the question.

Why in the hell had he come into *my* salon anyway?

Why had he left that damn coat, and made me start brooding

about things like…like…*him*. Him and that damn ring. Him and me. Not that there *was* a him and me, but just spending a few hours with him made me think about why things like him and me *couldn't* happen. And it had absolutely nothing to do with that ring.

That damn ring.

Had he proposed yet?

Probably.

I imagined it had gone perfectly, and I imagined she'd said yes. He wasn't the kind of man women said no to.

They'd get married, and after the appropriate amount of time, they'd have two point three kids and vacation up in the Hamptons. Eventually, Jal might even end up taking himself a mistress…like my father had.

That was, after all, how I'd come to be.

Oh, it was entirely possible my dad had loved my mother. I know my mom had loved him, and she'd told me that she loved him. It hadn't mattered to her at that time that he was married, rich, white…from a whole other world.

She'd just known that she loved him, and she'd stayed even after he made it clear that she would never be more to him that what she already was.

A woman to warm his bed.

The cliché maid and nanny rolled into one.

I knew all about men like Jal Lindstrom. Flirtatious, manipulative, so convinced that I'd fall prey to his easy charm.

I could have too, if I hadn't been looking out for that sort of thing my whole life.

Maybe it made me paranoid and cynical, but I'd seen how easily love could destroy a person. My mother had lost her sense of self for the longest time. Finding Tyson had been the first step to rediscovering herself, but sometimes, I still wasn't sure she'd picked up all the pieces.

I sometimes wondered if it'd ever affected my father. If he'd simply moved on to someone else as soon as Mom made it clear she was done.

Coming to a stop at the railing where I'd been with Tao and TJ just yesterday, I swiped my gloved hand over the back of my brow and slowed to a walk. From the nearby bridge, I heard horns and engines, their sounds carrying easily in the cold, quiet air.

It made me feel that much more isolated.

It had been years since I'd seen him or my sisters. I had two of them, although it had taken me a while to really understand that those two pretty little white girls were my *sisters*. Not that they knew, of course. They always looked so perfect, like elegant little dolls, dressed in their clothes so much nicer than anything I had. Not that I hadn't had nice clothes or nice toys, but there's nice and there's *nice*....

The kind of nice that only the very wealthy can afford.

I remembered seeing their presents one Christmas morning when they'd called the whole household in to the sitting room. It was an annual tradition – the household staff was given gifts, along with the family because they were part of the family. A nice idea…such bullshit.

While the girls sat there surrounded by their dolls and electronics and jewelry with authentic jewels, each member of the staff was given an envelope with some cash in it. I was given a sweater.

My father never looked at me that day.

Oh, he spent time with me when they weren't around. But I was the pariah. If his *real* family was there, then I was just…nothing. He didn't talk to me, rarely looked at me. It was likely I was something…other.

Not his daughter, just another one of his dirty little secrets. Like my mother.

That had been the way of it through my childhood. He'd spend some time with me, love on me and hug me, play with me and laugh with me – teach me things too, once he realized I loved to learn. Math and numbers had fascinated me. But if his *real* family was around, he didn't even acknowledge me.

Mom met Tyson when I was seven, then they got married. He was my step-dad and sometimes I called him Dad, sometimes Tyson. I never said he wasn't my *real* dad because I hated that word, like it meant some people were only figments of the imagination. But I never called my biological father "Dad." He'd never allowed it. After Mom and Tyson married, things had gotten even more tense, but Mom had stuck it out as long as she could. I hadn't seen my biological father since the day Mom and I walked out of the house and never looked back.

It was a rub against my nerves even now. Old wounds. They

never healed well, but I usually didn't brood over them quite like this. And I knew what had brought it on.

I'd always known that I didn't belong in that world, no matter how many times I had math lessons or got to listen to my father explain how his business worked. I was separate, different. I didn't fit.

I'd never cared about it really, though.

And it pissed me off that I was caring *now*.

All because some blue-eyed, sexy piece of work had smiled at me and made me wonder.

He was *engaged*. It didn't even matter if I might have fit and, why would I want to anyway?

"I don't," I said under my breath.

I'd kissed that part of my life goodbye when I was sixteen, when Mom had finally quit the job that had bound me to them, and I was glad for it.

"So stop thinking about it. Stop thinking about him."

Shoving back away from the railing, I turned to face the running path once more. The burn in my lungs was gone. About time to make it come back.

I snagged the paper off the front porch as I went inside. I was tired, my legs half-numb from the cold, my nose *all* the way numb. I wanted some coffee and a hot bath, but the hot bath would have to wait until I could actually feel my legs.

Caffeine first.

Inside the kitchen, coffee in hand, I dropped down at the kitchen table and flipped open the paper just as Mom came in. She smiled at me and asked if I was hungry.

Starving, I replied.

The coffee brought welcome warmth to my belly as I sipped it, and I wondered if this unending winter was *ever* going to end. March should start to show *some* sign of spring, shouldn't it?

A shiver racked me, and I rubbed my hands up and down my arms, chafing them to warm up. Over by the refrigerator, Mom was moving around. It wouldn't be long before I heard the sound of bacon sizzling.

Bacon. Eggs. Coffee. For a Sunday morning, it wouldn't suck.

Then I flipped open the paper, and my eyes landed on a picture.

My heart stopped for a few seconds before ratcheting back into something that resembled a normal rhythm.

It was Jal, and he wasn't alone.

Sitting on his lap was a woman with a sassy little flip of a haircut, a smile on her face that was decidedly smug.

The caption mentioned their names, along with an announcement about their recent engagement. *Philadelphia's golden son...engaged...*

Yeah. He was golden, alright.

Really, though, I didn't need the caption. I'd known he was getting engaged.

I just hadn't realized to whom.

Paisley Hedges.

My older half-sister.

Book 2

Chapter 1

Allie

"So which stock should we dump?"

Bent over the screen, I studied it, the numbers, arrows, and jargon that might have come off as a foreign language to some people made perfect sense to me. But then again, Daddy – *no*, I reminded myself, *Mr. Hedges; never call him Daddy* – had been helping me with this sort of thing for years. One of these days, I'd have as much money as they did and maybe then–

The door swung open before I'd made up my mind.

Immediately, he pushed away from me, and a cold, hard lump settled in my gut as his wife, Diamond, appeared there, along with one of my half-sisters. Paisley was the older one, and the one I liked the least. She saw me as she stepped into the room, although it was more of an acknowledgement that somebody was there. She didn't really *see* me at all. I was nothing more than background to her.

Diamond saw me though.

That made me shrink into the seat while my father got up and went to greet her.

"Hello, darlings. How are you? You're back early from your shopping trip."

"Mallory took ill." Diamond's mouth was tight around the edges. "It looks as though you've entertained yourself well enough."

"Oh…well, I'm just going over some things that she might

do to help her mother, love. That's all. She's old enough to start earning some of her own money, don't you think?" He brushed his lips against her cheek.

My face stung with embarrassment. I had money in my pocket from him. Fifty whole dollars. He gave me money all the time. Like it made up for not calling him *Daddy* like Mallory and Paisley did.

I said nothing though. I knew better.

Diamond stared at me, her eyes as hard as her namesake.

"Quite. If she's really interested in earning her keep, perhaps she could start working in the garden."

"She can clean my room," Paisley said, smiling sweetly. "Mine and Mallory's. As long as she doesn't steal from us."

Steal from her? Clean her room?

I wanted to shout something at her. I didn't even know what, but all the anger and embarrassment and misery were boiling inside me as I stared at my sister's smug little face. Did she know who we were to each other? No. I decided. No…she couldn't. If she did, she wouldn't be so mean, would she? I saw how she was with Mallory. They fought sometimes, but she wasn't mean to Mallory like she was to me.

"Should we show her where the bedrooms are, Daddy?" Paisley asked, looking over at him. "She could get started today."

Like I didn't already know where their bedrooms were. Like I hadn't spent my entire life wandering around this huge place, wondering what it would be like to live here, to be a real part of this family. If he said…

"Nonsense." He hustled them out the door. "I've got ideas on what she can do. Leave it to me. Now, let's go check on your little sister, shall we?"

He shut the door behind him, leaving me in the room with the computer still on and his trade account active.

For a minute, I was tempted to buy something that I knew would tank horribly. There was a hot, miserable ball of hurt in me, brought on by how he'd pulled away from me, by how Diamond had stared at me, by how Paisley had stared down her pretty little nose at me.

My sister. And she talked about me like all I was good for was cleaning rooms.

Moving closer to the computer, I studied all those numbers

and signs, that intricate language. I could hurt him now.

But I didn't.

Sighing, I studied the shares and then chose the one that had caught my eye. Normally, he didn't like me doing anything without his approval, but he'd told me to make a purchase. I was just doing what he asked.

I left a note telling him and slid out of the room. I'd planned on going shopping with the fifty dollars, but I didn't want to now. I'd just put it in the bank for when I needed something.

Present day

I'd retreated out to the front porch, claiming that I was still overheated from my run, and I'd taken the paper with me.

Mom knew I read it all the time, so she hadn't thought much of it.

But so far, I hadn't been able to do anything but stare at the picture.

Out of all the people in the world…

Suited.

I'd tossed the word back at Jal when he'd used it.

They *suited*.

Who the hell married somebody because they *suited*?

But even as I thought it, I knew the answer. My father had married Diamond because she *suited* him, the life he needed. His wife had to fit the life he'd laid out for himself. She *suited* him.

"That's how it's done in their world," I said, my voice thicker than I liked, for reasons I didn't want to think about.

My mother...she'd *suited* my father for other reasons. Maybe that's all it was, really, no matter how we wanted to spin it. Just some version or another of being *suitable*.

For some reason, I wished I hadn't asked Jal how he felt about his fiancée. It would have been easier to sit there, staring at their picture, Paisley looking so smug and happy if I could believe they *loved* each other. I hadn't seen her in five years. She could've become a whole different person than the one I'd always thought her to be. And it wasn't like I really knew Jal either. For all I knew, the two of them were perfect for each other. Maybe their love made them better people.

My mind spun back to the conversation I'd had with Jal just a couple days ago. How would things have gone if I'd realized *who* he was marrying? I wouldn't have gone to New York City, I knew that much. I would have told Alistair something. I would have lied through my teeth and told him that no one could pick up TJ. I would've stayed as far away from Jal as possible, even if it cost me.

But I'd gone, and damn it all, I *liked* the guy.

I'd been nervous at first, and I always ran my mouth when I was nervous. I'd told him a story that was highly inappropriate to be telling a customer, but he'd laughed, and that'd made me relax. Then we'd gone for a walk and ended up talking about his engagement and marriage. Both of us had been vague.

The idea of getting married any time soon was almost laughable. The last time I'd brought a guy home to my family, it had been so awkward I'd ended up never talking to him again. Hearing people weren't often comfortable around the deaf, and if somebody couldn't take my family, they weren't going to get me. On the flip-side, being somebody who could hear made a lot of the deaf men I knew not that interested in me.

It was no wonder I found my friends-with-benefits arrangement with Tao to be so much more appealing than actual dating. All of the pleasure of sex without any of the shit that came with pretending to believe in love.

Or risking having someone describe me as *suitable.*

Damn, that word rankled and it wasn't even about me.

The sound of a car blasting down the street drew me out of my memory, and I sighed, shoving my hair back from my face.

I was cold, so cold I was shaking with it, and I knew it was less because of the early March weather and more to do with the shock I'd had this morning.

Slowly folding the paper, I stood up. They did suit each other, I decided.

It was a bitter pill to swallow, staring at their picture, both of them so elegant and refined, Paisley with her perfect sweep of expensively cut hair and clean, classic beauty. Jal was just as beautiful in a clearly masculine way, and the two of them complemented each other. The picture looked candid enough, but my gut said it'd been a little more posed than that.

Before I could crumple the paper into pieces, I went inside and left it on the chair where Tyson would find it and read it. Mom might see the announcement or she might not. Either way, we wouldn't talk about it.

I headed upstairs, determined to get out of my clothes, into the shower, and try to wash away the feeling of inadequacy, that sense of being out of place.

Always out of place, no matter where I was.

Chapter 2

Jal

Cold air stung my lungs as I rounded the corner. My destination lay ahead although I didn't particularly want to go there. Not yet.

Pretty pathetic. My new fiancée was back in our warm bed, probably still asleep, and I could slide in next to her and warm myself up while *waking* her up, and I had absolutely no desire to do it.

I wasn't about to slip into bed with Paisley right now. I'd hoped the run would clear my head, and in a way, it had. But instead of making me feel better about how things were going, I just felt more certain that I was making a big mistake.

We'd come home after the proposal rather than staying at a hotel in New York, but that had been more my doing than Paisley's. She'd have been fine with upgrading to a more decadent room, spending tons of money on champagne and the most expensive room service she could order. But I wanted at least some of the comfort that came with being at home.

Even that wasn't the same anymore though. Paisley and I kept some clothes and things at each other's places, but I'd successfully avoided any conversation about us moving in together. I had a bad feeling that I wouldn't be able to keep that going for much longer.

As I slowed to a walk in front of the building, the doorman greeted me. "Good morning, Mr. Lindstrom. Did you have a nice run?"

"Good as you can expect in this cold," I said as I slowed to a walk. "I want warm weather, Dennis. You know that?"

"Don't we all, sir. At least you kept moving. Helps you stay warm a bit, I'd imagine."

"True. Miserable day for you. Maybe you should go for a run when you're done." It was an old joke between us.

He slapped at his belly. He wasn't what I'd call obese, but the man was as solid as they came. Running wasn't much his style.

"I don't think I'll be doing that, sir."

"On a day like today, I don't blame you." I clapped a hand down on his shoulder.

"Your paper." He held it out as I headed through the door.

I accepted it with a smile and little enthusiasm, although he wouldn't know that. Taking the paper and reading through depressing news or commentary on social tangles held no interest for me.

Once I was upstairs, silence greeted me. Paisley was still sleeping. I breathed a sigh of relief. I still had a little time on my own. Or at least I thought so until my cell phone rang. I really needed to get caffeine in me before dealing with the phone call, but if I didn't answer, she'd try again.

"Hello, Mom."

"Have you seen the morning paper?" she asked.

Good morning, son. I trust you slept well? How was your flight to New York? Did last night go well? What's the weather like?

No chit-chat, no greeting.

That was Ginnifer Lindstrom, getting right down to whatever she deemed important.

Normally, I would have just ignored the abruptness, but the foul mood I'd woken up in had me responding without thinking. "Why, good morning, Mom. I'm doing great...you? Yes, I was just sitting down with some coffee before I took a look at the paper."

She huffed out a breath. "Really, Jal. How are you?"

"Like I said..." I snapped open the paper. "I'm doing great." Like hell. "Afraid I haven't had a chance to look at the paper just yet, like I said."

87

"I assume you're looking at it now." She made it a statement rather than a question.

"Yes, of course." I flicked a look at the top headline, wondering if there was anything urgent that had her calling me so early. Nothing. Of course. With a fatalistic sigh, I unfolded the paper completely and then I saw it. It would be impossible to miss. "Well, I expect this pleases you."

"Of course it does," she said with a bright laugh. "That was very clever of you, arranging to have a photographer there."

"I didn't arrange it." The second the last word left my lips, I knew I should have kept quiet. Mom didn't like it when I interfered with my own life.

"You...didn't arrange for the pictures?" she asked.

"No."

"Well, I imagine it's just lucky coincidence that somebody was there."

Oh, now *that* was bullshit. Of course, I was more polite when I pointed that out. "That wasn't luck. Paisley had her hand in it, and I'm pretty sure that doesn't come as a surprise to you."

She didn't deny it. She didn't confirm it either, but I didn't need her to. "Jal, what's wrong with you this morning?" she asked. "You're very...out of sorts."

Out of sorts. That was probably the most accurate description I'd heard of how I felt. Everything was getting ready to change, and I had no way to stop that. There really was only one highlight about those changes.

"You're having second thoughts, aren't you?" Without giving me a chance to respond, she said, "Jal, there's no reason to be doubting anything. You and Paisley are so well suited."

Suited. I don't think there's anything she could have said that would've hit me harder.

With a bitter, hard laugh, I said, "Yes, Mom. We're suited." Something inside me felt like it was stretching to the breaking point. "Tell me something, Mom, are you certain you're fine with the fact that your son is marrying a woman because they're *suited* for each other because our lives are similar and she knows the right people and how to act at a dinner party."

"Jal, really–"

"Would you care if we ended up hating each other in ten years as long as we behaved in public so none of our friends realized anything was wrong?"

"Don't be silly, Jal. Besides, you and Paisley would never hate each other. You're too well matched." She sounded more annoyed than worried.

Disgusted, I shoved back from the table and moved over to the windows. I stared out at the city skyline, barely seeing anything. "Well matched. Well suited…how many people do we know that are well matched or well suited? And yet, they hate each other. You can't say it doesn't happen."

"Jal." She sighed. "I don't understand where this is coming from, or why so suddenly. But you must understand that you have a responsibility."

"Yes, I'm aware," I snapped. "And I expect you were just delighted with it too. You've only been pushing me further into this for how long now?"

I hadn't even been aware of how much bitterness I had in me, and now it was all spilling out. I wasn't sure if I wanted to stop it or if I simply couldn't.

"Jal. Son, I only want what's best for you." Her voice was sharp now, the familiar mothering tone I'd grown up with. The one that told me I was treading on dangerous ground.

A noise caught my ear, and I looked back, but the bedroom door remained closed, and everything stayed quiet. Paisley would likely sleep until noon if I didn't wake her. And since I wanted a peaceful Sunday morning, I'd probably let her sleep as long as she wanted. Monday would be fine.

"I know, but you're usually the one deciding what's best. Not me." I sighed. "Look, Mom, I need to go. I'll talk to you later. I love you." Before she could press the issue any further, I hung up.

Putting the phone on mute, I shoved it into the pocket of my pants and walked through the open doors to the balcony. Walking out into the bracing cold, I took a deep breath.

It didn't do much but remind me of how ridiculously cold it still was. Sometimes I hated living this far north. I wanted someplace warm, where the temperature never dropped below fifty degrees. No, better yet sixty – sixty-five.

I imagined booking a trip to the Bahamas, staying there until June, then going back at the first sign of forty-five degrees again. Maybe Paisley would go for a barefoot beach wedding, but even as I pondered the idea, I had to laugh it off.

That would never be Paisley Hedges. Not in a million years. Soon, we'd have to start making those plans. Then again, for all I knew, she was already making them. She might already have her dress selected, a date...

We didn't really have time to waste, after all. Aside from the scandal among our family's more old-fashioned friends, Paisley wouldn't want to be showing when we said our vows.

It'd been two weeks since she'd told me she was pregnant.

Two weeks since my comfortable life had completely shifted on its axis.

I was going to be there for my child, and Paisley had made it clear that if I wanted that at all, it had to come with a ring.

Mom, Dad, and Baby...a nice little family.

Leaning forward, I planted my hands on the stone balustrade and contemplated the changes coming up in my life. Things just kept spinning out of control.

After the initial shock, I was actually starting to look forward to the idea of becoming a father.

It was everything else that didn't appeal to me.

The thought of marrying Paisley, falling into the nice life that my mother had organized for me, joining a country club like Paisley kept insisting I should do. All of that just filled me with an ambivalence that was slowly turning into something even stronger.

What had changed?

That was easy.

I'd gone into FOCUS, sat in a chair, and talked to a woman who'd made me laugh, made me think.

What had changed?

The answer was simple.

Allie.

Chapter 3

Allie

"Did you see?"

Sonya showed me the paper.

"Yeah, I saw." Checking the supplies at my station, I headed to the supply room. Alistair and Sonya had already been talking about the engagement when I'd come in, and a few others had horned in, curious. I wasn't interested in all the hoopla surrounded him *or* her.

"She's pretty, don't you think? They look cute together."

I shrugged as I studied the bottles lining the shelves, took some shampoo and a deep conditioning treatment I liked. After signing them out, I headed back to my station, Sonya still trailing along with me, an expectant look on her face.

I sighed. I wasn't going to get any peace until she said what was on her mind. "What?"

"You spent half the day with him. He was a nice guy. Gorgeous. And you don't have *any* thoughts about this?"

"Sure." Rolling my eyes, I dumped my supplies on the counter and then took the paper. "I have thoughts. Good looking rich guy marries good looking rich girl. They'll have good looking babies who will grow up spoiled and over-indulged, and the cycle will repeat itself. Those are my thoughts."

"You're so cynical." She huffed a little and took the paper back. "You've got no romance in your soul."

"You're right," I agreed. "But there's nothing romantic about

91

that picture, Sonya. It was totally staged." People are so gullible.

She looked shocked. "No way."

I was about to point out all the ways it was staged when the soft tinkling music sounded through the salon, alerting us so subtly and elegantly that we had a customer. Turning to my station, I put away my supplies and checked my appearance. Time to get ready for the day.

A normal day in the life of a normal, hard-working person.

"Mr. Lindstrom!"

Shit.

I tensed, and then slowly looked up. In the large mirror over my area, I could see clear to the front and yes…there he was.

And he was smiling at me.

What the hell?

Alistair cut in front of me, blocking him from my sight. "Mr. Lindstrom. I heard about your engagement. Congratulations!"

Echoes rose up all around us. I kept my back turned to him. He had enough people fawning over him. He didn't need more over there offering him well wishes too. As Sonya gushed about how *romantic* the picture was, I snorted.

Staged, I thought. Totally staged.

I gave a vague smile in his direction so I didn't have to deal with Alistair telling me that I was being rude to somebody who was probably going to become a VIP here at the salon.

Dammit. I'd completely forgotten that he'd said he'd start using FOCUS, and somehow, I had a feeling he was the sort to stand by his word, as far as that went. Maybe somebody could get shampoo in his eyes, nick him, piss him off–

"Allie!" Alistair managed to make himself heard without yelling.

Lifting my head, I met Jal's eyes in the mirror for the briefest moment, and the small smile on his lips made my stomach sink even more. That smile should have been a warm, inviting one – and it was, really. But it wasn't an invitation I could accept.

He was taken.

By my *sister*.

Still, I didn't have much choice but turn and move to the counter where Alistair was waiting for me.

He gave me a beaming smile. "Mr. Lindstrom has requested

your services. He'd like a shampoo and massage."

"Of course." *You just had a shampoo and massage on Friday; don't you know how to wash your own damn hair?* I bit my cheek to keep from saying anything close to that and gestured for him to follow me.

Jal didn't do that, of course. He fell in step next to me, just like he had before. "Did you have a good weekend?"

"Of course. I imagine yours was as well. Congratulations on your engagement," I said, taking care to make sure my voice held nothing but good cheer.

"I take it you saw the paper."

I swept out a hand toward the seat and cocked my head. "The paper? Oh! Yeah. Sonya and Alistair were quite…" I pursed my lips, pretending I needed to think that over. I just couldn't seem to behave myself with him around. "Quite a flutter. You've made a few more conquests there. But yes, they showed it to me when I came in."

He actually looked a little disappointed. "That was the first you saw it? It was on the front page yesterday."

"Shocking, you being on the front page." It was far too easy to fall into that relaxed tone with him. I swung a cape around his neck and adjusted the chair before easing him backward over the bowl of the sink. What did it matter to him when I'd seen that damn paper? Since it did, though… "I don't spend much time reading the newspaper, Mr. Lindstrom. It's pretty tedious. News, most of it bad, social crap which is so very boring, and a lot of other stuff that doesn't really pertain to me."

"Hmm."

I'd already started to slick my hands through the healthy weight of his hair, but that *hmm* caught my ear. Glancing at his face, I lifted an eyebrow. "What's that *hmm* mean?"

"You struck me as the sort who seemed rather interested in keeping up with events. That's all." Light blue eyes caught mine, held, and for a moment, I felt almost…trapped.

It was like he was seeing right inside me.

The sound of splashing water drew me back. "There are other ways of keeping up with events. Besides, there are only so many events that are worth keeping up with. Why pay attention to the things that don't affect my life anyway?"

Before he could respond to that, I grabbed the nozzle and

started to rinse his hair. Settling into the massage straight after, I fell into that familiar rhythm. I actually went longer than normal just because he'd quit asking questions. He'd also closed his eyes, which meant he wasn't staring through me anymore.

"You keep that up, and you're going to put me to sleep," he said finally, his voice thick and soft.

A quick look at the clock told me I'd probably spent twice the normal amount of time on the massage than I normally did. At least with him, I knew Alistair wouldn't mind me being a little overindulgent.

"Well, you seemed to be enjoying yourself," I quipped. "Just trying to make sure you get your money's worth, Mr. Lindstrom."

I finished up and wrapped a warmed towel around his head before adjusting the chair. He was already sitting up, and I led him to my station so I could dry him. Once that was done, I could get him out of here.

Keenly aware of the fact that he was watching me again, I turned the chair so he wasn't staring directly into the mirror – and therefore, at me. "Would you like me to style it or just dry it?"

"Do I strike you as the kind of man who wants his hair fussed with?" he asked, sounding like he wanted to laugh.

"Well…you *did* come to a salon twice within the span of what…a few days?" The question slipped out of me before I could stop it and I winced, hoping like hell Alistair hadn't been around to hear.

Not even two seconds later, I was able to breathe out a sigh of relief because a bright, overly animated laugh filled the salon. That would be Esther Vosburg, one of the few clients that Alistair still saw to directly. Esther wouldn't have it any other way. Most of us suspected that she was trying to get him to ask her out. She hadn't quite figured out that he was gay. Which wasn't really a surprise since he flirted back, harmlessly enough, of course, but he kept her happy.

If he had Esther in his chair, then he'd be distracted for a good hour.

I finished my remark, "I think that alone says you're the kind of man who enjoys being fussed over."

"Ouch," Jal said. "You've got claws today."

"I've got claws every day." I reigned myself in, remembering where I was, who he was. "I'm just usually better at

94

hiding them. I think I'm having too much of a Monday. I apologize."

"You don't need to do that. I was just teasing you."

He was. I could hear the smile in his voice.

"Regardless, it's not appropriate for me to speak that way to a client." I turned on the dryer, silencing any further discussion and breathed out a silent sigh of relief. Being so close, I could smell the scent of him and it was…intoxicating. His hair was the color of cornsilk, soft and thick. Some women came in here and spend hundreds a month, or more, trying to get, then maintain this kind of color.

Once I'd finished, I turned off the dryer, smoothed his hair a bit more with the brush and then stepped back. "You're done, Mr. Lindstrom."

"Thank you." As he stood, I went about righting my station, trying not to think about how close he was standing. But the longer it went on, the more impossible it became not to acknowledge it. Turning, I pasted a blank smile on my face and tried not to take a step back.

"Is there something else you needed?"

He held out a hand. Familiar with the process, I accepted the tip, but when I saw the one-hundred-dollar bill, I shook my head and pulled my hand back without it. "I can't accept that kind of tip for such a small service, sir. It's outrageous."

"Please." He offered a smile that was both tempting and teasing. "I feel more relaxed after five minutes under your hands than two hours in a hot tub."

"Two hours in a hot tub isn't healthy." I shook my head. "A tip that size is excessive and you know it."

"Okay. Perhaps…" He dipped his hand into his pocket and withdrew a different bill.

Fifty still seemed ridiculous, but I was more comfortable with that than anything else. Besides, I'd gotten the impression he wasn't going to give up until he'd given me more than I deserved. "Thank you."

He nodded at me and turned to make his way over to the counter.

As he took care of his bill, I slid the money into my pocket and tried to steady my hands. Sonya's laugh, bright and fast, carried through the salon, and I tuned her out. I'd acted like I was above all of those people who'd been fawning all over Jal, but in reality, his hold on me was so much worse.

Ducking into the deli across the street, I breathed in a sigh of relief when I saw there was next to no line. I wanted a sandwich, some soup and some time to myself.

In short order, I had my meal. But within two minutes of sitting down, I realized I wasn't going to get the time to myself.

Somebody slid into the seat across from me, and I stiffened as Jal gave me his usual charming smile.

"Don't tell me you forgot something else in the salon."

"No." He gave me a sheepish smile. "There was something I wanted to take care of, but there really wasn't an opportunity. I had some business at the bank next door, though, and when I saw you ducking into here...well..." He finished with a shrug.

Even more nervous now, I leaned back in my seat. My Reuben sandwich and potato soup sat on the tray in front of me and my stomach, rumbling not five minutes ago, had begun to pitch in an altogether different manner.

"And just what was it you needed to take care of, Mr. Lindstrom?"

A look of frustration crossed his face. "Can't you call me by my name?"

"Mr. Lindstrom *is* your name," I responded. "Unless you lead a double life."

"Not what I meant, *Allie*." He leaned forward, elbows coming up to rest on the table with a casualness I wouldn't have expected from him. "Tell me something. Are you trying to be difficult or does it just come naturally?"

"Naturally," I snapped back. I wasn't at work, dammit. And I felt like I'd been...ambushed. "Now just what is it you need? I'm hungry, and I've got an appointment in thirty minutes."

Something flickered in his eyes, a frown dancing across his

face. I got the impression not many people gave him ultimatums on time.

"Some of us have to work for a living."

"I..." He stopped, blowing out a sigh. "Look, it's just...I have a function coming up in a few days. I thought you might like to go with me."

The noise around us faded into the background as a dull roar filled my ears.

"Excuse me, what?"

He repeated himself.

Yes, he'd said exactly what I'd thought he'd said.

"It's a fundraiser," he said, carrying on as though I wasn't gaping at him.

A fundraiser.

He was asking me to go to a *fundraiser* with him.

Had he lost his ever-fucking mind?

Chapter 4

Jal

She was looking at me liked I'd lost my mind.

In that moment, I couldn't really blame her. It was possible I had.

When I'd left the salon, I'd swung by the bank across the street to attend to a few minor business details. It wasn't the branch I normally used, but it was closer, so it would suffice. On the walk over, I'd told myself I needed to get over this bizarre obsession I'd developed for Allie Dodds.

I'd even agreed with myself.

Then I'd seen her hurrying across the street just as I came out of the bank.

Looking beautiful and carefree, not worrying that her shoes didn't match her purse and that her coat didn't particularly fit any certain *style*. She still looked beautiful, and she commanded attention.

She sure as hell commanded mine.

I wanted to know more about her.

I had no right to know more about her, I knew, but that didn't stop me from wanting it. It sure didn't stop me from following her. Sitting down at her table and asking a stupid question. And now I was hoping like hell that she'd say yes.

"I…" She drained half her drink in one gulp, then shook her head. "I'm sorry, I can't go with you. It would be inappropriate."

"Why is that?" I frowned at her.

"You're *engaged*." She glared at me. "Or have you forgotten already? Want me to go get another newspaper so you can remember what your fiancée looks like?"

Engaged.

As in...somebody had a claim on me. I had a claim on somebody too, but I guessed that was why it felt so foreign. I'd never wanted anyone to claim me, or wanted to claim anyone else. Except now Paisley had one by my own choice.

Uneasy with the path my mind was following, I pushed it all aside and focused on the here and now. On getting Allie to say yes.

When I didn't respond, Allie reached out and picked up her sandwich. It looked fantastic, and if I wasn't certain she'd run if I got up, I might have gone and gotten something myself.

"Don't you think you should be taking your fiancée?" she asked pointedly.

"Paisley already has plans." I lifted a shoulder.

It was mostly true anyway. Paisley had never particularly cared for this charity, which was odd, considering her father had been the one who'd introduced me to it.

"I could go alone," I continued, "but I prefer having somebody with me. In the past, I've taken other female friends. Paisley and I have an agreement when it comes to certain events. She loves to go to things like *Save the...*" What was the last one? "*Save the East Asian Hybrid Orchid*. Those things bore me stupid so she takes a friend from her social circle."

"And this...fundraiser you're attending on Friday? I take it that it's something that bores her stupid?" Allie nipped off another bite of her sandwich and then set it aside to pick up her spoon.

It took quite a bit not to stare at the sandwich. She hadn't even eaten half of it. I was starving. It was a Reuben and probably one of the best looking sandwiches I'd seen in ages. Sandwiches like that weren't exactly the standard fare any place close to where I worked.

"Ah..." Dragging my attention away from the sandwich, then having to drag it away from her mouth as she licked her spoon, I shot her an easy smile. "I wouldn't say that it bores her stupid. I'm a bit more of a social lout than she is, I'll be honest. But Paisley has her soft spots – the arts, for one. And I've got mine. I've got her father to thank for this one, though, really."

Allie tensed, something unrecognizable going across her eyes. "Is that a fact?"

"Yes. It's the *TomorrowU Foundation*. Are you familiar with it?"

She looked down as she nudged her tray away, reaching for the napkin and dabbing it across her lips. "Actually, yes. *TomorrowU* provided my brother's school with new computers."

"Really?" I couldn't stop the smile that spread across my face. I earmarked a certain percentage of my yearly income – and the company's – for the inner city charity, as well as several others that I'd discovered since I'd been introduced to it. It was one of the few things in my life that I could outright say I took serious pleasure in.

Well, that and sex.

It was the only unselfish thing I could say that I enjoyed. There was something about knowing that I could actually do something to make a difference in the lives of some kids who might not have a chance otherwise that just…well. It mattered. I couldn't figure any other way to describe it.

"Yeah." Looking a little disgruntled, she sighed and once more reached for her drink. "So the soon-to-be Mrs. Lindstrom isn't too keen on an inner-city charity, huh?"

Although her voice was neutral, I heard something there. Even though a part of me had felt the same way when Paisley had expressed her disinterest in the charity, I felt like I needed to defend her. "She has her interests. I have mine. We make it work."

"Let me guess," Allie said with a droll smile. "She's more about the pretty things. You said something about a flower, so I guess the others are cute little fuzzy animals, right?"

I couldn't help the smile. "How did you guess?"

"She just looks like the type." She glanced at me. "Look, I just don't think it's appropriate for me to go with you."

"There's nothing inappropriate about it. We're friends." She gave me a look. "Okay, so I think we could be friends." I gave her the same pleading look that had gotten me out of trouble a time or two. "Don't make me go by myself. You have no idea what it's like going to one of these solo. It's beyond a nightmare."

She gave me a skeptical look. "If you're used to doing these things with some other girl on your arm beside your fiancée, why don't you take one of them? Why me?"

"Because I'd like to take you," I said honestly. "Especially knowing that your brother's school has been one of the recipients of the charity. You understand what sort of positive impact it has. Wouldn't you like to talk to some of the people and let them know?"

"They won't care what I have to say." She brushed the idea off.

But I had seen a hint of interest in her eyes. Part of what made me so good at what I did was my ability to read people. While Allie was harder than most, on this, I knew I was on the mark.

"On the contrary, these are exactly the sort of people who want to hear from you. Sure, there are a few blow-hards that don't really give a damn about anyone other than themselves, but the rest really care, and they rarely get to talk to anybody who has benefited from there donations. Or family members," I added, smiling a little. "I realize it's your brother and his classmates who have benefitted, but you've seen what works and what doesn't. You would be able to share those observations with the people who can make a difference."

After a moment, she sighed. "You really do know how to push somebody's buttons, don't you, Mr. Lindstrom? I take it this is a formal event?"

"Yes, black tie."

"Aw, damn. And here I was thinking about saying yes, but I don't own any black ties." She clicked her tongue and gave me a snarky little smile.

It was adorable enough that I again had to remind myself not to leap over the table and kiss her. No kissing. She was off-limits that way.

Still, I couldn't keep from laughing. "As I'm the one strong-arming you into this, I'll handle your wardrobe. I can have a car to pick you up Thursday from your work…if arrangements can be made for your brother?"

"Some Thursdays he has an after school program with…" There was a faint hesitation, very faint, but I wondered what she was covering. "He stays after. Every other Thursday. But you don't need to buy my dress. I can handle it."

"I did mention it was formal, right? This is…" I hesitated,

not wanting to offend her.

"I have high society Philly princesses sitting in my chair all the time, Mr. Lindstrom." She looked amused. "I know what I'm getting into." She brushed her finger across the full lower curve of her mouth.

Man, that mouth…

"Okay, then. It's a date." The second I said it, I wanted to yank it back.

"No." Her eyes cooled. "Not a date. We're attending a function together. There's nothing remotely date-like about it."

"Relax…that's not how I meant it," I said easily, although I sure as hell wished I hadn't said it like that because now I almost wished it was a date. "We're just friends attending a function that happens to hold interest for both of us."

"We're not friends." She smiled as she repeated the words, but there was something almost sad about her. "We barely know each other. You're also a rich man engaged to a rich woman. I'm a hairstylist. We come from two very, very different worlds. We have nothing in common."

"Really? We both come from planet earth." That sadness in that smile got to me. Wondering where it came from, I touched the hand she had left on the table. "We breathe the same air, see the same sunset. We both eat, drink, laugh. I see kids in the city playing out in the streets with coats so threadbare they can't keep them warm. I bet you see them too."

Her lashes flickered. "I guess maybe you see a bit more of the world outside your own than I would have guessed. But that doesn't mean we have much in common." Then, before I could say anything else, "I need to go. See you in a few days."

She'd said yes. I couldn't quite contain the odd feeling of excitement as I met my driver out front. Thomas looked at the sandwich bag I held out. I'd lingered and finished the half she hadn't eaten before ordering another one for myself and one to go for Thomas.

"It's a Reuben. I had one just a few minutes ago. It was amazing."

"Thank you," he said, flashing me a wide smile. "I have to tell you, sir, I love a good Reuben. I don't get them too often. My wife doesn't care for them and…" His voice trailed off, and his smile went from appreciative to sheepish in a blink.

I didn't have to ask why. I slapped him on the shoulder. "Next time we're both hungry, maybe we'll head out here. I enjoy them too, and you can imagine I don't get sandwiches like that uptown."

"No, sir. I wouldn't think so." As I slid into the back of the car, I said, "Head down to the river and find a place to park. You can eat your sandwich, and I'll take care of some business so you can enjoy it while it's hot."

"Sir, that's not necessary."

I held up a hand to cut him off. "I can take care of things here just as well as anywhere else. Once you're done, then we can head up town. This way we can avoid the lunchtime traffic anyway. I hate lunchtime traffic."

Thomas found a spot near the river, and instead of staying in the car, I got out and walked over to the railing, looking out over the slow moving water.

Allie had said yes. Part of me felt a little strange about how I'd maneuvered her into it. I had never had to do that before. And even as I thought about that, I started to feel a different kind of guilt. This kind came with the realization that I was looking forward to seeing her again, spending time with her.

It's not a big deal, I told myself. It's not like we're going out on a date. Allie had made that clear. I had made that clear.

But in a way, it *was* like a date. I'd be picking her up. We were going to a formal function. There would be dinner, drinks, dancing. Those three *D*s usually added up to another *D*…date.

Turning away from the river, I shoved my hand through my hair and tried to shrug off the unsettling feeling in my gut. There was nothing to feel guilty about. It wasn't like I was deceiving her about what we were doing. I wasn't planning on ending my engagement. I wasn't planning on sleeping with Allie.

Although...just the thought of it was enough to make my mind conjure up an image and that image had my blood heating. Allie under me, those pale green eyes hot with need. Her body stretched out, her pussy wet and tight around my dick, her wrists pinned in my hand as I drove into her.

I turned and faced the river as my cock began to pulse, and my balls drew tight. That wasn't going to happen.

I was engaged.

Paisley was pregnant.

Allie was off-limits.

And even if none of the above were true, Allie wasn't interested. She'd made that more than clear. This wasn't a date.

This wasn't...anything really. Nothing remotely romantic about it, and I needed to get that through my head.

We were just attending an event together, and I'd introduce her to people...then probably retreat to the corner and watch her.

I had a feeling she'd charm just about everybody she met.

Not a date.

So why was I so damn excited?

Chapter 5

Allie

I had to go shopping for a dress.

Mom was going to get TJ after he finished up with his group today, and I usually got off early on Thursdays anyway, so I was going to take advantage of it and try to find something.

I did have some money I could spend.

While my father and I hadn't spoken since I was sixteen, he'd kept in contact. More or less anyway. Every few months, he'd send money – sometimes it was just a hundred dollars – usually cash. At least once a year, he'd send me some ridiculous amount, a check for a few thousand dollars. Once, it had been ten thousand. That had paid for cosmetology school as well as made sure TJ had the shoes he wanted for school that year.

Whatever he sent, if I didn't have a specific need, I put it away, just in case. The genetic condition that had made my mother lose her hearing, that might have caused TJ's hearing loss, could have other physical side effects. I wanted to make sure my family would be taken care of, no matter what happened.

I didn't just save it, though.

I was, after all, my father's daughter and Kendrick Hedges had been teaching me how to play with money and the stock market since I was five years-old. I'd made my first trade when I was nine.

I wasn't making millions because I wasn't investing high numbers. I was cautious in both the amount I invested and the trades I made. I wasn't trying for some get rich quick thing or anything like that. I kept most of what I made in a savings account that kept consistent interest, but I always set aside a percentage to use for investments.

How much I had and how much I could afford to spend fluctuated, but I'd been doing well these past few weeks, especially after my day trip to New York to return Jal's ring. So I'd go shopping. It had been a long time since I'd splurged on anything for myself.

The bottom line? I could afford to buy a nice dress...even if I would probably only wear it once.

Then again, I thought, maybe that was what I needed, to find other places and opportunities I could wear a nice dress to.

As I wrapped up my shift, Tao came strolling in, right on time. We'd been planning on hitting a few places together and then grabbing some dinner. I hadn't yet explained just why we were going shopping or just what I was looking for, and I was secretly dreading it.

He was going to smack me down to earth, and I knew it.

Maybe that was why I'd asked him along.

I *needed* to be smacked down to earth because I had to be fucking crazy to have agreed to do this.

"I'll be done in just a few minutes." Giving him a quick smile, I headed back to the employee's lounge and stowed my tunic, swapping it out for a blouse and some nicer flats that I'd brought with me. We weren't going to be heading into the local Dillard's or Macy's for what I needed. As it was, we'd both be lucky not to get kicked out for not looking the part.

When I came out, before I could say anything to Tao, Alistair came rushing over. "Allie, there's a man out front waiting for you. He says that Mr. Lindstrom sent him?"

My face went hot.

"What?"

Tao gave me a quick, surprised look.

The memory came back fast.

Jal's laugh. The way he smiled. Then his casual offer...*I'll handle your wardrobe. I can have a car to pick you up Thursday from your work.*

My face flushed even hotter. I'd told him I could handle buying my own dress. Apparently, he hadn't gotten the message.

"I'll handle it, Alistair. Tao, come on."

Hitching my purse up onto my shoulder, I headed outside.

Tao, ever curious, stayed close at my side, and at the sight of the car and driver, he gave a low, appreciative whistle. It could have been because of the car or the driver. Probably both. I would never hear the end of this, no matter how it played out.

"Damn, Allie. You're moving up in the world. That's a Bentley."

I could have jabbed him with a sharp stick just then – or smacked him on the head with one. I knew what kind of car it was.

Ignoring him, I focused on the man in the slick uniform. He approached me and gave me a polite nod. "Would you be Allie Dodds?"

"I would." I reached up, casually wrapping my fingers around the strap of my purse so I wouldn't fidget. "And you are?"

"Thomas, Miss Dodds. Mr. Lindstrom sent me. I'm to take you to Boyds. We're going to find you a dress to the charity function this weekend." He gave Tao a nod, so polite, so friendly. Sometimes, a client would come in with their assistants or drivers, and butter wouldn't melt in their mouths, but this guy was as friendly as he could be. Well, professionally speaking.

"You're here because Mr. Lindstrom sent you," I said slowly, ignoring the last part of his sentence.

"Yes." He checked the sharp timepiece on his wrist. "I believe we had an appointment for when you finished working for the day. Are you finished for the day?"

"No. I mean, I am finished, but no...we didn't have an appointment." Frowning, I stared at the car.

"What's going on, Al?" Tao asked, resting his chin on my shoulder as he smiled at the guy.

"Nothing, Tao." I nudged him back, but it didn't do much good. He just moved in closer and slung an arm around my neck.

"Mr. Lindstrom, huh? Come on, Allie. You shouldn't keep him waiting."

"Quite." Thomas gave Tao another polite nod and gestured to the car. "Miss, if you would...?"

"No." Jabbing Tao in the stomach, I sidestepped. "Look...um, Thomas. I told Jal – *Mr. Lindstrom* – that I'd take care of this."

Now the guy really looked confused. Just as Tao opened his mouth again, I caught his arm. "Be quiet." His incessant questions and the driver's persistent patience were threatening to do me in. Giving the man a bright smile, I held up my index finger. "Can you just give us one minute?"

Without waiting for an answer, I dragged Tao a few feet away.

"Would you stop? You're driving me nuts, and I have to think." Hands on my hips, I glared at him.

"You want to tell me what's going on?" The playfulness fell from his voice, and he stared past me toward the man in the suit, standing by the car, almost at attention with his shoulder back and straight, feet together. "What's up? Is this something about your dad?"

"No." I glared at him. He knew my backstory, was the only person besides my mother who knew it all. I didn't even know if Tyson knew as much as Tao. But we didn't talk about it.

"Then what's up?" He crossed his arms over his chest and stared me down.

Realizing that he wasn't going to back off until I explained, I gave him a hurried rundown of what happened and threatened his life if he said anything about my connection to Paisley. My stomach clenched when he slid a look back to the Bentley, then let his eyes linger on Thomas, who did a damn good impersonation of a statue.

"Honey, you know this is a bad idea, right?"

"It's about the charity," I said, brushing the idea that it could be anything else aside.

"I can believe that it is...in a way." Tao rested a hand on my shoulder, making it clear that he could already see how much bullshit was in that simple statement. "It's a great charity. They do a lot of good things at the college too. But it's not just about that. Is it?"

I started to deny it, and then after a second just gave up. "No. It's not. I just want…"

Tao pulled me in for a quick hug. "I know what it's about. It's me, remember honey?"

"I know." Sniffling a little, I hugged him back, then eased away.

"You're going to do this no matter what, aren't you?"

With my head tucked against his chest, I nodded.
I was screwed either way.

"No," I said again as Thomas gave me a pleading look.

True to his word, Thomas had taken me to the sort of place that threw girls like me out on their ass before they got two feet inside. Paisley would've felt right at home here, I was sure, which was yet another reason why I didn't. She and I had never moved in the same circles, and all this was doing was reminding me of how different we were.

As usual, Tao played peacemaker. "Look, I know you want to make sure Cinderella looks beautiful for the ball..." He winked at me before looking back over at Thomas. "But she can still be beautiful – and fit in – without shopping in a place like this."

"Mr. Lindstrom– " Thomas protested.

"Isn't the one wearing the damn dress," I interrupted.

"Allie..." Tao gave me a *shut-up and let me handle this* look. "Thomas, I'm sure your boss wants Allie to be as comfortable as possible, even when shopping for a dress, am I right?"

Thomas was on the fence, I could tell.

Tao pushed him over, leaning in with a conspiratorial wink. "I know just the place. Do you by chance know that song..." He hummed a few notes of a catchy new pop tune and then sang a few lines.

"Know the song?" Thomas rolled his eyes while I tried to figure out where Tao was going with this. "My seven-year-old sings it morning, noon and night."

"Oh, man." Tao shook his head. "Not my style, but I gotta tell you, that platinum blonde princess is a fashion queen...and I know her designer."

My jaw dropped as I swung my head around and gaped at him. He'd never mentioned anything of the sort to me. Though I supposed I shouldn't have been surprised. Tao was never one to name drop just for the hell of it.

Thomas looked intrigued.

"Yep." Tao buffed his nails on his shirt. "It's a friend of mine. Tarja. She designed the girl's last two dresses and after last night's award show, she's booked up for the next eighteen months, and looking to move to the Fashion District in New York. But she's still here in Philly right now, and I know she won't mind if we come in and take a look around her shop." Tao gave us both a pleased smile. "A design from Tarja will be every bit as good as anything you'd find in Boyds, darling."

Back in the car, I did a search on her name, and Tao, as always, was right. Tarja looked like she was on her way to fashion stardom.

Tao was busy too, texting back and forth, staring at my feet, my hair, my boobs critically.

What?" I asked, irritated after he'd leaned over to give my chest another intense stare. "You've had your hands on them a thousand times."

"Well, yeah." He gave me a patented Tao grin, his sapphire blue eyes sparkling. "But I wasn't exactly focusing on size before."

I supposed that was a good thing.

"Perve." Rolling my eyes, I went back to studying some of the dresses I'd been scrolling through. The country diva turned pop princess wasn't the only one who'd been wearing Tarja's designs. Two movie stars were now claiming they'd *only* wear her. That wouldn't last, I knew, but it was still high praise. Several socialites from New York, the governor's daughter. Tarja had quite the following already.

This might work...if she didn't charge me ten grand for a dress.

It took a little while to get there, and I had to admit, I was more than a little thrown by the building we stopped in front of.

"It's a train."

"Train *car*," Tao clarified. He'd already climbed out of the car and was waving at somebody who'd opened the door.

"Her store is a train car," I said as I got out of the car.

"Nah. Tarja doesn't haven't a store. She sells by word of mouth. Has for a while. People are going to be begging for her designs for years to come. I knew they would."

He grinned and held out his hands for the heavyset woman who approached, her hair slicked up into a rather fascinating beehive and her wide, deeply kohled eyes studying me the same way a scientist might examine a test slide.

"So you're Allie," Tarja said, pursing her lips as she circled around me.

"Yes..." I fought the urge to cover my breasts as she stopped dead in front of me, staring at my rack.

"I can work with this." She gave Tao a decisive nod. "You two boys wait out here."

"But..." I shot Tao a terrified look.

She caught my hand and began to walk. And since I was attached to that hand and she was insanely strong, I had to walk too.

"Sorry, sweets," she said. "I don't work with audiences."

Less than ten minutes later, I stood in front of Tarja wearing nothing but my underwear, trying to figure out what exactly just happened.

"Smart girl, you wore a strapless." She circled around me again, then stopped in front of me. She cupped my face and turned my chin from one side to the other. "What's the event?"

I had to rack my brains for a minute even though I knew I was familiar with it. Tarja seemed nice enough, but she was intimidating as hell. "It's a fundraiser thing for *TomorrowU*."

She grunted an approval. "Not a bad one, I guess. Better than some of the bullshit political stuff and most of the other *philanthropy* events where people just go to see and be seen." She walked over to a rack that held several pieces and began going through them.

Her little train car was an explosion of color, fabric and sparkles. I felt like I'd fallen into a rainbow. If I hadn't been so nervous, I would've enjoyed it. I wasn't an artistic person, but I definitely appreciated the beauty of things like this.

"Who you going with?" She asked as she pulled a dress of soft, misty gray green down from the rack and gave it a critical once-over before coming back to me.

I was so caught up at staring at the fabric and the way it shifted from a silvery, shimmery gray to misty green that I forgot to answer, and Tarja prodded me.

"Well? Is it a secret? I love secrets, Allie. I'll find out." She gave me a smile so much like one of Tao's that I felt myself start to relax.

"Um, no. It's not. Sorry…" I gave her a rueful grin. "The dress. I've got a weakness for pretty things, and I don't have many of them."

"There's not enough pretty things in life, I'll tell you." She held the dress up to me. "It's good with your skin – almost anything will be, really. Great for your body type too. So, your date?"

"It's not a date. He's going to introduce me to some people who donate. My brother goes to one of the schools that *TomorrowU* helps out a lot." I shrugged and couldn't resist stroking a hand down the dress. "His name is Jal Lindstrom."

"Lindstrom?" Slowly, Tarja looked up. "You're going with Jal Lindstrom? Well, shit. This dress won't work."

"Why not?" I fought the urge to snatch it away from her as she marched back over and put it on the rack.

"You said this wasn't a date, right?" She shot me a narrow look.

"No. He's engaged."

With a grunt, she started going through the few dresses on the rack before moving to another. A couple of the incredibly beautiful pieces ended up on the floor. Any of them looked fine to me, but I was going to leave it up to the expert. Besides, I had a feeling that questioning her wouldn't be the best idea.

"No, no, no…*hell*, no…" Finally, she turned back to me, hands on her hips. "I originally designed that for Miss High and Mighty Paisley based on measurements she gave me over the phone. Refused to come in for a sitting and when I told her I needed to see it on her to make any necessary alterations, she demanded I come to her. Then she tries it on and accuses me of making it too big across the chest, like I was the one who gave the wrong bust size. Girl didn't want to hear that she didn't have enough up top to fill it out right. Tried to make me refund her deposit but I reminded her that deposits are generally *non-refundable*. She sniffed her pretty little nose and said she'd never darken my doorstep again. Good riddance. But now she's calling me again…anyway." Tarja waved a hand. "I'm not putting *you* in one of her cast-offs. You, my dear, deserve something…better."

112

My heart fluttered a bit at that.

I couldn't explain why and I ended up lowering my head to hide the fact that I was suddenly fighting a rush of tears.

I hadn't even been allowed Paisley's or Mallory's cast-offs as a kid. My father hadn't wanted to risk anyone thinking he'd been paying too much attention to the help.

"Gimme a minute..." Tarja paced a few steps, forehead furrowed in concentration. "Oh, oh...I *love* it..."

She blew past me, and I wrapped my arms around my middle, watching her as she darted into a small area that had been sectioned off. "These are my babies. I made this one for a show, and then they went and changed the *theme*." The dry humor in her voice made it clear she hadn't been happy. "Paisley actually wanted it instead of the silver-gray, but no way would I give her this beauty. To make a living, sometimes I gotta sell to people I don't like, but nobody gets to wear these unless they're special."

She stepped out from behind the curtain, her arms full of something that shimmered in blue-green.

"And you, my dear, are the right kind of special for this. Let's get it on you and see if it looks as good as I think it will."

I was still staring at myself in the mirror when Tarja went to the door and called Tao in for his opinion.

He stumbled as he stepped inside, clutching at his chest. "Allie...you...I...I can't take the radiance."

"You're such an idiot," I said, grinning at him as I turned to stare at the back of the dress.

It swept low, revealing my back. It wasn't the typical floor length evening gown, and the high-low hem made my legs look endless, which was quite the accomplishment considering I was barely five-two. It ended a few inches below my knees in front before sweeping out into a train of sorts at the back.

"All you need now are the shoes, babe," Tao said after a critical study.

"I know just the pair." Tarja pulled out her phone and after a few seconds, showed me.

The price made my eyes go wide. "I can't spend that on *shoes*."

Hell, that was more than most of my shoes had cost all combined. Plus, she'd already told me what she was charging for the dress, and while it was a little over my budget, I knew she was practically giving it away. Besides, I had less problem giving my support to a local independent designer than some high-end store. But the shoes?

"Let your prince buy them," Tao suggested.

Tarja swept around us, pretending not to hear as she adjusted this or tugged that. I argued with him and let her turn me this way and that. But just as I was about to tell Tao to shut up, she caught my chin.

"Go get the shoes. Sounds like you're getting a fairy tale night. Let the guy be your fairy godmother since he can't be your prince."

"I…" I opened my mouth, closed it.

Then I looked at the picture of the shoes again.

Fairy godmother it was.

Chapter 6

Jal

If there was a time when I'd had this much trouble with my stupid cuff links, then I couldn't remember it. I also couldn't remember a time when I'd looked forward to an event this much either, and I knew the reason for both was one singular thing. One person.

Allie.

I was going to see her tonight, and I couldn't quit thinking about it.

After some prodding, Thomas had told me about how yesterday had gone, and I was both irritated and amused by the fact that she'd bought her dress from some woman in a train car. She'd invited Thomas to take a look so he could tell me that her choice was appropriate, and he'd assured me she looked lovely. I'd been a little annoyed that she hadn't just let me buy her a dress, but she had given in and gotten a pair of shoes on my account.

At my insistence, he gave me the name of the designer and I'd looked her up. The name had sounded vaguely familiar, which meant it was probably someone Paisley had talked about, although I couldn't see my fiancée having gone to a train car for a dress.

It wasn't the designer, however, that kept bugging me. It was how Allie had ended up with the designer in the first place. When I'd pressed the matter, Thomas had said Allie's...friend had recommended the woman. The pause had made something inside me twist uncomfortably.

I knew this *friend* was a guy without asking.

I couldn't push for more because it shouldn't *matter* that Allie had a guy friend. *Boyfriend*, some sly voice mentioned in the back of my mind. *He's her boyfriend.* And what should that matter? I was engaged. It wasn't as if I'd asked her out with romantic interests in mind.

"Doesn't matter," I said out loud as I finally managed to get the second cufflink into place. I shot a last look at my reflection, pushed a hand through my hair, and headed out the door.

My evening driver was waiting and greeted me with a smile. "Hello, sir. How are you?"

"Doing well, Eli. How's traffic looking?" Eli was a little older than Thomas but had only been my driver for the past couple years. He was nice enough, and professional, but I didn't have a connection with him like I did with Thomas.

"I've been checking. Shouldn't be much of an issue. I've already got the route planned out, and it shows just the typical traffic delays."

"Good."

He held the door open, and I slipped inside, noting the wine that had been opened and the glasses set out. No champagne. I'd been specific on that. Wine was a courtesy. Champagne was romantic. There was a cheese and fruit tray out as well, and while I hadn't had time to eat much since breakfast, I wasn't hungry. I wanted to see Allie.

I hadn't been this excited to see a woman since…I couldn't think of a time.

A few times in high school, maybe. The time when I'd asked out a junior even though I'd only been a sophomore, and she'd said yes. She'd also said yes when I slid my hand up her skirt, then inside her panties. I'd lost my virginity in the backseat of her car, and we'd dated for the next six months.

That first date was the only time I could remember being excited like this.

I knew I should feel guilty for feeling this way, and I supposed that, in a way, I did.

But I wasn't going to cancel the evening. I'd keep all of this to myself. I'd keep my hands to myself. I'd be friendly and polite, do nothing that could be considered inappropriate.

I couldn't ignore the fact, however, that I was going to spend an evening with a woman who made me laugh and think and…feel.

That was the problem, I realized on the drive to the address Allie had given Thomas. The minutes whisked away in silence as I turned the new knowledge over in my head. I hadn't *felt* anything with a woman in so long that it was a shock to do so now. I could feel pleasure with Paisley if I was fucking her, but even that was only a physical connection, not emotional. And I'd been surprised, then thrilled at the idea of a baby. But that wasn't even about her. It wasn't the idea of she and I having a child together that excited me. It was becoming a father. Paisley almost felt like an afterthought.

I knew that was a horrible way of thinking about my fiancée, but it was true.

It didn't matter to me if she was going out of town for a few days. If she was spending a few hours at the salon for a "massage." I suspected she was getting "personal" service from her preferred masseuse, Daniel, but I didn't care enough to ask. Paisley would never risk what she and I had by not being careful. Case in point, she'd already scheduled a paternity test after her fourteenth week to assure me that the baby was mine. Not that she'd been faithful, but that I was the one who'd gotten her pregnant.

And I still couldn't bring myself to really care about whether or not Paisley had another lover.

Allie, however, made me smile when I thought of her. I wanted to spend time with her, talk with her. Get to know her.

"We're here, sir."

This wasn't the best neighborhood in Philadelphia, but it wasn't the worst either. I looked up at the old three story building we'd parked in front of. I knew the type. I owned more than a few, and this one was in good shape although it was getting a little shabby.

Allie lived with her family, didn't she? She hadn't said whether that was in an apartment or a house.

"You sure this is the place?" I asked Eli.

"This is the address she gave Thomas." He exited the car and came around to open my door.

117

I was halfway out of the car when Allie came outside. She glanced back over her shoulder, talking to someone. I couldn't hear her, but I saw her lips moving. Her lips.

Her…everything.

Letting my eyes slide down her body, my heart began to race. The blue-green material drifted around her, and when she turned back, smiling toward me, my heart did a stuttering two-step in my chest.

Beautiful…

She started down the steps and was already on the third one before I managed to move toward her. Holding out my hand, I tried to find something casual and easy to say, but there was nothing casual or easy in mind.

Actually, I couldn't come up with much of anything.

My brain had turned into one giant void, and the only thought I could summon up was so simplistic, so *not* me, that I was better off not saying anything.

Allie put her hand in mine, smiling slowly. She'd slicked her mouth with a deep, wine red color that made me wonder how long I could kiss her before the color was gone...and then kiss her some more...

No. Idiot. Engaged. She's not yours.

But damn if I didn't want her to be.

I started to lift her hand to my lips but stopped just in time.

"You look…" I searched for anything that wouldn't be bordering on inappropriate, but I couldn't lie to her. "You look beautiful."

"Thank you." Her lips bowed up in a curve. "I hope you didn't give Thomas any trouble about the dress debacle."

My eyes dropped to the dress again. The bodice had a faint shimmer to it, something that sparkled under a thin mesh of fabric, and when she shifted, even when she breathed, those sparkles caught the eye and held it. "If this dress is the result, trust me, nothing was a debacle. You look lovely."

"Again, thank you." She glanced down and held out a foot. Like the dress, her shoes shimmered. It looked like she was walking on nothing more than air and crushed diamonds, the heel a clear material that I could see straight through. "You bought the shoes, if it makes you feel any better."

"They look like glass slippers."

"That's what I thought." She laughed and rotated her ankle, watching as they sparkled in the slowly fading light.

I wanted to kiss her.

I wanted it so bad, I could all but taste her already.

"We should go," I said gruffly, standing off to the side.

As she moved in front of me, my gaze slipped to her back. Her bare back. Naked, dusky skin that my hands itched to touch.

What in the hell had I been thinking?

Chapter 7

Allie

Taken…he's *taken*, I told myself again as Jal topped off my glass of wine.

We were still in the limo, waiting in line in front of the event venue, and while things were moving slowly, I didn't mind the wait. In fact, I was having more fun being stuck inside the limousine than I really had a right to. When it was just the two of us like this, I could almost forget about how different we were.

When Jal asked me more about the dream I had for opening my salon, I wondered how he'd even managed to get me to talk about it in the first place. I never talked about it. My mom didn't know. Tao didn't even know. It had been one of those things I'd always kept hidden away.

Until I'd somehow let it slip while talking to Jal.

"It's just a dream, Mr. Lindstrom," I said, offering a polite smile.

"Call me by my name, Allie."

"Okay, Allie," I parroted back easily.

Calling him by his name made things too easy, too intimate. He gave me a sigh of mock exasperation just as the car came to a stop and the door opened. I hoped I'd be able to get away without him asking again. Just the feel of his name in my mouth made my stomach twist.

There was a flash of cameras as I let him help me from the

car, the brilliant lights enough to almost distract me from the feel of my hand in his.

"Steady," Jal murmured as he wrapped my arm around his. "Just smile and walk. Don't stop to talk to anybody and it will be over soon."

That sounded a lot of like *smile and think of England*, I thought. My mom had told me that story once, and it'd always made me laugh. Now was no different, and I felt the laughter bubbling up again. I managed to stop it before it came out, knowing it would just sound hysterical, and that was the last thing I wanted.

Several people called his name and a few times, we stopped for pictures. Every time we stopped, the questions got worse, but he was gifted at being able to move along without giving them anything.

"You do this a lot?" I asked quietly as we kept walking.

"Not too often," he said. "There are more reporters here than usual because there's a rumor that a movie star's supposed to drop by to endorse *TomorrowU*."

We stopped just inside where he spoke quietly to somebody at the door, then shot me a smile.

The warm tingles that went through me were entirely out of place, but I told myself it was just a reaction to the right, or wrong, kind of stimulation. It didn't mean anything other than a completely normal physical reaction to an attractive man. I'd do the same if any other good-looking guy had smiled at me.

Except I knew that was a lie.

When we started to move again, he put his hand on the small of my back, and I felt the electricity shoot straight through me, down to the tips of my toes. I wasn't imagining it either. My toes curled inside my shoes and goosebumps broke out along my flesh. The dress left my back naked almost down to the base of my spine. Until his fingers rested there, I'd never realized just how sensitive that skin was.

"Are you cold?" he asked, bending his head down to murmur in my ear.

"No." I pretended a rapt attention on a piece of art that had been placed on a pedestal. There was a card placed next to it, with some information about a student. "This is nice."

"Would you like to have it?"

"No!" I shot him a surprised look. "I'm just making conversation."

"Well, it's for a good cause." He grinned at me. "Students from various schools who benefit from the charity have pieces up for auction. Whichever student pieces sell, the money goes into a fund for a scholarship for him or her, and it's matched by the foundation."

"Really?" Impressed, I studied the piece with renewed interest before turning to look for others. They were all amazing, but some of them were just staggering. "High school students did these?"

"Yes." Jal picked up the card and read it. "This was done by a ninth grader. I think I like it. It would look good in my office."

He looked up then, and that was when I noticed a young woman in a discreet black dress standing behind the sculpture. She smiled at him and held out an iPad. He punched something in, and then gestured at me. "Shall we?"

We made our way through the crowd, and from time to time, we'd stop and study a painting, or some sort of mixed media piece, or another sculpture. We were about halfway through when one caught my attention...and took my breath away. I wanted it so bad, it hurt, but there was no way I could afford anything here. I'd already splurged on the dress – the one I'd never really have a reason to wear again.

It was yet another reminder of the wide gap between people like me and people like Jal. They could buy pretty much whatever they wanted, whenever they wanted. Denying themselves something they wanted wasn't a notion they understood.

"Allie."

I turned, automatically smiling.

"This is Benedict Chambers – the brain behind *TomorrowU*." Jal indicated the man next to him.

Benedict Chambers was a black man, his age hard to determine, but I guessed he was in his fifties. He was tall and broad, with a face that looked like it had been hit – repeatedly – by a semi-truck. His tux was every bit as sleek as Jal's and when he spoke, his voice was rich and deep. "Hello...Allie, was it?"

"Yes, pleased to meet you, Mr. Chambers."

He covered my hand with his. "Jal was telling me that your brother and I have something in common."

"Oh…?" I shot Jal a quick look, confused.

"I went to the same school he attends."

"Ah…" I eyed the tux, trying to adjust the idea of a man who wore a tux like that attending a school anywhere that didn't require perfectly pressed blazers.

He chuckled, and I knew he'd followed my train of thought. "Let's just say I had some luck in life. That's part of why I started *TomorrowU*. Life has given me a lot. I believe in giving it back." He gestured toward a table tucked off toward the side. "Why don't you two join me for a drink? I must say, it's a been a while since I've actually been in school and things have changed…"

"I think you've made a conquest," Jal murmured in my ear as he took me into his arms on the dance floor. In my sky scraper heels, the top of my head actually came to his shoulders.

I told myself the dance was the sole reason my head was spinning.

Although, it might have something to do with the fact that I'd had some wine in the limo, then a glass of the most amazing champagne, and very little to eat. My nerves had destroyed my appetite most of the day, and now that the alcohol had dealt with the anxiety, I was too giddy to feel hungry.

With Jal's hand on the small of my back and his body warm against mine, I smiled up at him. "Mr. Chambers? Yeah. It's too bad he's married. Otherwise I might try to make him mine." I gave a low laugh. "He's a sweetheart. He wants to go in and talk to the kids at TJ's school. I gave him the name of the current principal."

"On a first name basis with him?" He shot me a teasing grin as he swept me around the dance floor.

His thighs brushed mine, and I shivered a little, wondering it might be like to feel him moving against me, without clothes…without the complications of a fiancée.

"No. I'm on a first name basis with *her*," I corrected him, hoping he assumed the blush in my cheeks was exertion and drink. "We talk often. There are...issues, sometimes with TJ."

"And you handle them? Not your parents?"

I shied away from explaining what it meant to be a CODA – a child of deaf adults. Jal knew that my mom and step-dad were deaf like my brother, but he didn't understand what that meant. Guys always acted differently once they knew, and even though Jal and I weren't involved like that, I *liked* how he treated me right now. I didn't want that to change.

I didn't want him thinking badly of my parents, so I kept it simple. "Communication with me is just easier."

"You do a lot for your brother." His fingers slid across the base of my spine in a caress, and it sent a shiver of awareness through me.

The song came to an end, and I eased away, curling my hands into fists to keep from reaching for him. "No. I'm just being a good sister."

Looking around, I licked my lips. My mouth was terribly dry, and even though it was stupid, when a passing server paused by us with a tray of champagne, I took a flute, downing half of it in a single swallow. The bubbles tingled my nose, tickled the back of my throat.

"It's part of being a family."

He took my arm and started to lead me back to the small table that had been set aside for us. My head went wobbly, and I held up a hand. "Whoa...I think that might have been a bit too much champagne."

"Maybe we should go." He stood closer and when I glanced up at him, there was a look in his eyes that made my heart race even harder than it already was.

And *that* had nothing to do with the champagne.

"Maybe." I nodded because if I didn't get out of here soon, I was going to end up doing something stupid.

Like not moving away ten minutes later when we were in the back of the limo, and he leaned toward me.

His mouth grazed mine, the touch almost too light to even be considered a kiss. I sucked in a breath, and all that seemed to do was draw him in closer. He slid his tongue across my lower lip, one hand resting on my knee as my mouth opened. The kiss deepened for several wonderful seconds before he drew back.

"We should stop this," he said, his voice rough.

"You're right." I caught his wrist, telling myself to push him away, telling myself to move away. I breathed in the scent of him.

The hand on my knee tightened, then eased. "Allie…" He kissed the corner of my mouth, an invitation. A warning, maybe.

I was doomed.

"Jal." I turned my mouth to his, taking that invitation, ignoring the warning.

I was lost, and I knew it.

Chapter 8

Jal

Her mouth was pure sin, her skin rich silk.

And when I pulled her onto my lap, she curled her body around mine like we'd been made for each other. Gripping her lush ass in my hands, I pulled her closer, felt her breasts press against my chest.

This was crazy. Insane.

I fisted my hand in her hair and tugged, drawing her back away from me. Then, eyes on her face, I used my free hand to loosen the clasp at her neck that held up the bodice of her dress.

Her breath hitched.

But she did nothing to stop the fall of the material.

She wasn't wearing a bra.

Fuck me.

They were firm and large, filling my hands as I cupped one in each. I leaned in, catching one nipple in my mouth. She arched her hips against me and my cock throbbed in response. With my tongue and teeth, I worked her nipple into a tighter bud, listened to her moan, felt her squirm.

Head spinning from her, from the alcohol, I tore my mouth from her breast and lifted my head.

Decision time.

If I wasn't careful, I'd fuck her right here in the car.

Eli would never say a word, wouldn't even peek back here, but I wasn't one to treat a woman like that. "I want you, Allie. Come back to my place."

She wouldn't say yes–

Her eyes widened a fraction.

I'd told myself that I'd make the offer and leave it at that, but I couldn't stop myself from continuing to speak.

"It's wrong. I know it. You probably do too. But I don't care. I want you." As her mouth fell open, I slid my hand up her knee to rest it on her thigh. "You want me too."

Her lashes fluttered, and my heart gave a wild thump. She wasn't pushing me away. Wasn't saying no. She did want me as much as I wanted her.

Shit.

I'd never craved anything as much as I craved her at this moment.

"Are you wet for me?" I asked, pressing my mouth to hers, easing my hand higher.

She whimpered, rolling her hips a fraction. I took the hint and slid my hand along the crease of her thigh, felt the lace of her panties. Nothing but lace and silk separated us. I pressed against her and stared into her eyes.

"You *are* wet. Decide, Allie. Tell me to stop...or say yes and let me take you home with me."

She closed her eyes, and I was sure this was done. That I'd never see her again.

Then she breathed out a single word, "Yes."

It was so faint, I barely heard it, but I *did* hear it. Something lurched inside me. It might have been guilt. It might have been anticipation. It was probably a mix of both, and I didn't care because no matter how guilty I felt in the morning, I wasn't going to turn back now.

I wanted her too much.

Hitting the button that would call Eli, I said, "Take me home, Eli."

"Of course, sir." There was nothing in his voice, no emotion, no censure.

Immediately letting go of the button, I turned and put Allie on the seat beneath me. She was soft, but strong too. Gripping her thigh, I squeezed and felt taut muscle under my hand. She arched up under me, her neck falling back. Unable to deny such an invitation, I bent down and scraped my teeth along the curve, felt her shiver. Her breasts were naked against my chest, and I wanted to slide down farther, worship those lush, ripe curves, but if I let my head go too far, I'd never stop kissing her, never stop touching her, and I wasn't going to take her on the seat of the limo.

She wasn't some quick fuck to satisfy my lust. I wanted more than that. I needed more than that with her.

So I kissed her, caught her lip between my teeth and bit it. She kissed me back, drawing my tongue into her mouth, whimpering when I ground my hips against hers. She shivered when she felt my teeth on her jaw and moaned when I bit her. Then her own teeth nipped at my earlobe, and a bolt of desire went straight to my cock.

I had to fight from pushing her skirt up and yanking her panties off. Just a few quick moves, and I could be inside her, have her wrapped around my dick. Feel that tight heat squeezing me.

"We're here, sir."

The voice came from out of nowhere, not making any sense. I cupped Allie's breast in my hand, ran my thumb over her taut nipple.

"Mr. Lindstrom."

I shoved upright, realized what had interrupted me – us. Or rather, *who*. The window was still up between us, but I still automatically moved to shield Allie.

"Thank you, Eli," I said, my voice ragged.

He climbed out of the driver's seat while I helped Allie sit up, helped her fasten the dress. Her hair was disheveled, but she still looked beautiful. Lush, sexy...all I could think about was getting her inside my house.

"Are you sure about this?"

"No." She licked her lips, her cheeks flushing a deep pink under the soft, delicate brown. "But I'm doing it anyway."

It took only a minute to get inside.

Even less for me to turn and put her up against the front door. I didn't keep a live-in staff. It was just me here and bringing in a housekeeper once a week was enough to take care of anything I couldn't. Now, I appreciated my privacy even more because I didn't think I could wait any longer for her.

Boosting Allie up, I pinned her between me and the aged oak. "I've wanted to taste your mouth since the second I laid eyes on you." I brushed my nose against hers. "I shouldn't be doing this."

"Then why are you?" She stared at me with level eyes.

"Because I can't stop thinking about this mouth." I cupped her face and, to prove what I'd told her, I kissed her. It was a deep, full-on kiss, and now I didn't worry about being seen or being interrupted, so I intended to keep my mouth on hers until neither of us could breathe.

As my lungs began to burn, she slid her hands under my jacket, and I caught them, pinning them over her head. She didn't resist, but when I lifted my head, her eyes were wide, startled. Our eyes locked as we both struggled to regain our breath.

"If you keep touching me, I'll lose my head. I'd rather see you lose yours."

The smile on her face set my balls on fire. "Well...that's just fine, Jal. But keep in mind...turnabout is fair play."

"I'll keep it in mind."

I used my free hand to unhook her dress again, but I didn't let it stop at her waist this time. I nudged it down over her hips until it fell in a blue-green puddle to the floor. She stood there wearing a pair of panties almost the same shade as the dress, and those fucking sexy Cinderella shoes. The punch of lust hit me so hard, I was tempted to spread her legs and fuck her right there against the wall.

But...no.

This was going to last.

This was raw madness, but I was going to make it last.

Taking a step back, I said, "Wrap your legs around me."

She did so, without hesitation.

Then I carried her down the hall into my office. I didn't want to make love to her in the bed I sometimes shared with Paisley, didn't want those memories in my mind when I took Allie.

No, I thought. If I was honest, I didn't want my memories of tonight to be marred by Paisley. I wanted Allie somewhere that would let me enjoy remembering what we had, somewhere I would never be with Paisley.

She eyed me nervously as I set her down on my desk. I was neat when it came to business. Almost excessively so, which meant I didn't have anything to clear off, and it was the perfect height for what I wanted to do first. The couch could wait until our next go.

I thoroughly planned on having her as many times as I could tonight.

She shivered a little as I guided her flat, the glass likely cool against her flesh.

"Are you cold?" I asked.

"A bit." Her nipples were hard points, and goosebumps ran across her skin.

I leaned down and flicked my tongue against one of those chocolate-colored nipples. "You won't be for long," I promised.

I stepped back and stripped out of my tuxedo jacket, vest, and tie, tossing them all on a nearby bookshelf. I didn't bother to look to see if they stayed. I freed the first few buttons of my shirt, and then grabbed the chair and brought it around so that I could sit down.

Her cheeks flushed when I tugged her to the edge so that I was between her thighs. I kissed one hipbone as I reached for her hand and tugged her upright. At this level, her breasts were slightly higher, a sweet, open invitation. I caught the tip of one, bit it. She whimpered, and I pulled back, concerned. I thought I'd read her correctly, but maybe not.

"Too hard?"

"No." It was a raw moan, full of hunger, while her fingers curled in my hair, urging me on. "More."

I moved to the other one and used more pressure. At the same time, I rested my free hand high on her thigh and stroked my thumb down her slit. She still wore her panties, but they weren't enough to keep me from feeling the rush of heat. She squirmed trying to get more pressure, but I pulled my hand away. Rising, I kissed her, harder, rougher, plundering her mouth. She was gasping by the time I lifted my head, and when I eased her back, she didn't protest.

She watched as I gathered her wrists into one hand, as I pinned them above her head. I pressed my mouth to her chest, just below the elegant notch of her collarbone. Her breath shuddered with each kiss I brushed against her skin, and by the time I'd reached the edge of her panties, she was breathing in hard, rough pants. I let go of her wrists but shot her a quick look.

"Be still." I didn't make it a suggestion.

She curled her hands into fists and gave me a quick nod.

Dragging her panties down, I revealed a neat patch of curls, already wet. My mouth watered, and I had to fight to keep from just tearing the underwear off, but I kept my movements slow – teasingly so.

By the time I dropped the scrap on the floor, we were both trembling.

She wore nothing but those wicked Cinderella shoes now, and I gripped both ankles, just above the straps and pushed her thighs wide. "I'm going to taste your pussy, Allie, and see if you're as sweet as I think you are."

Her eyes flew wide as I settled in the chair again, draping her legs over my shoulders. I blew a puff of air against her, and she shivered. She sank her teeth into her lower lip, letting it go slowly before her head fell back against the desk. It was a sign of total surrender, and my cue to see if I could make her scream.

I licked her, using my tongue to open her, exposing the entrance to her core and the hot nub of her clit. She whimpered. Then, leaning in closer, I pressed my mouth against her pussy and feasted.

She was sobbing by the time the first orgasm hit her, and I wasn't even close to done.

I used my fingers and mouth to bring her to the edge over and over. I knew I'd never sit at this desk again without seeing her spread open like this, without hearing the way she said my name.

My name. Not Mr. Lindstrom. Not Sir.

Jal.

And it sounded as amazing as I'd imagined it would.

I curled my fingers inside her, pressed against her g-spot. Her body jerked, then arched as she cried out, coming again. Her pussy tightened around my fingers even as I coaxed her higher.

When she finally went limp, I stood and picked her up. She blinked up at me as I carried her over to my couch, her attention focusing as I stripped out of the last of my clothes. Her tongue came out to wet her lips as her gaze dropped to my aching cock.

Damn, I wanted to fuck her mouth.

But, I wanted something else more.

The room seemed far too hot now. The wide, fat couch I'd bought was soft as a bed and almost as wide – I'd bought it so I could nap on it and I was never more appreciative of my preference for function over form than in that moment.

I settled over her, fighting the urge to simply drive into her,

131

rut hard and fast until I found my release.

The dim light glinted off the sparkle in Allie's shoes, and I caught her behind the knees with my elbows, rubbed my cock against her wet heat.

She moaned. "Quit teasing me, Jal."

Damn, I loved the way my name sounded coming from her mouth.

"It's all about making it last."

But she was right. I couldn't keep teasing her because I was dying. Bit by bit…I was dying. I needed to be inside her, to be a part of her.

Staring into her eyes, I shifted down and pressed against her. "Does this feel like I'm teasing?"

Her breath caught.

I'd put the condom on right after I'd taken off my clothes, but at this moment, I wished I could've sunk into her, skin against skin. Nothing between us. She felt *everything* and all those raw emotions seemed to flood into me and warm me. I wanted to feel that with nothing between us.

Except I wasn't going to be *that* stupid.

A hungry moan escaped her, and she reached up, sinking her nails into my shoulders. The small bite of pain made my blood flare, hotter, brighter. Made me push inside her faster than I'd wanted to. She wailed as I buried myself deep, her nails leaving scratches down my back as she writhed beneath me.

More pinpricks of pain, each one reaching for that primal part of me that I hadn't planned on tapping into tonight.

No…not good. Not good…

I let her knees go and caught her wrists, drawing them high over her head. The position arched her back, forcing her breasts higher. I bit one nipple, the other, felt her pussy tighten around me.

I groaned. "You've got the snuggest, sweetest pussy."

"You've got a dirty mouth."

"You don't seem to mind." I gave her a cocky smile.

"No…" The word trailed off into a moan as I circled my hips and then thrust deeper, harder.

I wanted to keep teasing her, keep bringing those smiles to the surface. But the feel of her – *all* of her – was dragging things out of me that I hadn't felt in a long time, if ever. I could feel the connection between us, binding us, changing us from two bodies into something singular.

Losing myself in her, I rode her faster, harder, staring into those pale green eyes. She rocked against me, raising her hips to meet me, but never trying to free her hands. Even when my grip tightened, I could see the trust in her eyes, feel it in her body.

She trusted me with everything she was.

Her body trembled as her orgasm approached, and I knew mine was just as close. I wanted to make this last, but it wasn't going to happen.

Later…I'd take her again and then we'd make it last.

Her eyes started to close.

"Don't," I demanded, cupping her chin and forcing her eyes to meet mine. "Be with me."

Slowly, Allie lifted her lashes and met my eyes. I kissed her then, crushing my lips to hers. Neither of us closed our eyes, watching, seeing.

This…just…*this*.

As the climax raced closer, I drove myself into her even harder.

It was like I was trying imprint myself on her. Maybe I was.

She'd already gone and imprinted herself on me.

"Say please…"

I scraped my teeth across her clit and smiled as she jolted, her hands tightening in my hair. I knew her entire body had to be so sensitive by now. Mine was. Every touch was magnified, the pleasure tinged with an edge of pain, but I wasn't going to stop. If this was all I had, I didn't want to waste a single minute.

"Please, you teasing bastard."

"That wasn't what I told you to say." I caught the hard little nub between my teeth and pulled. "How about…*yes*? Will you say yes?"

133

Allie's eyes were glazed with lust as they met mine. I rose up over and smiled, licking the taste of her off my lips.

"*Yes* what?" she whispered, her voice hoarse from screaming.

"*Yes, Jal...you can fuck me. Yes, Jal...I want you.* Just...*yes.*" I bent over and kissed her, sharing the taste of her, and groaning as she licked my lips, not shying away at all. She may have looked innocent, but her appetite was almost as insatiable as my own.

"Yes, Jal," she breathed.

I caught her thighs in my hands and pushed them wide.

"*Yes, Jal, you can fuck me,*" I instructed her.

"Yes, Jal, you can fuck me," she echoed.

I bumped the head of my cock against her opening.

"*Yes, Jal, I want you.*"

She said it back, her voice hitching as I pushed inside.

"Yes, Jal..."

"Yes..." The words became a wail as I thrust deep, hard.

"Now...scream it." I thrust deeper, harder, until she was doing just that.

I wanted to pull every last emotion from her, leave her as desperate for me as I was for her. Her pussy tightened around my cock, squeezing so tight, clamping down around me like a fist, and I shuddered as I withdrew almost to the tip before driving back in.

Allie sank her nails deep into my shoulders, and I swore, tossing my sweat-soaked hair back from my face. I was pretty sure she'd drawn blood, but I didn't care. In fact, I welcomed the pain.

Her eyes were closed, her lips open.

She looked like a work of art, a study in passion.

And when she came, my heart ached, and I knew nothing would ever be the same again.

Chapter 9

Allie

Some days, a person got to wake up feeling like a million bucks. Those were the good days.

But then there were the days where you could go from feeling like a million dollars to feeling like a husband-stealing tramp – okay, technically fiancé-stealing – all in the blink of an eye.

Memory crashed into me hard and fast, leaving me no time to dwell in the afterglow, no time to adjust.

"Yes, Jal." *His hands on my thighs...*

"Yes, Jal, you can fuck me." *His eyes glinting with a wicked light as he smiled at me.*

"Yes, Jal, you can fuck me." *You can do anything...*

"Yes, Jal, I want you."

Oh, man, did I want...

"Yes, Jal..."

"Yes..." *I could barely form the words, but I knew he wanted me to scream...*

The dream-memory shattered, falling apart around me, and then I was awake, shivering and aching...and aware. Aware of every single thing I'd done.

Sitting up, I swiveled around on the couch and looked around. My body felt used and abused in the very best of ways. The rest of me felt used and abused in the very *worst* of ways – and that was my own damn fault.

"What have I done?" I mouthed the question silently to myself as I dropped my face into my hands.

I was drunk–

Knee jerk reaction and immediately, I had to toss it aside, because I *hadn't* been drunk. Not really. I'd been lightheaded, tipsy, yes, but I'd known exactly what I was doing.

I'd slept with a guy I barely knew – stupid.

I'd slept with a rich white guy – also stupid.

I'd slept with a guy so far outside my league, it wasn't even comprehensible. *Stupid* didn't touch it.

And I'd slept with a guy who was engaged – *to my half-sister*.

That wasn't just stupid. It was wrong on more levels than I wanted to acknowledge. Part of me understood that I'd been caught up in all this because I wanted a little bit of *her* fairytale life. The life I'd never been good enough to have.

Then I'd gone and stolen her prince.

Not that I'd really *stolen* him.

He wasn't mine.

We'd just had sex.

But I'd still done something wrong, unforgivable. It didn't matter that Paisley didn't know. *I* knew.

My stomach rebelled, and I barely managed to keep myself from throwing up, but I couldn't do anything about the cold sweat that broke out over my body. Hand pressed to my mouth, I bit my lower lip and blinked back the tears. I didn't have the luxury or the time for tears. What I did have time for was getting out of this bed, finding my clothes and getting out of here before I had to explain any of this.

Easing the blanket back, I started to roll over. Jal moved with me, burying his face in my hair as he murmured something.

My heart broke a little as my ears picked up on it.

My name.

He'd said my name.

With his hand on my belly, he tugged me back to him, his big body pressed against mine and his chin resting on my shoulder. I felt surrounded by him…treasured, cradled. Like I was something precious. Something that mattered to him.

Squeezing my eyes tightly shut, I tried to figure out what to do. After a few more moments, he settled back in to sleep. I took

136

his hand and steadied it as I worked out from under his embrace. He made a few more noises under his breath, but then rolled onto his back and flung his forearm over his eyes, determined to stave off morning for a little bit longer.

Part of me wished I could settle down next to him, hide away from morning and reality too. But morning and reality were coming whether I liked it or not.

With every passing moment, my mind cleared, the details from last night becoming like crystal in my mind. I remembered tossing back champagne, most of it on an empty stomach, but I couldn't pretend anything had happened because I was drunk.

I *wish* I could blame it on that, but my head had been clear enough.

Dancing with him, I'd made a stupid, silly wish that he could be mine, wishing for other things I had no right to. A dance, a kiss…more.

Then he had kissed me in the limo.

He'd kissed me, put his hand on my knee, saying the very things I'd been thinking.

This is wrong.
We shouldn't.
I don't care.

It *had* been wrong. We totally *shouldn't* have.

And I hadn't cared.

Not at the time.

But now…

I'd said yes when he asked me to come home with him. Then I'd *screamed* yes as he teased me about wanting more. And I'd screamed it again as he made me come.

I shivered, desire a twisting knot in my belly.

I wished I could pretend I'd been just a little too drunk. That would have given me a little bit of solace, but as I lay there in the cold, hard light of morning, I had no one but myself to blame.

And the knowledge that if it were all to play out again, I would have made the same choices.

Guilt didn't describe how I felt.

Behind me, Jal rolled over onto his side and made a low noise deep in his chest. He sounded like a giant cat, stretching out and his sleep, and the part that didn't want to think about what I'd done wanted to turn back and curl up against him. I just wanted to forget about everything for a little while longer. It was a luxury I didn't have though.

Pushing up of off the couch, I stood up and looked around. The only articles of clothing I could find happened to be my underwear and my shoes. I grabbed them and eased out of the room after checking to make sure there wasn't anybody lying in wait.

The last thing I wanted to do was run into a housekeeper or a butler, but I didn't see anybody as I made it to the front door. My beautiful dress lay there in a wrinkled puddle. Grabbing it, I hurried into it before looking for my purse. My phone was running on low, but I was able to text for a car.

Wiggling into my panties, I used the step as a seat to put my shoes on, listening for Jal or anybody else.

A car would be there in less than ten minutes. It was cold outside, and I hadn't worn a coat last night. I didn't have a decent one for anything even remotely dressy, but I couldn't stay inside.

Still, I hesitated another minute. The silvery haze of frost clung to the trees outside, but I couldn't delay the inevitable without risking Jal waking up.

And I couldn't face him right now.

I was having a hard enough time facing myself.

That was enough to push me out the front door, and into the frigid not-quite-spring air. My arms were covered in goosebumps before I even cleared the porch, and by the time I'd navigated the long, twisting drive, my teeth were chattering. I'd asked the driver to pick me up a few houses down from Jal's, and I was going to have to hoof it to get there. Hopefully, that would warm me up.

My breath came in puffy clouds as I walked. All around me were elegant, stately homes. In this posh area of Philadelphia, houses didn't run in the six figures. It was more like seven and eight.

I was in luck. The black car with the uber sticker came pulling up before I'd gone more than a few feet past the drive. Waving at him, I sighed gratefully. Warmth wrapped around me as I settled in the back seat of the car.

I gave the driver the address to confirm...then I made the mistake of looking back just as Jal came jogging outside.

He looked down for the car just as we turned off the road. He didn't see me. But it didn't matter.

Pain lanced through me, bright and sharp.

I'd made plenty of mistakes in life – *plenty*. I had plenty of regrets to go along with them, but this one topped the list.

No matter how drawn I'd been to Jal, I'd had no business doing this.

I had no business wanting him, and I sure as hell hadn't had any business acting on those wants.

I'd grown up around this sort of thing, and I knew the misery it caused, the strife, the emotional bruises.

I'd made myself a promise that I wouldn't ever be the cause of it, and I wouldn't be on either side of it, either.

But here I was, the other woman.

And it wasn't enough that I had slept with an engaged man. I slept with the one who was engaged to my sister, even if that relationship was blood only.

I loved my mother, but that was one way I'd never wanted to be like her. But now I was. The billionaire's mistress. I'd destroyed Paisley's second family as surely as my mother had destroyed the first. Even if she never knew, it was still there.

Chapter 10

Jal

There were some dreams too sweet to wake up from.

Allie's hands gripping my hair, holding my face tight against her pussy as I lapped her up...that was one sweet, sweet dream.

Rolling onto my belly, I pulled a pillow in tight and buried my face in it. It was scratchier than normal, and that didn't help me settle back into the dream any better, but for a few more minutes, I kept reality at bay and tried to pretend I was still in that dream.

Allie...

Her legs around me. Her hands in my hair.

My cock pulsed and instinctively, I pushed my hips against the mattress. Soft leather gave under me.

Leather. I was on the couch.

Leather...the couch...just like in my dream.

Slowly, I started to smile. Maybe it hadn't all been a dream.

Maybe I was here trying to block out reality and the general fucked-up state of my life, and Allie was next to me. I swept out a hand. The space next to me was still warm.

The smile spread.

Allie...

I heard the front door close. It was quiet, but the sound echoed through my head. Jerking upright, my head spun.

What the hell–

Just like that, everything from last night tumbled into place.

I'd danced with Allie.

I'd laughed with her.

Kissed her.

Brought her back here and fucked her – on the desk, then on the couch, because I hadn't been able to stand the idea of taking her in the bed where I sometimes slept with Paisley. Because I'd wanted to have a place where I could remember without any other memories creeping in.

My cock pulsed again, this time in demand.

Allie...

"Stop it," I muttered, pressing my hand against it as I looked around, taking note of the things I'd missed the first time. My clothes were everything. I'd stripped Allie pretty much naked in the hallway, but I didn't see her shoes or her panties, which confirmed what I'd already known.

She was gone.

Will I was dead asleep, she'd left.

I'd slept better than I had since Paisley had told me about the baby, and Allie had just slipped out.

"Aw, hell." Dropping my head into my hands, I let the ramifications of what I'd done catch up to me. "The baby. Paisley...*shit*."

I hadn't had a decent night's sleep since Paisley had told me about the baby and I'd realized that I needed to marry her.

What in the hell had I done?

That wasn't me. I wasn't the kind of guy who ran around on his girlfriend. His fiancée. I may never have been one to have serious relationships, but when I did, I was faithful. I didn't cheat on women when I made them a commitment.

But that was exactly what I had done. I'd slept with Allie.

Worse, even *thinking* about her was enough to have me ready to do it again. If she'd been lying next to me when I'd reached for her, I would have had her under me and been inside her without a second thought.

It was good that she was gone, and the coward in me wanted to just let it go – let the whole thing just pass.

But...

I couldn't.

I needed to talk to her. To apologize.

It couldn't have been more than a minute or two since she'd

slid out the front door. Grabbing the wrinkled trousers from the floor, I pulled them on hurried down the hallway. The cold air hit my bare chest the moment I was out the door, and it was enough to remind me that Allie hadn't worn a coat last night.

Concern overrode everything else. Where'd she gone? I needed to take her back inside where it was warm.

The long drive was empty, but I heard a car. The cold pavement had already numbed my feet, but I didn't even consider going inside to get shoes. Once I caught up with her–

I stopped, spying a black car as it pulled away from the curb.

I wasn't going to catch up with her.

"Dammit!" I shouted. A couple of birds in the nearby hedge took off, tweeting indignantly at me. Turning on my heel, I stalked back to the house.

Once inside, I slammed the door and put my back against it, sliding down to sit on the floor. Glaring off into the distance, I fisted my hands and called myself a hundred kinds of fool.

I had been a selfish bastard last night, and a stupid dumbass this morning.

What was I going to do?

I had to apologize to Allie – had to find her first.

And Paisley…that was another nightmare altogether.

The last thing I wanted to do was *tell* her, but at the same time, the idea of not telling her was a weight I didn't want to carry. Shit like this always worked its way to the surface.

I needed to figure out what to tell Paisley.

I wasn't all that great at keeping secrets. Paisley was pretty decent at it, but I knew about the "arrangement" she had with her masseuse. She didn't particularly care about him – I knew that too. But all of that had been before the engagement. We hadn't talked about how things would work now that we were getting married, now that we had a baby on the way, but I'd always assumed I'd be in a monogamous relationship once that happened.

I'd never wanted to be *that* man. It was one of the reasons I'd always been so careful with the women I slept with, so a child wouldn't be involved. I wouldn't put a kid through all of that shit, no matter what I wanted. I could be a selfish bastard, but I'd never put myself above a child.

At least, I never thought I would.

"I didn't ask for this," I muttered, feeling sorry for myself and hating it.

I hadn't asked to meet Allie or to like her more than I'd liked anybody in a long time. I hadn't planned on Paisley getting pregnant, had done all I could to prevent it, short of a vasectomy.

Driving my fist into the mellow gleam of the hardwood floors, I swore out loud, listening to my voice as it echoed throughout the empty house.

"You have to deal with this," I finally said.

Man up and deal.

After a few seconds, I did feel a little…well, not better, but steadier.

I most definitely messed up last night, and in a big way. Ever since I'd met Allie, I'd fucked up one way or another, and it was time to start dealing with consequences.

I had to talk to Paisley, and I had to talk to Allie. I needed to make things right.

Or at least as right as I could, because I couldn't see a way out of this where no one was hurt.

Chapter 11

Allie

My pretty Cinderella dress was stuck in the back of my closet. I'd tucked the shoes away too. I'd never wear them again, but I didn't have the heart to give them away. Not yet. Maybe not ever.

Too bad I couldn't pack away the memories as easily.

I was in the shower now, in an effort to wash them away, but that wasn't working particularly well.

The pounding, hot spray felt wonderful on aching muscles, and it chased away the chill I hadn't been able to lose, but it did nothing to ease the guilt or my anger.

I knew I could stand under this spray for twenty years, and it wouldn't do anything. I could stand here for two *hundred* years, and it wouldn't lessen the guilt. Because I was guilty.

The water slid over my breasts, droplets gathering on my belly to slope down and collect in the nest of curls between my thighs. To collect in that place where Jal had done so much for me. One particular memory came back with enough force to almost hurt.

Jal on his knees in front of me as I lay on the couch, spreading me with his thumbs, looking at me as he bent low. *I'm going to eat this pretty pussy right up, Allie...say yes, say you want it.*

Moaning, I slid my hand down and cupped myself, because that memory alone made me burn.

Last night had been everything I'd been missing. Tao was a

good lover, knew how to bring pleasure to my body. But the passion I'd had last night had shattered everything I thought I knew.

Desperate, I hurried through the rest of my shower, turning the water down to cold so I wouldn't be tempted to remember more about last night, tempted to try to relive it.

Tears burned my eyes again, but I fought them back and won...again. I had no idea if the tears were from pity or something more, but once I gave in, it was going to be ugly and messy, and I didn't want to do that now. Maybe tonight.

I wasn't even sure if I deserved them.

My phone buzzed as I was drying off. For a moment, hope flared bright inside me at the thought of Jal calling me. Except it wasn't Jal. It was Tao, and I almost ignored it. He'd been texting off and on since nine, and I knew he wanted to know about last night. I didn't want to talk about it, but I knew if I put it off too long, though, he'd just show up.

Want to meet for breakfast?

I put the phone down after I sent the text and wiggled into my panties.

Yes. When?

I needed time to dry my hair so I asked for an hour and named our favorite meeting place. He shot me back a smiley face, then I set about dealing with the nightmare that had become my hair.

I wasn't going to think about Jal for a few minutes.

I really, really, really wasn't.

But I hadn't even managed to work the cream condition through my hair before he popped into my thoughts again.

This was going to be a fucking long day.

145

I had no sooner sat down when Tao leaned forward, pinning with a dark look. "You tramp. You slept with him, didn't you?"

Blood rushed to my cheeks. If I could have sunk into the cracked vinyl of the booth, I would have. "You asshole. Why don't you say it a little louder? People in Maine might hear it next time."

Tao waved a hand around the mostly empty diner. "*Hello*...it's Saturday and the place is dead. Now answer me."

The server appeared and offered coffee, which I gratefully accepted. After I had a few sips, I decided I could handle this without killing my best friend.

I still gave him a dark look, but Tao gave me a cheeky grin in return.

"I'm waiting."

I took another sip of coffee, sighed in satisfaction. In another hour, if I kept this up, I might feel warm again. I might feel alive. Too bad strong coffee did nothing to relieve guilt.

Just like that, my almost-okay mood plummeted and crashed.

"Hey..." Tao touched my arm, and I looked up, met his eyes. "You going to talk to me?"

"Not so sure." I gave him a weak smiled as I put the cup down.

Pressing the heels of my hands against my eyes, I tried to block out the memories. Jal's hands on me, his mouth...the way he'd whispered my name in his sleep. How it had felt to fall asleep in his arms. Safe. Protected.

"I don't know what the hell came over me, Tao. I don't know what drove me to do something so, so...*stupid*."

"How drunk were you?"

"I *wish* I could blame it on that. I'd had some wine in the limo, and then some champagne at the event. I was tipsy, maybe, but I wasn't drunk." Blowing out a hard breath, I shook my head. "The fact of the matter is, I knew what I was doing. I knew, and I just didn't care. I even knew I'd ended up regretting it." I held out my hands. "This is me. Regretting it."

"And yet..." Tao prompted me.

"I'd do it again," I whispered, that awful guilt swamping me once more, and I let it. I deserved it. "What does that say about me, Tao?"

"It says you made a mistake." Tao caught my hands, twined

146

our fingers. "It's not the end of the world, honey."

"No, it's just the end of my self respect. I told myself I would never do something like this." I squeezed my eyes shut against the tears. I'd have to cry them out sooner or later, but I wasn't going to do it here.

"Allie. Look at me." Tao squeezed my fingers.

I did, swallowing around the knot in my throat.

"You know, you weren't the only one in the bed."

On the desk, my mind automatically corrected. And then on the couch. No bed. The bed he shared with my sister.

Tao continued, "And you aren't the one who broke a promise. He's the one who's engaged. Not you. That's on *him*."

I wish I could say that made me feel better, but it didn't.

"He's engaged to my sister." Tao knew about the Hedges, about how I'd come to be. "Don't you get it? He's engaged to marry Paisley, and I slept with him."

Tao blinked, but I didn't throw him off stride much. I don't know if anything could really throw him.

"What kind of woman *does* that?" I shook my head. "No, we both know what sort of woman does that. I love my mom, Tao, you know I do, but I never wanted this part of my life to be like hers. But I am. I'm just like her. Ruining my sisters' lives just like my mother did."

Tao snorted, and the sound got my attention. Letting go of my hands, he leaned back in the booth. "Come on, Allie, you know better than that. Your mom's not perfect, but she's a hell of a lot better than mine. You know as well as I do that she never asked your father to leave his daughters, never wanted to hurt anyone. Yeah, she screwed up. You did too, but you didn't do it out of spite."

Hadn't I? And that was another part of the guilt, I realized. Had a part of me wanted to sleep with Jal *because* he was Paisley's fiancé? Had I wanted him to hurt her?

She can clean my room. I can still hear her voice, the look on her face as she said it.

"Look at me," Tao said. And he waited until I did. "You're not a bad person, Allie. No matter what you're telling yourself, you didn't do this because of Paisley. You did it in spite of her. You had sex with Jal because you wanted it. Wanted him. I'm not going to act like it wasn't a stupid thing to do, but don't beat

147

yourself up over something that wasn't a part of it."

"You act like this so simple."

"It is simple. And it's not." He jerked his shoulder in a shrug as the server came by, carrying our food. He paused as she put the plates down. He'd ordered for me, like always and I was glad because I didn't want to talk to anybody. Right now, I didn't know if I even wanted to keep talking to Tao.

Once she was gone, he said, "You want to make this more complicated than it already is because you want to think of yourself as the bad guy. Don't. You're not. It'll just make you feel worse, and you're already drowning in guilt." He paused for a moment, and then asked, "Now, are you going to eat that bacon or can I have it?"

"You are not touching my bacon." I sniffed and sat up, eying my plate with little enthusiasm.

Tao shot me a cheerful smile and patted my hand. "Cheer up, honey. Eat. We'll go to a museum, and I'll distract you with my charming self."

With a tired laugh, I picked up a piece of bacon.

"Sure. Why not?"

I doubted it would work, but I couldn't sit around and brood all weekend, could I?

Chapter 12

Jal

"I'm sorry, Mr. Lindstrom." The man in front of me wrung his hands, his eyes wide and over-bright. "You know I would do anything to be able to help you out, but there some things I just can't do."

If he'd do anything, then why in the hell wouldn't he give me her phone number? He was the owner of the fucking salon, and he wouldn't just give me some way to contact her. I could've gone to her house, I supposed, but I knew she lived with her parents, and I didn't want to get them involved in any of this. I just wanted to talk to her.

The near panic in his gaze had me turning away before I made it even worse. I didn't like using who I was to intimidate people, even unintentionally. Shoving my hands through my hair, I stared hard at her work area as if that would make her appear.

So far, it hadn't worked.

"When is she working again?" I demanded suddenly.

"Would you like to make an appointment?" Alistair asked hesitantly.

"No," I snapped. And a split second later, I realized I should have said yes.

"Well…" Alistair cleared his throat, then in the same, apologetic tone, he continued, "I really can't be giving out my employee's schedules…" The words trailed off, then he smiled at me, brightening. "Perhaps if you could leave your information? I could give it to Allie, and then she could contact you."

Somehow I didn't think she would do that. I had a feeling that if I didn't make the effort, I'd never see her again. She'd run away this morning because she hadn't wanted to face me.

The likelihood of her calling me? I placed my odds at about a million to one.

Part of me should've been glad, and I knew it. She'd saved us both the awkward morning after talk, and if I'd just let it go, I wouldn't have to worry about apologizing or seeing her again.

It would all just be over.

But I didn't *want* it to be over.

I wanted to see her again.

I wanted to touch her again.

I just plain *wanted* her.

And no matter what, I needed to apologize for the position I'd put her in.

Aware that the manager was still staring at me, I met his eyes. "No, that's not necessary. Thanks."

Two hours later, I stood at the curb in front of the house where we'd picked her up Friday night. I hadn't wanted to come here, but I knew I hadn't had much of a choice in the matter. I needed to see her.

A few people glanced my way, their gazes lingering. Then those gazes moved to the car and lingered even longer. Part of me wondered if the McLaren would be in one piece after I spoke with Allie, or if it'd even be here at all.

Tossing my keys up and down, I took the steps at a jog, feeling like a bug under a microscope.

I knocked on the door, but there was no answer. Blowing out a breath, I waited a minute, then tried again.

It wasn't early, but we'd definitely had a…busy night. But shouldn't her family have been home? What were the chances that she, her younger brother, and her parents were all out?

I tried again.

Still no answer.

Son of a bitch.

* * * * *

I went back Sunday morning.

150

The apartment was the only address that I had, but I now knew it wasn't where Allie lived. According to one of the nosy neighbors, no deaf people lived in the building. Which made me think that maybe Allie had asked us to pick her up at her friend's house.

Her *male* friend who'd gone with her to get her dress.

But it was the only place I could wait. It was Sunday, and her brother's school would be closed.

I couldn't loiter at the salon either. I had a feeling I'd give Alistair a heart-attack if I did that.

So I tried the apartment, again, waiting until ten, hoping that would be late enough I wouldn't wake her, early enough that she wasn't out.

Hands in my pockets, I stood at the door and waited.

No answer.

I pushed it again.

No answer.

Swearing, I leaned into it this time, held it for almost ten seconds before I let go.

Damn it, I needed to see Allie–

"What the hell?" a sleepy voice said through the speaker.

A sleepy *male* voice.

Son of a bitch.

Staring at the little box for a longer minute, I sucked in a breath, hardly able to process the anger that blasted through me. It was a man's apartment. Her *friend*. But maybe he was more than a friend.

A stab of jealousy went through me.

"Who's there?" the man demanded, a little less sleepy this time. "You wake me up, you can at least tell me what you want."

I turned and stormed back to the car.

What I wanted was to reach through the speaker and rip out his larynx. After, of course, I asked him where Allie was.

But I didn't think that was the right way to handle it. Especially since I didn't really have the right to be angry.

After all, I had a fiancée I needed to speak with.

After the day I'd had, the last thing I wanted to do was see Paisley. I'd even decided I'd wait until tomorrow to talk with her. Except, the moment I stepped into my loft, I knew I wouldn't have that luxury.

I heard the TV blaring from down the hall – one of those insane bridal reality shows. She did nothing but snark at them, but she loved watching them, and trying to make me watch them with her was her new current pastime.

I was tempted to just go straight to the bedroom, but that wasn't going to happen. On the way down the hall, I paused at my office door and stared in. I'd cleaned up enough that my weekly housekeeper wouldn't find anything incriminating, so there was no sign of Allie. But I could still feel her everywhere. I smelled her skin on mine, felt her hair against my body, tasted her on my tongue.

Staring at the desk, I remembered going to my knees in front of her, spreading her wide and licking her slit, holding her open. She'd moaned, arching against me.

Reaching up, I grabbed the carved oak door frame and squeezed. Hunger pulsed inside me as the memory played out, her hands in my hair, her lips on mine, tasting herself on and in my mouth.

A laugh rang out from down the hall, and the memory of Allie shattered.

With dread, I pulled away from the office doorway and started down the hall, on down the wide, arched entryway that led to the informal living room. Paisley sat curled up on the couch, her bare feet tucked under her, a smile on her lips. She started to lift a glass of water for a sip, then paused as she caught sight of me.

"Hello, darling."

She rose from the couch and came to me, pressing her lips to my cheek. I couldn't even find it in me to smile at her. Just looking at her filled me with this sense of resignation. How was I supposed to marry her?

I'd been apathetic about this from the start, but since I met Allie, I knew there was something more out there.

Not love. Certainly not that. But something *more* than what I had with this woman.

"I missed you," she murmured, her lips still against my skin. She slid her hand down my chest, and I reached up to catch her wrist.

I hadn't missed her. I hadn't seen her since we parted ways the weekend I proposed, and I'd barely thought of her.

Guilt twisted into slippery knots, and I felt even worse now than I had yesterday. I'd been debating all weekend – did I tell her? How much? Did I pretend it hadn't happened?

Now, face to face, I still didn't know. The insane thing was that part of me suspected Paisley wouldn't give a damn, as long as I was discreet and as long I kept it all away from her.

She didn't love me.

I didn't love her.

We both knew that.

We're suited... I'd said those words to Allie, and she'd said it sounded insulting. I'd disagreed at the time, but now I thought she was right.

Now, standing there as Paisley leaned against me, all I could think about was how much fun I'd had with Allie, how easy it had been to laugh with her and talk to her. How often I'd thought about *her* during the day.

This wasn't working, I realized.

Paisley drew away, head tipped back as smiled up at me. I returned the smile because it was expected, but I knew the smile was every bit as strained as it felt.

This wasn't working.

And I couldn't lie and pretend it was.

I had to do what was right for our child, and that meant not making him or her a part of a lie.

"What's wrong, Jal?" Paisley asked, her cool grey eyes searching my face. "Don't tell me that you and Daddy got into another argument about the stock market. And if you did...never mind." She turned away, making a dismissive gesture. "Don't tell me. I don't want to hear all those figures and facts. They hurt my head."

It was a game between us, a tedious one in my opinion, but a game regardless. Paisley knew more about the stock market than she let on and it was no surprise to me. She was Kendrick Hedge's daughter, and he was a financial genius.

It might not be possible to grow up in that household and not learn a thing or two about the stock market, but Paisley preferred to pretend otherwise. Her world was limited to the social world, who to know and where to shop and what shoes one mustn't wear.

"No. I didn't even see him Friday night," I answered honestly.

"Friday night?" Her brow puckered, then she waved her hand. "Oh, yes. That charity for poor kids."

"It's an inner-city project for schools, Paisley." I'd told her that a hundred times.

"Of course." She shrugged and sat back down on the couch. "Father decided not to go. Mama wanted him with her at a banquet for the Conservation Hall, then they went out of the Franklins."

I didn't care. Clearing my throat, I moved over to the bar setup and poured myself a stiff drink. It wasn't stiff enough though, so I made it a double before I turned to look at her. "We need to talk."

I had to get this done now.

Something flickered in Paisley's eyes, and the guilt in my gut twisted just a little bit harder. Had she just paled? Her mouth had gotten tighter.

Did she know–?

Stop. How can she know?

"Of course, darling." She gave me a smile, her composure perfectly in place. Maybe I'd imagined it. She patted the seat next to her. "Why don't you come sit down?"

I stayed where I was, shoving my hands into the pockets of my jeans as I mentally rehearsed things once more.

I had to do this.

For everyone involved.

"First, I want you to know that no matter what, I'm going to stand by my responsibilities."

It was pretty obvious she had no idea what I was saying. At first, at least.

Then she did and red creeped up her check and to her neck before settling on her cheeks. She kept her composure though.

After all, this was Paisley Hedges. She didn't *lose* her temper. It just wasn't done.

"What, exactly, does that mean, Jal? Of course you're standing by your responsibilities. We're engaged." She stroked her thumb over her ring and smiled at me, but it was strained, too tight at the edges.

Looking away, I took a drink from the glass in my hand before I spoke again, "Paisley, I'm not so sure about the engagement. I'm not so sure about any of this. I need some time off."

"Time *off*?" she demanded, her voice rising.

Shit. Her composure *was* cracking.

"You want time off." She flung out a hand. "That's just great, Jal. Great. You do realize I'm pregnant. I'm planning a wedding. Those sort of things don't really allow for *time off*."

Her voice hitched, then broke.

Shit.

"Paisley…"

I started for her, but she turned away, grabbed her shoes, her purse. "Leave me alone, you bastard!"

She slammed the door behind her, and I knew that I'd made a second choice that would change my life completely.

Book 3

Chapter 1

Allie

TJ tried to disappear down the hall the second the door slammed shut behind us, but I caught the back of his hoodie. He came up short and turned around to glare at me.

"Wha?" His signing was sharp, brisk, his impatience clear.

Placing one hand on my hip, I pointed at the backpack and lunch bag he'd dropped in the middle of the floor. With an exasperated roll of his eyes, he grabbed his things and turned toward the closet to hang them up.

"No. You need to clean out the lunch bag before whatever is in there turns into your next science project." At home, I didn't always speak when I signed since I was the only one who could hear it. Sometimes it felt a bit too much like talking to myself when I did it.

My comment teased a faint smile out of him, although he fought not to show it.

"Your cooperation is duly noted." Sometimes it frustrated me how some tones simply couldn't be translated into sign.

He rolled his eyes – again – I'd counted five times just since I'd picked him up from school. *"You keep on doing that, making it out..."* I stopped signing as he turned his back on me and finished my thought by shouting at the back of his head. "Make me out to be some slave driver, TJ! You're so rude sometimes!"

Mom's soft laugh caught me off guard.

Turning, I saw her standing a few feet away, an amused smile dancing around her lips.

"Why are you yelling? How much good does that do?" she asked, speaking while she signed.

159

She'd been talking to me more than normal lately as if she'd finally realized how much I'd missed hearing another voice. She was talking louder than normal, and I knew the only reason she'd heard me was because I'd been yelling. While not completely deaf, enough of her hearing was gone that speaking even close to normally wasn't enough for her to understand what I was saying. Still, it was nice to have another voice to go along with the sign language.

"It does a lot of good – for me. He's being a brat today."

"How so?"

"Moody. Argues with everything I say. Doesn't want to do anything."

I turned as I heard a thump and sighed at the sight of his backpack, now on the floor, half of his books and papers spilling out of it. *"See?"*

I shook my head. It wasn't any wonder half the stuff had spilled out. I'd told him to zip it closed, and he'd ignored me. I knew he was having a rough time at school, but that didn't mean he had to act like a brat at home.

Mom gave me a small smile as she came closer. *"You realize you weren't all that much different. It's a stage. You all go through it."* She gave me a peck on the cheek. I was only an inch taller than her five feet one inch, so she didn't have to stretch far to do it.

"I wasn't as lazy as he is." I scowled.

"No." She gave me an indulgent smile. *"That's true."*

TJ and I were only half-brother and sister, but we never really paid much attention to that fact. My step-father, Tyson, was the only true father figure I'd ever had, even though I'd always known my biological father. Sometimes, however, I felt like my being the only hearing member of the family wasn't the only thing that set me apart. TJ and I had clearly received very different upbringings, and I knew that our mom often coddled him because of it, wanting to shield him from a lot of the shit that I'd had to deal with. I wasn't so sure that was always a good thing.

"By the way, you have mail."

Turning, I saw a brown and white envelope in her hand. An overnight delivery, it looked like. Frowning, I accepted it, studying it curiously. Who would overnight me anything? I hadn't ordered anything online recently so it couldn't be that.

Mom's gaze lingered on me, and I knew she was curious too. When I didn't offer to explain, she signed that she was going to start dinner, and then walked away, leaving me alone to read my mail.

In the relative privacy of the empty living room, I tore open the envelope and reached inside where I found another envelope, this one made of heavy vellum, the paper textured and elegant, the kind used for wedding invitations and the like.

I frowned. I couldn't think of any reason why somebody would overnight a wedding invitation, or any invitation for that matter. Especially to me. Other than Tao Maki, I didn't have any close friends, and Tao would never send something so pretentious. The women I worked with at the salon might invite me to things, but not like this.

A few seconds later, though, I realized that I'd forgotten to include one of the people I did know who had the money and the arrogance to pull off something like this. I dropped to sit on the couch, staring dumbly at the words on the elegant white textured linen.

You are invited...Saturday...Sponsored by the Lindstrom Foundation

That right there told me everything.

It most definitely *was* an invitation, and to the biggest fundraiser for the deaf community in the entire city. I knew about it. Mom and Tyson had even gone once as representatives of the deaf community. People respected them, listened to their ideas, looked up to them for their constant involvement in deaf issues.

Me?

Not so much. I mean, I supported all of those things, but I'd never been on the front lines. And the deaf community didn't want a hearing person representing them. I completely understood the reasoning and never felt slighted by it. I just did my thing and stayed in the background.

Which meant there was really no logical reason for me to have this invitation.

But I knew why I had it, and logic had nothing to do with it.

Jal had arranged for me to get it. How he'd gotten my address, I didn't know, since the only time we'd gone out together, I'd had him pick me up at Tao's place. Now I was even more glad that I hadn't had him at the house. I didn't want my family involved in any of this. Not when I'd fucked up so badly by sleeping with the man my half-sister was engaged to. My mom had worked so hard to distance herself from my biological father and his family. I didn't want to bring the Hedges back into our lives.

My heart began to race as my chest tightened. What was he doing? Why was he doing it? And, most importantly, what the *hell* was he thinking?!

Carefully, I put the invitation down in my lap and pressed my fingertips to my eyes. Blood rushed and roared in my ears, and the way my thoughts were racing had me wishing I could just do the day over again. Except this time, I'd throw the envelope away without even looking in it.

I wasn't going.

That's all there was to it.

I *couldn't* go. That much was obvious. The last time I'd gone to something with him as friends, I'd ended up in his bed. He was turning out to be a fatal weakness for me, and that was just bad. Something clanged in the kitchen, reminding me of my mother's presence, and with that came a sudden realization.

"Dammit."

Tightening my grip on the invitation, I wondered how I could rationalize not going. Mom and Tyson, they'd gone every time they'd been invited. Not because they enjoyed it, but because they felt they owed it to the community. How could I do any less for my family? So much money was raised for the local deaf community at this fundraiser.

And I doubted I'd be able to hide what the invitation was for. Mom would ask me what had come in the mail, and I hated lying to her. I could, I knew, but it wouldn't stop me from adding another layer of guilt to my already guilt ridden life.

"Shit."

There was a dinner banquet. Cocktails. Well, that wasn't bad, although if there was booze involved, I'd have to stay away from Jal. I didn't trust myself around him sober. Even the slightest bit tipsy would be a danger.

Except...the invitation read *plus one*.

I could take a plus one. That would keep me on the straight and narrow. Why Jal had invited me would no longer matter. I'd stick with my date and ignore Jal. I'd spent the past few days

162

trying to put Friday night out of my mind. Not that I'd had much luck, but I'd tried. I even had myself almost convinced that if I kept trying, I'd succeed. Sooner or later. Like in two or three decades.

"And now this," I muttered. For once, I was glad no one in the house could hear me.

A sly little voice spoke up even as I was debating what to do. *It's just a dance. Dinner. You can take a date. You might not even see him. And if you do...don't talk to him.*

"Yeah, right."

Dinner. Drinks. I could take a date.

I took a slow breath. "I can do this."

Yes, you can do it. Go and show him that screwing him wasn't a big deal. A mistake you never intend to make again.

The little voice in my head was right. It was like facing my fears. I just needed to get on with it and make sure that it was clear to Jal that our one crazy night was done, over, and it would never happen again.

To do that, though, I needed to make sure I had someone at my side who'd ensure that I didn't do anything stupid.

Again.

When faced with important decisions that need answers quickly, sometimes there's only one thing to do. Call your best friend, go out, and have a drink.

This was definitely one of those times.

And, as always, Tao was happy to help. The fact that I promised to pay for his first couple drinks helped. So, after dinner with the family, I met up with Tao at an out-of-the-way bar we went to when we needed a drink but didn't want to go to a club.

After getting our first round of drinks and an order of the bar's amazing onion rings, I quickly explained the situation and then waited for the comments I knew would be forthcoming.

"You know I love you, right, honey?" Tao reached across the table and took my hand. His sapphire blue eyes were filled with concern.

My free hand was locked around the tall pilsner of beer, and I wasn't letting go until I'd emptied it – and maybe downed a refill. Eying him over the rim, I prepared myself for what he was going to say. His pint of beer sat in front of him untouched, a sign of just how serious he was.

163

"Because I love you, I feel the need to point out that I think this is a very bad idea. Capital *B*. Capital *I*. Bad Idea." He waited a moment as if to make sure I'd gotten the message, then he picked up his pint and took a healthy drink.

"Okay." Tipping my glass in his direction, I said, "Point made. Now are you going with me or not?"

With a groan, he rubbed at his face, then shoved straight, shining black hair out of his eyes. Making a dramatic show of throwing his arms open wide, he said, "Who else will go and protect you from yourself? You certainly aren't going to be watching out for your own cute ass, are you?" Before I could even form a properly scathing retort, he asked, "Why are you doing this to yourself?"

"I'm not doing *anything*." I flicked a dismissive hand as I scowled at him. "And stop it with the drama. You keep this up, I'm going to think you need to shelve the nursing school idea, head to New York City and try out for the soap operas or something, the way you carry on."

He gave me a patented Tao grin. "With my luck, I'd end up being cast in a role where the studio would want me playing straight off the clock too." He winked at me. "And you know I'd want to have my hands on pretty boy candy every now and then."

I rolled my eyes. "Then go play with yourself. *You* are pretty boy candy."

"That's just not as much fun, honey. You know that." He ate the last onion ring and ignored my glare. "But you can play with me whenever you want."

Grabbing a pretzel from the bowl between us, I tossed it at him. "You're such an ass." I gave his hand a squeeze. "But, seriously, thank you for agreeing to go with me."

"No problem. Now, answer my question. Why are you doing this? You're already in too deep with this guy, Allie." He cupped my cheek and gave me a sad smile. "It's not good for you. I don't want to see you falling for someone who's only going to hurt you."

"I'm not..." Stopping myself, I looked away. "That's not what this is about, Tao. I'm going to prove to myself that I'm *not* falling for him."

"If you wanted to prove that, you would have tossed the invitation."

"But…" Faltering, I shook my head. "I couldn't, Tao, you know that. I've got to support these things. It's…"

"Honey." He leaned forward and pinned me with a brutally honest stare. "I support the rights of the LGBT community, but that doesn't mean I have to go to a march, a dinner, or any other thing unless I *want* to. You've never wanted to go to one of these events before, so don't force yourself to do it now just because you got an invitation. You don't have to martyr yourself for your family."

I flushed as I stiffly replied, "I'm not." Taking my beer, I tossed back half of it to ease the tight knot in my throat.

"Yeah, you are," Tao countered, his tone gentle. "You go ahead and fool yourself if you need to, but I see how things are. Your family knows you love them and support them, even if you aren't sacrificing your own happiness for theirs. Half the time, I think you do it because it's easier for you to live your life for them rather than live it for yourself. But this deal here? With this guy? You're going to get hurt."

The heat still suffused my face but for different reasons now. Looking away, I half-wished we'd gone to a club so I could've disappeared on the dance floor, forgotten my problems that way.

"He's getting married, Tao. I know that. I won't make the same mistake twice." With a sour laugh, I added, "I know better, trust me. I just feel like I have to prove to myself that I can be around him and *not* cave in again. I have to…"

I didn't finish.

I couldn't let myself.

I was ashamed to be even thinking it, but the thought was there all the same.

I had to know I wasn't like my mom.

She was a wonderful woman, and I adored her. But I knew without a doubt my life and hers would have been very different if I hadn't been conceived with a man who was already married with two legitimate daughters to dote on. I knew how much my parents' decisions had hurt everyone involved.

Maybe Tao was right. Maybe I should just stay away.

But I knew I wouldn't.

"Hey." Tao squeezed my hand, drawing my eyes to his. "I know what you're thinking, and you need to stop. So, yeah. Your mama played the other woman for some rich, married white guy.

You've got issues. But if she hadn't? Allie, you wouldn't be here. And I kinda like having you here. So suck it up and deal." He smiled at me. "Now, let's discuss wardrobe."

Chapter 2

Jal

"Mr. Lindstrom?"

I looked up at Janie Beck – Mrs. Beck – as she smiled in at me. She'd been my father's assistant before she was mine, a stable figure in my life. I could remember coming in after basketball practice and then going back downstairs with money for cookies and milk from the bakery across the street.

Mrs. Beck was a sweet lady, and her kids had lived halfway across the country even back then, so she'd sort of adopted me. Thus the cookies and milk. My dad had always fussed at her not to spoil me, and she'd told him that he did it, so why couldn't she? She was one of the few people who'd never been intimidated by who my father was or how much money he had.

She was right. My dad had spoiled me, although not enough that I could always go buy cookies and milk whenever I wanted. One thing he'd done was make sure I understood the value of a dollar. Sure, maybe I'd gotten my first Porsche when I was sixteen. A month later, I'd wrapped it around a tree and broken my leg. So my next car had been a beater, and I hadn't gotten another decent car until I'd been able to pay for it with money *I* earned.

That entire incident had changed things for me, made me realize that I needed to stop taking things for granted. I started applying myself in school, at work. If I was asked to pinpoint a specific event that changed the direction of my life, that would've been it.

It very well might be how I got to be head of Lindstrom Enterprises, why I had my father's former assistant working for me now. And why I was dealing with a bunch of bullshit from a company I was looking to take over.

Janie winced when she heard a voice come over the speaker. *I'm sorry,* she mouthed.

I waved it off and waited until the blowhard on the other end of the line paused to take a breath. Then, I did my thing. "Listen, Malcolm. What you're trying to tell me is that you've got a piece of real estate that nobody wants and that you'll give it to me on the cheap...because nobody wants it. I can get your company, and everything else on top, because you're feeling magnanimous, is that right?"

Mrs. Beck pressed her lips together to keep from smiling. Apparently, I played a harder game than my father had.

"Jal, listen…" Malcom Hardesty came back with a schmoozing sort of tone that made me want to hang up. But he *did* have a piece of real estate that nobody wanted right now. That was going to change, and soon. I wanted it before that happened, and I would get it.

"How about you listen?" I asked, cutting him off. "You have my deal in front of you. Look it over. Call me back. Offer expires at five. You won't get another one this good. I'll treat you and your people right, Malcolm. You know you won't get as good an offer from anyone else." I ended the call and sighed, ran my hand through my hair, and then looked up at Mrs. Beck. "If it's time for milk and cookies, you'll have to order in. And I want coffee."

She laughed, a loud, bawdy laugh that didn't fit with her demure appearance.

"No, sir." Mrs. Beck patted at her beehive hairstyle.

She'd always had it, even though it'd gone out of fashion long before I'd even been born. It might've even gone out of fashion before she'd been born. But she didn't care. I didn't either. It suited her, just like the cat-eye glasses and the fifties-style dresses. She sat down in the chair in front of me and folded her hands on her lap.

"Jal, honey."

Ah, shit.

She only got *that* tone in her voice for a few reasons, and they rarely meant good things for me.

My phone rang as if on cue. I hit the ignore button and turned it face down.

Mrs. Beck wagged a finger at me. "Now, boy. You can't ignore her forever."

"Why not?" The words popped out of me without any conscious thought and briefly, I wondered just why it was so easy to talk to a woman like Janie Beck and so hard to talk to the woman I'd just silenced on the phone. My mother.

"Because it's impolite." Janie sniffed, then rolled her eyes. "And because she'll just keep calling. You know that."

"Yeah, I know that, Mrs. Beck." Sighing, I eyed the phone. I would have to talk to her. With a short nod, I met the eyes of the woman across the table. "Okay. I'll talk to her. Next time she calls."

She arched an eyebrow that was penciled darker than they were naturally. "Will you?"

"Yes, but only because you asked."

She gave me a skeptical look, and I grinned, laying a hand across my heart.

As she rose from her chair, she shook her head at me. "One day, boy, you'll find a woman who'll set you in your place. Mark my words."

As she left the office, I reached for the paper I'd kept folded on the side of my desk. I knew that was, in part, why Mom kept calling.

The other part had everything to do with Paisley. She'd called, texted, emailed almost a dozen times. Finally, sometime Monday, she'd stopped. But Mom hadn't stopped, I knew she wouldn't, not until she said what she had to say.

It didn't help that some of the media had become slightly obsessed with the charity banquet. There'd been some pop sensation there, so the press had shown up. There were dozens of pictures of her, but my problem was that there were also a couple of me...and my *unnamed partner*.

None of the pictures of Allie had gotten a clear shot of her face, and I was thankful for that. She wouldn't appreciate the intrusion on her privacy.

But there was no doubt about the fact that the two of us looked...cozy.

In one of them, I looked downright dazed. And that was a

good way to describe how Allie made me feel.

Dazed.

Had she gotten the invitation?

I'd ended up going through all the contacts I had at my disposal, and to my surprise, one of the charitable arms actually had her address. They wouldn't release it to me, but they did mention that her family was active in the deaf community. That was when I remembered that Allie had said her family was deaf.

That could be my way in.

The company had an event this weekend, so I'd told them to overnight an invitation to someone I'd missed. They'd been happy to do so even though they'd still refused to give me the information.

Privacy reasons…bullshit.

I was about ready to just hire a private investigator, but I had a feeling Allie wouldn't thank me for that, so I held off.

If she came to the event, then it wouldn't matter.

If she didn't…well. Then I'd reevaluate–

The phone rang.

Swearing, I almost silenced it. Again. But I'd told Mrs. Beck I'd talk to my mom the next time she called. And I never lied to Mrs. Beck.

"Hello, Mom."

"Jal, darling."

The ice in her tone would have had more of an effect if I hadn't been so used to it. After all, I disappointed her on a regular basis. Well, except in business. She appreciated how good I was at making money. And I knew she loved me. In her own way.

"How are you?" I asked, falling back on the social niceties she'd drilled into my head since before I'd been old enough to understand them.

"Wonderful, dear. You?"

"Busy. Got a few deals I'm trying to square away – one of them has an expiration date." *So can we just get on with this…*

"You're always up to something."

I got the feeling she wasn't talking about work.

"Tell me, son, I was talking to Paisley, and heard something rather upsetting. She seems to think you're not so certain about your engagement now. She's wrong, isn't she, Jal?"

Shit. I should've known to pre-empt things by letting Mom

know what was going on. Of course Paisley had gone right to her.

Closing my eyes, I leaned back in the seat. Soft leather cupped me, the chair steadying under me as I kicked my feet up on the desk. "No, Mom. She's not wrong. We aren't right for marriage, I don't think. I need time to make sure we're doing the right thing. Not just for us, but for the baby too."

"How can there be any question of that?" She snapped. "You have a *child* coming. You should be married before that child arrives."

I closed my eyes and pinched the bridge of my nose. "People should marry for reasons other than a child. I can be there for the baby *without* being married to Paisley. It'd be worse for a child to be raised in a loveless marriage."

There was nothing but silence on the other end for several long moments. Her response, when it came, grated on my ears.

"Nonsense." Her voice was brisk, matter-of-fact. "Listen, Jal...you've always been a...*sweet* boy."

Sweet?

I bit back the curse words that I wanted to let loose.

"I know you might have some idea in your head of a passionate kind of love, something crazy and wild...heaven knows I had those ideas a few times myself. And your father?" She laughed, the sound trailing off into a gusty sigh. "But there's more to life than...fantasy. You need to have a *good*, solid foundation. Like what you have with Paisley."

Was she seriously accusing me of being a romantic? Did the woman not know me at all? I'd never been the sort of person who'd searched for love. There was sex and lust. There was friendship, companionship. But I didn't believe in the sort of love my mother was accusing me of wanting.

Right?

And how in the world could she say that Paisley and I had a solid foundation? What made it solid? The fact that both of us came from wealthy families? That we knew the same people in the same social circles?

But we weren't alike in other ways.

For Paisley, no remark was too cutting, no insult too cold. No dress was too fine, and nothing was too good for her.

Matter of fact, *most* things weren't good *enough*.

Despite my upbringing – or maybe because of it – I

appreciated the things I had. I liked nice things, and I could sometimes be a bit abrasive, but I wasn't cruel.

Was our background enough to give us common ground?

"Do you really think we have a solid foundation?"

"Of course I do." My mother rushed to assure me, but I knew she didn't understand that it wasn't doubts I had.

What I had were certainties. Certainties about the ways it wouldn't work. Nothing she would say would change them. But I didn't want to argue with her. I knew from experience that it wouldn't change anything with her.

Mom continued, "Now, I realize how…intriguing it might be to have some pretty thing clinging to you."

I stiffened. "What?"

"Don't play the fool. It doesn't suit you, Jal." She sniffed. "I saw the paper. I'm sure you did too. The *girl*, Jal. I saw you dancing with that girl. And you looked like you were…were…" She sputtered now, unable to come up with something apparently fitting.

"I looked like what?" I stared at the picture. I know what I looked like.

I looked like a man who actually *felt* something. I didn't need a picture to know I never looked like that when I was with Paisley because I never felt much of anything when I was with her.

"To be honest, Jal, you look like you're being led around by the dick by some cheap whore," she said, her voice cold.

Anger flashed through me, bright and hot. *Hell, Mom. Just tell me how you really feel*. But I remained calm as I replied, "That's enough."

"*Really*, Jal. Have you looked at those pictures? What are people going to think? What are our friends going to think?" Mother carried on as if I hadn't said anything.

I wasn't surprised. How often did I really say anything? But I wasn't going to listen to her talk about Allie like that. What we'd done was on me, not her.

"Mom, please stop." I put more emphasis in my voice, and when she continued to keep talking, I said, "Fine. I guess I'll just hang up. You didn't call to talk to me. You called to talk *over* me."

That got her attention.

"What…no, wait. Jal, darling. Of course I want to talk to

172

you." Surprise showed in her voice, but she managed to cover it well.

"Then we can talk. What did you want to talk about?" Still frustrated, I leaned back in my chair.

On the other end of the line, my mother laughed. "Do I need a specific topic in mind? I just wanted…well, Jal. To be honest, I'm worried about you. I can't believe you told Paisley you needed time to think. You're about to be a father. The two of you have been together a long time."

"Not really." *Six months. Barely.*

She carried on as if I hadn't said anything.

"It's perfectly understandable that you might be getting cold feet. That girl in the paper, she probably scented you down like a shark scents blood."

"Mom…"

"When do you think you'll be ready to talk to Paisley?"

I didn't say the response that immediately leapt to my lips. I could only imagine what my mother would think if I told her I'd just as soon never talk to Paisley again outside of conversation related to the baby. That wouldn't go over well.

But she wasn't going to let it go. "Jal?"

So I lied. "I don't know, Mom. I told you. I need time. When two people get married, it shouldn't be because there's an unplanned pregnancy. There should be…more. I don't know what, exactly, but I do know that Paisley and I don't have that." I sighed. "I need to go, okay? I'll talk to you later."

I hung up before she could respond and sat there, staring at the phone. I hadn't planned on saying any of that, but now that I had, I had no intention of taking it back.

I couldn't, not without telling some sort of lie.

A few weeks ago, a month ago, maybe I saw a different sort of truth, but the bottom line was, there *wasn't* any kind of connection between Paisley and me. And I could no longer stomach the thought of being in a relationship that felt more like a business transaction.

It's one thing not to believe in love. It's another thing to feel hopeless about the rest of your fucking life.

And that was how I felt.

I had no idea what to do about it either.

Chapter 3

Allie

That's a lovely dress.

I got the impression that my mother had been standing in the doorway waiting for me to look up for several minutes. I smiled my thanks and went back to studying my dress. There were times in my life that I had friends I just didn't deserve. This was one of those times.

The dress Mom had just complimented was actually an Armani. It was a couple of years out of fashion, but new off the rack, it still would have cost a couple of thousand. Thanks to Tao's friend, Tarja Caldwell, however, I paid barely a couple hundred. I didn't know what Tao had told her, but she'd sold the dress to me at cost. Now, because of her, my outfit looked like a one-of-a-kind designer piece straight off the runway.

The once-open back of it was now mesh and seeded with tiny little stones that caught the light. There were inserts along the skirt echoing the design. The bodice had the shimmery little stones as well. Pretty, elegant and sexy, with a vague hint of retro to it, the dress was feminine without being fussy. I was playing off the vintage tones by sweeping my hair up into a twist reminiscent of the fifties. I had a strand of pearls as well. The pearls were one the few rare gifts my father had given me that had nothing to do with money.

I thought I'd blend in rather well. At the very least, I wouldn't look like some street urchin. Maybe I wouldn't fit in, but I wouldn't stand out, either. Then I reminded myself that I didn't actually want to fit in with those people.

Sometimes, I still had to tell myself that daily. I'd spent way too much of my younger life trying to fit, to shape myself into whatever mold I thought would please my father, make him love me. When I'd finally realized that wasn't going to happen, it made me go in the complete opposite direction and not want to be a part of his world at all.

And now I was stepping into it voluntarily.

Mom came up behind me and rested her hand on my shoulder.

Meeting her eyes in the mirror, I started to smile. But she asked quietly, *"Why are you so sad?"*

"I'm not." I spoke the words, knowing she could read my lips via my reflection. She wouldn't hear the tremor in my voice, but if I signed them, my hands might shake a little, and I didn't want her to see anything I wasn't ready to share with her.

But this was my mother. And mothers, damn them, they could always tell. She leaned forward and gave me a kiss on the cheek. Then, softly, she spoke and sighed, *"You let me know when you're ready to talk. You know I'm always here for you."*

"Oh. My heart." Tao clutched at his chest, pretending the organ in question pained him. "Baby, I can't take it. You look too beautiful for the likes of me."

I'd put a petticoat on under the skirt, and it swished around my legs as I walked. It made me feel insanely girly and sexy in an odd sort of way. As I came down the last few steps, I rolled my eyes at Tao's behavior.

"Are you going to fall to the floor? If you plan to do so, hurry up and get it over with. We'll need to grab the lint roller because I haven't swept in here."

He looked affronted. "I give you a compliment, and you're worried about lint? Allie, where's your sense of romance?"

"It died a long time ago," I said tartly. I came a little closer and watched as he adjusted the cufflinks on his rented tux.

When he caught sight of me watching him, he grinned at me and shot me a lascivious wink and did a little spin. "Do I look good or what?"

"Not to add to your overblown ego, but yes. You look fantastic." I leaned in and kissed his cheek before settling back down in front of him. A quick glance assured me I hadn't left any lipstick on him.

"What?" He reached up to brush his cheek. "Do I have anything on my face?"

Mom came up behind me, laughing. *"No. She's checking to make sure she didn't leave lipstick on your cheek. I guess she plans on doing a lot of kissing later tonight."*

Tao wagged his eyebrows at me. *"Excellent plan, Allie."* He signed as he spoke so my mom could get it too.

My cheeks flushed, and I turned away without responding.

Not because I planned on kissing Tao. *That* wouldn't make me blush. The things Tao and I had done together made the two of us insanely comfortable with each other. It was the thought of kisses and...*him.*

"Come on, Allie." Some of the humor had faded from Tao's voice, although when I looked at him, he was still smiling. His eyes had sobered, but he kept the mask up for my mom. Holding out a hand, he angled his head toward the door. "I begged and bribed a friend of mine, and we've got a nice ride for the night."

When I met his gaze, I could tell he'd known exactly who I'd been thinking about. My mom, however, didn't know about any of that.

A few minutes later, we were heading down the stairs, my hand on Tao's forearm. We'd been just about to leave when Mom abruptly insisted we wait while she rushed into her bedroom. I'd been convinced she was taking off to get a camera, or something and I'd almost pointed out that this wasn't the prom, but she'd emerged almost immediately, carrying a fluffy bundle of soft lavender – not a camera.

"It's too cold for you to be out there without a wrap," she'd signed as I unrolled the bundle. It was silk and something else – all of it woven together in layers that were soft and thick and warm as I threw it across my shoulders, drawing it around me. I'd

smiled my thanks before we left and now, as a cold wind cut through the streets, I was even more grateful.

"So…what do you think of our ride?" Tao asked, leaning in and nuzzling my temple.

I came to a stop, looking for his car. Except all I saw was a sleek, sexy red Stingray.

My jaw dropped.

"That?"

He grinned.

"Who did you kill or what did you steal?" I demanded.

"Nothing. I just called in a favor." He said it nonchalantly, but I knew Tao. The man was pleased with himself. *Beyond* pleased.

He opened the door for me, and I slid in. He helped me tuck the skirt in around me, giving my leg a little lingering caress. From anyone else, it would've been lecherous, but from him, it was comforting.

When he spoke, I knew why he was offering me comfort. "Just remember, Cinderella, no matter how charming the prince is, your kingdom isn't ever going to fit with his."

"How is Malla doing?"

Smiling at Charles Bailey, I signed, *"Mom's doing fine."*

"And your brother?" He paused, frowning. *"How old is he now?"* He tapped his temple. *"The old head isn't what it used to be."*

I laughed. *"I think you just have too many schemes going on up there, Mr. Bailey."*

He grinned.

I launched into a story about what was going on with TJ at school, moving into some of the issues that my brother was facing with the bullies. Charles Bailey was one of the driving forces behind some of the programs we now had for the deaf community in our neighborhood. Even now that he'd stepped back and retired from almost everything, he was still a key figure. He'd also been friends with Tyson and my mom for years. It was nice to see a few friendly faces.

By the time I finished, Charles was shaking his head.

"I wish you folks lived closer to me and Maureen. TJ would get along great with my youngest son. Amar hears, but with all of the rest of us not being hearing, he understands our culture as much as you do."

"Maybe we should just set up some time for them to get together," I suggested, signing.

"That's not a bad idea." Charles nodded, his lips pursed. A moment later, he reached into his pocket and withdrew a card. He also took out a pen and wrote something down. *"My private email,"* he said after he gave me the card. *"Get in touch, Allie. We'll set something up. Maybe TJ can come to one the ballgames with us."*

He hugged me, and I nodded at him before we both moved in separate directions. I saw another familiar face, and she smiled, waved at me, but before we reached each other, somebody cut her off.

"Who is *that?*" Tao asked, sipping from the mug of craft beer somebody had given him earlier.

"Liz Carter. She runs a sign language class through the library system. It's the one I help out with when I'm not being worked into the ground," I added dryly. I studied the crowd around her. "We'll catch up with her later."

As we moved off into the crowd, Tao shot me a look, clearly amused. "Look at you. All hobnobbing with the rich and..." He frowned. "You know, the rich and elite just doesn't sound quite as good as the rich and famous, does it?"

I rolled my eyes at him.

"How many other mega impressive personages do you know?" he asked.

"Does your big ego count?"

"We can count my ego if we can also count my..." He wagged his eyebrows at me.

"Would you *hush?*" Laughing, I leaned and pressed a quick kiss to his mouth. "You are incorrigible, I swear!"

As I hooked my arm through his, some of the tension in my

body fell away. Everything was going fine. Nothing to be nervous about, nothing to worry about, right?

But when I began to scan the crowd again, everything changed.

I looked right past her at first, but her eyes brought me back. She was staring dead at me like she could just will me off the face of the planet. I stumbled a little, thrown off track. No, that was a lie. It felt like the entire *world* had been thrown off track, not just me.

"Allie?" No humor existed in Tao's voice now. He knew me so well. He steadied me, his hand immediately moving to my waist.

Tearing my eyes away from the woman across the room, I swallowed and made myself look at Tao.

"Are you okay?" He touched my cheek. "You look like you've been stabbed with a hot poker or something."

"Worse," I said wanly. Needing a few moments of privacy, I tugged him off to the side, hoping the crowd – or the floor – would swallow us up. Why was *she* here?

"What's wrong? You see *him*? If you did…well, honey, you should have expected–"

"It's not him." Well, not just him. Because I had seen Jal too. Standing next to *her*.

He'd seen me too.

Both of them had.

Jal's light blue eyes had lit up.

The woman with him had looked like…I didn't even know how to describe the look on her face, but it didn't fall anywhere near the realm of pleasant. She'd recovered quickly though.

No surprise, really. After all, Diamond Hedges knew how to hide what she was feeling.

She wouldn't *dare* to be caught off stride, not by something insignificant as seeing her husband's bastard at a gala with her friends.

I swallowed the panicked laugh bubbling in my throat as Tao stroked a hand up my arm. "Tell me what's wrong, honey."

From the corner of my eye, I saw her moving off into the crowd, away from me.

"Kendrick Hedges," I managed stiffly.

Tao jerked as if I'd stabbed him. "What? He's here? Your

179

dad?"

I didn't point out that he wasn't really my father. Not in any way that truly mattered. Even the time he'd spent with me as a child, any money he'd sent, all of it came from curiosity and guilt. But it didn't matter right now. Shaking my head, I glanced back toward the direction where I'd seen Diamond.

"No. Worse." I cleared my throat and managed to speak with some strength. "It's his wife – and she hates my guts."

Chapter 4

Jal

She wasn't here yet.

A little voice in my head suggested that maybe she wasn't coming at all.

Like hell. She'd come.

She had to. I went to a lot of work to *get* her here.

Even as I thought it, I hated myself for it. How fucking arrogant was I?

As one of the guests – I think his name was George Spieth – stepped up and held out his hand, I shot another look at the door. For all I knew, she'd looked at the invitation and tore it into confetti. Or she might have already come and gone, slipped in while I was making the rounds and left just as quickly. I couldn't exactly watch the door nonstop when I was hosting this gala.

Maybe I should've thought this out a little more.

"Your fiancée shared with me the happy news–"

I jerked my head around and stared at George. Shit. "She did?"

"About the engagement." He clapped me on the shoulder. "She's a lovely one, that Paisley. Hope to hear news about the wedding soon."

I gave him a strained smile. Paisley had been showing her damn ring off all night. It seemed that my request for time and space had fallen on deaf ears. She was cooing about wedding plans and a honeymoon cruise that would take us halfway around

181

the damn world.

At the moment, she was standing across the room with her mother. They glanced my way, and I had no doubt what the subject of the discussion was or perhaps I should say *who*.

Of course, the look on Diamond's face was pure ice.

When George caught sight of her moving our way, he chuckled. "It's the mother-in-law...I'll be upfront, son. I don't pity you on *that* front." He clapped me once more on the shoulder and passed me a card. "Let me know what your people think of that proposal."

Proposal – I didn't even remember him talking about one, but I was sure he must have. I gave a vague answer. "Just get the information to my team."

As he moved off, Diamond took his place.

I pushed the card into my pocket and gave another casual look around the ballroom. No such–

Son of a bitch. She was here.

I let my gaze devour her while Diamond started to talk.

"Hello, Jal." The cool tone barely made an impact as I took in the lush curves of Allie's body, the pearls around her neck...the *guy standing with her*?

Son of a *bitch*! She'd brought a date? I ground my teeth.

"What in the *world*?" Diamond said in a low voice. I hardly noticed. No doubt she was pissed off at me for not paying attention to her.

A date.

Why in the hell had she brought a date? Her gaze flicked my way in just that moment, although she didn't seem to look straight at me. Her eyes widened, her lips parted. Before I could do anything, her date put his hand on her arm, the gesture clearly protective. And she didn't shake off his touch.

Oh, *hell*, no.

"The *nerve* of that–"

"Yes," I said to Diamond, not really understanding a word coming out of her mouth. "Absolutely. We'll talk later, of course."

I moved, straight toward Allie – and her *date*.

If Diamond bitched, I'd just tell her I had to greet people. And I did. The one person I wanted to talk to was over there, and I had to talk to her. Courtesy dictated I say something to the asshole with her, so I'd say hi, then fantasize about ripping his balls off. After, of course, I made sure he understood that Allie was off limits.

As I crossed the floor, I nodded and waved and greeted the people who stood like tuxedoed and formally-gowned obstacles, but I wasn't exactly greeting them. I had no desire to talk to anybody, save for Allie. She was the only one I saw now.

I sure as hell wasn't going to let her know that though.

I nodded at a few people standing between me and Allie as I strode straight to her. I tried not to stare too intently, but it was hard. She looked beautiful. Elegant and refined, her dress looked like it'd been made for her, and the strand of pearls around her neck completed the look.

Her eyes came to mine, and a smile that was both reluctant and pleased curled her lips. "Hello, Jal."

I hoped nothing more than friendship showed when I returned her smile. "Allie. How are you? Enjoying yourself?"

"Well…yes. I suppose." She laughed and the sound was…strained. The life I had come to associate with…well, everything about her seemed dampened.

I glanced over at the man standing with her, unable to do a very good job at hiding my curiosity. Curiosity – the word seemed so mild for what I was feeling. It really didn't touch on this overwhelming urge I had to shove him aside and take over the space he had at her side.

His lips twitched, like he knew exactly what I was thinking. A moment later, he leaned over and murmured something in her ear, his lips brushing against her skin. Another rip of envy tore through me and again, his lips twitched like he was following my line of thought.

Asshole, I decided. He was an arrogant asshole.

Whatever he said had her cheeks flushing a pale shade of pink, and she averted her gaze for a moment, shaking her head. Then she looked over at me and nodded. "Jal, this is my date for the evening, Tao. Tao, this is Jal."

"For the evening," I echoed. There was no denying the edge in my voice. It was too pointed and obvious. I held out a hand, and he cocked an eyebrow before slowly accepting it. It was a total dick move, but I didn't care. I squeezed his hand as I stared into his eyes.

183

Except he didn't look impressed or intimidated. He just squeezed right back, and the look in his eyes was as clear as day.

He was laughing at me.

Son of a bitch.

Tugging my hand free, I looked back at Allie. "Would your…*date* mind if we had a dance?"

"I doubt he would." She slanted a look over at him.

Tao leaned in and kissed her cheek, murmured something else that made her blush, and she shook her head at him.

I held out a hand, and she accepted. Her gaze slid past me, lingering for a few seconds. It was long enough to tempt me to look back and see what it was she was looking at. Was it whoever had her less…*her* today?

Whoever it was, I wanted to make them go away. They could disappear from the face of the planet for all I cared. First, though, I needed to know who it was.

But before I could look, her gaze came back to mine, and I was more interested in her than anything else. Leading her out onto the dance floor, I guided her hand to my shoulder and folded the other in mine.

I was about to mention something about the waltz and how she could just follow me when she started to move.

"You never cease to amaze me," I said.

"Why?" She smiled up at me. It was still strained, but she wasn't pulling away from me, so I counted it as a win. "Because I can waltz?"

"Where did you learn?"

Canting her head to the side, she replied, "Where did you?"

"Point taken."

I had one hand on her waist, and I wanted to tug her closer. Wanted to pull her up against me and move until our hearts beat together. But I stayed...platonic and guided her to the music. As I swept her around on a turn, she smiled, and some of the shadows fell from her eyes.

"You look beautiful tonight. I'm glad you came."

"Why did you invite me?" She held my gaze.

"You left." My body heated at the memory of what had preceded her leaving. Then the negative emotion followed. While the word *pissed* wasn't exactly the right word, I was…irritated. "You just left. I wanted to talk to you."

184

"Why?" She turned her head, staring out over the dance floor, although I doubted she saw anything. "What was there to talk about really? We didn't have anything left to say. We'd agreed it was a mistake. We'd agreed we shouldn't have done it. What was there to talk about?"

"When did we agree on any of that?" I had my hand resting on the small of her back, and I was holding her closer than I should. I heard her words, but all I could think was how *wrong* her words sounded, and how *right* she felt in my arms. How easily we moved together, like we were made for each other.

"Before we even got started, we agreed it was a mistake," Allie said, smiling at me, but it wasn't a nice smile. She gave a slow shake of her head.

"I don't regret it." I never should have said those words, never should have given her that truth. And I knew it. But it was another thing I didn't regret. She deserved to know.

Her pale, soft gaze slid away. Whatever – no, *whoever* – it was that had her so upset caught her attention again. I knew it because her spine stiffened. Immediately, she forced herself to relax, but the tension that filled her sweet body was undeniable.

"What is it?" I asked, leaning down and murmuring the question next to her ear. *Tell me and I'll fix it.*

"Nothing." She gave me a tight smile.

"You're not acting like yourself."

"I'm fine, Jal."

"No, you're not."

But that shuttered look in her eyes made it clear that she wasn't going to share anything with me. It pissed me off. My gaze landed on the man standing on the edge of the dance floor. Tao. The date she'd brought with her. There was a closeness between them. A connection I couldn't overlook. Jealousy bubbled inside me, and I nodded toward him.

"What's the matter, did you and your boyfriend have a fight?"

"My boyfriend." The words were cool, almost remote, reminding me how much of a hypocrite I was.

Somewhere over in the grand ballroom, Paisley was showing off the damn rock I bought her. I'd told her I needed time, but I hadn't technically ended it, had I?

And I was angry because she'd come with a guy.

"My boyfriend." She repeated the words again as she tipped her head back, staring up at the ceiling overhead. It exposed the delicate arch of her neck, the pearls against her warm, dusky skin.

Damn. I wanted to see her naked, wearing nothing but those pearls.

"No, Tao and I didn't have a fight. We *never* fight, Jal. We might disagree on a few things – whether or not we're getting popcorn or nachos at a movie or whether we'll see some drippy drama – Tao loves them – or an action flick – my preference. But we don't fight."

"How long have you two been together?" I couldn't resist the challenge in my voice.

"Tao? Oh, man…let me think." Her forehead furrowed for a moment. "We've known each other almost our entire lives."

The music came to an end, and she stepped away.

"Wait," I said, reaching out a hand.

"You've got to go mingle." She glanced back over her shoulder for Tao, then smiled at me. "It was…nice seeing you, Jal. But you've got your thing to do. I'm just here to eat, drink and dance. You go do your thing."

"We haven't talked."

"We've talked as much as we need to." She inclined her head. "You're engaged. Your world…it isn't mine. We already established this. There's no need to go over it again."

As she turned away, I bit back a couple of ugly words – okay, a couple dozen. I didn't want to go do my thing. I wanted to follow Allie, find some place private to talk to her. I wanted to make her understand that the only world I cared about was one with her in it.

But I couldn't shirk my responsibilities, either. And Paisley had a very big responsibility growing inside her right now.

Chapter 5

Jal

Moving off the dance floor, I fought the urge to look back, to catch one more glimpse of Allie.

I might have done it if it I hadn't crashed into a petite blonde. The tipsy socialite shot me a beaming smile as I caught her arms, steadying her.

"Hi, Melanie." I managed to keep the annoyance out of my voice.

"Jal!" She flung her arms around me and pulled me down for a sloppy kiss. "I'm *sooooo* happy for you and Paisley."

She giggled and pulled away, stumbling again and forcing me to steady her once more. Fortunately, her fiancé emerged from the crowd just as I got Melanie onto her own two feet, and I was able to release her.

"Melanie, there you are, sweetheart." He slid an arm around her waist and nodded to me.

"Evening, Jared."

He nodded at me. "Hello, Jal. Great party. Have your office get in touch. I'll make a donation."

"Yes. Get in touch." Melanie giggled and reached out, grabbing my hand. "I saw Paisley's rock, it's *amazing*."

"Come on, Melanie." He offered me an apologetic look. "She's not feeling very well."

"Of course." In our circle, "not feeling well" commonly translated to "drunk off her ass." Not that I really needed an explanation. I'd known Melanie for years, and she always overindulged at events like this. Fortunately, she was at least a charming drunk. "Would you like a car...?"

Jared smiled. "No. I've already arranged for mine to be brought around."

We parted ways, but I hadn't even taken five steps before I was cut off again. This time, instead of a pair of random guests, it was by a very irate Diamond Hedges. Paisley's mother stood in front of me, her cheeks pale, save for two flags of color high on her cheeks. Her ash gray eyes glinted as bright and hard as her name, while her mouth was compressed into a thin line. She stared down her nose at me, which she somehow managed in spite of the height difference, an imperious look on her face.

"Jal." She spoke in icy tones.

"Is there a problem, Diamond?" I gave a polite smile and worked to keep my tone just as cordial. People were all around us, and more than a few slid discreet glances our way. I had no doubt everyone was curious about what the future mother-in-law wanted to say.

Normally, that would have given her pause, made her carefully choose every word she said, guard her expression.

But whatever it was that had her so worked up had changed the circumstances from normal to...whatever this was. She sniffed as though there was something foul in the air.

"Just who were you dancing with?" Her tone was icy, accusing.

I was tempted to walk around her without answering. Maybe if Paisley had been there, I'd give her an answer. Paisley...well, yeah. I owed her an explanation. I'd been an ass to her.

But I didn't owe Diamond a damn thing. I knew her though. She'd either follow me until she got the answers she wanted, or she'd possibly hunt down Allie, and I wasn't about to put her in the middle of all this. It was my fault Diamond had Allie in her sights, and I would take care of it.

"She's a friend of mine."

"Oh?" Diamond's eyes narrowed. "She's quite lovely. What's her name?"

"Allie Dodds. Her family's deaf, so I thought she'd be interested in the gala." I was almost certain I didn't imagine the flash of something dark across Diamond's eyes, and I wondered if there were rumors going around that I didn't know.

"How long have you known her?"

"Is that really your concern?" Maybe I should have just answered, but Diamond was pissing me off. I had a pretty long fuse, but the look Diamond was giving me coupled with her infuriating tone was pushing every button I had. I didn't like my own mother prying into my business, much less my future mother in law.

Diamond took a step closer and the fury in her voice might have cut some men off at the knees, but most men hadn't grown up with someone like my mother. It took a hell of a lot more than a nasty expression to get me.

"Why exactly do you want to know?" I let my smile drop away so that my face was perfectly blank.

"Let's take a walk." She stepped forward and held out her hand.

I eyed her narrowly, considered just walking away, but again, I knew if I didn't answer her, she'd keep after me, or go after Allie. So I held out my arm, and she took it. We began to walk, easing away from all of the curious eyes and ears.

"You and Paisley seem to have finally connected," she said as we walked around the edge of the dance floor. "The baby, you're engaged…then you tell her that you need some space."

She lapsed into silence, but I didn't rush to fill it. I could feel her watching me, but I just continued to walk, nodding at the familiar faces, greeting one or two.

She continued, "It's understandable. You are, after all, still young. You're nervous. You were reckless, or you wouldn't be in this boat, but I can understand why you're still hesitant to commit, even if you two are perfect for each other."

As she continued to talk, I wondered if she was going to get to the point or if she just wanted to drive me crazy by talking at me for the rest of the night.

Her tone shifted to something harder than usual. "But then I see the pictures in the papers. You dancing with that…*girl*. And I have to admit, I'm confused."

We came to a stop, and I looked down at her. She stared at me, her expression cold. At least we were getting down to it. I suddenly wanted it all over with. Everything. This discussion. The engagement. All of the things that I knew were keeping Allie and me apart.

189

"Now, we're at this event, and you're dancing again with another girl, and you won't discuss it. Worse, it's only days after you've decided to put my daughter to the side." Diamond's face was flushed. "When did you meet that girl?"

"I told Paisley I needed time," I said, keeping my voice just as icy. "And since I've gone to several functions with female friends and it's never been an issue in the past, I don't see why it is now. I don't owe you an explanation."

Diamond took a step back.

"So, you won't answer me?" she demanded.

"How about you tell me why you're so interested in Allie?"

She drew her shoulders back, frigid and remote like some blue-blooded ice queen. The resemblance between Paisley and her mother was striking. "Well. If that's going to be your response, I suggest you ask *that girl*. She should have quite a story to tell."

She walked away, and I passed a hand back through my hair. When I turned, I could see Paisley standing close by with a few of her friends. When she caught sight of Diamond, she said something to her friends, and then started toward her mother. No surprise there.

What did surprise me was the sight of Allie just a few feet away. Tao had his arm around her, holding her close. He was talking to her, and it was pretty clear she was upset.

And she was looking at me...and Diamond.

What the hell was going on here?

Chapter 6

Allie

"Come on." Tao caught my hand, tugging me away from the dance floor. "You don't need to stand around here worrying about what the Diamond bitch is doing."

I managed a weak smile. My stomach was in knots, and I was grateful I hadn't eaten much of anything tonight.

"Let's go get a drink, honey." Tao already had me halfway to the one of the numerous champagne fountains before I could respond.

"I don't want to get a drink," I said. I couldn't see Diamond anymore, but could only imagine what she had said to Jal. What had she told him? What was he thinking? "Maybe we should just go. You were right. Coming here was a bad idea. Capital *B*. Capital *I*."

I shot a look over my shoulder but didn't see Jal or Diamond. That only made it worse. I knew how Diamond was around her kind of people. She'd probably pulled Jal into some side room where she could give him my whole sordid past. By the time she finished, I had no doubt Jal would think I was just like my mother, and not in a flattering way.

The tension in my neck and shoulders was enough to leave my head pounding, and all I wanted was to find some place dark so I could crawl in and hide. Preferably for a week or two.

Tao was insistent. "You need a drink, and then you need to dance with me and quit worrying about her, about him."

I looked up, met his eyes. Clear and steady, they rested on

mine, and I wish I could have the calm assurance that always seemed like a part of him. "What if she told him who I am? What am I going to do then?"

"What if she has?" He took two flutes of champagne and pushed one into my hand before taking a sip of his own. "Come on, Allie. What could she tell him? That your mom fell for a rich older, married man and they had you? It's not like that's your fault. Hell, for the first part of it, you weren't even there. You came along after the fact. A bystander, not a participant."

A bystander.

More like a by-*product*. Diamond had always acted like I was some sort of disease. And my sisters...hell. They didn't even know about me. They'd always thought I was just the help's daughter. Barely a blip on the background radar.

"Drink up, honey," Tao said. "We're dancing and dining and debauching the rest night away. You got me all dressed up, so we're going to make the best of it."

He gave me a lascivious look, and if anything could have stirred me out of my grim mood, it would be him. It *would* have been him, too, if a familiar figure hadn't appeared in my peripheral vision.

"Oh, hell," I muttered.

Tao glanced up.

I put my champagne down. "Let's just *go*," I said, giving him a pleading look. "I'm not...I can't do this, not here. Not like this."

"Too late," Tao said softly as Jal drew nearer. Tao dipped his head and kissed my cheek as he slid his arm around my waist, offering me comfort and support. "If you really need to cut and run, we can."

Cut and run–

Shit. I wanted to so badly. Except now, Jal stood in front of me, and there was no way out without it being obvious that I was running.

Jal glanced at Tao, then down to where my friend's hand rested on my hip. His jaw tightened as he raised his eyes to meet mine.

He held out his hand and asked, "Would you take a walk with me?"

"I..." Shooting Tao a quick look, I searched for an answer to that question. But Tao couldn't tell me the right or the wrong thing to do here. It had to be my choice. And I just didn't know.

One thing I did know...if Diamond *hadn't* told him anything, or even if she had, I didn't want *her* version of events to be the only thing that Jal knew. Even if we could never be together, I didn't want him to think badly of my family.

Slowly, I moved away from Tao. Glancing back at him, I managed a weak smile. "I won't be too long."

He nodded. "I'll see if they can get the car brought around if you want to meet me near the door when you're done."

"Great."

I followed Jal in silence as we made our way up the staircase to the mezzanine level where we could look down over the ballroom itself. Others were up there as well, but it was quieter, dimmer, with the illusion of privacy. Only when he'd led me to a private alcove did he finally speak.

"I was speaking with Paisley's mother a few minutes ago." He glanced down at me but then quickly looked away. "Paisley is my fiancée. A few days ago, I told her I needed some time to think. Neither she nor her mother are very happy with me."

My heart started to thud. Maybe Diamond *hadn't* remembered me. Maybe she'd looked pissed because of Jal and Paisley. While part of that was my fault, it didn't mean she'd been talking to him about me.

"Do you know her?"

Shit.

I took a step back and stumbled.

"What?"

Using the excuse of my clumsiness, I eased away from him, and steadied myself against the long, marble balustrade, lifting one knee and rubbing at my ankle. It didn't even twinge, but if I could use it as a reason to move further away from him, to give myself a moment to process what was happening, I'd go for it. I glanced up at him while I did it, and his eyes were no longer on my face. He was staring at my legs.

An electric thrill went through me.

"Did you..." His voice was rougher now. "Is your ankle okay?"

"It's fine." The small twinge of guilt I felt was nothing compared to the misery I knew was coming. Rotating my ankle one way then the other, I put my foot down and took a step. It did ache a bit more than I liked, so with a scowl, I slid my heels off and picked them up.

The music from below had changed again, settling into a low, sexy jazz tune that pulsed and throbbed, inviting, coaxing.

"Do you know Diamond Hedges?"

I took a step over to the railing and stared down at the dance floor. I couldn't see Paisley or Diamond from here, but it didn't matter. I could practically hear them talking, hear what Diamond was saying about me.

"Did you ask her?"

"She told me to ask *you*," he said, his voice sharp.

Slowly, I turned and met his eyes. "Did she now?"

His eyes were hard, angry even, and there was a thread of distrust in his voice that I'd never heard from him before. It made my gut twist, and I suddenly wished that Tao was here with me. I'd always considered myself a strong person, but at the moment, I could've used some support.

"I'd appreciate it if you'd just be straight with me, dammit. I'm supposed to be downstairs mingling, not trying to figure out what the hell is going on with you." He moved in closer, and if I hadn't backed up a step, he would have put his hands on me.

And I would have let him.

Crazy things happened when he put his hands on me, and with all that negative emotion flickering in his eyes, there was no telling what would happen this time. I suspected I probably would end up hating myself even more.

"She thinks you're the reason why I told Paisley I needed time. She's pretty convinced, and that makes me wonder why? Is this a common thing for you?" Jal shoved a hand through his hair.

"Just what are you implying?" I asked, something sick settling in my stomach.

"I want to know how the hell you two know each other. Why she thinks there's something up with you." He scowled. "I had things arranged in my head up until you barged into my life, and now I'm second-guessing everything. You act like you want to break things off, and then the second I look your way, you come running back to fuck with my head again. It's one hell of a play, Allie. I'll give you that."

"You son of a bitch," I hissed as I realized what he was

194

saying. Taking a step toward him, I jabbed him in the chest with my index finger. I wanted to hit him, and with every passing second, it became harder not to do so. "You think I set this up? That I somehow forced you to pick FOCUS for a haircut that day? That I tricked you into leaving your engagement ring at the salon so you'd invite me to New York to give it back? That *I* asked *you* to invite me here tonight? I sure as *hell* didn't ask you to tell your spoiled little fiancée you needed time! If you're regretting telling her that, by all means, *go*. Run off to Atlantic City and get married right now, you stupid asshole! I'm sure the two of you are well *suited* to each other, you spoiled little prick!"

I was almost shouting, tears burning against my eyelids.

"You don't know a thing about her," Jal said, his voice scathing.

"Like hell I don't," I snapped back. I usually prided myself on my ability to contain my temper, but my control had snapped. "I know her better than you *ever* will. She's manipulative, controlling, and cares about *nobody* but herself." I paused a beat. "Am I wrong?"

A muscle tensed in his jaw. "So far, *manipulative* can apply to quite a few women I know."

I jerked back, feeling like he'd slapped me.

"You're one to talk about manipulation." I was almost shaking now, every word torn out of me. "You went and left that damn ring, and then you tell my boss you'll blackball his place if you don't get the ring back. Of course you left it behind on purpose so I'd have to come to you, and you have the nerve call *me* manipulative. You son of a bitch!"

He opened his mouth to say something, and I shoved him.

"And even worse? You did all of that *while you were engaged*." I took a step closer to him. "You invite me to a fundraiser for special needs in schools. Then a fundraiser for the deaf." I shook my head. "It's like you're keyed in on how to work people, you know that? You knew exactly what to do to get me to attend. Not once – but *twice*. And you call *me* manipulative?"

He reached out, grabbing my arms hard enough to make me gasp.

"How do you know Diamond? How do you know Paisley?"

I should have known better. I had known better. He was just another rich bastard who didn't give a damn about anyone but himself. He made demands, not requests. He thought the world owed him everything and that he could take what he wanted from whoever he wanted.

I yanked myself away from him. "You want to know?"

"Isn't that what I've been saying?"

"Fine. I'll tell you, but once I do, I want you to stay the *hell* out of my life. Stay away from me. You hear me?" Without giving him a chance to respond, I continued, "Twenty-two years ago, my mother worked for Kendrick Hedges. They had an affair. I was the result." Lifting my chin, I met his gaze. "Paisley's my half-sister."

His eyes widened, and I could hear the shocked, audible intake of air.

"There. Are you happy now, Jal? You know it all. But then again, you already know everything about who I am, right?"

Flinging those words out, I turned on my heel and ran for the stairs, thankful I'd taken off my shoes. I was more than halfway down when I heard him shout my name, but I ignored him and kept on running.

As soon as I reached the entrance, I saw Tao there, waiting with my wrap.

"Let's go," I said, my voice thick.

He caught sight of my face and nodded, his expression a mixture of concern and anger. We didn't do the jealousy thing, but we sure as hell were protective of each other.

"Allie!"

I flinched at the sound of Jal's voice, and I fought back the tears threatening to choke me. I felt Jal as much as I heard him grow closer, and then Tao was between us, shielding me.

"That's enough," Tao said, his voice flat. "I think you've done enough damage, don't you, lover boy? Go find your fiancée, okay?"

Jal snarled something I couldn't understand. Then there was another voice, one I wanted to hear even less than Jal's.

Diamond.

"Tao, get me the hell out of here," I said, almost desperate now.

"Sure thing, honey. Let's go." He wrapped his arm around me and led me away. Right then, I was damn glad of that unfaltering, unwavering confidence of his, because I couldn't have done any of it on my own.

Within two minutes, he had me in the car. In another ten, we were parked in a parking lot somewhere. I had no idea where, and I didn't care. I was just glad to be away from *those* people.

"Come here, you." He hooked an arm around my neck and tugged me as close as he could in the snug little car. "I guess that didn't go very well."

I buried my face against his shoulder. "Next time..." I caught my breath and forced myself to breathe out slow and steady. "Next time...please don't let me be so stupid."

He knew I wasn't really talking about going to a party.

"This is life." He rubbed his cheek against my hair. "Sometimes, being stupid is part of it."

I sniffled, fought the sobs burning the back of my throat. *Why?* I wanted to scream it, shout it, cry it. But I didn't let myself because I wasn't exactly sure what I wanted answers for or who I wanted them from. All I knew was that everything in me was begging for some sort of peace.

"Allie?"

"What?"

"Go ahead and cry, honey. You'll feel better."

So I did.

I let my best friend, my sometimes-lover, the only person who knew all of me, hold me while I cried. Cried over Jal, over what I knew I could never have. And I cried over the child I'd been, the one who'd always known that there were some things I would never be able to reach.

Chapter 7

Jal

As Tao escorted Allie outside, her words kept echoing in my head. *Sister. She's my sister.*

What in the hell did she mean by that?

I wasn't stupid. I understood what she was saying on an intellectual level, but it was everything else that I was having a hard time comprehending. Like how in the world I could've known the Hedges my entire life and not known about Allie.

But the doors, already closing in front of me, offered no answer. I turned, ready to make my goodbyes and leave, but came up short when I realized that Diamond was standing right there, glaring up at me.

"I see you took my advice and asked her."

Paisley stood next to her, her face pale and strained.

"What's this all about?" I demanded roughly.

Several people were eyeing us, and Diamond raised her chin, apparently having had enough of us making a public spectacle of ourselves because she looked around before shaking her head. With a sniff, she turned on her heel and beckoned for me to follow.

"If you want to know, you'll have to come with me. Paisley and I do not believe in airing our dirty laundry in public. Unlike *some* people."

That certainly hadn't stopped you earlier, I thought sourly. But I went to Paisley's side. I needed answers.

After Diamond failed to find any private place on her own, I flagged down one of the staff helping out with the event and spoke to them. Within a few moments, we were escorted into a small, private room.

Diamond shot the tuxedoed server a dirty look. "Did you really have to make me wander around for five minutes before you showed us a private room?" she demanded.

I stepped between them. "The staff can't read minds, Diamond, and you barely looked for two minutes," I said before he even had a chance to offer some unnecessary apology. I turned to him. "Thanks for your time." I pulled a bill from my pocket and pushed it into his hand. It was more to make up for her rudeness than anything else, and I suspected he knew that.

A faint smile tipped up one corner of his mouth. "No trouble at all, Mr. Lindstrom. Please let me know if you need anything else."

Once he left, I walked straight to the mini bar. I'd been in here earlier when I'd gone over last minute details with my assistant, the head event planner, and the heads of the foundation. I hoped to hell they hadn't removed the alcohol yet.

I was in luck.

Splashing some scotch into a glass, I swirled it around before turning to face Paisley. She wasn't looking at me, or her mother, but rather staring at the far wall as she twisted her engagement ring around her finger. I'd never seen her like this before, and for a moment, I felt a pang of guilt for what I'd done. What I was doing.

"It's true, isn't it?" she said quietly.

I wanted to ask what she meant, but before I had a chance, Diamond moved to her and wrapped an arm around her shoulders. Paisley stiffened. If I hadn't been watching them so closely, I wouldn't have noticed. But I saw it. It lasted only a second, and when Diamond leaned in, murmured to her softly, Paisley nodded.

I took a sip of my scotch, waiting for one of them to fill me in on whatever the hell was going on.

When, after a minute, neither of them did, I plopped down into the closest chair. Focusing on Diamond since she seemed to want to run the show, I leaned back. She was entirely too much like my own mother, and if I let her set the rules, then I'd have to play by them. I wasn't in the mood to have her lead me around by the nose.

"I'd like an explanation," I said quietly, hoping the calm control in my voice hid the riot that was going on inside. "Allie said that she's…" I glanced at Paisley, but she was still looking away. "She said Paisley is her sister. Is that true?"

"Don't you *dare* imply there's a relationship between that miserable little tramp and *my* daughters," Diamond said, her face screwing up like she'd had a lemon shoved in her mouth. "That bastard is not a part of my family."

I curled my hands into fists even though, if what Allie had said was right, the term was actually applied correctly. I had a feeling, however, that Diamond wasn't using it because it was accurate.

"Just because her whore of a mother seduced my husband one night doesn't mean she can claim any sort of relationship with my girls." Diamond stared down her nose at me, as if daring me to contradict her.

I swirled my scotch in my glass, a hundred things running through my mind. The very foremost thought was the plain and simple fact that Diamond was wrong. Whether she liked it or not, if Kendrick Hedges was Allie's biological father, then Paisley and Mallory Hedges were half-sisters.

My next gut response was that Allie wasn't responsible for what her parents had done. Before I could say any of that, Diamond was forging on ahead.

"And *that girl* is no better. Even as a child, she manipulated Kendrick, luring him away from his children, stealing his love, stealing his devotion. She was a threat to my marriage from the moment she was conceived." Diamond lifted a hand as if she needed a moment to continue. "You'd think it would be impossible, wouldn't you? And I didn't blame a child for my husband's indiscretion, not really. How could I? I wanted him to be a father to her even though it hurt so much that he'd been unfaithful. But seeing him as often as she did wasn't enough. She wanted more. She wanted everything…"

Diamond started to sniffle as she sat down on the divan and reached into her small evening bag. Someone else might've been moved, but I was too used to the theatrics of women like her.

Finally, she continued, dabbing at her eyes, "Even then, though, I couldn't blame her. Her mother was…" She reached over and cupped Paisley's cheek. "Not much of a mother. Malla had so many chances to better herself, to offer her daughter a better life, but she was more interested in trying to get back into my husband's bed. She didn't even love her own daughter. I often suspected that she'd planned to get pregnant to try to convince my husband to leave his family, and when that didn't work, she didn't have any use for the poor child after that. It's no wonder the girl latched onto Kendrick. But she was driving us apart – all of us."

I felt like I was going to be sick. Was what Diamond was saying really true? Had Allie really been the product of an affair intended to drive a family apart? Had she been raised to think that was how to get what she wanted? To scheme?

Now Diamond looked at me again. "Can you imagine how humiliating it is to beg you own husband for attention? To beg him to pay attention to the children you gave him? But he'd rather give money to *that* girl. Rather spend time with her than his own flesh and blood."

I wanted to argue that Allie was as much Kendrick's flesh and blood as the daughters he'd conceived with Diamond, but I knew if I did, I'd never hear the end of the story, and right now, I needed to hear it all.

"Mallory and Paisley were lost. And there I was, struggling for him to notice me while he had his whore and their child living under my own roof."

Confused, I shook my head. "Wait, what? They lived there?"

Diamond scowled, as if my question was something untoward.

"Allie's mother, Malla, was my nanny." Paisley stared at her hands, as if this was part of some shameful secret of hers. "I loved her. I thought she loved me. But things started to change, and she spent more and more time with my father, less and less time with me. She hardly ever spent *any* time with Mallory at all. Then she had *her* baby, and everything changed. I felt like she'd abandoned me. I had no idea what was going on or who the baby was." She laughed and reached up to wipe at her eyes. "She was supposed to take care of me, and all of a sudden, I just didn't matter!"

"Hush, darling," Diamond murmured.

Paisley rested her head on her mother shoulder.

It was the most emotion I had ever seen from the two of them, but I still wasn't sure if I should trust it. I got the feeling that

Paisley was trying to use what had happened in her childhood to garner sympathy, playing up things that had barely been there.

I felt like a heel for even thinking it, but there it was.

When Paisley looked back at me, her eyes were wet and bright. "I suspected, you know, that Allie might be my sister. That's not the sort of thing you discuss, of course. And I didn't want to ask. It was horrible in our home for so long, but it got better when Malla started dating some other man. She wasn't there all the time, and Mom and Daddy began to reconnect. I thought it was all behind us."

"Allie didn't like not having Kendrick there to wrap around her little finger. She's just as much a money-mongering tramp."

"Mama," Paisley said, turning her gaze from me to her mother.

"Hush. You always try to see the best in people, darling." Diamond patted Paisley's cheek, leaning in to kiss her daughter on the forehead. Then she rose and turned, facing me. The lingering grief I had seen in her eyes was gone, replaced by the ice I had come to associate with Diamond Hedges.

"They left our household for good when Allie was sixteen. I finally insisted. The girl would come over after school and stay there while her mother worked. Kendrick would make time in his schedule to see her. Never our daughters, of course, but he'd visit with *her* two or three times a week. She'd demand he give her money, more and more of it as time went on. Anything that Paisley and Mallory had..." Diamond narrowed her eyes, hesitating just a moment.

Paisley flicked a look my way, and I pretended not to notice. I still wasn't sure how much I believed.

Diamond continued, "If they had it, she wanted it. Boys from high school and college would come over to visit Paisley and Allie would make a spectacle of herself. She was an embarrassment and a bad influence. She was younger than my two girls but there she was, flirting with boys who were far too old for her. Then, one day, we...well, I had to come down hard on her after a particular incident, and that night, I told Kendrick he would have to decide who mattered most – the family who loved him or the girl who only wanted to use him."

Her description of Allie left a bad taste in my mouth. Guilt and anger and mistrust churned inside me. Shaking my head, I rose and started to pace, sipping my scotch as I turned things over in my head.

I had to say something.

"Look, I certainly haven't known her for as long as you guys, and I know nothing of the history, but the woman I've gotten to know isn't anything like that."

"Of course she isn't," Diamond said softly, her tone almost understanding. "Allie is adept at presenting the face she wants people to see. A poor, sweet girl, abandoned by her father. Whatever will get her the most sympathy. To be fair, I think she had to become that way, what with her mother being the way she was. If she didn't learn to manipulate, she never would have survived."

Frowning into my scotch, I waited for her to continue.

"She'll show you a face that is just fun and laughter – make no mistake, Jal. She's very intelligent, and she knows how to read people. She won't make any sort of move until she decides whether a person may be of use to her or not. But she's not what she makes herself out to be."

I wanted to argue, to stand up for Allie, and I even turned to do so.

But then I saw Paisley sitting there, looking lost and hurt, and I couldn't bring myself to do it.

"Jal," Paisley said, her voice far more hesitant than I'd ever heard from her. "I'm almost afraid to ask, but the two of you...I saw you dancing. Was she the woman you were dancing with at the last event you went to? I saw the pictures in the paper. The woman was wearing a dress..." She laughed bleakly. "I wanted that dress. I recognized it immediately. It was from the designer I used to use. I no longer use her, of course. She was very...vulgar. But I saw that dress – the client who'd ordered it couldn't use it and I offered an...well, it was almost embarrassing, really. But the designer wouldn't sell it to me. The woman who was wearing it, the woman with you before...was it Allie?"

Now the guilt was about ready to choke me because I was forced to remember what had happened after that event. Even so, I couldn't help but wonder how Allie had gotten the kind of money to get a dress that *Paisley* hadn't been able to buy? It made Diamond's story more believable.

I couldn't lie to Paisley, not again. "Yes."

Her soft intake of breath was another punch of guilt, and she closed her eyes. "And you…you two, are you just friends? Or are you attracted to her?"

"Paisley, I…"

Her soft, strained laugh kept me from saying anything else. If I'd any decency at all, I would've confessed everything, right then right there. I would've told Paisley that I'd slept with Allie. That I wasn't only attracted to Allie, I wanted her so badly that it hurt, even now.

But I couldn't do that, couldn't tell Paisley any of that, not when she already hated Allie so much. The betrayal of my having slept with Allie would be so much worse than if it'd been with anyone else. I couldn't do that to Paisley.

And if I was honest, I couldn't do it to Allie, no matter what Paisley and Diamond said about her.

"When did you meet her? Was it before or after we announced our engagement?" Paisley's voice had risen, and I could hear the sharp note of accusation in her voice.

I answered those questions honestly, "She and I met right before the engagement. She had no idea that you and I were involved." I wasn't sure why I felt the need to make it clear that Allie hadn't been trying to get to her.

Diamond was quick to butt in. "And this event, where Allie was wearing the dress…" She let the words trail off. "Was it after the engagement was announced?"

"Yes."

Paisley made a sound, but I didn't look at her. I kept my eyes on Diamond. The expression on her face told me that while Paisley hadn't yet figured it out, Diamond had. She knew that Allie and I had been intimate.

Diamond arched one perfectly plucked eyebrow. "Is that a fact?"

"Yes." Refusing to look away, I held her gaze. "I invited her to the event as a friend." That, too, was the truth. I'd been attracted, yes, but I hadn't planned for anything to happen. I continued, "As you're well aware, Diamond, there are a number of functions that I attend that Paisley doesn't like, and I don't care to go alone. We agreed quite some time ago that I could invite a friend to go with me. So that's what I did."

"Yes. She and I have talked about that at length." Diamond

still had that pinched look on her face, as though this whole thing was distasteful. "And I've made my feelings clear. As your fiancée, Paisley should be the only one attending functions with you from here on out. Perhaps that's something else the two of you should discuss. And might I add, it's funny how you invited this *friend*, but she says nothing about her connection to Paisley or our family."

Paisley made a pained noise in her throat, her hands moving over her stomach, as if cradling our unborn child.

I still didn't know how much of this was real, but the guilt over what I'd done was eating me up. I knelt down next to her, resting a hand on her shoulder.

"I'm sorry, Paisley," I murmured. Then I looked up at her mother. "You've already made it clear you don't believe there's a connection to your family. From where I'm standing, you view your husband's part in Allie's conception to be more of a...biological donation."

Paisley flinched, and I could have hit myself for my crudeness. I hoped she didn't think that I thought of our child that way. No matter how complex this situation was, our child would always be a part of us both.

Her shoulders hitched, and she sounded like she was about ready to start crying. Awkward with this kind of emotion from her, I smoothed a hand down her back.

"Paisley, I'm sorry. If I had known..."

"I know, Jal, I know." She nodded, but she didn't look at me.

"Perhaps you should take your fiancée home," Diamond said. "I think you've upset her enough, and I highly doubt she wants to return to the gala."

Rising, I met Diamond's hard gaze. "I think I can handle this myself."

She opened her mouth to respond, but I glared at her. "I'm not one of your little minions, Diamond. Don't get it into your head that I am."

Then, without saying anything else, I offered my hand to Paisley.

There were a lot of things I didn't know, that I still had questions about. There was, however, one thing I did know. I'd done enough damage. It was time to start making things right.

Chapter 8

Jal

"Come inside, baby."

Paisley had curled up against me for the entire drive home, her head pressed against my chest, and now, as the driver came to a stop in front of her townhouse, she looked up at me, her light gray eyes wide.

"I can't bear to be alone tonight."

I wasn't sure I was up to *not* being alone, but since it was my own damn fault she was this upset, I couldn't be even more of an asshole and leave. "All right."

I left her in the back as I stepped out to speak with my driver. After a word, he moved to the trunk to grab the bag I kept there for occasions like this. Then I reached down and held out my hand to Paisley. She gave me a wan smile as she climbed out, staring up at the townhouse for a long moment before looking up at me.

"You'll stay all night, won't you?"

The beseeching look on her face had me nodding without thinking about it, and she turned into me.

"Thank you. I know you like your time to yourself, but I…I just can't bear the thought of being alone right now. I've spent so much of my life *feeling* alone and isolated."

"Come on." I put my arm around her shoulders and pulled her against my side. "Let's get you inside."

Leading her to the front door, I cursed every step I'd taken that had led to this.

Switching stylists – yeah, big mistake.

Flirting with Allie, bigger mistake.

Flying her to New York…

Every choice I'd made lately seemed to be one wrong choice after another. Now that I was here with my fiancée, it should seem like I was doing the right thing. So why didn't it feel right?

Why did I feel like I was in the *wrong* place? Doing the *wrong* thing.

206

Being with the *wrong* person.

"Come on."

Paisley took my hand and tugged me along behind her, into a room of soft blues, greens, and whites. It was her favorite room, but I always felt like a drowning fish in there. She kept the lights off but turned on the fireplace to take the chill out of the air. She'd gone on a tear when the designer had told her the building wasn't up to code for a real fireplace. She'd fired that one and two others before she finally realized that the only way to get the fireplace would be to tear the building down and buy a new one. Since some of the other tenants hadn't wanted to sell, she'd tried every trick in her book.

When that hadn't worked, her father had sent her off with her mother on a girls' weekend, and when she came back, it was to find that the original designer had come in, done the project as they'd planned with a realistic-looking electric fireplace. She'd been delighted – mostly – and had declared she had the best father ever.

Since he owned the building as a whole, Paisley had the top floor, and this particular room took up almost a quarter of the unit. Her bedroom took up half, and the rest was her kitchen and dining room.

I frowned at the memories, trying to bring together how much I'd personally witnessed her father spoiling her with the story I'd just heard from Diamond and Paisley. I supposed it was possible that since Allie and her mother had left, Kendrick had been trying to make things up to his daughters.

But none of that mattered at the moment. I needed to make things right with Paisley before I worried about the rest.

She collapsed down onto the couch and pressed her hand to her forehead, a heavy sigh escaping her. "This entire day...it's been horrid."

"Yeah." I could agree with her there.

I moved to the windows and stared outside, wondering where Allie had gone. Was she alone or had she gone home with Tao? And who *was* he? She said he was her date, but it was clear that they were close. I was willing to bet he was the same guy who'd gone with her to get her dress.

The dress that I'd been wondering how she'd bought.

Had he bought it for her? Who was he to her that he would

buy something that expensive? Did they have some sort of *arrangement*?

The thought made me sick, and I hated myself for even thinking it, but with Diamond and Paisley's words dancing through my head, I couldn't stop myself. If Allie really was as manipulative as they said, was it possible that she was sleeping with Tao so he would buy her things? Had that been what she'd intended for me? Or was I more personal? Had she chosen me to get back at her father's family? To get back at them for having what she never did?

"Come sit with me, baby."

Paisley's voice brought me back to the present. Pushing the other thoughts from my mind, I went. I sat next to her, closing my eyes as she cuddled up against me. It should've felt natural, but it didn't. Paisley's body was thin, long, not the soft curves I wanted.

"It's been such a horrid day." She pressed her lips to my neck.

"So you've said." I thought of how Allie had looked at me, the way she'd set her jaw before turning and walking away, shoulders squared.

"Just awful." She kissed my neck, the light caress soft.

And I felt nothing. My mind stayed caught on Allie, on the things I'd learned, the things Diamond and Paisley had said. The girl I'd come to know.

It didn't fit.

She'd been aware that I had money, and it hadn't impressed her. I'd seen that. I'd seen the truth in her eyes.

"Make me forget," Paisley said, her voice rough and low.

Before I could react, she climbed into my lap and took my hands, lifting them to her breasts. My hands completely covered them, felt her nipples harden against my palms.

Staring up at her in the dim light, I realized I could see similarities between the sisters. In the line of her jaw, the slope of her nose. If I really tried, I could almost pretend–

I stopped myself right there. I wasn't going to betray either woman that way. I'd always prided myself on not being *that* guy, the one who had to fantasize about another woman to get off. I wasn't going to start here.

"Please, Jal." She ground down on my lap, the friction barely getting a twitch of interest from my cock. "I need you."

Slowly, I slid my hands down to her waist and tugged her closer. She kissed me, her lips cool against mine. Paisley tugged at my tie, pulled it over my head. Once she had it free, she went to deal with the buttons on my shirt, and I remained still, watching her. Seeing what she was really doing.

She wasn't looking to make herself forget anything. She was trying to distract me, and I knew it was because she didn't want me thinking about Allie. She might not have known the specifics of what happened between Allie and me, but Paisley knew I cared, that I wanted.

And still, I couldn't bring myself to stop her.

"I know she's pretty," Paisley murmured against my mouth.

My entire body stiffened, and not in a good way.

"What?"

She reached up and freed the fastening at the back of her neck. The front of her dress fell to her waist, baring her breasts. She cupped them, rolled her nipples between her fingers.

"I know she's pretty, Jal. Everybody always talked about it, even when she was a little girl. That mixed skin and Daddy's eyes." She kissed me again, then moved her mouth to my ear. "But I'm pretty too. Aren't I?"

I could answer that honestly. "Paisley, you're beautiful." My voice was rough as I added, "You don't–"

She pressed her finger to my lips. "Hush. It's okay. Whatever it is, I don't need to know. It's okay. You're mine. That's all that matters."

She slid off my lap and onto her knees in front of me. Her eyes darkened as she pushed my knees apart.

Shit.

"I want to show you what I can do for you. I want to show you what I can make you feel."

She undid my pants, her eyes still locked on mine. I should stop her, but I knew what she wanted. She wanted to show me that she was desirable, that she could make me want her.

I was still soft when she wrapped her hand around me, but she gave me a couple hard, quick strokes, the rough friction making me suck in a breath. I didn't let myself close my eyes though. I wasn't going to pretend she was somebody else. I owed her that much.

I wasn't so convinced that I was *hers*, but I wasn't going to

209

use her like that either.

Guilt made it easier.

But when you have to remind yourself to stay on target, it takes some of the fun out of getting a blowjob, even one from someone as skilled as Paisley.

Pushing my hands into her short mahogany hair, I kept my gaze on her. She leaned down, took the tip between her lips. Her teeth lightly grazed the crown and I tugged hair. Her eyes flicked up to me as I arched up so she'd take me deeper. She let my cock slide across her tongue and bump against the back of her throat. I moaned as she held me there, unable to stop my body's natural response to the wet heat of her mouth.

My cock glistened as it emerged from her mouth. "That's my boy."

My stomach clenched at her words, and I knew what I said next would either break us completely or give us a chance. Right now, I didn't know where we would end up, only that I didn't want to risk alienating the mother of my child. I'd asked for time, and now I realized that I needed more. And I needed Paisley to know that I was still trying to figure it out.

"Suck on it, Paisley."

Heat flared in her eyes at the command. She liked to play it rough, but she never admitted to it. When it was all said and done, it was my fault for talking her into whatever kinky thing we did.

Women like her didn't do things like *that*.

My fingers tightened in her hair. "It's not going to suck itself."

In response, she slid her mouth down slowly, pretending reluctance. I gave her head a push, shoving my cock deeper into her mouth. She worked me up and down, cupped my balls and rolled them. Her teeth scraped me again, and I swore, yanked her head off of me.

"Ready to fuck me now?" She grinned at me. "Take me hard and fast? You want me to bend over the couch so you can spank me, or take me to the bedroom so you can tie me up?"

I glared at her. "That's enough. We're not getting that rough. You're pregnant."

"But you're not." She pouted up at me. "Besides, pregnant doesn't mean *fragile*."

"You heard me. Be nice." I stroked my thumb across her

lower lip, swollen now and wet. With another light tug on her hair, I guided her back to where she'd been. She slowly opened her mouth and went back to business, sucking and licking until I finally exploded in her mouth.

After she swallowed, she stood and dropped her dress to the floor. She straddled my legs, putting her pussy right at level with my face. "Now it's my turn."

Later that night, as I lay next to Paisley in her bed, my mind refused to let me relax. The orgasm should've been the precursor to a good night's sleep. The one I'd given her with my fingers and tongue had apparently done the trick. My brain, however, refused to turn off.

While I'd been going down on Paisley, I'd managed to keep Allie from my mind and focus on my fiancée – or whatever she was. Now, however, all I could think about was the woman I didn't have next to me.

I was in bed with one woman and dreaming about her sister.

I'd found myself in probably what was one of the more awkward situations in life. Engaged to one sister. Crazy about the other.

And that was the bottom line. It wasn't about the grass being greener, or getting cold feet. I wanted Allie, plain and simple. When I was with Paisley, I was thinking about her sister. And when I was with Allie, she was all I could think about.

If I'd known about the relationship between the two of them, I wanted to believe I never would have pursued her, but the truth was, I didn't know. I had an almost obsessive desire for Allie, and nothing was going to change that. Even if I didn't act on it, it would still be there.

So…what to do?

Was I supposed to ignore the one woman who had ever really gotten to me?

Marry Paisley and ignore whatever this was with Allie?

Could I do that?

And aside from all of that, none of it even made sense.

Definitely not the way Diamond presented it.

Granted, she had reason enough to pretend things in her own way, so I knew I couldn't take anything she said at face value. Something told me Allie wasn't going to be all that open with me, even if I did ask.

One thing was certain…I had to figure out what I was going to do.

It would help, though, if I could figure out exactly what happened to begin with. At least that was a place to start.

Chapter 9

Allie

Tao held out a glass of wine, ignoring me when I tried to push it away. I reluctantly took it, knowing that he wouldn't stop until he got what he wanted. Despite his usually easy-going nature, Tao could be quite stubborn when he wanted to be.

"Just one," he said, sitting down next to me with his own glass. "I think after tonight, we both deserve it."

"Why didn't I think about them being there?" Slowly, I sipped at the wine I didn't really want. "Seriously, what was I thinking?"

Tao pressed a kiss to my temple. "You were thinking, honey, just not with your brain."

Miffed, I shot him a dirty look. "Hey, I'm not the one here who has a penis. I don't think with that part of my anatomy."

"Allie." He shook his head as he pulled me into his lap, somehow managing to do it without spilling my wine or his.

He was laughing at me, but it was a nice kind of laughter. I leaned against him as he took another sip of his wine.

He set down his glass and cupped my cheek, his expression soft. "I wasn't talking about sex. I was talking about your heart. I always knew that when you fell, you would do it hard, and you're falling for this guy."

I shook my head, protesting. "No. He's hot but..."

Tao gave me a look that said he wasn't buying it. Setting my jaw, I looked away from him. What did he know?

Except...he knew me. Tao knew me better than anyone else

in my life. Better than my family even. No matter how close my mother and I were, Tao was closer.

Groaning, I dropped my head onto his shoulder and sighed. "My life would be easier if you and I could just fall in love. You'd be happy. I'd be happy. My parents would be happy."

"Love is a fickle bitch," he said as he smoothed a hand down my back. "She isn't worried about people being happy." He sighed. "Maybe it'll all work out, Allie."

I snorted, a decidedly unladylike sound. "Yeah. Maybe. And I'll wake up tomorrow tall and thin and rich."

"While we're wishing," Tao said, "we'll both be madly in love, pleasing both our parents. We'll get married and sail off into the sunset going *fa-la-la-la*." Tao rested his chin on my shoulder.

I laughed. "Sure. Fa-la-la-la-la."

"Any fa-la-la-la-la yet?"

My cheek rested on Tao's sweaty chest, my breasts pressed against his side. One of his arms was wrapped around me, his fingers tracing patterns on my skin. His other arm was behind his head as he stared up at the ceiling. My entire body felt like I'd just run a marathon, and I was pretty sure his fingers were imprinted on my ass.

I chuckled, the sound coming in short bursts as I worked for my breath. "Nope. Sorry. A lot of *yes, right there* and *fuck me*, but no fa-la-la-la."

"Damn. I was sure those *fas* were in there somewhere."

I laughed and curled closer to his side. The position was comfortable, familiar. All of this was comfortable and familiar. The way he fit inside me, how he knew exactly the right amount of pressure to put on my clit, the perfect way to bite my nipples. He knew exactly how to get me off in every position, and loved to draw it out so that we used more than one. He had stamina, and thoroughly enjoyed every part of sex. Foreplay, oral, all of it.

When it came to fucking, Tao participated enthusiastically.

I just wished there was some of that *fa-la-la-la-la* he'd been teasing me about. Some feeling beyond platonic love and basic physical attraction. If I could just fall for him, if he could fall for me...sex with him was great. Being with him was great. But when we weren't together…

Just like that, the lightheartedness of the afterglow passed, and a cold knot of misery settled inside.

I was starting to think Tao was right in the worst way. That I wasn't simply lusting after Jal, but that I'd actually fallen in love with him.

It was one of my worst fears, not just falling for somebody who was so totally wrong, but falling for somebody who was completely out of my reach. I'd always told myself that I wouldn't repeat my mother's mistakes, but the events of the past couple weeks had blown that vow all to hell.

The hand I had laying on Tao's chest closed into a fist, and he covered it. "What's wrong?"

"I…" The moment I opened my mouth, for reasons I couldn't even explain, I started to cry.

Without needing an explanation, Tao pulled me into his arms, rolling us onto our sides so he could stroke a hand up and down my back. He kissed the top of my head.

"I'll tell you what, Allie. I don't think I've ever sexed you right into tears before."

The comment did what I knew he wanted. I smacked his chest.

"Jerk," I managed to get out between sobs.

"Just trying to help." He ran his fingers through my hair as his tone shifted. "It's okay, Allie. It's all going to work out."

"How?" I couldn't think of anything that would make any of this better.

No matter how much I wanted to deny it, the sinking feeling in my gut said that I'd fallen for the wrong man. And I had an equally bad feeling that after I'd left, he'd gone to Diamond for answers. I didn't even want to think about what she would've told him.

Diamond had never liked me, and she'd hated my mother. Granted, I couldn't really blame her. My mother had carried on a long term affair with a married man, and I was the result of that.

Diamond, however, hadn't been satisfied with hating from afar, or even confronting her husband. She'd never been physically abusive – that sort of thing was beneath her – but biting insults and other forms of verbal abuse had been constant whenever my father wasn't around.

No child should learn the meaning of the term *bastard* because they were one.

And I knew Diamond had shared all of that with Jal. Told him everything from her twisted point of view. As much as I felt for her as the woman who'd been cheated on, the way she'd treated me made any real sympathy nearly impossible. The thought of Diamond pouring out all of that venom and hate to Jal made me cry even harder. If he didn't hate me already, he would after Diamond was done.

Even as Tao's arms tightened around me, and I knew that Jal and I could never be together, I couldn't help but wish that he was the one comforting me, telling me that it would be all right.

Chapter 10

Jal

The morning was cold, wet, and gray. Pretty much the usual for March in Philadelphia.

Any other Sunday, I probably would have just rolled over and slept another few hours, then done all I could to avoid going outside. There was nothing good out there, I was sure of that.

Now, however, I knew there were necessary things out there. Like answers.

I'd spent most of my life balancing the life I wanted with the life I was expected to have, hiding the truth of who I was behind the public image I was supposed to maintain. Because I did it so well, my mother rarely interfered in the things I did behind closed doors.

But now, all of that was blown to hell. I was trapped by expectations I didn't want, and I knew that whatever I did next would shape the rest of my life.

A soft sigh came from the woman next to me, a reminder of just how very true all of that was. I was in bed with Paisley after a night of dreaming about another woman, and I couldn't deny that the idea of spending my life like this left a bad taste in my mouth.

That was the impetus I needed to sit up and kick my legs over the bed.

Paisley didn't stir. No surprise there. She'd always slept like the dead. Even me getting up out of bed and walking around, gathering up the few clothes I'd discarded didn't stir her.

I showered in the guest bathroom, although it wasn't much

bigger than a closet. Some people might've thought the disproportionate sizes of the rooms was strange, but I knew how Paisley thought. She wouldn't waste space on anything she wouldn't personally use. Her bathroom boasted a tub big enough for several people, and an even bigger shower, but any guests she might have wouldn't need much more than the basic necessities. Right now, that was all I needed too. I had to wash away the scent of her perfume, of her.

Since they were for spontaneous situations, the clothes I'd packed in my overnight case consisted of jeans, a t-shirt, and a pullover. It took little time to dress, and by the time I was ready to head out the door, I had a message from my driver that my car was already out front.

I didn't plan on being driven around today, so when I got to the curb, there were actually two cars waiting. The Bentley and my Bugatti. I didn't drive the Bugatti much. It was a hand-built, custom-made piece of machinery that was badass enough to make even the biggest automotive aficionado weep with envy. To be honest, I didn't drive any of my cars much. It was easier just to let somebody else drive me so I could concentrate on other matters, business mostly. But the last thing I wanted to do today was give my mind time to think.

What I needed was to feel the power of a good, solid piece of automotive art, the wheel in my hands, the way it hugged the curves. Basically, I needed to let the miles tear away, and hope it burned out some of the stress chewing at my gut.

As the Bentley pulled away from the curb, I climbed into the Bugatti, not lingering to look back up at Paisley's townhouse. I'd be back, sooner than I liked, most likely, but I hoped I'd have some answers by then.

The drive to the sprawling, somewhat ostentatious estate where Paisley's parents lived was almost thirty minutes outside of the main city. That gave me time to focus my brain and figure out exactly how to do this. I didn't want to walk up to Kendrick Hedges and flat-out accuse him of being a selfish prick.

I had a feeling he deserved it, but it wouldn't do me any good. I owed it to myself, to Paisley – to Allie – to find out the truth. Whatever decision I ended up making needed to be based on the facts of what really happened, who Allie really was, not rumors and biased statements.

Although it was still fairly early when I arrived, I was told that Mr. Hedges was in the library and had just finished breakfast, but I was welcome to have some myself.

I declined the breakfast invite but did request some coffee as the butler led me back to Kendrick's library. There wasn't really any point to calling the room a library, in my opinion. There was one wall that boasted a couple of floor to ceiling bookshelves that were filled with first editions and classics, but I'd be willing to lay money down that none of them had ever been read. They'd been bought solely for their value or their visual appeal, no other reason.

I didn't spend much of my own time reading, but if I were going to spend money on books, it would be so I could read them, not so I could look pretentious.

I pushed all of those thoughts aside as I stepped into the library. I wasn't here to critique Kendrick's decorating or spending habits.

Kendrick rose and came forward, holding out his hand. "Jal, good to see you, son."

"Kendrick."

I shook his hand while the butler moved to the sideboard and poured me a cup of coffee. He brought it to me and then gave us both a polite nod before retreating. I took a sip, felt the jolt of caffeine hitting my system. I needed about ten cups of this before I'd feel somewhat normal. Then again, normal might not be in the cards ever again. Not what I'd always considered normal, anyway.

"How was the gala last night?" He gestured for me to join him in front of the fireplace. "Are you hungry?"

"No. I'm good with just the coffee, thanks." I sat across from him in a comfortable armchair. At least now I didn't have to figure out a way to ease into the subject. "I take it Diamond hasn't talked to you about the party."

He blinked, confusion showing on his face. "No, she hasn't. Diamond got in rather late and I was already in bed. I'm afraid I'm not up for socializing as I used to be. More often than not, Diamond goes to events with Paisley or one of her friends from the country club." He gave me an expectant look. "Did something happen?"

"Well..." I blew out a breath and looked down into my cup. Part of me had hoped that he'd at least be aware of some of the events so I didn't have to explain them, but now I was thinking that it might be better that he wasn't prepared. It was harder than most people realized to come up with a lie on the spot. He might be more likely to give me honest answers this way.

"Your daughter was at the gala last night."

Kendrick chuckled. "Of course she was. She went with her mother. I know the two of you are a bit on the odds right now, but..." His voice trailed off as he realized that I wasn't talking about Paisley. "Was Mallory there with her girlfriend? Diamond can be...harsh at times. She just wants what's best for the girls, and that doesn't always match what the girls want."

I cut in before he could continue along the same vein. "I'm not talking about Paisley or Mallory."

For a moment, his eyes went blank before understanding dawned. He tried to hide it, pasting a look of confusion on his face, but I'd seen the slip. That was the first confirmation I needed. He knew he had three daughters, not two. That much of the two stories I'd heard was true.

"I'm talking about Allie, sir."

Kendrick got up and moved over the windows that dominated the far western wall. Tension radiated off of him, and I knew he wasn't admiring the view of his grounds. He'd just needed to move, to give himself some space to think. I remained silent, letting him take in what I'd told him.

Several minutes passed before he finally broke the quiet. "I take it Diamond saw her."

"Yes. Paisley saw her too."

To my surprise, Kendrick shrugged. "Oh, that's no concern. Paisley doesn't know anything about Allie."

That was interesting. I leaned forward. "On the contrary, sir. She does."

He turned, his frown cutting deep grooves into his features. "Pardon me?"

Rubbing my hands down my face, I stood up and met his eyes. "She said she suspected for a while, but when Diamond confronted me, Paisley was there. She heard it all."

A heavy breath escaped him, and he came back to his seat. Sitting down, he met my eyes. "I think it's best you tell me exactly what happened last night."

So I did. Occasionally, he would mutter under his breath or

swear outright, but he didn't interrupt with questions or explanations.

When I finished, I reached for my coffee – lukewarm by now – and took a healthy swallow. Figuring he needed a moment to process, I got more coffee and then turned back to face him. He was staring at nothing.

"Kendrick."

At the sound of my voice, he started.

"I'd like to know the truth," I said softly.

A deep frown creased his cheeks. He was a fit man and didn't look his age until he frowned. I hadn't noticed it until now. "The truth, Jal?"

"According to your wife, Allie's mother, and Allie herself, have little concern for anything but themselves and money. Now, I've only known Allie a short time, but that doesn't sound like the woman I've talked to."

"That's because it's not." Sounding tired, Kendrick leaned back. "Sit down. Let me tell you things as they really happened. Diamond…well, I didn't do right by her. I won't pretend otherwise. But there was no reason for her to take it out on Allie."

I had a feeling I was going to end up really pissed off by the time his story was done, but I sat anyway, determined to keep my temper. This was what I'd come for. Real answers.

"Contrary to what I'm sure Diamond said, Malla didn't seduce me." His jaw went tight, and he was silent for a moment before continuing, "I loved her. When she left me…"

He had one hand resting on the table, and as he spoke, he clenched it into a fist so tight, it was almost bloodless. The pain in his eyes was still raw.

"It wasn't some one-night stand or drunken fling. We were together for *years*. I loved her. I gave her…everything." His expression hardened. "And she left me for somebody who would never be able to appreciate her."

I couldn't keep my mouth shut. "It sounds like she left you for a guy who would actually marry her."

A wash of red flooded Kendrick's face. "What do you know about it?" he demanded.

My own temper rose, but I kept my voice even. "I know that your wife hated having your mistress living here, and that made her treat your daughter like shit." Guilt started to twist inside me as I remembered all of the horrible things I'd said to Allie, the accusations I'd made.

"You don't understand–"

I interrupted, "I know that Allie's a wonderful person, and Diamond treated her like she was garbage. And I'm willing to bet that you never did a thing to stop it, did you?"

Kendrick looked away. It was answer enough.

And I'd let Diamond manipulate me into doing the same thing.

I was an idiot.

I glared at Kendrick. "She was just a kid."

"I love Allie," he protested. "I treated her the best I could under the circumstances. I still write to her. I send her money." He looked even more tired than he had earlier. "She's a strong, stubborn, independent young woman."

"I've noticed." My head was spinning with what he'd said and what I'd done. "I'll leave you to the rest of your day, Kendrick."

I was halfway to the door when he called my name. I turned back to him without a word.

"I never did ask…just how did you meet Allie?"

I wasn't going to give him the truth. He didn't deserve it. "Happenstance. We got to be friends. After learning about her family being deaf, I thought she'd be interested in the gala last night." I rubbed at my jaw and looked away. "If I'd known she was your daughter…"

"So you're simply friends."

I stared him down, refusing to confirm or deny. It wasn't any of his fucking business. Not when he hadn't protected Allie. He didn't deserve to be a part of her life.

"You're committed to Paisley," he murmured.

"Like you were committed to Diamond?" I shot back.

His jaw clenched as my question hit the mark. I turned and left before either of us could say anything else.

I wasn't going to be like him. I would make a choice and live by it. I wasn't sure what the choice would be, or how I was going to make things right with everyone involved, but I was determined that I wouldn't put Allie in the same position that Kendrick had put her mother. And I wouldn't do to Paisley what her father had done to Diamond.

Both women deserved better than that.
Hell, they both deserved better than me.

Chapter 11

Allie

"Mama."

I laid my hand on her shoulder as I spoke. I'd deliberately walked into the kitchen with hard steps, making sure my footsteps struck the floor to alert her to my presence. She'd known I was there and had already been half-turning to meet me. She had a smile on her face, but it faded when she saw my face.

She cupped my face. *"Baby, what's wrong?"*

Instead of saying anything, I leaned in and put my head on her shoulder, needing the comfort. She wrapped her arms around me and for a few minutes, I just let her hold me, hoping it would do something to ease the ache inside me. I'd finally fallen asleep at Tao's last night, had even slept in late, but once I woke up, it'd all come rushing back to me.

You act like you want to break things off, and then the second I look your way, you come running back to fuck with my head again. It's one hell of a play, Allie. I'll give you that.

A play.

He thought I was playing with him. Fucking with his head.

That was the kind of woman he thought I was.

A sob caught in my throat. Mom brushed her hand down my hair and made soothing noises.

I didn't feel soothed though. If anything, the sounds made me cry harder.

She didn't stop. Didn't even speak for several minutes, but

225

when she finally did, she kept it simple. *"What's wrong, sweetheart?"*

When she pulled back, I didn't have any choice but to meet her direct look. It was a mother's look, and I knew she would get the truth out of me one way or another. I needed to tell her.

"I'm such a fool, Mama."

Her eyes went to my mouth since I hadn't signed, and I'd kept my voice low. I didn't really feel the need to shout something that was so humiliating.

After a moment, she smiled and patted my cheek. *"Come on, baby. Let's sit down, and you can tell me about it."*

I let her guide me to the table and sat, trying to figure out where to start.

But she made it easy on me.

"Who is he?"

I looked up, met her eyes.

"Oh, honey." She shook her head. Then, she signed. *"You're my daughter. Do you think I don't know when you're in love?"*

"I'm not." I signed back as well, but I needed to say the words. I wanted to say them, hoped I'd find the truth in them, but they sounded as false as they felt. Maybe I wasn't *in* love yet – I sincerely hoped I wasn't – but I was damn close, and I hated it.

"If you're not in love, then why are you hurting so much? Love is the only thing that will do that."

I hadn't quite cried myself dry yet, and a few more tears spilled free. Burying my face in my hands, I told myself *again* that I should have just walked away from anything and everything connected to Jal Lindstrom. Not that it mattered now. What was done was done. Lifting my head, I met Mom's eyes.

"This guy..." I took a deep breath, and then signed alone because I didn't trust my voice not to crack. *"I met him at the salon. He's engaged, Mama."*

She closed her eyes. When she looked back at me, she shook her head. *"Baby, that's bad news."*

I wanted to laugh but knew if I did, I'd never stop. I could feel myself on the edge and forced myself to keep on track. *"That's only the beginning of it. Mama, he's rich. Like–"*

I couldn't say it.

I surged upright and paced over to the window, staring outside. Clutching the edge of the counter, I stared at the thick, leaden clouds that had piled up over the course of the afternoon. It was brutally cold and ugly, making the thought of spring seem far away.

I had to get it all out, tell her everything. The whole, ugly story.

Turning back to face my mother, I began to sign.

I told her about how Jal came to the salon. How he left his coat and the ring. I told her about how he called the salon and told Alistair he'd pay me a thousand dollars if I'd get him the coat that next day.

Her features grew harder and harder to read as the story progressed, and more than once, she started to say something, only to stop and indicate that she wanted me to continue.

I told her about the first event he'd invited me to, the dress that had been the one Paisley had wanted, and for once, *I* was the one who was picked first.

She stopped me then. *"Honey...you were always first with me."*

"I know that." Or, rather, I knew that she thought that. I gave her a sad smile. Of all people, she should've understood how I felt. Then again, she'd eventually found Tyson. Had TJ.

I had Tao, but I knew that, someday, he'd find the person who'd make him happy – okay, maybe more than one knowing Tao – and I'd become second in his life. I wanted Tao to be happy, so I was okay with that, but it still hurt knowing that the one person with whom I still came first, I would eventually lose.

Mom clapped her hands, startling me.

"Please tell me that you don't want this man because he's with your sister!"

The accusation stung. Glaring at her, I said, *"I didn't even know who he was engaged until we'd already started spending time together. How could you think I'd be so petty?"*

I tried to hide how much her words bothered me, but I knew she saw it. Her face softened, and she moved toward me.

I backed up. I was struggling to keep the anger and pain back, but a touch from her would undo me.

Her shoulders slumped, and she stopped. *"Allie, honey...I'm sorry. I shouldn't have said that. But you can't live your life comparing yourself to Kendrick's other daughters. Your life isn't theirs. I can't give you the things Diamond and Kendrick can give*

Paisley and Mallory."

"It's not about things." Pressing my fingers to my eyes, I tried to find a way to explain, but I didn't know how. *"You don't get it, Mama. You just don't."*

I started signing before I looked up at her, the words coming sharp and fast.

"You fit. I don't. I never have. Kendrick loved you more than me. He gave me money and taught me things, but as soon as Diamond or his real daughters showed up, he was done with me. I didn't belong there. Tyson's a great step-father, and I love TJ, but I've never been a part of the same world as the rest of you. I don't fit. Not anywhere. But for a few minutes, with Jal...I almost did."

My heart lurched, twisted. Shaking my head, I skipped to the rest of it.

"It doesn't matter now. It's over. Diamond was at the party last night. So was Paisley. They saw me dancing with Jal. You can imagine how well that went over. Diamond demanded to know what was going on, and when he asked her why she wanted to know, she told him to ask me. And he did."

My anger shifted to Jal.

"And guess what...I'm the one who was manipulating him. I'm gaming him, playing him the fool. There's a surprise, right? That it's my fault? Apparently, he'd told Paisley he needed time, and it's my fault. I've been using him, somehow setting this whole thing up. Because that's the sort of woman he thinks I am."

Mom started to sign something, but I shook my head and turned away. I didn't want to talk anymore. I didn't want to cry. I wanted to hit something, hurt something. I was tired of being the odd one out, never fitting in, never belonging.

I had been played. Played my whole fucking life, and Jal was no different. Maybe he hadn't done it intentionally, but it happened anyway.

"Honey."

A lifetime of respect had me turning to face her.

She brushed my hair away from my face, her milk chocolate eyes full of concern and love. *"I can see that you care about him. But if he'd think you would do that sort of thing, then he's definitely not good for you. Never mind the fact that he's engaged. Forget your sister, even. We won't even discuss the fact that the sort of men the Paisley Hedges of the world go after don't marry girls like you."*

I managed not to flinch, no matter how much her words hurt. She was only saying them because they were true, but that didn't make them any softer, any kinder.

She continued, *"He doesn't deserve you, Allie."*

That may have been true, but it didn't stop me from wanting him, even now.

Chapter 12

Jal

The time I'd spent talking to Kendrick, and then the time I'd spent thinking over everything I'd learned over the past couple days, was enough to give me a headache. Thinking about what I'd said to Allie was enough to make me a little sick.

Despite all of that, I'd managed to come to a few conclusions.

First and foremost, I was an asshole. I'd had an easy life. Both of my parents loved me, although my mother spent way too much of her time trying to control me and make me into who she wanted me to be. But still, she loved me. Things had always come easily for me too. Work. School. Women. I'd always thought I was smart, people savvy, but I could see now that it was arrogance. All of those things came together to make me blind. Blind and careless.

Aside from the realization that I was an asshole, I'd also accepted the fact that I was more easily manipulated than I cared to admit, particularly when it was easier to give in than to fight. And with Paisley, it'd been easy to give in just like I did with my mom.

I loved my mother, but she looked at life as a battlefield, and she was the general. Granted, her battles were dinners and balls and galas and the social circles she'd chosen to move in, but she treated them like war. Everything she did, every move she made was one strategic choice on that battlefield.

I didn't want to marry a woman who looked at life the same way.

I didn't want to raise my child to view life the same way.

Paisley could be just like my mother if left unchecked, but what I didn't know was if she could be any other way.

I had to talk to her. That's all there was to it.

I couldn't let Paisley see our child the way my mother saw me. A pawn in the giant chess game that women like my mother played.

The final realization, however, was the most brutal one, and that was saying something since none of them had been easy. But acknowledging this last one was taking the wind out of me, leaving me feeling more than a little empty.

I wasn't any better than Kendrick Hedges, and I despised what he'd done, both to his wife and the girls he'd had with her, as well as to Allie and her mother.

I didn't want to be like him. I didn't want to be the sort of man who pitted two women against each other, craving one to the point that I chained her to me, even while I married another.

I had to face my responsibilities when it came to Paisley, but I had to find a way to do that and balance the need I had for Allie…or let her go.

I didn't know if I could let her go. Just the thought was tearing me apart.

"Shit."

Leaning against the car, I stared out over the river and drew in a breath of cold air. The scent of rain was heavy in the air, and I knew once the downpour started, it was going to be miserable and freezing. If I were smart, I'd get in the car and haul my ass back to my place before that started, but I was still trying to think my way through what I needed to do.

Rather, *how* I needed to do it.

A cold fat drop of rain fell on my nose. Tipping my head back, I stared up at the sky just in time for another raindrop to hit me square on the chin. The sky opened up in the next moment, but I didn't move.

The bracing cold felt…*good*.

After nearly a full minute, I finally shoved away from the car and moved around to the driver's side to get inside. I started the car and then blasted the heat, even though I knew it wouldn't really reach the cold deep inside me. I had to go see Paisley and in all likelihood, the conversation would be a pain in the ass. The two of us were going to have a heart to heart, and I doubted I'd like how it went.

I knew she wouldn't like it either.

But it needed to happen.

Before I could talk myself out of it, I pulled out onto the street.

The rain didn't let up for the entire drive, but I was glad because that meant I had to concentrate on what I was doing, which didn't leave much room for obsessing.

Once I reached the protective overhang in front of the townhouse, I tossed my keys to the valet and headed inside.

Even that warmth didn't do much to penetrate the chill of my bones, but I'd spent the past fifteen minutes sitting in clothes that were soaked, so that didn't help much. Inside the elevator, I pushed my hands through my damp hair and attempted to straighten my clothes.

Not that there was much point.

A hot shower, some strong coffee and a change of clothes were the first things I had in mind. Then I'd confront Paisley.

Confront.

Even thinking it made my skin feel tight, but it had to be done, and the longer I put it off, the worse it was going to be.

The longer it would be before I could figure out how to deal with things with Allie.

Allie.

That made it easier to focus as I strode off the elevator.

So I kept her front and center in my mind as I headed for the door and unlocked it. Absently, I noticed that the alarm system wasn't on, and I shook my head. I'd have to remind Paisley to set it – again.

Striding down the hall, mind focused on the hot shower, I almost didn't notice her.

She definitely didn't notice me.

Of course, if she hadn't been staring down into a nearly empty glass of wine, if there hadn't been a half empty bottle next to her, maybe she would have been a little more aware.

Wine.

What the fuck?

My gaze locked on the glass and I stared at it for the longest time.

Blood roared in my ears.

I wasn't sure if I'd spoken, or if she just felt me looking at her, but suddenly she was turning toward me.

"Jal." A guilty flush danced across her cheeks. Her hand fluttered to her throat, and she looked down at the glass, pushed it out of the way as if that would hide what she'd been doing.

"You're drinking." Shrugging out of my overcoat, I threw it on the nearest chair and strode over to her.

"No." She picked up the glass, then lowered it. "I…well. Jal, it's just a glass of wine. Really."

"*A* glass?" I grabbed the bottle and lifted it, studying the bottle for a moment before turning it back to her. "Funny, this bottle was full when I noticed it earlier."

Again, her eyes fell guiltily away.

The anger inside me bubbled up, and I struggled to keep myself from shouting. "How often have you been drinking?"

"Don't worry about it." Paisley got up and carried her glass over to the sink. She tossed back the rest.

"Dammit, Paisley!"

She put the glass in the sink and turned back to me. "It's wine, Jal. A glass or two never hurt anybody!"

"It can hurt the baby!"

"The baby, the baby! That's all you care about!" she shouted, throwing her arms wide. "It's not *me*. You wouldn't even be marrying me if it wasn't for the baby, would you?"

I didn't even hesitate. "No."

Her jaw dropped, eyes widening. "You can just say that so easily? Don't you even care about me at all?"

I sighed, trying to stay honest without hurting her. "I care about you. But that doesn't mean I ever planned on marrying you, Paisley."

She threw back her head and laughed. "This…oh, this. It's just rich. First, I find out you've been seeing my little bastard half-sister behind my back."

"Hey–" I took a step toward her.

She spun and grabbed an apple from the fruit basket and hurled it at me. She missed by a mile, but it was so out of character that I lapsed into silence, and she continued, her voice

233

shaking. "Then you disappear for hours, leaving me alone, and you're actually *angry* with me because I needed a glass of wine?"

"You drank half the fucking bottle, Paisley!" I shouted. "That's a hell of a lot more than a glass!"

"So what!" She stormed over and jammed me in the chest with a fingernail painted a harsh, wicked red. "Let me guess…you're worried about the *baby*!"

I grabbed her wrist. "Newsflash, Paisley. Alcohol isn't good for a baby. The baby inside you doesn't need that fucking wine."

"I need the fucking wine!" She jerked away from me and took a step forward. She grabbed the bottle from the counter and spun around, glaring at me.

"Give me that bottle." I strode over to her, but before I could grab it, she circled around the island and smacked a hand down on it.

"I'll drink the whole damn thing if I want." Her eyes narrowed on my face. "You know what? I'm tired of this…tired of this…this…this *bullshit*. I don't even know why I'm doing this anymore. You're all moon-eyed over my trampish little sister. She's going to be just like her mother, but *I* will *not* be like mine. I'm tired of this, do you hear me?"

"Give me the damn bottle and stop your ranting, Paisley!"

"No." She brought the bottle to her lips and started to drink, lowering it with a sigh. As I came around the island, she held it out to me. "Here…have a drink. You might want one after I'm done."

The glint in her eyes had a chill of trepidation racing down my spine.

"What's that supposed to mean?" I demanded.

"You want a drink or not?"

I hesitated a moment too long because she spun away and sauntered off, lifting the bottle for another long swallow.

She turned back to me once she'd reached the doorway. "What, aren't you going to rant on me some more? She took another drink. The bottle is more than half empty now."

"What's going on, Paisley?" I approached her slowly, unable to figure out what the hell was going on. "You're up to something."

"No. Not really. I'm just…well, let's just say I'm going to come clean." She wagged the bottle. "After all, I don't want you fretting over a baby and booze. That wouldn't be very kind of me, now would it?"

"Paisley. Enough."

She sighed, tipping her head back. "Why did I ever even bother with you?"

Then she looked at me, lifting the bottle to her lips. She didn't drink though. She just stared at me over it. The ring I'd given her sparkled on her hand, cold, bright...lifeless.

Her voice was flat, emotionless as she spoke, "I'm not pregnant, Jal. So, here's to me. Bottom's up!"

She tipped the bottle back, and without pause, drained it while I stood there, trying to absorb what she'd just said.

I'm not pregnant...

Book 4

Chapter 1

Jal

I'm not pregnant...
Not pregnant.

"Not pregnant," I said as my brain struggled to process the bombshell my fiancée just dropped. "Did you..." Taking a slow breath, I looked from the wine to her flushed face. Maybe there was a rational explanation for her behavior after all. I forced my voice to soften. "You lost the baby?"

"No." Paisley slammed the bottle down and stormed across the few feet that separated us. "I didn't lose the baby."

Sucking in a deep breath, I turned away and shoved the heel of my hand against my eye. My patience was wearing thin, but I didn't want to react based on a misunderstanding. "Spell it out for me, Paisley."

She gave the sort of unladylike snort that I would've thought was beneath her. "You know, I never thought you were as smart as everyone seemed to think."

I ignored the insult and waited.

"Can't lose what you never had to begin with."

My stomach dropped. "You were never pregnant."

"Bravo. Now you got it." She gave me a smile of mock pride, clapping her hands. "Good job, honey!"

I curled my hands into fists. "You made it up. All of it."

When she didn't respond, I closed the last of the distance between us, putting my hands on the counter on either side of her

239

waist. I wasn't touching her – I never wanted to touch her again – but she was effectively caged in.

She swallowed hard, apparently realizing how pissed off I was. A bit of the alcohol haze left her eyes, and I could see her trying to compose herself.

"You made it up," I said again.

I needed to hear her say it, needed to know that I wasn't jumping to conclusions. Still, a part of me was hoping that it was a misunderstanding. That she'd honestly thought she was pregnant, and by the time she discovered that she wasn't, things had gotten away from her. I could forgive her for that.

Her expression hardened, and she practically sneered her answer, "Yeah. So what? I'm not pregnant. We'll get married and sooner or later, I will be."

"Seriously?" I shoved away and started to pace.

I ran my hands through my hair, trying to calm their shaking. For the past few weeks, there had been only one positive thing when I looked at what I thought was going to be my future.

One.

And it turned out that one tiny thing had never existed.

Everything I'd done over the past few weeks had been because of the baby. Every choice I'd made, every painful decision. I'd changed everything for that future, and now it was all ripped away.

Maybe it didn't make a difference to her, but it made one hell of a difference to me.

"Does my mother know?"

Paisley gave me a distracted look, one that clearly told me she didn't see why it mattered. The threads of my temper stretched taut, and I could all but imagine them snapping, one by one. Taking one step closer, I asked my question again.

"Of course she knew," Paisley snapped, waving a hand in the air. "Do you really think I'd do something like this on my own? It was her idea. Well, hers and my mother's."

I stared at her in disbelief, hoping I'd misunderstood what she said. "They both knew? You were lying this whole time, and my mother knew? It was her idea?"

I thought that repeating the statements would make them seem more ludicrous, less believable, but that wasn't the case.

"Of course." Paisley leaned against the island, tapping her

nails on it in an aggravated rhythm. "Really, Jal. It's not like anything else was going to get your attention, now was it? We'd been dating for almost a year–"

"We went to a couple of functions, and my mother was always pushing you at me at family events. That's not *dating*, Paisley." I didn't understand how my entire world could have shifted on its axis in just a few short minutes.

"And what did you think we were doing when we were sleeping together?" She shoved off the island and glared at me. She seemed angrier that I was pushing the issue than contrite about lying about something so important.

"It's called *sex*, Paisley! I told you I wasn't looking for any kind of commitment." I paused a beat and then asked sarcastically, "Or did you think I was just making that up? Apparently you do it as easily as breathe."

She had the nerve to look insulted.

As she sputtered for a response, I moved into the living room and headed for the bar service. I'd left a bottle of twenty-five-year old scotch back there and now was the perfect time to break it open. I'd been considering saving it for the baby's birth, but apparently this was more realistic.

"So exactly what was the plan, Paisley? Pretend you were pregnant, get me to propose, and then *lose* the baby? A miscarriage would've made me look like a heel if I left you then. Or were you going to tell me the truth somewhere along the way and hope I'd just go with it to avoid the embarrassment of admitting I'd been tricked? Maybe try to get knocked up and fake a super-short pregnancy? Do I strike you as that much of an idiot?"

Her face had paled, as if she'd only just realized how badly she'd fucked up. "I...Jal, I don't see why you're so upset about this. We're now where we should've been all along. It's the natural progression..."

I'd been about to pour the scotch into a glass, but at those words, I stopped, lifting my head to stare at her. Her words trailed off, and she nervously cleared her throat, then opened her mouth as if she meant to continue.

I held up a finger, stopping her. "You don't see why I'm so upset. So..." I splashed the scotch into my glass and took a slow sip, savoring the taste and the feel as it burned a smooth path

241

straight down. "You got this idea in your head that, at some point, you and I were going to end up on this road, so you decided to take a shortcut to get us there quicker. Am I right?"

She gave me a smile that wobbled at the edges nervously. "Of course. Not the best idea, I can see that now. That's all it was. A shortcut."

"Wrong." I tossed back the rest of the scotch like it was pure moonshine and slammed the glass down so hard it was a wonder it didn't shatter. Bracing my hands on the bar, I glared at her across the expanse of the room. "When I said I wasn't looking for a commitment, I meant it."

She twisted the ring on her finger, and the sight of it reflecting the light back at me hit me hard.

I was still technically engaged to her.

She wasn't pregnant.

I no longer had a responsibility to stay with her.

There was no baby.

"I had no plans to marry you, Paisley. At all." I splashed more scotch into my glass and studied her over the rim. "See, unlike you, unlike your mother, my mother, when I say things, I mean them. The only reason I proposed was because of the baby, because I thought it was the right thing to do."

Because I was going to be a father.

Her throat worked. She backed up a step, her heel hitting the island at her back. I watched her putting together just how badly things were going for her, but I didn't feel any sympathy as her new reality sank in.

"Since there's no baby..." I shrugged and looked down, watching the amber liquid swirl around in the glass. My anger drained away as quickly as it had arrived. Now, all I felt was numb. "There's no reason to get married, is there?"

"What are you saying?" she demanded, her voice shaking.

"It's not so hard a concept. Keep the ring if you want. I don't care. But the wedding is off." I shot her a look over the glass. "And I don't mean *off* as in I need time to think. I mean we're not getting married, not going to any events together, not fucking. Ever. If I had my way, I'd never see your face again."

"You son of a bitch!" she shouted. "You immature, self-centered bastard! We were doing you a *favor*!"

I couldn't hold back the sharp laugh that burst from my

242

throat. "Next time you feel inclined to do me a favor? *Don't*. And I suggest you educate yourself on immaturity and self-centeredness. I don't think you'd recognize what it's like to think of others if your life depended on it."

Face flushed pink, Paisley flung a hand toward the window, as though the whole of Philadelphia society could see us fighting. "And what am I to tell everybody? People are expecting a wedding!"

"You could try the truth for once," I suggested. "Tell them you lied, and I found out and thought marrying you wasn't in my best interest."

She gaped at me for a moment before starting in again. "You insufferable ass! I can't...you...*you* won't do this to me."

"It's already done. Now..." I put my glass down. "If you'll excuse me, I'll see myself out. And if you know what's good for you, you'll stay away from me, or I'll have you arrested."

I slammed the door behind me and headed outside as I tried to absorb everything that had happened in the last few minutes.

Minutes.

It felt like years.

No matter how long it'd taken, it'd been long enough to change everything.

She wasn't pregnant. Hadn't ever been pregnant.

A headache pulsed at the base of my skull, pounding and threatening to explode, but things kept coming, one after another.

Paisley.

My mother.

Diamond.

They'd all lied. Planned it together.

Then, my mind circled around to Allie.

Allie.

The things I'd said to her, accused her of. The stricken look on her face before the anger had covered it.

I suddenly felt like I was going to throw up.

Man, when I fucked up, I did it well.

Chapter 2

Allie

It had been one of the worst weekends of my life

Things were awkward between Mom and me, although I knew most of that was my fault. She wanted to protect me from the mistakes she'd made, and I understood that. *I* wanted to protect me from those very same mistakes. But I was already in a little too deep for that.

Aside from my personal drama, TJ had gotten sick, and we had to take him to the clinic late Sunday night, which was always a hassle. He'd had chronic ear infections as a toddler and had hated doctors ever since. It didn't help that the clinic was training students, and even though I'd been as polite as possible when I explained who I was, the girl we'd been assigned copped an attitude and tried to make me leave. It'd taken the threat of a lawsuit to get her to let me stay, and even then, she'd deliberately ignored any questions I asked. I ended up having to flag down someone in the hallway to insist on another doctor.

All in all, we were there for nearly six hours before TJ was diagnosed with strep and sentenced to home with antibiotics until the fever cleared.

The only upside was that I got to sleep in an extra twenty minutes Monday morning since I didn't have to walk him to school.

I treated myself to a double caramel latte on my way in and thought it might not be quite as cold as it had been. The sun was even shining, and I heard birds calling. Spring. It was the last week in March. About time spring showed itself.

I made it to work with five minutes to spare and sat in the back, finishing up my latte and flipping through a supply catalog to see if there were any clearance items.

"Man, if the prices on these raise much more, we'll have to start having bake sales or something just to cover the costs," Sandy said in disgust as she tossed her catalog down.

I grinned at the thought. "I'd love to see the look on Alistair's face when you suggest that."

The other girls laughed, knowing that our uptight boss, Alistair Hopkins, would throw a fit if any of us suggested something as common as a bake sale.

"I'll do my strawberry lemon cake," Sonya offered. "He loves that. He'd pay fifty just to have it all to himself."

"Keep it up, girl." Shaking my head, I focused on the poppy seed muffin I'd picked up with my latte. "You're going to make me hungry, and it's not even close to lunch."

I didn't need any help either. As moody and depressed as I'd been all weekend, I'd wanted nothing more than wine, chocolate, and ice cream. I'd been fighting myself tooth and nail not to give in. With the money I'd spent on clothes over the past couple of weeks, I couldn't justify a splurge on even cheap wine. Popping the last bite of muffin into my mouth, I tried to pretend it was strawberry lemon cake.

Tried. Failed.

The sound of a chair scraping against the floor had me looking up. It was time to get to work.

"He hated it," Daisy Caldwell announced as I wrapped the cape around her shoulders.

She was my first appointment this morning – switching from her normal day and time because she was going on a cruise later this week. With her newest boyfriend. He was only forty-six. She'd taken great pleasure in telling me that.

She was also planning on sleeping with him.

She'd told me that too.

Now, I was hoping she wouldn't tell me too much more. She loved regaling all of us with the details of her trysts with her younger companions. Sometimes I thought she did it just to see how much it took to get us to blush.

As she grinned at me in the mirror, I asked, "Your son didn't like your new style?"

"He *hated* it." She said it with relish and reached up to pat at her coif. "I'm going to do it again closer to the family picnic this summer."

"You are bad, lady." Tsking under my breath, I fought not to laugh. She had a devilish gleam in her eyes, and I wondered if I'd be as much fun in my seventies as she was.

Then I had to mentally fight a bit of sadness. I wasn't as much fun as she was now, and I was barely twenty-one.

I forced myself to focus on my customer. "What are we doing this time? Vamping you up for this stud you're taking on the cruise?"

She started to laugh, but to my surprise, her cheeks turned the prettiest pink.

"Well now, Daisy." I propped a hand on my hip. "If I'm not mistaken, you look a little nervous there. You actually like this guy, don't you?"

"Oh, hush." She flicked the cape draped across her like it was a velvet gown. "Just make me beautiful, Allie. That's all you need to do."

"That makes my job easy, Daisy. You're already one of the most beautiful souls I've ever known." I winked at her and got to work.

Less than an hour later, she pressed several bills into my hand on her way out the door. While it wasn't unusual for her to tip with cash, it seemed to be more than usual. I didn't look though. Alistair drilled it into our heads that we weren't supposed to check tips where customers could see us. I tucked it away and told her to have fun on the cruise.

"You be a good girl, Allie." She paused and then hugged me. "You make sure you're having fun yourself."

I nodded at her, wondered why she suddenly looked a little sad but didn't ask. Even if I'd felt comfortable asking something so personal, she was busy chatting with Alistair, making his cheeks burn as she told him about her upcoming cruise and her new stud.

I returned to my station and went about setting things to rights. I had forty-five minutes to kill, thanks to a last minute cancellation.

Using the time to restock my supplies, I didn't even notice him come in. If I had, I would've snuck out the back until he left.

But I was right there, and at the sound of Alistair's voice, I froze.

"Mr. Lindstrom!"

Squeezing my eyes closed, I tucked my chin down low. *No, no, no*...I mouthed the words to myself like they were some sort of magical incantation and just saying them would make him disappear.

A weighted silence fell across the room, and although I couldn't see him, I knew he was walking my way. Bracing myself, I pushed away from the cabinet and turned to face him.

"Hello, Mr. Lindstrom." I silently congratulated myself for how even and professional I sounded.

Everybody around us seemed to get terribly busy doing absolutely *nothing*, including Alistair. Jal didn't pay any of them a single bit of attention as he came toward me, his eyes rapt on my face. For all the interest he showed them, I might as well be the only person in the room.

"Allie." His voice was rough, lower than normal. There were dark shadows under his eyes, like his weekend had been as bad as mine.

After a few seconds, he hadn't said anything else, so I asked, "Is there something I can do for you, sir?"

I put a slight emphasis on the *sir*, reminding myself as much as him that there was a clear gap between us. Two very different worlds, no matter how he tried to act otherwise. No matter how much I wanted to pretend otherwise.

"Yes...I..." He glanced around, finally noticing all the people who were pretending *not* to watch us. "Do you have a few minutes?"

I wanted to lie, tell him that I was booked solid, and he needed to leave. I didn't want to talk to him. Didn't want to feel the hurt I'd locked away.

But, of course, Alistair came hustling over. "Allie, your next appointment isn't for forty minutes. You know what? I bet

247

everybody would *love* it if you went and got us some coffee. My treat. Go on up to my office and get some petty cash. You and Mr. Lindstrom can talk on the way." He looked over at Jal with polite blandness. "Will that work, Mr. Lindstrom?"

"Of course."

Feeling deflated, I gestured to the seating area. "I'll be right back."

"Nonsense." Alistair cut in. "Just go on up with Allie." He made a shooing motion at us both. As I turned away, I tossed a glare over my shoulder, but he beamed at me, all innocence.

Alistair's office was the most private place in the building, up two flights of stairs, and the only room with an official purpose. The second floor was more storage and currently in a half-finished state. He kept talking about adding more services. Full-body massage, mud-wraps, salt soaks, but he didn't have the capital just yet. Inside the office, I went straight to his desk and pulled out the cash I'd need to get coffee for all. It wasn't unheard of for Alistair to treat us, but it wasn't an everyday occurrence either. This time, I knew, was because of Jal, not any magnanimous gesture on my boss' part.

I started to shove the cash into my pocket, and then stopped, flashing it in front of Jal. "Would you like to count it, make sure I'm not helping myself to extra? You can let my boss know if I'm being dishonest."

Apparently, I hadn't boxed up my feelings quite as tightly as I thought. I could feel my temper bubbling just under the surface.

I walked toward him. "Here, go ahead." I held the money out.

He reached out and closed my fingers over it. His touch and voice were gentle. "Stop. Look, I came...I want to apologize."

I yanked my hand away, unable to think clearly when he was touching me.

"You apologized. Fine." I jutted my chin toward the door and walked over to the window. "You've done that. You can go now."

"No."

Eyes burning, I stared through the sheer curtains that covered the single window. "There's really nothing else to be said."

Behind me, I sensed his movement and fought the urge to turn. If I looked at him, whatever it was he wanted, I just might give it to him. And more. For the first time in my life, I felt a flash of sympathy for my mother and how she must've felt about my father.

"Look at me, Allie."

Closing my eyes, I leaned closer to the window and rested my forehead against the glass. "Why can't you leave me alone, Jal?" The question came out much quieter than I'd wanted it to.

"If it were that easy, I would have done it already. You've made everything so complicated."

He put his hand on my hip and my entire body tensed. I gritted my teeth, trying to ignore the heat from his palm. He put his other hand on the wall next to me, leaned in until I could smell the spice of his aftershave.

"I spoke to your father. I…Allie, I messed up. I'm sorry. I said terrible things to you. I made awful assumptions. I was an ass, and the word *sorry* doesn't really cover it, but it's about all I've got."

I wished I could say those words covered all the hurt and made everything better, but they didn't. The reason he'd said those things, the reasons that made it okay for him to talk to me like that, those still existed between us. They always would.

"Okay." I didn't open my eyes or turn to look at him, hoping he'd take the hint and leave. He was absolved. He could go back to his life without whatever guilt he'd wanted to get rid of.

He pressed his lips to my shoulder, and I suppressed a shiver, swallowing back a whimper. I wanted to feel that mouth all over me. *All* over me. Before I could give in, I twisted around, extricating myself from the tight little spot between him and the window. I needed space between us.

"You've said what you needed to say. Now…I need to go—"

I'd been walking away from him, focused on the door and escape. I should have been paying more attention to him.

He caught my arm and spun me around. Suddenly, for the first time since we'd come into the room, I was facing him, looking directly at him. His light blue eyes cut into me, glittering with intensity. Harsh flags of color rode high on his cheekbones.

"Stop walking away from me, dammit." His voice had lost all of its previous gentleness.

He cupped my cheek with one hand and buried his other hand in my hair. I'd left it down and loose today, letting it go a bit wild. His fist tightened, and he used that hold to tug my head back, urging me to hold his gaze. Not that I needed any urging. I needed help to *stop* looking at him, the bastard. And here he was making me do the impossible.

"Jal." I could hardly breathe. "Please. You've got to stop this."

He stroked his thumb across my lower lip, watching that small action as though mesmerized. I swallowed a whimper.

"Your mouth," he whispered. "I can't tell you how much I love your mouth."

"Jal…"

He repeated the caress with his thumb, and I almost opened my mouth, licked his thumb, sucked on it.

Even thinking about it made me want to do *more*, take other things between my lips. My mouth started to water, and a moan escaped me. He moved closer, and I turned away as he dipped his head to kiss me. His hand in my hair prevented me from completely turning aside, and he didn't let my movement deter him. His mouth landed on the corner of mine, and his tongue swept out in a quick, light caress.

"Allie…"

In that moment, I was torn between hunger and hate.

I wanted him more than I'd ever wanted *anything*.

And I hated him for how weak he made me.

Hate won.

I shoved him – hard.

The force behind it caught him off guard, and he let go, moving away.

"Enough," I said, breathing hard. "Enough. Okay? You've got a fiancée."

Just thinking about him with Paisley hurt. It was like having jagged, broken bits of dirty glass shoved straight through my chest, my ribs, right into my heart. He was tearing me apart, and he didn't even care. The pain gave me the strength I needed.

"You need to go. I hope you and Paisley are happy together."

"I'm not done," Jal said, his voice tight. He grabbed me again, pulled me against him.

Clenching my jaw, I brought my hands up to shove him away. Then his mouth came down on mine, and I found my

250

fingers curling into his shirt, pulling instead of pushing.

I was royally screwed.

Chapter 3

Allie

I couldn't do this. I knew I couldn't.

I felt fractured, like there were three different parts of me. One part was enjoying his kiss, wanting more. Another part was standing apart, watching everything like some sort of observer. And the other was screeching, raging at me to stop, telling me that I was better than this. That I deserved better than someone who would cheat on his fiancée.

That thought had me going rigid under his kiss.

"Allie...." Jal whispered my name against my lips.

"Stop. We're not doing this, okay?" I pulled away, and this time, he let me go.

I pressed my back to the door. Laying my hands flat against the smooth wooden panels, I sucked in air, then blew it out slowly, willing my racing heart to calm. I had to make him understand that this couldn't happen, that he needed to leave me alone so we could both move on. Him with his fiancée, and me with my regular life.

"I'm not going to be the other woman," I said. "I wouldn't do it to a stranger, and I sure as hell won't do it to my sister. You made your choice."

Jal caged me in against the door, his arms on either side of me, his expression intent. "Listen to me, Allie. The only reason I asked Paisley to marry me was because she told me she was pregnant."

I sucked in a breath, staring at him. Was he fucking kidding me? Did he really think that would make things better? "She's...you're...the two of you..."

He pressed his finger to my lips, silencing the jumble of words.

His face softened. "She lied, Allie. There was never a baby. It was all some crazy, bullshit idea she cooked up with my mom and her mom. They all thought it was time I settle down, and for some insane reason, they all thought Paisley would be the one." He leaned in, his mouth brushing my ear as he added, "She's not."

Heart now hammering against my ribs, I slowly met his eyes as he straightened. The air between us began to crackle, all but sizzling now. I didn't want to dare to hope.

"What are you saying?" I asked. I had to know, I had to be sure.

"The engagement is over. I was only marrying her because of the baby, and lately, I haven't even been all that sure it was the right choice to begin with. But now? Hell, no." He cupped both sides of my face with his hands. "You've never been the other woman, Allie. *She* was. You're all I've been able to think about pretty much from the moment we met."

I searched his eyes for some hint that he was lying. Maybe it would be easier if he was. If he were lying, it would make it easier to push him away next time.

Next time…

I was crazy. That's just all there was to it.

But, still...

Slowly, I reached up and curled my hands in the front of his shirt. "The engagement is off?"

"Yes," he said, the relief in his voice clear. "It's off. And not just the engagement. She and I are done. Over with. Forever."

Jal nuzzled my neck, his breath hot against my skin. I arched my back, shuddering. I told myself I needed to think, figure out what all of this meant, but how could I possibly think when he was touching me?

It was then I realized that, for the first time, he was touching me without a shadow between us. No fiancée. No ring. No Paisley.

"You're not engaged," I said. Hearing the words again sent a rush through me.

"No."

"It's over?"

His hand slid under my shirt, his fingers shockingly hot against my skin. Why was he so hot? I whimpered as those fingers skimmed higher, over my ribcage.

"Yes, baby...it's over. Now..." He closed his teeth around my earlobe and bit down gently. "Can we stop talking? I've got other things I want to do. Namely, *you*."

I groaned, partially because I wanted him, but mostly because I knew we needed to stop. "I've...Jal, I'm at work."

"Your boss said you had forty minutes." He made a dramatic show of checking the pricey watch on his wrist. "We used eight talking already." His eyes narrowed, but the heat in them was all lust, not anger. "Now be quiet."

His voice came out harder, stronger, and the command in it surprised me enough that my mouth snapped shut. His mouth took mine in a fierce, quick kiss that was over all too soon. Before I could catch my breath, he spun me around and grabbed my hands, bringing them up and pressing them to the wall.

In a matter of seconds, he had my pants down to my knees, the cool air shocking against my bare skin. I heard the familiar sound of a condom wrapper tearing, and anticipation twisted inside me. Nudging me forward, he canted my hips, and then thrust, shoving halfway inside me. My shocked, startled cry was caught against his hand as he covered my mouth. He moved closer, forcing my body to straighten as he pinned me between him and the wall.

"Fuck, I want to hear you scream so bad."

I bit down on the fleshy part of his palm instead as he withdrew, groaning as he thrust back inside. It was excruciating, how aware I was of him. I could feel *everything*. The hard plane of his chest. His muscular thighs. The thick weight of him filling me.

Hot shivers of sensation raced through me as he reached up and caught my wrist, dragging my hand down, urging it between my pinned thighs.

"Play with yourself."

Mindless, I did as I was told as he moved his hand to my hip, my fingers falling into the familiar rhythm I'd perfected over the past couple years.

"I'm going to let go of your mouth, but you can't scream."

I wanted to, felt like I had to as his strokes became faster, deeper. He hit all those places inside me that only Tao had been able to find before, and only with practice. Jal instinctively seemed to know where they were, and all the right ways to play them.

"Don't scream, Allie," he reminded me.

I nodded, mindless answering a command that I wasn't sure I could follow. Circling my fingers over my clit, my body rocked under the motions of his, but it wasn't enough. Moaning in frustration, I shoved back against him, needing something more.

Jal muttered something harsh and raw under his breath. Then, a moment later, he pulled away. I cried out, my pussy throbbing in protest, suddenly and achingly empty.

"Quiet," he said against my ear as he dragged me to the ground. On my hands and knees, I swayed backward, all but ready to beg him just to be full again.

But it wasn't necessary. He gripped one hip, and the blunt head of his dick probed at my entrance. Then he was driving inside me again. Deeper, harder, faster.

Over and over.

My head fell forward as I bit my lip to keep from crying out. He pressed his thumb against the entrance to my ass, and I shivered, chills rushing through me, threatening to dissolve my very bones.

The climax blindsided me, and I gasped, desperate for oxygen as the orgasm raged and tore through me. My entire body spasmed, shook. He swore, and I felt his cock jerk and throb inside me as he came too. The head of his thick shaft pressed against my G-spot, setting off a series of mini aftershocks as he emptied himself into me.

Blood roared in my ears, and I shuddered. His fingers tightened on my hips as he ground against me, milking out every last drop of pleasure. Another shudder went through me, and my arms gave out. The only thing holding me upright was the solid strength of Jal's hands as he gripped my hips, his cock still rigid inside me.

Jal smoothed a hand down my back as I straightened up over the sink. Our eyes met in the mirror as he came closer and slid an arm around my waist. It was crazy how completely natural the move felt, as if he'd been doing it for years.

"I have to get moving." My forty minutes had shrunk down to nineteen, and I still hadn't gotten the coffee.

"Yes." Jal continued to stand there, his face buried in my hair, his arm holding me snug against him. He didn't seem like he was in any particular hurry to go anywhere.

Realizing I was going to have to move first, I pulled away from him and slid out of the minuscule bathroom. I'd managed to clean up fairly well, although I had a bad feeling everybody I worked with would be able to take one look at me and know what had happened up here.

"What now?" I asked as he followed me out of the bathroom.

"Now, we go get that coffee."

I rolled my eyes. "Not what I meant."

As he edged around me, he shot me a look. "I guessed as much, but we can talk about that on the way. We've already been up here much longer than what it would take to get some money. Speaking of which…" He bent over and picked something up from the floor.

When he turned, I saw it was the money I'd gotten from Alistair's desk.

I scowled and snatched it away, spinning on my heel. I was suddenly annoyed at him, at myself. "A bit late to think of that, isn't it?"

I tossed the words at him over my shoulder as I hurried down the steps and straight toward the back. I might be in luck, and nobody would be in the breakroom. No one would have to know that I'd gone out the back way long after I should have already been gone. They'd think the line at the coffee shop was just long.

Jal followed me out into the cool spring air, catching up with me easily, his long legs eating up the distance between us.

"I want to see you again."

That calmly uttered statement almost made me stumble.

Keeping my eyes straight ahead, I clenched my jaw and remained silent for a few seconds before responding. "And you're telling me this…why?"

"Seems to be the polite thing to do." He sounded slightly surprised that I was asking a question. "I'm asking you on a date."

This time, I did stumble. He steadied me, his hand going to my elbow. I shot him a quick look before easing away, checking the traffic before darting across the street.

"Playing chicken in the middle of the morning isn't the best way to avoid giving me an answer," Jal said, irritation evident in his voice as he caught up to me again.

"I'm not playing chicken." Glaring at him, I checked the time. "I've got twelve minutes until my appointment shows up, and I still haven't gotten the coffee."

"Or given me an answer." He settled a hand low on my back as I reached for the door to the coffee shop.

There was no line.

When the barista saw me, she waved. "Want your usual?" Her eyes strayed to Jal before returning to me, and I managed not to laugh when she wagged her eyebrows at me.

"Actually, I need everybody's usual, Cathy." I named off the girls who were working and then added, "And one for the boss too."

"You got a nice boss, kid. Lucky you."

Cathy's boss smacked her on the back of the head as she walked by, but it was a friendly gesture, not a harsh one. "Your boss is going to leave you a coffee shop one day, so don't complain."

Cathy turned her head and stuck her tongue out.

"I saw that!" The older woman called over her shoulder.

"Moms." Cathy was still rolling her eyes as she got to work on the list of drinks. One of the other baristas came in a few seconds later and started working alongside her. Both of them kept shooting Jal and me sidelong looks.

"You still haven't given me a yes or no," he said, keeping his tone neutral.

I sighed. "For crying out loud."

He dipped his head, pitching his voice low enough that the others wouldn't hear. "Well, *crying out loud* is one of the things I

257

plan on making you do a lot. If you'd say yes, we can set a date and time."

Heat rushed to my face.

"Whipped cream?"

"What?" My voice cracked.

Cathy eyed me, a hint of a smile on her lips as she repeated herself, "Whipped cream on yours, Allie?"

"Um, no. No, I'm good."

Like hell I was. Now my heart was racing all over again, my thoughts scattered. Every nerve in my body felt like it had electricity racing across it. I was overly aware of every inch of him, the sound of his breathing, the unique scent of him.

"I knew I should have steered clear of you," I said under my breath.

Jal shot me an amused look. "What?"

I just shook my head and checked the time. Down to seven minutes now. I'd need three of those minutes just to get back to the salon. Alistair wouldn't fire me if I were late, but it wouldn't be good either, especially if he figured out that the reason was because I'd been having sex in his office instead of getting coffee like I was supposed to have been doing.

"Relax." Jal dropped a kiss on my head.

I stiffened in surprise, and he slid a hand down my back, then back up before closing his fingers around my neck and massaging at the tension gathered there.

"If you're a few minutes late, what will it hurt?"

"Seriously?" With a roll of my eyes, I checked the tray of drinks. Only one left. I might make it. "Let's put it this way, Jal. If your mother was kept waiting by her hair stylist, would it go over well? I've never met her, but I doubt it. And who do you think would pay for it? The stylist."

From the corner of my eye, I saw him grimace. He shouldn't have been surprised that I could accurately guess his mother's behavior. I might have been from different social circles, but I knew how the upper class worked, how they thought.

"Point taken." He nodded at Cathy. "If you can rush that, I'll make it worth your while."

In another forty-five seconds, I had Alistair's double espresso mocha latte steaming in the tray, and Jal passed several bills over. I heard the startled gasps behind me as he hustled me out the door, taking one of the trays. Remembering how well he tipped me the first time we met, I had no doubt he'd just made their day.

He kept pace with me as we hurried down the sidewalk. "Now. We're outside. You didn't seem to want an audience to our discussion, so make it quick or I'll just follow you back into the salon, and we can keep talking there. I'm sure your friends won't be too interested."

When I watched for another gap in traffic, he remained at my side, ignoring the man in the Beemer who started honking at us when he had to slow down. He was tenacious, I had to give him that.

"Will you have dinner with me, Allie?"

Chapter 4

Jal

Wanting shouldn't be like this.

Want was easy and shallow and simple to satisfy. A quick fuck. A physical release.

But the want I had for Allie was hard, gut-wrenching, and unending. There was nothing easy about it, and although I could still taste her, still *feel* her around me, I wanted to take her again…and again.

Still waiting for her to answer my question, I pressed the tip of my finger against her lower lip, the smooth, lush curve making me ache to kiss her all over again.

Would I ever have enough of her?

"The clock is ticking," I said, keeping my tone light.

"You're a nag."

The words startled a laugh out of me, and I could see the corners of her mouth quivering in an answering smile. She reached up and caught my wrist, the touch scorching my skin.

"Fine. Dinner. When?"

I grinned. I would have demanded she just leave with me now, but I didn't see that happening. Besides, I needed to get my head together. "Tomorrow."

Once she disappeared inside the salon, I dragged my hands down my face and leaned against the rough brick of the wall for a minute. I had never gotten so stupid over a woman in my life. I'd never gotten so stupid over *anything* in my life.

I needed to focus. I had two meetings between now and three

o'clock, and I hadn't even gone over my notes. As I started for the car, my phone buzzed. Tugging it out, I checked the screen. My mother.

Fuck me.

I hit the *ignore* button and jammed the phone back into my pocket. I knew I'd have to deal with her, and sooner was probably better than later, but now wasn't the time. I wasn't sure if I could keep from exploding.

It took a lot to make me lose my temper, but after what she and Paisley had done? Yeah, that had pretty much done it.

Whenever I thought I could finally manage to talk to her without losing it, I would, but only so I could tell her to leave me the hell alone for a little while.

The drive to my office passed in a blur, and it wasn't until Thomas said my name that I realized he'd parked in front of my building and was holding open the door. Offering him a crooked grin, I said, "Sorry. My mind is elsewhere."

He gave me a polite nod.

I headed to the front door, and then stopped, turning back to him. "By the way, in case Paisley Hedges tries to call and have you pick her up for some sort of little surprise, you should know that we're no longer together."

It may have sounded a little paranoid, but I knew it wasn't. Paisley had done the surprise thing once or twice before. Thomas knew I wasn't too fond of them, but Paisley had always been persistent. I didn't want that same quality to make things even more awkward than they already were.

"Oh. I'm sorry, sir."

"Don't be."

I sure as hell wasn't.

As soon as I stepped off of the private elevator, Janie Beck leaped out of her seat and came rushing in my direction. She held several multi-colored bits of paper in her hands, and she looked very flustered, which was strange for her because she was rarely ever flustered.

"Oh, my word. Jal, of all the days for you to come in late." She pressed her lips together and shook her head. "Not that you aren't entitled to do whatever you want. You work too hard as it is. But this morning has been insane. The phone won't quit ringing and if that girl Paisley–"

She stopped speaking, clamping her lips shut. She was usually good at keeping her personal opinions to herself, but she was clearly at her wit's end.

I slid her a look. "Yes?"

"I apologize, sir. It's just been a very hectic morning, and every third phone call seems to be her." Ms. Beck flushed, the flustered look on her face growing more intense.

"It's okay." I kept my voice calm. "I take it Paisley's called a few times?"

"A few?" She laughed, but it sounded strained. "She called a *few* times before nine-thirty. I'd say she's called six times since, every twenty minutes, give or take. And her mother has called as well."

Shit.

She pushed the notes into my hand. "Mrs. Hedges is quite adamant that she speak to you. Your mother has also called twice."

Double shit.

"That should be it for personal matters. Then the Wheeling Group called, and Lester Wheeling is insisting you make room in your schedule for him this week. I told him that you're very busy, and we could work him in next week for a half hour, but he wouldn't accept that. He…" She stopped and pursed her lips. "Jal, I don't like how that man speaks to me. How a person treats subordinates shows a person's true colors, and *he* treats everybody who actually has to be employed like pure trash."

"Be sure you don't hold back." I patted her shoulder.

"Don't tempt me." She pressed her lips together so tightly, they went bloodless. "Otherwise, when he calls again, I'll tell him where to shove his demands."

While that would amuse me, and he definitely deserved it, having Janie go off on Lester would probably cause more problems than it'd be worth. Flipping through the messages, I said, "Why don't you order us lunch? Pick the spot. My treat."

"It won't make up for this morning." Her face softened a little. "But it's a start. I'm afraid there were a few more calls though. A few were just reschedules or confirmations about matters later this week. We can go over them later, but your two-forty-five called. They need to know if you can possibly meet them at three. There was a family emergency."

I cocked an eyebrow. We'd been trying to close this deal for weeks. "What sort of family emergency?"

"I thought you'd ask. The lawyer who helped set everything up, Brant Garland, is at the hospital. His younger sister went into early labor, and her husband is out of town. The husband is flying back and is expected to land by two, but Mr. Garland can't leave his sister alone."

"Hell." I dragged a hand down my face. I couldn't be annoyed at that. "Fine. But they better be ready to move when they get here. I'm not hanging out until seven with the owners dancing around the bush."

I flipped through the messages, separating a couple out. Paisley's, Diamond's, my mother's. I didn't have to read them to know they said pretty much the same thing.

Holding them up, I smiled at Mrs. Beck. Then I crumpled them in my fist.

"If Mrs. Hedges calls back, let her know that the two of us have nothing to discuss. If she has questions, I'm sure her daughter can answer them, but I have no desire to talk to her."

Speculation danced behind Mrs. Beck's cat-eye glasses, then was gone almost as quickly as it had appeared. She nodded.

I continued, "If Paisley calls, tell her that we've discussed everything we need to discuss. We have nothing else to say to each other, then see what we can do about blocking her calls. Tell security that she's banned from my offices. Oh, and find someone to change the locks at my place before I get home tonight."

Now Janie was giving me a wide-eyed look. I said quietly, "It's over. I ended things."

I wasn't about to go into any more detail. Not with her, certainly, and hopefully not with anybody other than the little I'd told Allie. They'd lied. I'd believed them. I felt like a fool, and it stung.

Some of the edge I still felt showed in my voice as I went on, "As for my mother…" I hesitated, because out of the three, she was one I couldn't ignore. At least not forever. There were holidays to think of. "Tell her that it wouldn't be smart for us to talk until I've had a chance to cool down. I need a few days. At least."

Mrs. Beck nodded and started to turn back to her desk. Then she looked at me, the professional expression on her face slipping into something more personal. "Sir, is everything okay?"

"Yeah." With a tired smile, I said, "It's fine. I'm just still…adjusting to some things."

Standing in front of the bathroom mirror, I adjusted the collar on my shirt one more time. Then, I thought maybe I should wear blue instead of black. I'd heard more than a hundred times that women loved the way I looked in blue.

But I wasn't dressing for any other woman.

I was dressing for Allie.

"Stop it," I said, glaring at my reflection. I'd already changed shirts three times.

I'd even debated on whether or not I should wear a suit. The place I'd picked for tonight was a low key Italian restaurant, definitely more upscale casual than fancy, but a confident man could wear a suit anywhere he damn well pleased and be just fine.

The problem?

I wasn't comfortable. Not in the suit. Not in my own skin.

Not tonight. I was downright nervous for the first time since I was a kid. And the fact that I hadn't been able to stop thinking about Allie wasn't helping matters much.

She'd been trying to ease back, insisting on how different our worlds were, how different our lives were. Logically, I knew she was right, but when it came to sexual attraction, those kind of differences didn't matter.

Except I knew this was going a lot deeper than mutual sexual attraction. I'd experienced a few relationships that had been built on mutual lust. None of them had ever felt like this.

After one more study in the mirror, I checked my watch.

Then I swore, a good long line of words my mother would have frowned at.

I was going to be late.

I'd made the decision to drive myself, wanting the time alone with her, but without a driver to hurry my ass along, I'd lost track of time. I swore again and practically ran down the stairs.

And I still arrived late.

Ten minutes late. Fortunately, Allie had finally given me her phone number so I was able to send her a message and let her know so she didn't think I'd stood her up. She was out front waiting for me when I finally pulled up to the apartment building. She hadn't given me a new address, and I hadn't told her that I'd been here on my own before.

"I meant to ask," I said as I opened the door for her. "How well do I have to behave before I get to come in and meet the family?"

Allie glanced at me as she climbed inside. "Oh, I don't live here. A friend of mine does."

As I walked around to the other side of the car, I told myself not to look back. Things had just clicked for me. The friend who'd gone with her to get the dress. The man who'd answered me the last time I was here. The man she'd been with at the gala.

Tao.

What had she said…*oh, we've been together forever.*

What were they to each other?

Friends, definitely, but was there something more? It seemed like it. There was something…intimate between them. Shoving it out of my head, I focused on the fact that she was here, with me.

"Nice ride," she said, slipping me a wide smile.

"Thanks. It gets me from point A to point B." I made a turn and then asked if she liked Italian.

"Who doesn't?" She smoothed her skirt down, calling attention to her lovely legs.

Keep your eyes on the road, Lindstrom. "Good." I had to clear my throat and yet again, I found myself wondering just what it was this woman did to me. "It's a bit of a drive – half hour. That

265

okay?"

"Hmmm." She rested her head against the back of the seat. "You can drive to Disney for dinner if you want. As long as we're in this car."

I laughed, enjoying the little flare of pleasure I got from knowing she liked my car. Out of the corner of my eye, I watched her smooth that sexy, flirty little skirt down again.

I had a feeling it was a nervous habit, and I was starting to think maybe I should have used one of my drivers. Then I could have been the one smoothing my hands up and down her legs. Of course, then I would have wanted more, and that could've been very awkward...for the driver.

"What's wrong?" Allie asked.

I gave her a quick look. "What do you mean?"

"You just..." She laughed. "Well, you made this weird noise."

"Did I?"

After all the deceit, she deserved honesty, even if it were just about this. As she went to smooth her skirt down again, I reached over and covered her hand with mine.

"You keep playing with your skirt. It's making me want to do the same thing. Only more. Push it up over those thighs of yours. Then I want to pull your panties down. And well, you get the idea. It's getting very distracting."

Slowly, I let go of her hand and flashed her a wicked grin. My blood rushed south as her skin flushed. "Maybe you should save our sanity and quit playing with your skirt."

Chapter 5

Allie

"Another bite," Jal said, his voice low and seductive. He held a spoonful of decadent tiramisu in front of my lips, his eyes darkening as he watched.

I shook my head. "No. I'm so full I feel like I'm going to pop." As he slid the spoon between his lips instead, I added, "That stuff is pure sin."

"Watching you eat it isn't any better." He leaned over and murmured softly, "I've got a hard-on just from watching the way your mouth closed over the spoon, how you licked your lips. I'm tempted to get some more and take it with us."

The implication had me leaning back, staring at him.

He hadn't planned on saying that – I could tell by the look in his eyes – but he didn't seem opposed to making the most of it, either.

"Come home with me tonight, Allie."

My heart banged against my ribs, and my mind went blank. I had no idea what to say. None whatsoever. A waiter clad in black appeared like a shadow at our table and laid down a leather folder holding the bill, letting me know that I didn't have much time to make my choice.

"I won't be upset if you don't want to," Jal said, his gaze intent. "But I'd be lying if I said I didn't want you."

It would be just one more idiotic choice I'd made in a line of them, but I did it anyway.

I nodded.

Jal pulled out some bills and tossed them inside the bill fold. He rose, holding out his hand.

We were moving way too fast, I knew that, but I couldn't seem to stop myself. Not when it came to him.

At least, this time, there was no fiancée.

"I can't begin to tell you all the ways I want to touch you." Jal stood behind me. We'd driven to his place in silence, and now we were standing in what I assumed was his bedroom. I hadn't been in here before, and a part of me wondered if Paisley had been the reason why.

I shoved thoughts of her out of my mind and focused on the reflection of us in the full-length mirror.

His teeth scraped the shell of my ear, and a shiver raced down my spine as his fingers played over the fourth button on my blouse.

He'd undone three already.

Only three and my skin was burning up. I was dying for him to touch me, but he was taking his time, having fun as he tormented me.

"Would you quit teasing me?" I demanded.

"Anticipation just makes it all that much better." He raked his teeth down my neck.

A red mist washed over me, and I thought my nerve-endings would implode, one by one, burying me in a sea of sensation. Even as skillful as Tao was, he'd never been able to make my body sing like this.

"Do you want to hear what I fantasize about doing to you?"

"I'd rather you just do it." My breath hitched, trapped in my lungs as he finally lifted his head and met my gaze in the full-length mirror that hung next to the dresser. Most of the lights were off, but a few still glowed, bathing us in a wash of soft, amber light.

"You didn't answer the question, Allie. Do you want to know?"

With a groan, I covered his hands with mine. "Yes."

My breath locked in my lungs as I waited. Seconds drew out, and I became intensely aware of every breath I took, of how my clothes rubbed against my skin, his chest rising and falling. Maybe this anticipation thing had some merit.

But he didn't *say* anything.

Instead, he took my wrists and dragged them back to the base of my spine.

"Have you ever been tied up?"

The question caught me off-guard, and I laughed a little. "Yeah." I barely stopped myself from saying Tao's name. This wasn't the time to have *that* particular conversation. "I indulged in a bit of kink with a previous lover."

His eyes flashed. "I'm not talking about a fuzzy pair of handcuffs or some scarf you got out of a kit, Allie." His grip tightened. "I mean tied up. Face down with your hands tied behind your back, and your legs restrained so you can't move while your lover fucks you into oblivion."

"Ah…" I wasn't sure how to answer that.

Jal didn't seem to mind. "Did he ever bring you to the point of climax, and then back off, only to repeat it over and over until all you can *think* about is coming, until your whole *world* is that climax, and you're begging, screaming, ready to do anything he asks if he'll just let you come?"

I could see my own reflection in the mirror, and the answer was written clearly on my face. Yes, Tao and I'd had some fun, and he was an amazing lover, but we'd never had anything quite like he was describing.

"Well?" he asked, pushing.

"I…" My mouth was so dry I could barely speak. Clearing my throat, I tried again. "I don't think I've taken it quite as far as that, no."

He cupped my breast, sliding his hand inside my partly opened blouse and lightly squeezed my nipple. "Do you want to?"

I didn't even have to think about it this time. "Yes."

Less than five minutes later, he finally had me stripped naked.

And had given me a safe word.

Apple.

Standing in the middle of his bedroom, he cupped my face in his hands. "Close your eyes. And remember what we talked about."

Slowly, I let my lashes drift shut, feeling the slight shift as he moved away.

He'd told me I'd need a safe word. He didn't plan on doing anything extreme, but he said it was a good idea to make sure I was comfortable at all times. I appreciated that.

Now, eyes closed, alone in a strange room and naked, I felt more vulnerable than I could remember feeling in a long, long time. I wasn't sure how I felt about that.

When I heard the faint sound, I turned my head toward it.

"Have you opened your eyes?"

"No." I shivered a little and fought the urge to cover myself with my hands. I wasn't cold. It was just nerves, but they were getting worse, and I shivered even more as he approached.

"Are you cold?" He brushed his lips down my shoulder. I felt a responding tug in my nipples, then lower.

"No," I answered honestly.

"Nervous then." He rested his hands on my hips, then slid them up until he was cupping my breasts. "We won't do anything you don't like."

I wanted to ask him how he knew that, but before I could summon up the courage to speak past the onslaught of nerves, he had caught my hands, lifting them. My mind went blank as I felt something being tied around them. Around and around – a *rope*?

"I'm tying them in front of you tonight. You'll feel a little more control."

"Okay." I nodded, vaguely aware that everything had taken on a surreal sort of slant.

"You know I've fantasized about this, about seeing you restrained?"

"You get off thinking about tying me up?" The words flew out of my mouth, and in all honesty, I should have been freaked out. Weirded out. Instead, I felt that weird tug in my nipples again, and a pulsating ache settled in my pussy.

"Yes." He pressed his mouth to my ear. "And I think you like hearing that. Do you?"

Heat flooded my face.

"Tell me, Allie." He finished tying my wrists – holding them between us, rubbing his thumb across my skin.

"Yes."

"Yes, what?"

"You're a bastard," I muttered. Shaking my head, I forced the words out. "Yes, I like knowing that you've fantasized about me…" I tugged on the ropes. "Like this."

He kissed me then, deep and rough, and I was moaning against his mouth by the time he pulled away.

"Good girl." He took my arms, guiding me forward. "Now I want you on your knees. Do you understand what I'm saying?"

"Yes." Heat raged in me now, a brutal storm of it.

"Any objections?"

I shook my head.

A few moments later, I was kneeling in front of him with his legs splayed out on either side of me. One hand in my hair guided me forward until the head of his cock bump against my mouth. I opened for him, moaning at the feel of him pressed against my tongue, the weight of him in my mouth.

Without thinking, I lifted my bound hands. After some awkward maneuvering, I was able to hold him steady between my hands. But before I could glide back down on him, his hand tightened in my hair and pulled me up.

"Did I say you could touch me?"

Dazed, a little disoriented, I whispered, "No."

He rubbed his thumb over my lip. "If you want to touch my cock, then you should ask."

I didn't even hesitate. "May I touch your cock, Jal?"

"And with proper grammar, too, baby. That's so nice." His hand loosened in my hair. "Yes. Do it while you suck me off, Allie."

I took him in my mouth again, let my fingers run over his silky skin, through the curls at the base of his cock. I moved my head in a steady rhythm, letting myself enjoy the sensation of having my lips stretched wide around him, the feel of him sliding toward the back of my throat. I rolled his balls in my hands, hollowed my cheeks to increase the suction.

When his hips jerked, I knew he was close. But before I could finish him off, he stopped me.

My breathing was ragged as his cock slid out of my mouth.

His hands moved over my arms, lifting me, positioning me. He bent me face down over the chair he'd been sitting on.

"Don't move."

He released me and the loss nearly made me protest. He'd barely touched me at all tonight, and my body was on fire.

Dimly, I heard foil tear, felt him pressing against me. Once more, he fisted his hand in my hair. I'd always liked it when Tao pulled my hair, but this went beyond a little bit of rough play. This was commanding, taking control.

Dominating in a way I'd never understood before.

"Open your eyes," he ordered as he dragged me upright.

Now that I could see, I realized he hadn't been on a chair. He'd been sitting on one of those fancy, padded benches some people put at the foot of the bed. He'd moved it so that it was in front of the mirror, and as he thrust into me, I was watching myself and him.

He wasn't looking at me though. He was staring downward, watching where he entered me.

I cried out. The feel of him entering me, stretching me, knowing that he was watching where my body stretched wide around his overloaded my system.

He brought his hand down on my ass and in shocked surprise, I yelped. He did it again and slowly lifted his eyes to meet mine in the mirror. He thrust into me again, harder. Again, harder.

When he hit my ass harder than before, I came, my orgasm hitting me hard enough to make my vision go white, then gray.

And then I blacked out.

"That's it, baby."

Jal had me on my knees again, his hands back in my hair. This time, however, he wasn't being quite so gentle. He wasn't letting me suck and lick at my own pace. He was fucking my mouth, making me take him deeper than I'd taken anyone else before.

My eyes burned.

My throat felt bruised.

And when he pulled back and then thrust back in, slow and sure, I took him, desperate for more. He could have fed me his cock just like this for the next few hours, and I would have loved it. Mostly because of the low and rough sound of his voice as he kept talking to me.

I was pretty sure he could make me come from his voice alone.

"You like sucking my cock, Allie?"

I nodded as best as I could. I wrapped one hand around the base of his cock and pumped, but before I could do it a second time, Jal pulled on my hair. "I didn't say you could do that."

Pinpricks of pain went through my scalp as he pulled me off him, arching my head back.

"Do you remember what I told you about touching?"

"May I touch your cock?"

Jal smiled, the sexy slant pulling at something deep inside me. "Yes, you may."

I dragged my hand down again, then back up before leaning in and wrapping my mouth back around his cock. His thigh muscles tensed, and his cock pulsed against my tongue.

"Aw, yeah…do that again, baby," he growled as I sucked on him. His fist tightened in my hair, urging me to move faster.

I needed very little urging though. I'd always enjoyed giving head, but this was better than anything before. Raking my teeth along the vein along the underside of his penis, I moved quicker.

My clitoris was throbbing, pussy clenching. I could almost imagine myself coming, just from this.

"Allie…" It came out in a groan this time, one that shuddered and then faded into nothingness as he started to come.

His hand tightened in my hair, holding me steady as I drew the climax out.

When he finally released my hair, I pulled back and lay my cheek on his thigh. I was all but shaking with my own need, but I was content to just sit there for now.

This…I felt like everything I had with Jal was what I'd been missing my entire life. I started to lift my head, words I didn't fully understand already forming on my lips, words that could maybe explain the vastness of emotions welling up inside me. I wanted him to know what this meant to me.

Jal was staring at me, a faint smile on his lips, eyes sparkling. "You know, baby, you suck cock better than any woman I've ever been with."

The words that had been dancing inside me started to die. I felt frozen. Such blunt, basic words. Here I was thinking this all *meant* something to him.

And I guess it did.

It meant he liked fucking me.

He liked the way I sucked cock.

And he apparently didn't care enough to even notice the change that came over me. Instead, he reached for me, bent me over his bed. My brain was still numb when he thrust inside me.

"Oh, baby," he groaned.

My body reacted to the friction, to the feel of him inside me, pleasure stretching through me until sensation and the exquisite torment he brought me was all that mattered.

Physically.

But my head was in another place entirely.

He brought his hand down on my ass, spanking me and I jerked automatically, a weak cry escaping my throat just as the climax broke over me. A purely biological reaction with no emotion behind it.

Just like him, I now realized.

It donned on me that we hadn't used anything.

That was a mistake.

Yet another one.

One I didn't intend to make again.

You suck cock better than any woman I've ever been with.

I didn't say anything as he pulled me up onto the bed and stretched out behind me. I needed a moment for my treacherous body to recover.

"You're still not out of my system." He ran his hand down my spine.

The words made the ache inside me spread. "Is that what this is? You trying to get me out of your system?" I asked, my voice hollow.

He didn't even notice.

"If it was, it sure as hell isn't working." He gripped my hip and pressed his semi-hard dick against my ass. "I wasn't like this even when I was a teenager. You're addictive."

The bed shifted as he got up.

As soon as he disappeared into the bathroom, I got out of bed and started grabbing my clothes. He came out again just as I was buttoning up my shirt. Still naked and half-hard. He really was insatiable.

"Hey…" He frowned. "Where are you going?"

"I have to work tomorrow." Shrugging, I sat down on the edge of the bed to slip my shoes on, grateful for an action that allowed me to look away from him. "I've got to drop my brother at school, shower…too many things to do and I'll never get it all done if I stay here."

"I'll get you a car." He came closer, but I edged around him before he could touch me.

"Don't be silly." I hurried down the hall, determined not to let him touch me. I couldn't. I was barely keeping it together as it was. I had to get out of there before I broke down. I couldn't let him see what he'd done to me.

I'd learned that at a young age. Never let them see how much they can hurt you.

But when he reached out to touch me, I flinched and practically ran down the stairs.

Something flickered in his eyes as he followed. "Allie?"

I grabbed my purse. "I need to go," I said again, forcing a smile.

"What's wrong?" He sounded completely bewildered.

I paused at the door. "I'm glad I suck good cock, Jal."

His eyes widened. "Allie, wait–"

I made my voice ice. "Don't ever touch me again."

I slammed the door behind me and ran toward the elevator. I wanted nothing more than to take a hot shower, scrub away the feel of his hands, the smell of his body. And then crawl into bed and forget I'd ever met Jal Lindstrom.

Chapter 6

Allie

My call to Tao went to voicemail, and in a fit of borderline desperation, I threw my cell down on the bed and dropped down next to it. Grabbing my pillow, I buried my face in it and started to cry.

...you suck cock better than any woman I've ever been with.

I wasn't an idiot. I knew what a comment like that meant, how it defined what I meant to him. Sex. I gave him physical pleasure because I was skilled at oral sex. That's what I meant to him.

If I'd only wanted a fuck, I would've stuck with Tao. At least, with him, I always knew where I stood, and I knew that he loved me. It wasn't romantic love, but Tao would never pretend what we had was anything other than what it was. My feelings, who I was as a person, mattered to him.

...you're still not out of my system.

I rolled onto my side, hugging the pillow to my chest, as if it could somehow ease the pain in my heart. I'd put myself out there, trusted that when he said I was the only woman he was thinking of, it meant something. Or, rather, that it meant the same thing to him that it did to me.

Once again, that was my mistake. I'd put us on the same level, assumed that our social differences were simply material. I'd let myself forget the most basic lesson I'd learned when it came to rich men like my father, like Jal. They never thought about women like me as anything more than a body to use for their pleasure. Even when they were giving pleasure, it was still all about them, about their prowess as a lover.

Jal's words had reminded me of what I was to him, and I hated myself for forgetting.

The night played over in my head, a video on repeat. My chest started to ache, the pain building and building until I could barely breathe.

I'd knelt in front of him like some naïve little fool, spinning daydreams and fantasies while he'd been mentally comparing me to all the other women he'd fucked, rating my skills. He'd asked if I trusted him, but I could see now he meant it only in the physical sense. I'd been an idiot to think any different.

It was my own fault. He'd taken me out to dinner, and he'd offered a night of sex. He'd made it clear that it hadn't been expected, that it was my choice. It was my own damn fault for seeing it as something more than what it was.

The knowledge, however, didn't stop the pain or the tears, and after a while, I stopped fighting them.

I lost track of the time.

And eventually, I lost track of consciousness, sliding off into sleep and losing my misery to the darkness.

Morning came too early, and my head was killing me as I woke. Curled onto my side, I stared dully at the window. Maybe I could call in dead since that was how I felt. I didn't want to do anything except lie here and be miserable for a day...or three. Of course, that wasn't an option. I had responsibilities that didn't allow for self-indulgence.

TJ wasn't awake yet. I'd woken up a good hour earlier than normal, but I knew there wouldn't be any going back to sleep, and if I just laid in bed, I'd start thinking again, and that was the last thing I needed to do.

Sighing, I sat up and swung my legs over the edge of the bed and knocked something to the floor. My phone. I scowled as I picked it up. Several notifications popped up. Messages from Tao and the last one had come in less than ten minutes ago.

Relief flooded me. He was awake.

I sent him a text, asking if he could come to the house and walk with me while I dropped TJ off. My shift didn't start until ten so we could get some breakfast, and I could talk.

His response popped up less than a minute after I'd sent the text.

Sure thing, gorgeous.

At least I had one man in my life I could count on. Okay, technically I had Tyson. He was a good step-father, but it wasn't the same thing.

I took longer in the shower than I usually did, letting the white noise of the water drown out the chaos in my head. Unfortunately, it was still waiting the moment I stepped onto the bathmat. Thoughts of his touch, the way he'd felt inside me, all the things I thought I meant to him. The pain that came with the realization that I didn't.

I muttered a curse under my breath. I couldn't let him do this to me.

Jal Lindstrom was bad for my sanity, bad for my soul. Bad for me.

I had feelings for him. There was no denying that, no going back to before. I could only move forward. I needed to get past it, move on with my life. My real life, the one where people had to work for a living and rarely had the money to spend on frivolous things. The world where the best I could hope for was a friends-with-benefits relationship with my best friend. The life that revolved around taking care of everyone around me, and ignoring the things I wanted, because that's what I was supposed to do.

I'd let myself get too twisted up about him time and again, and each time, all I got was hurt. I was tired of being burned by people who said they cared about me. I knew the four people who truly loved me, and they were all that mattered. I didn't need anyone else. I was done with all of the rest.

I was at the window waiting for Tao, still working on boxing up my feelings for Jal, when a strange car pulled up in front of the house. Tao popped out of passenger's seat but didn't come up to the house immediately. Instead, he waited as a guy climbed out of the driver's seat and walked around. They appeared to be finishing up some sort of conversation.

Tao smiled, and then the guy hooked his fingers in Tao's belt loops and yanked Tao toward him. Their kiss wasn't the quick peck between friends. This was a long, deep kiss that said the two of them were parting after what had most likely been a great night.

After a couple of minutes, they separated, and I stood so I could greet Tao when he came in. Unfortunately, he stepped inside just as my little brother came crashing down the stairs, sounding like a herd of elephants.

Tao came up short at the sight of me, and his mouth tightened.

"Not right now," I warned him as TJ threw his arms around Tao's lean body. With TJ's back to me, no one but Tao knew what I said.

TJ's hands were already moving when he took a step back, the brisk, harsh movements clearly saying that he wasn't happy. *"Where have you been? You haven't come around much lately."*

Tao laughed and responded, talking as he signed, *"Busy, kid. School, work, dates."*

"Girl or boy?"

"Both." Tao winked. *"You know me. I don't like to restrict myself."*

TJ rolled his eyes, then asked, *"Are the girls pretty?"*

I smacked him in the back of the head. He grunted and looked back at Tao.

"Well?"

Tao slid me a look, his expression sobering. *"There's more to a woman than looks, TJ. But of course...she's a knockout. Sadly, though...that's all she had to offer."*

I arched a brow at him and nudged TJ. *"Get your stuff ready."*

As he turned away, Tao told me, "I'll tell you later."

It looked like we both had things we needed to discuss.

He went first.

"So let me get this straight. You've been out with this chick twice – and by the way, I'm a little pissed I'm only hearing about her now. So after two dates, she thinks she can decide you two are serious enough that she wants you to stay away from men, not even check them out, because she's not comfortable with it." I shot him a look. "Did I get that right?"

Tao grimaced. "In a nutshell. Look, it's some girl I know through work. We haven't even really been *out* twice. We had lunch together one day, and we all know that's not a real date." He rolled his eyes theatrically. "Then she asked me out to a movie. Hell, she's gorgeous. How was I supposed to know she'd start laying out the rules five minutes later?"

"Sounds like you got a stalker."

He shuddered. "Don't joke."

"I'm not." Sliding him a look, I added, "Be careful."

Not that I was in any position to be telling other people the best way to handle their romantic entanglements. I'd proven more than once over the last couple weeks that my own judgment sucked when it came to the heart.

Up ahead, TJ jammed the button for the crosswalk. While we waited, Tao hooked his arm through mine. I leaned my head on his shoulder, thankful for his familiar presence. I didn't even want to think about what I would do when he finally found the love of his life. Or loves, since he did tend to lean toward the polyamorous way of the heart.

"She might've been a mistake, but last night? Much better. Honey, this guy…" Tao gave me the dirtiest look his sapphire blue eyes could manage. "You'd want to be a gay man if you knew what he could do. Or at least a bisexual man, like myself."

"I'll take your word for it." Amused, I eyed him a little more closely. "So you had a good time?"

"Yeah." He smiled. "I did. He's easy on the eyes, but…" Tao shrugged. "It was more than that. For once."

"Good." I was happy for him, but seeing how happy he was

made me a little sad.

We were nearing the school, and I walked faster to catch up to my brother. I didn't want to talk about the whole Jal thing until Tao and I were alone. I tried to keep TJ from seeing any negativity in my life, and this was definitely negative. As if he sensed what I was thinking, Tao changed the subject and started teasing TJ about the girls in school, firing off a hundred questions that I barely tried to keep up with.

By the time we got to school, I'd settled my thoughts and was able to face my brother with an easy smile.

Chapter 7

Jal

I hadn't slept worth shit, and at somewhere between misery and dawn, I decided to go for a run, hoping to clear my head. To get rid of the memory of the hurt I'd seen on her face, the last words she said to me.

I'm glad I suck good cock, Jal. Don't ever touch me again.

The misery in her eyes gnawed me the entire five miles, which completely nullified any good the physical activity might have done. I deserved it though. Deserved every painful mile, every sickening punch to the gut that the memories brought.

What kind of guy would say something like that to a woman he cared about? A total bastard, that was who. Part of me thought that maybe I'd been driven by fear. She'd gotten under my skin, made me nervous, so much that my mouth had run away with itself.

I didn't know how to handle anything about her. Even the gut-wrenching need between us that should have been easy, wasn't. There was nothing more fundamental than sex, but what we had wasn't *sex*.

It was...everything.

And I'd gone and screwed it all up – *again*.

I came back from my run even more exhausted than I should have been, completely drained to the bone, an emotional wreck.

After a quick shower, I collapsed face-down on my bed and sent Mrs. Beck a text, telling her I'd be in late. Being the doll she was, she didn't ask questions. I had no idea what my schedule was like this morning – she hadn't updated me with meeting notes or anything important, so I had to assume there was nothing major, but things would be shuffled around regardless.

I needed sleep.

I also needed to quit thinking about Allie.

Despite my resolve, my mind was on the taste of her lips as I slid into a restless sleep.

I woke up with a hard-on, my hand wrapped around my cock and the sound of a fist hammering on the door.

Disoriented, I lay there, the dream of Allie replaying through my mind, and for a brief second, I almost forgot what an ass I'd been, and how fucked up my life had gotten over the past couple weeks. Tightening my fist, I dragged my hand up my shaft, remembering how amazing Allie's mouth felt as she sucked on me.

Then came the memory of her voice.

I'm glad I suck good cock, Jal. Don't ever touch me again.

My hand froze, but before I could process, a familiar, strident voice sliced through the haze in my brain and shattered the memory. My erection deflated instantly.

"Harold Lindstrom, Junior, you open up this door right *now!*"

My mother, still talking to me like I was eleven years-old and peeking at a Victoria's Secret catalog. The cool anger in her voice put my teeth on edge. That, combined with the decidedly *not* cool anger that had just exploded to life had me up and moving in seconds.

Most of the time, I didn't like getting involved in arguments. I was just too damn lazy. I especially didn't like arguing with my mother. She was as manipulative as any politician, and ten times smarter. And, honestly, it just wasn't worth it half the time with her.

But I was done.

The three of them – my mother, Paisley, and Diamond Hedges – had manipulated me, tried to trick me into marriage I didn't want, and now my mother actually had the nerve to sound pissed off at *me?*

No. Fucking. Way.

She knocked again, her voice loud through the intercom. "Jal, I said open this door! If you don't–"

"I'll be right there!" I bellowed, cutting her off.

Surprisingly, she went silent.

I yanked on my pants and grabbed my shirt from the floor. I was comfortable with nudity, but there was something about my mother that made a man feel like he needed to have certain important parts of his anatomy covered or he might lose them. Striding out of my bedroom and down the hall, I gritted my teeth as I descended the stairs and walked over to the front door.

I told myself to count to ten before opening the door, but it didn't make my anger lessen.

Jerking the door open, I stared at my mother.

She brushed past me, despite the fact that I was standing in the middle of the doorway. I clenched my jaw. No way in hell would this go the way she probably thought. I rarely confronted her so she likely assumed this would go the same way as any other time I did something she didn't like. That I'd shrug and give in because it was the easier thing to do.

Like hell.

Slowly, I closed the door, forcing myself not to slam it. When I turned to face her, she had her arms crossed and one eyebrow lifted.

We were clearly cut from the same cloth. My mother, without a doubt, was one of the most beautiful women I've ever met. She was fifty-two, but could easily pass for forty. She was still slim, and if there was gray in her long dark blonde hair, I'd never seen it. Her eyes were a sharp emerald green, glinting with an intelligence far beyond what most believed she possessed.

Usually, her face was a cool, composed mask, the sort of flawless expression that could've made her a model despite the fact that she was barely five-seven. Mom didn't do emotions.

But on rare occasions, something set her off. And today, that something was me. Her eyes were narrowed, nostrils flaring.

"Jal, would you care to—"

I pointed at her as I cut her off, "Don't."

She sucked in a breath as color flooded her cheeks.

"Don't you dare look at me like I did something wrong." Shaking my head, I moved around her to the window and stared down at the busy street hundreds of feet below. "You, Diamond, and Paisley set me up. Do you have any idea how humiliating all of this is? I felt like I was sucker punched in the gut."

"Jal, don't you think you're overreacting?"

Slowly, I turned and stared at her. "No. I don't. I don't actually like Paisley all that much. Not that you bother to consider that I might have my own feelings about her since *you* like her. You also didn't bother to think that I might actually fall in love with the baby." The smile on my face must have looked as ugly as it felt because Mom's eyes fell away from my face and she shifted her gaze. "A baby that doesn't even exist." When she didn't respond, I added, "You set me up. You *lied* to me. All of you."

Again, my mother tried to interrupt. "Jal, darling. I simply wanted–"

"I know what you wanted," I snapped. "I don't want to hear it."

A mix of disgust, fury, and a multitude of other emotions I couldn't even begin to identify swirled inside me, an insidious mess that just couldn't wait to spill out.

Unaware of the thoughts running through my head, my mother turned on her heel, her Ferragamos clicking on the floor as she strode over to the couch and sat down. Clearly, my surliness had only briefly slowed her down.

"Jal, I will not have you speaking to me this way. What would your father think?"

"He would be surprised as hell," I snapped. "But not because of me. I doubt he thought you'd ever do something like this. I know I sure as hell didn't. I don't know why though. It's not like you've ever cared about our thoughts, our feelings. All you've ever cared about is yourself."

Her nostrils flared, and she pulled her head back as if I'd slapped her.

Oh, sore spot.

Mommy dearest didn't like it when people questioned her motives. It made her look bad.

"I am your mother, and you will not speak to me like that."

"Newsflash, *Mother*," I said, drawing the word out. "I'm an adult now. You don't get to dictate my wardrobe. You don't get to discipline my behavior. And you sure as *hell* don't get to pick my *wife*."

She flinched, and some part of me knew I needed to rein it in, but I had too much of it pent up, and it was all coming out now. I'd let this go on for far too long. Maybe if I'd stood up to

285

her sooner, she never would've thought she could get away with what she did.

"You had *no* right to do that to me."

"*To* you?" She had the audacity to look shocked. "I was trying to help you! You need to settle–"

"Don't say it!" I pointed at her. "Don't you *dare* say it. This isn't some royal family where you need an heir to pass everything on to. I'm not sixty years-old and doddering along. And if I choose to live the life of a bachelor, that's *my* choice. It's *my* life!"

"Aren't you even going to listen to my side?" she demanded. Her own temper was starting to fray.

Nobody stood up to Ginnifer Lindstrom. She was so used to getting her own way, she didn't seem very well-equipped to deal with any type of opposition.

Too fucking bad.

The anger burning in me was hotter than I'd realized and I was only now scraping the top layer.

"Your side." I rubbed my chin, stubble scraping against my hand. "Tell me something, Mom. What side could you possibly have that makes it all okay for you to lie to me about something like this? Did any of you even think that I might end up wanting the baby? Did any of you care that I was flipping my life upside down and forcing myself to marry a woman I didn't even like for one reason…that baby? Did it occur to you how I'd feel when I realized *all* of you – including my *mother* – had lied to me? What did you think I'd do when I realized I was married to someone I didn't want for a reason that didn't exist?"

She fluttered her hand. "Oh, don't be absurd. You and Paisley are perfectly suited–"

"No, Mom, *you're* suited to Paisley. The two of you move in the same social circles. I can't stand ninety percent of the people the two of you spend your time with. You both think I waste my time and money on lost causes and degenerates looking for a hand-out." I ran my hand through my hair. "The *one* bright spot in all of this was a baby. My baby. By child, Mother, that was nothing but a figment of your imagination!"

"Well, go and fuck her and make that damn baby exist if you want it so fucking bad!"

The crude words coming from my mother's mouth was

286

enough to give me pause. I could count on one hand how many times I'd heard my mother swear, and I was pretty sure I had never heard her drop an F bomb, let alone two of them in a row.

She got up and began to pace, agitation clear in every step. She wasn't ready to give this up. She wasn't ready to admit she was wrong. I almost laughed at that. My mother didn't give up on anything. Ever.

"You haven't heard anything I've said, have you?" Or had she heard it...and just didn't care? "I don't love Paisley. I don't even like her. And right now..." I couldn't even finish. I couldn't describe how enraged I was. "This entire thing *disgusts* me. All three of you disgust me."

She sucked in her breath, her porcelain skin going completely white. "Jal, sweetheart...really."

"Why do you look so shocked?" I demanded. "When Paisley told me the truth...shit, Mom. I think you could have punched me in the face, threatened to disown me, and it would've hurt less. *Anything* would have been better than what you did. Why can't you understand that?"

She pressed her lips together, blinking rapidly.

"Do you know one of the things I hated to hear from you or Dad when I was growing up?"

She looked away, twisting her wedding ring around. I got the impression I was finally starting to get through to her.

"When you told me that I'd disappointed you. I would've rather had one of you spank me and get it over with, but that's not what *Lindstroms* did."

Shaking my head, I shoved my hands through my hair again. I'd never been good enough for her. Her expectations were impossible. I'd increased the company's net worth by ten percent within two years, and now it was at a nearly thirty percent increase. I had men my dad's age coming to me for financial advice. And it wasn't enough for her. Being a good student hadn't done it. Being considered a financial genius wasn't enough.

I was a social disaster in her eyes, and *that* ruined all the rest.

"You told me time and again that I'd failed to live up to your standards, that I disappointed you. So I'd try harder. And harder." I looked back at her. "And you gutted me each time, even though I knew, every time, that I'd failed you before you said a word."

"Jal, that's not–"

287

"I don't want to hear it." All of the fight went out of me. I was so tired, the sort of tired that went down to the bones. "And here's the thing, Mom. Maybe I never lived up to your standards. I always thought that was why you pushed me so hard. You had this standard in your head, and you wanted me to fit it. But I can see now that it had nothing to do with an ideal. You just wanted to control me. That ideal doesn't even exist. I guess I can't even say I'm disappointed. I'm just…disillusioned."

She lifted a hand toward me. "Sweetheart…"

"Don't." It came out hard and brittle, and this time, when she flinched, I didn't care. She'd spent too long jerking me around like a puppet on its strings. "You need to leave. And do us both a favor. Stay away for a while. I love you. You're my mother. I know you love me. But I need to…let this settle. If you don't give me some time to do that, I'll say something we'll both regret."

I didn't look back as I headed up the stairs. Part of me thought it might've been a better idea to kick my mother out, but I had a feeling that would've been pressing my luck. Better she thinks it was her idea.

After a few seconds, I heard the front door closed.

One hurdle down…the biggest yet to come.

Chapter 8

Allie

I needed to buy new shoes. My hamstrings were killing me. Working on my feet all day was a real bitch.

The good news was that today had been completely and utterly miserable, with everyone in such bad moods it kept me from thinking too much about Jal. Now, all I wanted to do was take a long hot bath and go to bed.

But Mom had book club later tonight, and I needed to get dinner together if any of us wanted to eat before the meeting.

When I heard her footsteps on the kitchen floor, I glanced over my shoulder and smiled at her, but I turned back to what I was doing in the hopes that she'd be too busy thinking about book club to talk.

No such luck. As I began to dump the vegetables into a bowl to rinse them off, she joined me.

"How was your date?"

She nudged me out of the way so I could respond, taking over the small task. Trying to buy time, I grabbed my bottle of water and drained half of it.

Finally, knowing I couldn't avoid it forever, I answered, *"It doesn't matter. It's not going to work out anyway. I won't be seeing him again."*

I couldn't bring myself to say the words out loud.

While she finished with the vegetables, I got an iron skillet down and oiled it, putting it on medium heat before turning to dig out some garlic from the fridge. The rice was already cooking. Once I had the meat sizzling along with the garlic, I turned to get the vegetables. Mom had already mixed up some soy sauce and orange juice to toss in once the meat and veggies were done.

She was waiting for me to meet her gaze, and now that I had a brief lull, I couldn't avoid it.

"What happened?"

"I...nothing happened." With a half-hearted shrug, I forced myself to speak while I signed, *"I just saw the light – saw reality. It won't work. You were right. We're too different. A guy like him won't ever be happy with a girl like me."*

Please, I thought desperately. *Just take that and let it go.*

But I knew she wouldn't, and I tried to steady myself. I didn't want to cry over this anymore, and I definitely didn't want to cry in front of my mom. Not about this.

Mom touched my shoulder. When I didn't look at her, she asked, *"What aren't you telling me, Allie?"*

All kinds of things, I thought hysterically. *"Nothing, Mama. I'm fine."* The smile I gave her felt hysterical and wild, more than a little sharp around the edges.

Her dark eyes narrowed. *"Don't give me that."*

I eased away to get some distance between us. *"What do you want me to say?"*

I saw the flash of triumph cross her face and knew I'd confirmed for her that something was wrong.

Mom pursed her lips, pulling them slightly to the right as she studied me. *"What do I want you to say? How about you tell me the truth? Or if you don't want to talk, tell me that, but don't lie to me or say it doesn't matter when it clearly does."*

The ache inside me grew, expanding until it seemed that I no longer existed. I was just that ache, nothing but pain and sadness. Tilting my head back, I stared at the ceiling to try to keep the tears out of my eyes.

Why was I trying to hide this from her anyway?

She'd been right. She'd warned me about men like my father, men like Jal. And I didn't learn.

Maybe that was part of why I didn't want to talk about it.

"You were right, Mama." I signed. *"Things between him and Paisley are over, but that doesn't mean I stand a chance with him."*

I didn't want to explain about Paisley and the baby that never existed. Her scheming hadn't surprised me, but it had nothing to do with what was between Jal and me. Or rather what *wasn't*.

He wanted me, but that's all it was.

My mother's face softened, and she took a step toward me. I held out a hand and shook my head, offering a weak smile. *"It's okay. I'm fine. Like I said, it doesn't matter. You need me here anyway."*

If I'd hoped to end the discussion, I should have tried something else.

"Don't," she told me, signing the single word slowly and deliberately.

When I didn't respond, she gave me that look mothers must learn instinctively when they give birth.

"Don't even try that route, Allie. Am I helpless? Is Tyson? TJ, when his head isn't up in the clouds, I wouldn't call him helpless either."

"Mama, I didn't mean that–"

"Oh, I know what you meant," she snapped, cutting me off. *"You're using us as an excuse. If you trap yourself here, you're safe. You tell yourself that it keeps you safe. But it's all you, sweetie. We've never held you back. You stay here because you want to, because you want to hide."*

My spine stiffened, and heat flooded my face. *"That's not true,"* I said defensively.

"The hell it isn't," she spoke her words as she signed them, as if she wanted to make sure there were absolutely no misunderstandings. *"You are so afraid of being rejected again, you prefer to just stay here where it's nice and safe."*

"You don't...that's bullshit, Mom."

"Is it?" She smirked. *"You would know bullshit as well as anybody. You are spouting it to me right now. Don't tell me that this is about us."*

She sighed then and looked away, wrapping her arms around her middle. After a moment, she looked back at me, and her face was sad. *"I know you love us, and I know you want to be here for us, but sweetheart, I took care of you for a long time all by myself. I'm perfectly capable of being TJ's mom...and it's a little insulting that you'd think otherwise."*

"Mom, that's not what I meant," I said, shame and regret filling me.

She reached out and squeezed my hand. "*I know.*"

But it didn't make me feel any better. I knew that a part of it was the way society behaved, always choosing to go through a hearing person whenever possible, treating the deaf like they didn't understand anything. It was too easy to fall into that role, too easy to simply be the voice instead of making other people work for communication. I should have stepped back, forced people to stop being ignorant about my family.

"*This is your home, Allie. You'll always have a place here. But you aren't going to hide behind us.*" She brushed my hair back. "*You've held yourself back from life for too long already, baby.*"

"*I'm sorry,*" I said.

"*Don't apologize to me. You love us, and I know that. But if you want to apologize, then apologize to yourself. You're the one holding back on yourself.*" She gave my hand a squeeze. "*Baby...what do you want?*"

I gave her a puzzled look.

"*Maybe I made a mistake, giving you advice about this man.*" Then she scowled. "*Of course, him being engaged...*"

"*That's over.*"

"*I know you said they ended it.*"

Nodding, I looked away.

"*Is he what you want?*" Eyes narrowed, she pushed on. "*And do you want him because of who he is or because he loved your sister?*"

"He never loved her," I said automatically. Realizing my mom wouldn't understand unless I explained, I quickly told her about the fake pregnancy in as few details as possible.

Mom's eyes widened, then narrowed again. Anger twisted her features as she signed, "*That girl. I swear, I never knew a girl who needed a mother as bad as she.*"

"She has one," I said.

"*No.*" Still looking disgruntled, Mom said, "S*he has a creator who self-indulgently shaped her into a mirror image of herself, never giving her limits, structure, or discipline. Paisley has no idea what a real mother is – or a father for that matter. Kendrick screwed up with all of his kids.*"

For the first time in my life, I realized that my half-sisters might not have had the fairytale relationship with our father that I always thought they had.

With a shake of her head, she continued, *"I have to say this. It sounds like this Jal is a decent enough boy."* After a few more moments of quiet, she went on, *"Allie, do you want him for the right reasons?"*

Heart aching, I looked away for a long moment, and then turned back to her. I couldn't lie anymore.

"Yes."

She smiled. *"Then go get him."*

Chapter 9

Jal

The past week had been one fucking insane roller coaster, and the last few days had been all downhill.

I was dragging so close to the ground, it was pathetic. As impossible as it seemed, I'd discovered an all new level of low. I'd thought that what happened with Paisley was as bad as things could get.

I was wrong.

And this time, I had no one but myself to blame.

You know, baby, you suck cock better than any woman I've ever been with.

"Shit, you might as well have told her you kept a little black book with notes about each of your scores," I muttered as I moved over to the window and stared outside.

It was finally warmer, the temperature hovering in the mid-fifties, and the sun was shining, but my mood was so sour, I almost wished a thunderstorm would blow in. That would suit me a lot better than the sun that glinted off all the high-rises.

I had an appointment with some investors, and I needed to be thinking about an upcoming trip to New York, but instead, I was brooding over Allie and trying to figure out where to go from here, how to fix things with her. How to make things right.

Leaning forward, I braced my forehead against the glass. It was treated so the sun's rays hadn't warmed it at all. The cool surface felt good against my pounding head. I hadn't slept worth shit since Allie had left, tossing and turning as I tried to think of how to approach her.

I just didn't know what to say.

Yet I knew the longer I waited, the harder things would get. *Sorry* wasn't going to cut it.

I was deep into the darkness of my thoughts when the knock came. I ignored it. I rarely brooded. I was just too lazy to waste time on it. But sometimes circumstances called for it, and this was one of those times.

I was justifiably surly, in my opinion, when Mrs. Beck knocked again, then finally came inside. "I don't want to be disturbed," I said, struggling to keep my voice polite. She hadn't done anything wrong.

She sniffed, clearly disapproving of my behavior. "I'm aware. However, you have a guest. There's a young woman here to see you. She says it's important, and that she'll wait all day if she must."

Without thinking, I snapped, "Didn't I say Paisley wasn't allowed on the premises anymore? What does it take for people to understand a simple fucking message?"

"*Mr. Lindstrom!*"

The sharp edge in her voice cut through the haze in my head, and I turned, guilt immediately flooding me.

She narrowed her eyes at me, giving me the kind of look I'd rarely ever seen from her. It was the look a mom gave a kid when they'd stepped over the line. And Mrs. Beck, for all intents and purposes, was probably the closest thing I had to an actual mom when it came to setting me straight.

"I am well aware of what you said about Ms. Hedges. And, while I may technically be your employee, you will not talk to me that way." Her voice was stern. "I will give your father a call if I have to."

Shit. While I knew my father would be on my side when it came to what my mother and the Hedges had done to me, he'd have my ass for taking it out on Mrs. Beck. My father was easy-going about most things, but when something struck him as wrong, he was adamant about it.

"I'm sorry, Mrs. Beck. I shouldn't take any of this out on you. It was wrong of me to snap at you."

"Apology accepted." She looked satisfied and moved on.

"Now, the young lady isn't Paisley. She's—"

"I don't want to see anybody just yet," I said, cutting her off as politely as possible.

The door was pushed open. "How about I just come in and handle this?"

That voice hit me like a fist to the heart.

Mrs. Beck looked almost as surprised as I was. Nobody ever breached what she considered her territory without her say-so, but Allie came strolling in without so much as batting an eyelash.

It took the older woman a few moments to find her voice. "Miss, you cannot—"

"It's okay, Mrs. Beck," I said.

I wanted to stare at Allie and ignore Mrs. Beck, but I forced myself to look at my assistant and nod. "It's fine. It's all fine. Why don't you take an early lunch?"

"Sir, it's nine-thirty."

"That's fine." Reaching into my desk, I fished out my wallet. I had a gold card in there I kept specifically for business related expenses. I held it out to her. "Your anniversary with the company is coming up. Go buy yourself a nice anniversary gift. The sky's the limit. Then take a nice long lunch. It's on me."

Allie hadn't spoken again, clearly waiting for Mrs. Beck and me to work out what we were doing. I couldn't take my eyes off of her. She looked like a rock star. She wore a fitted black top with the shoulders and elbows cut out, so her smooth, dusky skin peeked through. More skin was revealed by the jeans, slashed strategically to reveal the flesh underneath.

My stomach clenched.

Her hair was tousled, spilling down to her shoulders. She wore make-up around her eyes, making them so smoky and mysterious, I thought I'd get lost in them. Her mouth was a rich, wine red, and I was suddenly dying of thirst.

Vaguely, I realized Mrs. Beck was still standing there watching us. Flushing, I looked at her. A strange smile curved her lips, and she nodded at me. "You know, Mr. Lindstrom, I think I'm quite famished. I believe I'll go have that early lunch after all." She started for the door but right before she reached it, she looked back at me. "I'll let the front desk know that you're unavailable for the remainder of the morning and that they'll need to check with me before allowing anyone else in." She didn't bother to wait for an answer as she glanced at Allie. "Have a nice day, miss."

After locking the door, she pulled it shut behind her. The sound of the lock echoed in the room, and suddenly, all the tension was bearing down on me.

Rising up from behind the desk, I placed my hands on its smooth surface and met Allie's eyes. "I was going to call you this evening."

I hadn't made any definitive plans exactly, but I'd known that I needed to talk to her, to make things right. I was just still trying to figure out what to say. Relationships consisting of more than just sex weren't my thing.

"Is that right?" Allie gave me an insolent smile and started forward, hips swinging lazily with each stride. She was pure sex, and my hands itched to pull her up against me. Not yet, I thought. Not yet. She'd come to me. She was in charge right now. I would follow her lead if it meant we could work things out.

Clearing my throat, I tried again. "Yeah. I…uh…look, I needed to talk to you about…um…things. Specifically…"

Shit. This really sucked.

"Things like how I suck good cock?" Her smile didn't reach her eyes. Actually, there was nothing in her eyes at the moment. They were guarded, masked. "How I'm better at it than any other woman you've been with."

She circled around the desk and nudged me until I fell back into my chair.

"Yeah." I swallowed. "Look. About that–"

"You know something, Jal?" She bent down, placing her hands on the arms of my chair. Her eyes drifted down to where my cock was straining against my zipper. She leaned in and pressed her lips to my ear. "It might not surprise you, but you're not the first man who's told me just how skilled my mouth is."

An explosion of jealousy and anger went through me. I caught her arms, wanting to demand just how many men would know what it felt like to have her lips around their cock. Was her 'friend' Tao one of them? Had she slept with him? Was she still sleeping with him?

Questions raced through my mind, one after the other, but she simply stared me down until my anger deflated. I had no right to make demands of her, to feel jealousy toward the other men she'd slept with.

"Allie, I wanted to–"

She reached up and placed her finger on my lips. "I'm talking," she said quietly. Her voice was gentle, but the words were decisive and firm. "Something tells me that your mom is probably quite a bit like Diamond Hedges, and I know how much a parent like that can mess with someone's mind. You probably do relationships about as well as I do. We isolate ourselves. I did it because of my father. He pretty much made it clear that I was second best. Yeah, he loved me in his own way, still does I guess, but he made it clear I wasn't the important one. I bet you do it so you don't get pulled into the drama, to avoid conflict with your mother."

It hit a little closer to home than I liked. "Allie–"

She kissed me, hard, rough. Need shot through me, painful in its intensity. She bit my lip, then pulled away before I could grab her.

"Let me guess..." My voice came out thick and harsh. "You're talking."

"Exactly." She stared at my mouth and licked her lips. "Here's the deal, Jal. I like you, a lot. Probably more than like. But what I do know is that I refuse to be another in a long line of women. You're not going to compare the next woman to me. Because there won't be a next woman. I'm it, or I'm walking."

I stared at her, a little stunned. I'd spent days trying to understand what was going on between us. Days trying to figure out why she had me so twisted up.

And then, in just a few short words, she summed it up. As it all sank inside me, the knots started to fade.

There won't be a next woman. I'm it or I'm walking.

Fuck me. She was right. It wasn't even a real choice to make. She was it.

Slowly, I reached up. She took a step back, but I followed, rising to my feet and cupping her face in my hands.

It was so simple that it wasn't really a surprise that I hadn't realized it before.

This was why she scared me, why she fascinated me.

This was the reason for all of it.

She was everything.

"For the past month, I've only had one woman in my head.

You've been there even when I didn't want you there." I dipped my head and brushed my lips across hers. "Sometimes it pisses me off because I can't think about anybody but you. I can't concentrate, can't work. You're like my drug."

She closed her hands around my wrists. She smiled, and I felt it against my mouth. "That's one hell of an endorsement, Jal Lindstrom."

"Yeah, well, I'm addicted." I tried for a kiss, but she pulled her head back enough that I couldn't. I shook my head. "I'm addicted, and I don't want a cure. You're not walking."

"What does that mean?" She was pushing me, and I knew she wouldn't stop until she got the truth.

"You're it for me, Allie." I met her eyes. "I think I knew it almost from the beginning."

I bend my head to kiss her, but she backed away, releasing my hands as a mysterious smile curved her lips. She pushed me back into the chair, and I let her do it. "Do you always have to be in control?"

I didn't pretend not to understand her question. "I'm not a hardcore Dom. Sex doesn't always have to be BDSM for me."

"Now Jal…that wasn't what I asked." She gave me a sly grin. "Do you always have to be in *control*?"

Instinct demanded I say yes, then tell her to get naked and bend over. But if I'd learned anything over the last couple days, it was that, sometimes, I needed to think before I spoke, and to think about what she needed rather than what I wanted. So I shook my head and waited to see what she was up to.

She reached up and fiddled with something at the neckline of her shirt. A moment later, it felt away.

I felt like my brain was about to explode.

The shirt must've had some sort of built-in support because she wasn't wearing a bra, which meant she now stood in front of me half-naked. Lazily, as if it had just occurred to her, she glanced at the windows. "Are they treated or can people see through?"

"If I said people could see right through, what would you do? You're already standing there with those gorgeous tits bared for me." I put my hand on my crotch, readjusting my rigid cock.

Allie swept her gaze lower, watching me for a moment before she answered, "True enough. There might be people looking at me right now."

Jealousy flared again. She was trying to drive me insane. "There aren't. The glass is treated. And that's good because I don't want anybody seeing you like this but me."

With that same smug smile, she stripped out of her jeans and panties, then stepped back into her shoes. I hadn't noticed until that moment that they were a pair of sexy black heels. I wanted to take her just like that, her naked, save for those heels. Right up against the glass windows of my office.

I started to reach for her, but she backed up. The smile on her face said that she wasn't angry, but rather taking control.

"No touching," she said, shaking a finger at me.

Then, as I watched, she took that same finger and dragged it down between her breasts, over her stomach. When it reached the thin layer of dark curls between her legs, I gritted my teeth.

"You're enjoying this, aren't you?"

"Damn straight."

She leaned forward, her full breasts swaying with the movement. Her nipples slowly hardened into hard points, practically begging me to suck them. Then she went to her knees, and I had to grip the arms of the chair tighter to keep from grabbing her.

As she put her palms down on my knees, she licked her lips and asked, "What do you want me to do?"

The question wasn't exactly what I expected. "Weren't you the one who wanted to be in control?"

Allie lifted her shoulder and my gaze dipped to her breasts. "Aren't I already? You're dying to touch me, to have me touch you. You're all but shaking with it. And I think I could turn over all that control to you, let you do whatever you wanted – right up until I wanted you to stop. And then you would, wouldn't you?"

She was right. No matter what illusions I told myself, she had the power to stop me, which meant she was technically in control, even if she gave it over to me. The fact that the realization didn't fill me with fear said more than anything about just how far gone I was over her.

"Yes."

"So." She reached forward and trailed her finger up, then down the fabric of my trousers. "What do you want?"

Fuck.

I gave it all to her, my voice raw. "I want your mouth on me. I want to feel your wet pussy gripping me. I want to sink my dick inside your snug ass and feel you break for me. I want everything you have and more. I want *you*."

Her eyes darkened. "Open your trousers and take out your cock."

I did, my hands shaking with the intensity of my need.

"I'm going to suck you off for a while, Jal, and when I'm done, you won't be able to even *think* of another woman."

Fuck me. The moment she put her lips around the head of my cock, I knew she was right.

Up and down, wet heat encompassed every inch of my shaft. Fingers and teeth and tongue made my eyes roll back in my head. Minutes stretched out until I wasn't sure how long we'd been there, how long I'd had her mouth on me, teasing me. How long I'd needed relief.

I was right there – right on the verge.

Again.

And then Allie pulled back, squeezing the base of my cock tight, staring at me until the blistering need to come eased back.

Again.

"You're a witch," I said, panting.

I'd lost track of how many times she'd done this. I was so ready I could have brought myself to orgasm with a few rough strokes, but that wasn't what she wanted – that wasn't what I owed her.

"And don't you forget it." She stood, eyes still on me, as she slid a hand down until she cupped her sex, dipped her fingers between her folds. Desperate, I stared as she teased her clit, then as she slid her finger inside her pussy.

My dick twitched, remembering what it felt like inside her.

"Let me do that," I said. "I can fill you up a lot better."

"Yes…you can."

But when I started to rise, she shook her head. I sank back, my cock still bobbing in the air, swollen and glistening. My stomach tightened as she moved over me, straddled me.

She gasped as I pressed up against her, and I groaned at the liquid heat of her pussy kissing the head of my cock. I thrust up, hard and fast, even as she moved down, and then I was buried deep. The sound of her crying out my name was the sweetest damn sound I'd ever heard.

She braced her hands on my shoulders, grinding against me as though she couldn't bear to pull too far away.

"I'm *it*," she said, her voice ragged. "Tell me."

"You're it. You're *mine*." I fisted a hand in her hair, yanking her closer. "And I'm yours."

I rolled my hips, letting the friction send waves of pleasure through us both. Her cunt fisted around me as I slanted my mouth over hers, kissing her deep. The driving hunger faded with that kiss though. It turned into something slower...sweeter...softer.

I understood sex. I was good at it, and I'd been playing with it for years. Making love was something else, something entirely new.

It left me feeling bare and exposed, but the way she looked at me made me clear I wasn't alone in this. That she felt the same way. That we were going through this together.

Chapter 10

Allie

In some ways, it was a typical club, although a little more upscale than what Tao and I usually went to. There was dance music, low lights, roaming people with trays of drinks.

But there were also raised platforms with *different* kinds of performances on them.

One of them held a man and a woman. He was being tied in what Jal told me was shibari. Shibari style? I had no idea. But it was intense and judging by the look on the man's face, apparently erotic. And it wasn't just his face that said how much he was enjoying things either. The tight pants he wore left nothing to the imagination when it came to the long, thick erection he was sporting.

One dais, wider than the others, had a woman bound to a pole, her body bare of everything but the rings through her nipples and the chain connecting them. It ran between her legs as well, and I was pretty sure she had a piercing down there too. Clit or labia, it didn't matter. I was more transfixed by the semi-clothed woman behind her who was using a whip. I stiffened when I heard the crack against the bound woman's flesh, but Jal urged me closer, and when I saw her face, I realized she was enjoying it. Her cries were of pleasure, not pain.

Behind semi-opaque screens, there were couples in various stages of sexual activity, including a threesome between two women and a man, and one sexual position I wouldn't have thought possible.

My heart stuttered a little, and despite myself, I found myself getting wet, my nipples tightening. The ache between my legs increased with every step, with every new experience I took in.

We'd been there less than a half hour when Jal pulled me into a dark corner. One hand gripped my throat while the other tipped my head back so he could take my mouth. And taking was what it was. Fierce and hard, demanding.

His voice was ragged when he finally pulled away. "You look like you're on the verge of coming. I can't decide if I'm jealous, or if I want to take you to the screens and get a private booth there. Slide my hands inside your panties and *make* you come."

I swallowed a groan. I'd seen the booths. They were only semi-private. People wouldn't be able to see my features, but they would see my body, his body, as he coaxed an orgasm from me.

"No." Shaking my head, I did my best to make it clear that wasn't what I wanted.

He bit my lip. "You sure?"

"Yes."

I straightened, and I looked for any sign that he was disappointed. I didn't see any. He took my hand and raised it to his lips, smiling. "Okay. Dance with me then."

He led me onto the dance floor, and when he pulled me up against him, his cock pressed against my belly, sending a shiver through me. I pressed my cheek against his shirt and tried to handle the arousal that had been burning inside me from the moment Jal said he wanted to take me to a club.

I should have kept my eyes shut.

The couple next to us was dancing with her back pressed against his front, and he had his hand resting torturously low on her belly. As he whispered something to her, she nodded, her pretty blue eyes glazed with heat. The hand on her stomach slipped underneath the waistband of her skirt. Her legs parted, and she arched against him. I could see his hand moving under the fabric, stroking her. When her hand moved behind her, he whispered something else. Something that had her body writhing against him.

"You like watching," Jal whispered in my ear.

I jumped, startled. Heat rushed to my face.

"I–"

"Watch. If they didn't want anyone to see, they'd get one of the private rooms." His cock was hard and hot against my stomach.

I whimpered...and kept on watching. The man shifted so that he could use his free hand to deliver a hard slap to the woman's ass. It was an awkward position, it had to be. But Jal was right, I realized. Half the draw, half the arousal for them both was being watched. And I wasn't the only one.

The man brought his hand down on her ass again. His other hand was moving almost violently between her legs. I could imagine his fingers thrusting into her, pressing against her flesh.

And then she came. Hard. I thought I could actually hear her cries of pleasure.

He spun her around, squeezing her ass as he ground himself against her. He pushed his fingers into her mouth, the fingers that had been inside her, and the look on her face was one of complete bliss. He said something to her, and she nodded again. The two of them disappeared down a hall – the one that led to rooms behind the screens.

"They have rooms where you can actually...watch. All of it. Do you want to?"

I jerked my head up to see Jal watching me carefully, as if gauging my reaction. I was breathing as if I'd run a marathon. My nipples were hard, and I felt as aroused as if *I* had been the one being worked over.

"How does that work?"

"It's live streamed into a side room so that there's no physical contact with the couple, and they have complete control over whether the camera is on or off." He ran the back of his hand down my cheek. "Do you want to watch?"

I couldn't seem to say the words. I'd never thought of myself as a voyeur. Until now. But I still couldn't bring myself to say it.

Jal seemed to read my thoughts anyway, and he led me toward a different hall. We went downstairs, and although there was a desk – of sorts – the woman there said nothing. She didn't even seem to notice us. Jal swiped a card, and I realized he was taking me to a space for special members only.

Once we were through the door, another woman, clad in an elegant black dress, gestured to a door.

The couple from the dance floor was displayed on three

305

walls, from three different angles.

I'd expected it to be tawdry.

But the room we were in looked like an expensive hotel suite. Each screen was easily life-sized, so it was almost like being in the room with them.

I looked over at Jal and asked, "They know we're here, right?"

"Yes. Anyone who wants to use one of those rooms signs a consent form, and anyone who comes in here agrees not to record anything. When someone rents one of these rooms, a light goes on, letting them know they're being watched."

He stepped behind me and slid his arms around my waist. I'd called Tao to give me a suggestion for what to wear, and he'd selected a fairly revealing deep purple dress with a low neckline and high hem. The lust in Jal's eyes told me that it had been the right decision. Now, he moved his hands up to cup my breasts, taking advantage of the revealing cut to brush his thumbs over the bare swell.

"I'm in control this time, Allie," Jal said against my ear. "I'm not going to fuck you here. But you'll wish I had. Take off your panties."

Hands shaking, I did, still staring at the screen in front of me. The man was tying his partner to a bench. That much I understood. She had a gag in her mouth and a scarf in her hand, prompting a question.

"Can I ask questions?"

He kissed my fingers. "Yes. Always."

"Why the scarf?"

"She's gagged…can't talk. If he goes too far or tries something she doesn't like, she drops the scarf, and they're done. It's a non-verbal safe word."

It made sense, but a bit of anxiety twisted my stomach. "What if he doesn't stop?"

"They're married, Allie. I know them. He'll stop. But…" He ran his hands over my ribs, down to my hips. "There are safeguards in place for random hook-ups. These rooms are monitored. The private rooms are monitored via audio. If something alarms one of the security guards, they'll enter the room. They aren't…polite with people who try to take advantage of places like this. Consent is taken very seriously here."

I nodded, watching the screen as the tension inside me eased. The man had moved to stand between the woman's legs. He held a bottle in his hand.

Jal answered a question I didn't actually have. "Lubricant. He's going to put his cock in her ass. Have you ever had anal sex, Allie?"

Licking my lips, I nodded. "Once or twice. It's...not my favorite."

My last boyfriend had wanted it, so I'd agreed. Since Tao had known my distaste for it, he'd never suggested it, though his fingers had occasionally wandered there. Though I knew Tao could probably have made the experience more pleasant, I'd never had the inclination to ask.

"Will you let me try to change your mind?" He cupped my breast over the dress, lightly pinching my nipple.

I reminded myself that part of being in a relationship was compromise. I trusted him not to hurt me. "Yeah. If...well, if you like that."

"I want to show you that *you* can like it to." He slid his hand down and squeezed my ass. His knee nudged against my thigh, and I moved my legs a bit farther apart. "Keep watching."

The man on the other side of the screen had finished preparing the woman and now had one hand on her cheek as the other hand steadied his cock. Slowly, he began to fill her. She was shaking, her feet kicking up and down in mad little flutters, the most exquisite sounds coming from her mouth.

A faint electronic hum had me jerking my head around.

Gaping, I saw that the screen on the right had gone up into the ceiling, and there was an entire *wall* of sex aids. Jal pushed a button under one. There was a clunk and a faint, startled laugh sputtered out of me.

"A *vending* machine for dildos?"

"Why not?" Jal turned back to me, grinning. He held up something. "But this isn't a dildo. It's a butt plug."

My face went hot. "I know what it is."

Something that looked a lot like jealousy flickered across his face, and for a moment, I wondered what would happen when he realized that Tao had been my lover for the past three years. Somehow, I didn't think that would go over very well.

"Go to the bench." He gestured toward a padded bench at the

foot of the bed. It looked identical to the one the woman on the screen was using.

Nerves twisting in my stomach, I looked over at him, at the toy he was holding.

"Trust me," he said, his lips twisting into a decadent smile.

Oh, hell.

I moved toward the bench, suddenly very aware that I was now bare under my dress.

The bench was wide, with the top of it rounded and thick, almost pillowy soft. The part I knelt on was soft as well, but I could feel a bit of give and realized that the covering could be taken off if someone wanted to kneel on the hard wood.

My gaze was once more drawn to the screen, and I groaned as I realized how fast he was going. They'd come soon, and it would be over. I felt like I'd only barely started to understand a part of me I'd never explored before. Tao had opened me up to some of it, but the intensity of this world was overwhelming.

"What's wrong?" Jal asked, bending over me.

I shook my head, my face hot. I'd been bold, confident when I'd gone to Jal's office this morning, but all of that was gone now. I was out of my depth, embarrassed by what I was feeling, by what I wanted.

"Tell me." The words were a command, not a request.

"They're going to come soon. I don't want them..." The words trapped in my throat as another wave of embarrassment washed over me.

Jal moved away, and I gasped in utter shock as he pushed a button on an intercom I just now noticed.

"I don't suppose you two might be interested in making this...last?"

The man's face turned toward the camera unerringly, then bent over his partner, his cock still buried in her ass. He released the gag and spoke to her, his voice too low for me to hear the words. She nodded in response to whatever he said and lifted her head to face the camera.

The look of ecstasy on her face was enough to have my belly going tight, almost enough to make me forget how strange and new this all was.

The man smoothed the woman's hair back into a ponytail, then wrapped the dark locks around his fist. He pulled, using her hair to tug her upward until her spine bowed, putting her full breasts on display. Her skin was smooth, pale, nearly translucent, and the contrast to his tanned body was beautiful. They looked like a work of art.

"Tell me you wouldn't want to feel like that, Allie," Jal said as he came back to me. "Open, exposed...so vulnerable to me."

He knelt behind me, and flipped up the bottom of my dress, exposing me to his gaze, to his hands. I whimpered as his finger slid between my cheeks, slick with lubricant. My eyelids fluttered as he started to work his finger into my ass, but I forced them to stay open. I didn't want to miss a thing.

On the screen, the woman was panting, begging her partner to ride her harder, faster. Begging him to make her come. His pace, however, stayed steady, control and restraint radiating off of him.

His voice was even as he responded, "No, baby. You want to be watched, so we're going to make it a good show for our audience. Talk to them, baby. Tell them how it feels having my cock in your ass."

"So good...so full...please, baby...make me come." Her voice was breathless, almost pained. "Please..."

He ran his hand over her hip, then brought his hand down on her ass. She cried out, writhing as she tried to push back against him.

I twitched as he did it a second time, harder than the first, then cried out when Jal echoed the movement. It was more a sharp sting than actual pain, and then warmth followed.

"I can make you feel like that," he said as he added a second finger, twisting them. "All you have to do is tell me."

A shudder ran through me. I'd had a finger in my ass before, had even enjoyed the way it intensified things, but what he was doing was something new.

And I wanted more.

"I want to feel it. Jal, please..."

"Good girl." He pressed the plug against my anus, and I instinctively tensed. "Watch them, Allie. Watch and relax."

On the screen, the man stood and pulled the woman to her feet as well. He nudged her legs apart, positioning them so we could see everything. His hands were on her hips, steadying her as he began to thrust up into her hard enough to put her on her

309

tiptoes. I moaned as I watched his cock emerge, then disappear back inside. He moved so slow, filled her so deeply, I could almost feel it.

"Take a deep breath," Jal order.

Without thinking, I did.

I watched as the man drove back into his partner – and then I cried out, my hands tightening on the bench as Jal twisted the plug and pushed. "Push down on it, Allie. And *watch him* – see him taking her. Imagine it's us."

I whimpered, the line between what I was watching and what was happening blurring away into nothingness. Without thinking, I pushed back onto the plug, the way she was pushing back onto her partner's cock.

"That's it, baby." Jal's voice.

"Do you like my cock in your ass?" The stranger's voice.

She moaned out a raw yes.

I made a sound that wasn't a word. I knew the plug wasn't a large one, hardly more than the two fingers Jal had been using, but it was solid, unyielding. The prior boyfriend with whom I'd tried anal sex before had been about this size, but it didn't feel the same at all. I gasped in ragged breaths, my hands opening and closing as I struggled to process all the sensations.

"I changed my mind." Jal's voice low in my ear, words not quite covering up the sound of a wrapper tearing, a zipper being lowered. "I'm going to fuck you."

I barely had time to register what he said before he was burying himself inside me with one rough thrust. I wailed, every muscle in my body quivering with overloaded nerve endings. On his own, he was big enough to make me see stars if I wasn't prepared. With the plug still in my ass, I felt like I would surely explode. I was too full. It was too much. I couldn't take it.

One of his hands slid under my dress and up my spine, the touch soothing, calming.

"Relax, baby. Let me make you feel good." His hand moved around to my breast, and his fingers gave my nipple a tug, drawing a moan from me. "Keep watching…and don't you dare come before she does."

I made a sound of protest, curling my hands into fists so tight my nails marked my palms. I couldn't hold back. I knew I couldn't.

"Let me come," the woman pleaded. "Please, Master, say I can come."

"Please," I moaned along with her. Jal had just barely started to move, and I was already burning with the need to climax.

"Don't come yet, Allie. When *he* says she can, then you can."

Jal's strokes were long and deep, reaching every inch of me. The plug moved with every thrust, sending painful pleasure to mix with the sensations of Jal's cock dragging over my g-spot, stretching me. I'd never considered doing anything like this before, but now, I could only think of how good it felt, how the pressure inside me was building until I could barely breathe.

The man on the screen was pounding into the woman, sweat glistening on both their bodies. As I watched, he dropped a hand between her legs.

"Come!" He made it a command as he shoved three of his fingers into her pussy.

She screamed, and I was vaguely aware that Jal was saying my name, but all of that was lost as the command gave me permission for release. My orgasm overwhelmed me, claimed me, made me lose all sense of self, of reality. When the darkness claimed me, it was almost a relief.

Chapter 11

Jal

"I can't believe you expect me to keep this thing in."

I risked a glance over at Allie. Looking at her was dangerous, especially since I knew the only thing she had on under that gorgeous dress of hers was the thin silicone buried in her ass. She squirmed in her seat as she glared at me, and my already hard cock twitched. Damn, she was dangerous.

"Just until we get back to my place." I reached over and took her hand, lifting it to press a kiss against her knuckles.

"I don't understand why I couldn't just take it out at the club."

"Because it needs to keep you stretched so that when we get to my place, I can replace it with my cock."

A beat of silence. Then, "Oh."

My grip tightened on the steering wheel as I reminded myself that it wouldn't be a good idea to pull over on the side of the street and take her ass right there. One, I didn't think getting arrested for public indecency would be a great way to end the night. And, two, she'd already said that she hadn't enjoyed anal sex the previous times she'd tried it. I wanted to make sure she enjoyed herself this time.

Hell, I didn't want her to just enjoy it. I wanted her to crave it. Wanted her to crave me in every way possible.

But I wasn't about to push her further than she was willing to go. "Do you remember what to say if it's too much?"

She nodded. "Apple."

"Good." I glanced at her again. "And I mean it, Allie. I don't want you to stay quiet because you think it's something I want."

She nodded again, a thoughtful expression on her face. Part of me wanted to ask what she was thinking, but a greater part was terrified to know what was really going on in her head.

I took her hand to help her from the car when we arrived at my house, grateful that no one else was around to see the glimpse of bare skin she flashed as she swung her legs around. For a brief moment, I considered bending her over the hood of my car, but I filed that thought away for future consideration.

She made a startled sound as my mouth came down on hers as soon as the front door closed behind us, but then she leaned into me, those lush curves soft against my hard body. We were a rash of contradictions. Everything about us said we shouldn't fit together. Race. Social status. Finances. Family. But she was mine in a way I'd never known existed before her. A way I'd never believed could possibly be real.

I fed my hunger as my tongue plundered her mouth, reveling in the taste of the champagne we'd had at the club. My hands ran down her back to her firm ass and my stomach clenched in anticipation. I wanted so badly to be buried in her ass, but I would hold back, take it slow, prove to her that she could enjoy this too.

I eased down the zipper at the back of her dress and then took a step back so that the garment could fall to the floor. Her panties were already in my pocket, and the dress had built-in support, so she was completely bare in front of me. Unlike this morning, however, she stepped out of her shoes, making her more than a foot shorter than me.

Without a word, I pulled off my shirt, kicked off my shoes, and stripped my pants and underwear off at the same time. Her eyes flicked down to my cock, and she licked her lips.

I groaned. "As much as I want your mouth, I want another part of you more tonight."

I held out my hand to her, and when she took it, I led the way to my bedroom. In the past, I'd always insisted on my sexual encounters taking place in either a guest room or my playroom if we wanted to use toys. Paisley had wormed her way into my bedroom with her pregnancy lie, but I was taking Allie there of my own volition.

"On the bed." I walked over to my bedside table and reached into the drawer to pull out a tube of lube and a condom. I wasn't surprised to see that my fingers were trembling. I felt like my entire body was humming with anticipation. Allie was a tantalizing combination of innocence and sexuality, like no one I'd ever met before.

"How do you want me?"

I closed my eyes. Fuck me. Her words alone would've been enough to make me hard if I hadn't already been that way.

When I turned to look at her, she was on her hands and knees, looking at me over her shoulder. Her knees were parted enough for me to see her glistening slit, and above that, the flat black end of the butt plug was still tucked in between her cheeks.

"Just like that." My voice was hoarse as I stared at her. I'd never seen anything so beautiful.

I walked over to the bed and tossed the condom and lube onto the bedspread. We would have to talk soon about getting tested so we could stop using condoms. I wanted to slide inside her with nothing between us, feel that wet, hot pussy of hers without a layer of latex.

But right now...I planned to show her just how good it could feel to have her ass fucked.

She shivered as I ran my hands up her legs and over her hips. Her head dropped down, and I felt her tensing under my touch. She hadn't said that the man she'd tried this with had hurt her, but it was clear she was nervous.

"It's okay, Allie. Remember, you're in control. Say the word and we stop."

She nodded, her muscles relaxing slightly.

I took hold of the plug and slowly began to twist it. She shuddered, then moaned as I eased the plug out. My stomach clenched as I watched the tight ring of muscle stretch. When the plug came free, I set it aside.

I took a moment to prepare myself, then turned my attention back to Allie. I ran one finger along her slit before slipping it into her pussy. I moaned at the same time she did. I hoped she wasn't planning on going home any time soon because I fully intended to spend the rest of the night taking her in every possible way.

As I began to tease her clit with my thumb, I worked my

middle finger into her ass, then added another. She gasped as I stretched her, her hips rocking forward onto one hand, then back onto the other.

"You're going to come for me, Allie," I murmured, breaking the silence between us. "And while your body is all nice and limp, that's when I'll slide inside."

"Yes. Yes, Jal." Her words were breathless, telling me that she was closer than I thought.

I leaned down and pressed my lips to the base of her spine. "Come on, baby."

I slid two fingers into her pussy and pressed the heel of my hand against her clit. Her body jerked, and she whimpered. When I pressed my fingers against her g-spot, rubbing it with just the right amount of friction, she came. She cried out my name as her cunt and ass tightened around my fingers.

As soon as she relaxed, little tremors of aftershocks running through her, I removed my fingers and positioned my cock against her asshole. She groaned as I eased my way inside.

"Jal...Jal..." she panted as she dropped onto her elbows. "Fuck."

"Breathe," I said.

I kept moving forward, one inch at a time, even though everything inside me screamed for me to just slam into her, ride her rough. I wouldn't though, not right now. One day, maybe, but she had to learn to enjoy this first.

"Jal," she whimpered. "It's too much."

"Then you know what to say, baby," I reminded her. I prayed she wouldn't use her safe word because I didn't want to stop. I would if she said it, but I didn't want to.

After a moment, she shook her head. "Keep going."

I reached under her, cupped one of her breasts, and gave it a squeeze. As I teased her nipple, I moved forward again. The trick, I knew, was to combine the pain with pleasure, to let them merge into something intense and full. I was half-way inside when Allie began to swear, her muscles spasming around me as her body struggled to adjust to the intrusion.

"Relax, baby." I ran my hand around her hip and down between her legs. She was slick with arousal, and I ran my fingers through it, then up to her clit.

She cried out as I ran my fingers in circles over the swollen

315

bundle of nerves. Her hips jerked backward, shoving me deeper. I groaned as her muscles gripped me.

"Fuck, babe. You're like a vice."

"Please, Jal. Please," she begged.

My hand left her breast and tangled in her hair. I held her tight as my balls brushed against her skin. I rested there for a moment, fighting for self-control. She was so tight, so hot.

And then there were the sounds she was making...

It was almost enough to make me come right there.

When I began to move, I took it slow, long strokes that stretched and filled her. After half a dozen, she was moving back against me, making little sounds of pleasure.

"Talk to me, baby." I slid a finger into her pussy, felt my cock through the thin membrane separating the two.

"Feels so good," she moaned. "Burns. So full."

"I need you to come for me, Allie." I pulled her up against me, the change of angle making her gasp. "I'm so close, baby. I need you to come first though."

I pressed my mouth against her throat, nipped at her skin. She reached behind her to grip me, her nails biting into my thigh. I pressed my hand harder against her clit, pushed into her as deep as I could go. I tried to hold back, to wait for her, but she felt too good. Even as I started to come, my cock pulsing inside her, the muscles in her stomach twitched. She was on the edge.

"Come for me, Allie. Now!" I barked out the last word.

Then she was coming around me, and all I could feel, smell, see, was her. She was everything, and now that I finally understood what that meant, I would never let her go.

Chapter 12

Allie

"Would you *stop?*" I said, laughter thick in my voice. "You're making me make a mess!"

Jal stood behind me, his mouth pressed to the side of my throat, his teeth and lips doing dangerous things to my skin.

Waffle batter now liberally splashed the counter and my hands. I'd been getting ready to pour out the first one when he caught me off-guard with a kiss to the back of my neck.

"No." He took the bowl and set it down, then spun me around and boosted me up on to the counter, wrapping his arms around me.

"You got my shirt dirty," I protested. "And the batter's cold."

"So what? You're warm...hot..." He kissed his way down my neck and then, before I could stop him, he pulled the shirt off and tossed it to the floor. "And, technically, it's my shirt."

His kisses moved down my collarbone, and my nipples tightened with the knowledge that he was going there next. Then my stomach growled, reminding me that I hadn't eaten yet.

"No...nuh-uh." I pushed him back. "I'm getting food first. You clearly have no idea what a monster I turn into when I'm hungry."

He heaved out a sigh and leaned back. "Fine. But only if you finish breakfast and eat...like that."

I looked down reflexively even though I already knew I was naked from the waist up. "You're serious."

His challenging smile was all the response I needed.

I grinned. "Fine by me."

His eyes widened, and I knew I'd caught him off guard.

Doing my best to keep myself from chickening out, I asked him to get out plates and start the coffee, and before too long, we were sitting down to waffles, eggs, and bacon.

"Do you cook?" I asked him from the opposite side of the island.

He'd tried to put us next to each other, but I'd insisted on space until I had food in me. He'd sulked good-naturedly, but had given in.

He shrugged as he answered my question. "Not really. I can do basic stuff, but I've got a cook who comes in three or four times a week and prepares meals ahead of time. If it were up to me, I'd live off fast food or whatever I could scare up at the closest restaurants to my job."

"You eat fast food?" I asked dubiously.

"I'm addicted to a couple of places." He gave me a self-deprecating grin. "My mother sort of loathes my 'low-brow' tastes, but give me some McDonald's fries, and I'm a happy man."

I laughed. "Me too."

I was about to take a bite of my waffle when the bell rang.

Jal ignored it, snapping a piece of bacon in two, his gaze on my breasts. "I'm going to enjoy spreading you out on the island here in a little bit and having some dessert with my breakfast."

I blushed as he winked.

There was another knock – harder this time. "Mr. Lindstrom, you need to open up."

He frowned, and I crossed my arms over my chest, suddenly self-conscious. "You know who that is?" I asked.

"No." Sighing, he nodded toward the stairs. "Why don't you grab a clean shirt and I'll get rid of whoever it is."

I hurried up the stairs and into Jal's room. I grabbed the first shirt I could find, my gut telling me that something was wrong. By the time I reached the top of the stairs, I heard raised voices, the kind of voices that had authority in them. I hurried down the stairs and into the living room where I stopped dead.

Cops surrounded Jal.

Gaping at him, I took in the uniformed patrol officers and the men in plain clothing. Detectives.

"This whole thing is bullshit!" Jal's face was flushed, the muscles in his jaw tight.

One of the detectives gave him a mild look. "That may well be, and you're entitled to a lawyer who can help you figure it out."

A uniformed officer looked at me, his gaze sliding down and up again, his expression making it clear that he knew what we'd been doing. He looked back to Jal. "Do you really want to make this any uglier than it has to be?"

Jal looked at me, his eyes meeting mine, and he shook his head. Without looking away, he put his hands behind his back.

"Harold Lindstrom, Junior, you're under arrest for insider trading. You have the right to remain silent..."

This couldn't be happening.

Except it was.

Book 5

Chapter 1

Allie

Arrested.

Jal was being arrested.

The words repeated in my head, but my brain refused to accept them.

This whole thing felt like a set-up for some awful reality TV show, and some hot celebrity was going to come rushing out from around the corner any moment to tell us that we'd just been punked.

But the officers were slowly and *politely* walking Jal toward the front door. Soon, they'd be outside, down the steps to the police car that was surely waiting.

I couldn't let that happen.

"Jal, what do you want me to do?" My voice sounded louder than I thought it should, but it had the desired effect of stopping everyone.

Jal jerked his chin toward the kitchen. "Get my phone. It's on the counter. Call my lawyer, Adam Abbott. Tell him what happened."

"Where…where will you be?"

I looked at the detective behind Jal. He scowled but answered, "The thirty-ninth."

Then they were all gone, leaving me staring at the closed door.

Gone.

He was gone.

He'd been *arrested.*

Hell, it wasn't like I'd never known anybody who'd been

arrested. But Jal Lindstrom? He came from the kind of family who could pay to make arrest warrants go away. Not that I thought Jal would ever do that, but I was shocked this had gone through without him even getting a head's up. I'd spent enough time in the Hedges' house to know how things like this usually worked.

They didn't get arrested for things like this without a hell of a fight from some high-priced lawyer.

Lawyer. Right. Jal wanted me to call his lawyer.

I moved into the kitchen, my limbs feeling stiff and abnormal. Jal's phone was lying on the counter, and I picked it up, sliding my thumb across the screen until it came to life, and I was able to get into the contacts. Fortunately, he didn't use a passcode, or I would've been in trouble. It dimly occurred to me that I should tell him to add one since this wasn't exactly safe, but that was neither here nor there. I scrolled through the contacts twice before remembering that the man's name would be at the top.

I was in shock, I was sure, but a part of me thought it was more than that. Something just didn't feel *right* inside me. All sorts of things felt wrong *outside* me too.

Two rings buzzed in my ear and then a man's voice boomed out. "Jal, son...where you been, you lousy fuck?"

I blinked. "Ah. Um..."

"Oh..." There was a soft chuckle. "I'm sorry. I expected...well, Jal."

"The lousy fuck."

The man laughed again. He was loud, but something about him eased the knot in my chest.

"Yes. Exactly. How can I help you, and why are you calling from Jal's phone?"

"Because he told me to. He's been arrested."

For a second, there was absolutely no response. Then, the man on the other end of the line said quietly, "Would you please repeat that?"

I did, then told him every single thing that happened from the moment the cops knocked on the door. I even told him why I hadn't been in the room when Jal had let them in. Adam Abbott seemed like the sort of man who wouldn't get distracted by details but would rather know them so he wasn't caught off guard.

When I finished, he was quiet for a few seconds, then spoke,

"Thank you, Miss…I don't believe I caught your name."

"Allie," I said. "Allie Dodds."

"Thank you, Miss Dodds. Will you be meeting me at the police station?"

I hadn't thought of that. I hadn't thought of anything beyond getting a hold of the lawyer. Now that I'd done that, I had to figure out what to do next.

Not that it was really even a difficult decision to make. "Yes. I'll meet you there. I need to get a cab–"

"That won't be necessary. In Jal's contact list, you'll find the name Eli. He's one of Jal's normal drivers, and he'll take care of you. I expect Jal will want to see you once I get him out of this mess."

I would have argued.

But I wanted to see Jal too.

I'd never been in a police station, and it wasn't something I would look forward to repeating any time soon. The lights were too bright, the floor too white, the noises too harsh and voices too strident.

One girl came through the doors crying, begging the officer who was holding her by the arm to call her mother. In the next breath, she pled with him to please just let her go, she'd only had the one beer.

Of course, if she'd only had that one beer, she wouldn't have been in this position to begin with. I could tell by the way she was half falling against him that she'd passed *only one beer* about ten beers ago.

One woman came in, demanding to know where her son was. She was dressed in clothes almost fine enough to rival Diamond's. When she tried to slap an officer who told her she'd have to wait her turn, I watched as she was restrained.

"Miss Dodds?" The voice was familiar.

The man standing in front of me wasn't, but I figured out who he was pretty quickly. He was older than I would have expected, black hair going silver at the temples, dark brown eyes, and dimples that had long since deepened to grooves bracketed his mouth as he smiled.

"Mr. Abbott," I said, rising.

"Call me Adam, please." He held out a hand.

I shook it, but my focus had already shifted back to Jal. "What's going on? Have you seen him yet?"

"Currently, we're in the process of me being jerked around out here, and Jal being jerked around in there." He flashed me a quick smile. "That's very technical talk, by the way. Make sure you remember it."

"In legalese, it translates to no, right?" Feeling a little drained and hollow, I fought the urge to drop back down the bench and just cry. I did sit though. I felt like I'd been through an emotional wringer over the last couple weeks.

He sat with me. "It does indeed translate to no. You might be a natural at this legal talk thing."

"What's taking so long? They showed up almost two hours ago. I've been here almost an hour." I didn't try to keep the frustration from my voice.

Adam patted me on the shoulder. "I know it feels like a long time to you, but it's not. They won't keep him waiting much longer, but they have to process him and go through all the procedures. You said this was about insider trading, but between you and me, that's bullshit, because Jal is the most honest person I know. Plus, he's too competitive to win anyway other than the right way. He wants to know that he can beat everybody just by being smarter and better."

"He *is* arrogant," I said with a soft smile.

"He is," Adam agreed. "And with good reason." He rubbed his hands up, then down his face before folding them in his lap. "But insider trading is a big deal. The police will be looking at this the way they look at any crime, crossing all *i's*, dotting all *t's*."

"You got it wrong. You dot your *i's* and cross your *t's*."

"Right..." The grin he gave me was crooked and warm. "Please excuse me. Part of me is still half asleep, Ms. Dodds."

I wished *I* was still half asleep, Jal's lean body wrapped

around me.

Looking away, I told myself not to think about it, not to wish or worry or wonder. I'd drive myself crazy that way.

"It will be okay," Adam said. "I'm a good lawyer, and Jal's an even better man."

I nodded.

Then they called his name, and he gave me a quick pat on the shoulder before disappearing through a set of double doors, leaving me to wait. Alone.

But I wasn't going anywhere without Jal.

Not again.

Chapter 2

Jal

I was pretty sure there wasn't a single experience on the entire planet as humiliating as being arrested. Except, of course, being arrested in front of the woman you'd been working your ass off to impress.

For the first twenty minutes or so, I kept trying to convince myself that it was all a bad dream. Or a mistake that would be remedied as soon as I stepped into the police station.

One of the uniformed officers walked alongside me, his hand gripping my inner arm like he thought I was going to bolt. I supposed plenty of people did, but I wasn't going to. I wasn't an idiot. I knew I was innocent, and I'd never gotten on the wrong side of anyone at the DA's office or the police force. The smart thing to do would be to wait it out and let my attorney fight my battle for me.

So while a part of me wanted to argue that I was innocent, I responded to their questions politely, even if it was only to say that I didn't want to discuss anything until I spoke to my lawyer. I didn't yell or threaten or even curse, though I was tempted. Fortunately, thanks to my mother and some of the business associates I'd worked with over the years, I'd had a lot of practice controlling my temper.

"Would you like some coffee, Mr. Lindstrom?"

I looked up to see one of the uniformed officers standing in the doorway. I'd been escorted to a plain white room several minutes ago, and I already felt like I was going to suffocate. It wasn't small, but there was only a table, two chairs, and the door. And, of course, the two-way mirror that took up a good portion of one wall.

"No, thank you." I was pleased to hear that I still sounded polite. "Will I be able to make a phone call soon?"

The officer nodded. "Yes, sir. Although if you're looking to call your lawyer, you can save the call. He's already here."

"He's here?" Relief rushed through me. Allie had gotten through to Adam. One of my hands was handcuffed to a hoop on the table, and it rattled when I pulled too hard on it, giving me a reminder that it was there. Still, I felt better than I had only a few seconds ago. "Good. That's...that's good to hear."

The cop nodded. "Still want to make a phone call?"

I considered it for a moment. If Adam were here, the only other person I could think of to call would be my father, but what in the hell would I tell him? I didn't actually know that much. They'd read me my rights, which had included telling me what I was being charged with, but I had no idea what possible evidence they could have since I was innocent.

As the door shut, I brought my free hand up and braced my elbow on the table. With my head in my hand, I tried to think everything through. The whole thing could've been a mistake, but that would be one serious ass mistake. It wasn't like I was a mid-level employee whose log-in information or phone records could've been switched around.

The next question, of course, was who had I pissed off? That was the only thing that made sense, really. I'd pissed somebody off, and they'd decided to go for the balls.

I was still trying to figure it out when the door opened abruptly, and two men in suits entered. One of them, I didn't know, but the other one? I knew him, and I was so relieved to see him that I surged up right. I would have hugged him – except I was restrained. The chain clinked, reminding me of the leash, and I gave it a disgusted look as I held my free hand out to Adam.

"Thanks so much for getting out here as quick as you did."

Adam didn't respond. Instead, he gave the cuffs a look of supreme disgust and turned toward the other man.

"Joseph, you and I go back a long way. I've always considered myself a fair man, and you as well."

Joseph lifted his chin. "I like to think so."

"Then why in the hell is a man arrested on *suspicion only* for a white collar crime sitting here handcuffed like a hardened criminal? He's barely even had a speeding ticket."

After giving Adam a less than friendly look, the detective came over and unlocked the cuffs.

"I'd like to speak to my client alone," Adam said.

Joseph scowled but didn't argue. A few seconds later, Adam and I were alone in the room.

I rubbed at my wrists and Adam came up, clapped me on the shoulder. "Damn, kid. You're having one hell of a day, aren't you?"

That was an understatement, to say the least. "Yeah. I guess Allie got a hold of you?"

He nodded. "Once we get this wrapped, she's out front waiting for you."

For a split second, a wash of embarrassment washed over me, and I wanted to tell him to go out there and make her leave, but other thoughts stepped up and took over. I hadn't done a damn thing wrong, and I wasn't going to act like I had.

And it would definitely be nice to see a friendly face when this was done.

"Okay." I met Adam's eyes. "What do we do next?"

Logically, I knew it didn't take forever, but it sure as hell felt like it.

By the time the cops agreed to let me go, I wanted to take an hour long shower, burn the clothes I was wearing, and down about half a bottle of aspirin.

Adam advised against the last part, but I only halfway heard him.

Allie was still here.

I'd lost track of time while Adam was dealing with all of the paperwork. In reality, it had only been about eight hours, though it'd felt like weeks. Adam told me that if the cops had wanted to, they could've kept me longer, but between who my family was and Adam's own connections, he'd managed to work some magic so that I was released after eight hours.

Eight hours.

And Allie had waited.

Crossing the floor to her, I pulled her to me and held on tight. I hadn't realized until that moment how afraid I'd been that this would ruin everything. She curled her arms around my neck and buried her face against my chest. Her body shook, and for the first time, I found myself thinking of her as delicate.

"It's okay," I murmured against her hair. "It's all going to be okay."

"I should be telling *you* that," she said, her voice muffled.

I kissed her temple. "Okay. You can tell me."

She didn't say anything. She just hugged me, tighter and tighter. "It was taking so *long*."

"I know." Smoothing my hand over her hair, I half turned us, giving my back to the people in the waiting room. It wasn't much privacy, but it was better than nothing. "Are you okay?"

"No," she answered honestly as she looked up at me. Her pale green eyes were rimmed with red.

I gave her a partial smile. "Me neither."

Adam cleared his throat politely, and I sighed, reminding myself that there were things I needed to deal with. Reluctantly, I pulled back, keeping one arm around Allie's shoulders as I met Adam's eyes over the top of her head.

He had a faint, curious smile on his face and more than a little speculation in his eyes. We were friends, and he knew about the engagement with Paisley, though I doubted he'd heard it was over. I'd have to deal with his personal questions, I had no doubt, but that would come later.

"I'm going to start digging around, see if I can get some hard data on this alleged witness, a copy of his statement…something." He kept it professional. That was one of the things I'd always liked about Adam – his ability to separate friendship and business. "And while the judge released you on your own recognizance, it would make things look…tidier if you would turn over your passport voluntarily. As a show of faith."

331

I didn't like the idea of doing anything that even suggested I shouldn't be trusted, but I could see Adam's point too. Handing over my passport meant I wouldn't try to avoid fighting the charges against me.

"Fine."

He covered a few more things, some of which I agreed to, while others I flat-out refused. All the while, Allie stayed at my side, her hand making soothing circles on my back, though I wasn't sure which of us she was reassuring more. Finally, when I couldn't take anymore, I told Adam that I'd discuss it more with him later and took Allie home.

Everything was too quiet.

For a few seconds, I stood near the door, keys clutched tightly in my hand while Allie moved around restlessly just a few feet away. The cops hadn't had a search warrant, so the place wasn't turned upside-down. In fact, it looked exactly the same as it had when I left. And the silence wasn't anything new, but for some reason, it grated on my nerves.

Tossing my keys down on the table near the door, I moved over to the entertainment center and hit a button. Music began to pump out.

Too fast. Too loud. Too vibrant.

I changed it to something lower. Soft jazz came spilling out, and I braced my hands against the wall, letting the music flow over me. The fading sun shone in through the windows, turning the living room shades of gold, warming my skin as I stood there.

Too many things going on inside my head.

None of this made sense, and I needed it to.

They'd asked me about accounts I didn't work on. Hell, I was the CEO of the entire company. I barely worked hands-on with any accounts anymore. Sure, I technically had access to everything, but any time I wanted to check out an employee's accounts, I went directly to them. I'd always run the business that way.

"Are you okay?" Allie stroked her hand up and down my back.

Reaching around blindly, I caught her wrist and tugged, pulling her into my arms.

"*Okay.*" Turning the word over in my mouth, I pondered the question. Such a simple one, so mundane and...ordinary. *Okay*. It was the type of question you'd ask anybody after they went through something rough, be it big or small. Somebody trips and you ask *are you okay?* Somebody loses a family member, and they take a few days off. Next time you see them, you ask, *are you okay?*

And if you get arrested for insider trading and fraud, somebody will ask, *Are you okay?*

"I don't know," I said truthfully.

"Should I..." She hesitated, then tried again. "Would you like me to leave? I can...well, I can catch the bus if you'd like to be alone."

"No." I shifted us so that I trapped her body between me and the wall. I didn't want her to leave. I needed her here, needed her presence to center me. "No. That's not what I want."

"What do you want?"

"For now, I only want this."

I might have gone on holding her for the rest of the night, taking some small comfort in her presence, but my landline rang. She let her hands slide from my back to my hips, but I didn't release her.

"Aren't you going to answer that?" she asked.

"No."

The call went to the antiquated answering machine I'd kept for the rare occasions I wanted to have a conversation on the record. A voice, strangely muffled and muted, came rolling out.

"Hello, Jal. I understand you've had a trying day."

Slowly, I lifted my head and looked over at the phone.

The voice continued, "You don't have anyone to blame but yourself. You made a promise, and I can't have you backing out of it. Should you decide to rectify the situation, I'm sure you'd find that your current problem would disappear. You'll want to hurry though. I'm not a patient man. And don't even think of

333

trying to fuck with me, Jal. In this game, I don't care what I have to do to get the win. I will always come out on top."

The line went dead just as I lunged for the phone.

Too late.

"What the ever-loving hell?" Allie breathed out.

I tried callback and got nothing but noise. Caller ID showed that the call had come from a blocked number and probably re-directed so it couldn't be traced. The robotic voice had sounded familiar, but I couldn't place it.

"No. He couldn't have..."

Allie's voice was shaking, and I turned around, immediately concerned. Her face had gone ashen, her eyes wide. "Allie?"

She looked at me blindly, not truly seeing me.

"It's me," she whispered.

Shaking my head, I went back to her, put my hands on her shoulders. "What are you talking about?"

"It's my fault. That call...my dad..." She cleared her throat, trying to speak and failing. "That call...it was from my father. Kendrick."

"How do you know? The voice was all muffled and synthetic."

"I've heard him saying that phrase before – ...*in this game, I don't care what I have to do to get the win. I will always come out on top.*

Allie turned away and started to pace, smoothing her hands restlessly over her hair. Her gaze darted to the phone and then to me. She started to speak, but stopped, chewing on her lip. I wanted to take her in my arms, tell her that her father wouldn't do something like this, but the sick feeling in the pit of my stomach acknowledged that this was exactly the sort of thing Kendrick Hedges would've done.

It's my father for sure. He's doing it because of us – because of *me*. It's my fault." Allie's eyes swam with tears.

"No."

Catching her in my arms again, I pulled her up against me. "No." I shook my head and said it again. "No. He's doing it because of me. Because I broke things off with Paisley. None of this is your fault."

Pressing my brow to hers, I closed my eyes. I'd always gotten along with Paisley's father, more than her mother anyway,

334

but I knew he'd never been above twisting things to get what he wanted. I just never imagined that he'd go this far.

"I should go," she said, her voice wooden.

Something like panic gripped my heart. I couldn't deal if she left. She was the only thing keeping me sane. "No. I want you to stay."

"But–"

I nipped at her lower lip, and when she gasped, I took her mouth. I didn't hold back, didn't try to be gentle. I poured every ounce of my need and desire into the kiss. After a moment, her arms circled around my neck, and she pressed her body against mine. Slowly walking her backward, I shifted and guided until the couch was just behind her, then I lowered us both so that I was stretched out over her.

"Stay," I said, sliding my lips down the elegant line of her neck. "Please stay, Allie. I want you to stay. I need you to stay."

Chapter 3

Allie

Stay...I want you to stay. I need you to stay.

The words wound through my head as Jal caught my hands and dragged them over my head. When he stared down at me, our gazes met and locked. I nodded without a moment's hesitation.

He pushed himself up on his knees. His eyes never left mine as he reached for the buttons of my shirt, freeing them one at a time. Once it lay open, he moved lower, going to work on the snap of my jeans and working them down.

I'd had Eli take me to the salon so I could grab the bag of extra clothes I kept there. I hadn't wanted to go home and risk having to try to explain to my mother why I was running back out again. After the third hour sitting at the station, I'd been glad I'd gone through the extra trouble. Now, however, I was more than ready to get out of my clothes.

My jeans were still wrapped around one ankle when I started tearing at his clothes with hungry, desperate hands. I managed to get the shirt off, but I was still working on trying to shove down his jeans when his self-control snapped.

Catching my hips in his hands, he urged me flat on my back even as he frantically rolled on the condom. "Allie?"

"Please."

He drove into me hard and fast, and it was everything I needed at that moment. His teeth scraped a line down my neck, and I shuddered. I dug my fingers into his hair and pulled him toward me for a kiss. His tongue delved between my lips even as he thrust into me and I moaned.

He swiveled his hips, lifting up just enough so that each stroke had the base of his cock dragging back and forth over my clitoris. The oxygen in my lungs seemed to dwindle down to nothing, and I couldn't breathe. Every weak breath I did manage to draw in smelled of him. He flooded my senses. When I licked my lips, I tasted him.

He lifted up, light blue eyes searing into mine and I bit his collarbone. He swore, slamming into me hard enough to drive a scream from my mouth. The next thrust knocked me breathless.

The one after that made my vision spark and my body shake as I came. His eyes darkened, and he whispered my name as he came too.

A moment later, he pulled out, all sticky and wet against my thigh for the briefest second before he was disposing of the condom. Then he stood, stripped off his clothes, yanked off my jeans, and swept me into his arms. He carried me up the stairs and into his bedroom.

"I can't think straight when it comes to you," he confessed as he stretched me out on the bed. "I never think to slow down and do things right." He cupped my breasts in his hands, plumped them together, and eased lower until he could kiss one nipple, then the other. "More. I want more…"

"Take it," I breathed. "Take everything."

He wrapped his lips around my nipple, tugging and biting on the sensitive flesh until it was swollen and throbbing. Then he moved to the other side, sucking and licking until I was writhing beneath him. His hand slid down my stomach, and I opened my legs for him, desperate for his touch.

I whimpered as his fingers grazed my overly sensitive flesh, but when two fingers hooked inside me, I arched up against him, crying out. I didn't think I'd ever get enough of him.

I'd always enjoyed sex, but it had been like any other appetite. Feed it and the hunger stopped.

Except when it came to him.

"Roll over," he ordered.

Then, without waiting for me to do it, he rolled me over and pulled me up, wedging one knee between mine and forcing me to open, to yield. And I wanted to. I wanted to submit to him, to let him take control.

337

His hands held me steady as he slid inside me again. I moaned as he filled me as my body conformed to fit his like a glove. He moved in and out a couple times and then pressed his thumb against my ass. I whimpered at the brief flare of pain and he stopped. His hand went down to where we were joined and one of his fingers slipped inside. Then it was back, slick with our combined arousal, our natural lubricant. When he pushed his thumb against me the second time, it slipped in more easily, with little burn. I shuddered as he began to ride me, twisting his thumb in and out of my ass in time with his strokes.

"So perfect," he murmured. "You're so fucking perfect, Allie. So beautiful."

He began to move faster as my muscles shivered and strained. Hot little pinwheels of color blazed behind my eyes as I came, forcing me to close my eyes as waves of pleasure washed over me. Sagging forward, I lost the ability to think clearly, to form any sort of coherent thought. Nothing else mattered, except that pleasure, except that bite of pain that made everything more intense.

He was still rocking against me, the twitching fading from his semi-erect cock when I finally relaxed against him.

"When you play the game, you play to win. Now, that might not always make you the most popular person in the world, but when you win, it doesn't matter."

I nodded, not looking at my father as I finished going over the papers he'd put in front of me. I didn't know what they were, not exactly, but I had a pretty good idea.

The name of a company caught my eye, and I frowned.

He must have been waiting for me to notice something, because when I looked up, he was right there.

"What did you see?"

"I...I'm not sure. This company." I tapped the name. "They

sound familiar, but you've never dealt with them before."

"Yes, I have." Now he smiled, looking pleased with himself.

Not with me. With himself.

*"You've only been given so much data, Allie. You're young –
brilliant, but young – and I can't exactly trust you with highly
confidential data, now can I? It's unethical. These people expect
me to be the one looking at their confidential financial
information. Not my sixteen-year-old daughter."*

But it's fine for me to offer stock advice, *I thought sourly.*
*He was right though. Even if it had been the pretty, perfect
Paisley offering the advice, he wouldn't let her do it for long
before the novelty wore off.*

*He had to be the smart one, the winner. Even if he was only
playing against his daughter.*

*He might teach me how to play the game, and how to win,
but he would never let me beat him. Nor did I expect to. He'd hold
back enough information to make sure that never happened.*

*There was a knock at the door, and Diamond came strolling
in.*

*When she saw me, she stiffened, her shoulders going back,
her mouth tightening in a line like she'd just scented something
foul. Kendrick subtly stepped between us, although whether it was
as a shield or merely a buffer, I didn't know.*

Or, rather I didn't want to know.

*"There's a gentleman downstairs looking for you. Heath has
attempted multiple times to send him away, but he refuses to
leave."* Diamond looked pissed, but I was pretty sure that was
because she was playing messenger. *"He says to tell you that he's
ready to play ball. I assume you know what that means."*

*From where I was sitting, I could only see my father in
profile, but I had a clear enough view of his eyes that I could
make out the avid glint there. Yeah, he knew what it meant.*

*He started to turn toward the door, but then stopped and
gestured at me. "Come on, Allie. I'll show you how it's done."*

*Diamond stepped between us before I could decide what I
wanted to do. "You can't be serious, Kendrick."*

"This doesn't concern you, Diamond."

"It damn well does." She sniffed, clearly pissed. *"I'm your
wife, and you want to take your* bastard *to a business meeting.
Keeping her around is bad enough. I will not let you humiliate me*

in this way."

I flinched, blood rushing to my cheeks at her harsh words, but neither Kendrick nor Diamond noticed. I should be used to it. Should expect it.

Tears burned my eyes, and I fought them back.

It wasn't like they were wrong, anyway. I was Kendrick Hedge's bastard.

Twisting the pencil I'd been using around and around, I waited to see if he was going give in and change his mind. He usually did when Diamond confronted him about anything to do with me.

Except, this time, he looked at me and gestured for me to follow. "Come along, Allie. You should follow up on this and see if you understand."

As I followed, I could feel Diamond's gaze digging holes into my back with the intensity of that glare. I was still trying to figure out why Kendrick had stood up to his wife, so it took me a little while to figure out what was going on with my father's visitor.

I'd been introduced as an intern, which was his usual cover for me whenever he'd asked me to come by the office. "It's an inner city project," he'd say. "Low income students who show promise, and I try to help out..."

And they'd praise him for being such an upstanding citizen.

I might not have lived in the best part of the city, but my family wasn't low income or inner city.

But he had to make sure there was no possible connection to me, so the truth didn't matter.

This was no different, and after a few moments of the usual niceties that preceded a meeting like this, I watched as my father got down to brass tacks.

"Bill, I'm going to level with you. You've got nothing to offer in this deal but the company. Rushing Limited is about to fail–"

My brain clicked on, and the figures I'd been looking at earlier started to run through my mind. Figures, names, facts.

Rushing, LTD.

Slowly, I looked up at my father, then over at the man. My mind started to spin, then whirl. Various phone calls I'd heard, notes I'd seen. I started putting the pieces together even as I took in new information from the conversation my father was having.

The meeting ended without me saying a word, and I dutifully followed my father back up into his office.

"And that's how you play the game," he said, closing the door, and turning to me with a satisfied smile.

"You cheated."

He blinked, looking caught off-guard by the disapproval in my voice. While I'd always understood the truth of the relationship between my parents, I'd tried very hard to give him at least some measure of leniency.

"I heard you talking to somebody on the phone a few days ago. I saw some of the notes. You've been lying to that guy – you just lied to his face. You're not going to restructure his company. You're going in, liquidating everything, and firing everybody. That's not winning."

His face hardened, and he crossed his arms over his chest. "The game is about making money, Allie. And in the end, if you've made it, then you've won."

It wasn't a dream. Not really. It was a memory.

What happened with Rushing, LTD fell in that gray shade of legal, and it still haunted me in ways I can't explain.

In the end, it had been the echoes of that afternoon that had finally pushed me and my father so completely apart.

My father was still one of the top execs at the investment firm, but before he'd *slowed down*, he'd helped out friends on the side. Rushing, LTD had been about helping out a friend. And Bill Rush, the man I'd met that afternoon, had gotten in the way. My father's friend had wanted a particular technology that Rushing, LTD was developing, and Bill Rush hadn't wanted to sell it.

Rush hadn't been prepared for the cut-throat business world he'd waded into, and a hostile takeover had happened before he realized it. My father had been behind it.

A couple weeks after that meeting, I'd sat on the steps in the grand foyer and read about Rush's suicide. While I'd been

341

reading, the family had come parading in. Kendrick and Diamond, followed by the two perfect princesses, Mallory and Paisley. They were all dressed in elegant black and laughing, chatting about things that didn't matter, fresh from the funeral. Well, Mallory hadn't been laughing, but it was clear that she hadn't known the truth behind what happened.

I'd been wearing jeans and a faded hoodie from my public high school on the other side of Philadelphia.

My mind slid back there, playing that scene out again.

Diamond took one look at me and sniffed, then glared at Kendrick. "It's bad enough she feels she has the right to walk around this house like she belongs here, but must she dress like such a waif?"

"I'm sorry if I don't meet your standards," I said, interrupting before my father could say anything. "What should I wear? A maid's uniform, maybe?" Shifting my attention to my father, I swallowed hard around the knot in my throat. "If I'd known you were going to his funeral, I would have met you there. After all, I helped you figure out some of the approach, didn't I?"

Kendrick looked at Diamond, then his other daughters. He spoke to them, but while the girls left, Diamond didn't. Finally, he looked at me. "Allie, this isn't the time."

"He committed suicide." I pressed the subject. "You told him you'd keep his company together. You lied, and he killed himself. Was that *part of the game?"*

He flinched. I saw it. So he did feel some guilt at least.

"Young lady, you will not *speak to him—"*

Kendrick touched Diamond's arm, and she fell silent. "Allie, this is an ugly world."

"His world was just fine until you tore it apart!" My voice cracked. "Did you have to use me *to do it?"*

He'd been teaching me about the stock market for years, and for the past few months, he'd actually been asking my advice, *praising me when I got things right.* You're a natural, *he'd told me.*

"You made me *part of this."*

He scowled. "You're blowing this out of proportion, Allie. You're not seeing things in the right light."

"He's dead. He blew his damn head off. *I don't think you're seeing it in* any *light."*

342

I wasn't supposed to leave until eight, but I couldn't stay there anymore.

He reached out to touch my arm, and I took a step away. "Don't touch me. You make me sick. All of you." I looked at him and then at Diamond. "Did you all stand around chatting at his visitation, sipping wine, and talking about how sad it was...then making a date with friends to get together and have coffee? It's your fucking fault!"

Diamond slapped me.

She would have done it again, but Kendrick caught her wrist. "That's enough."

"She will not speak about us like that. She has no right. She's not a part of this family."

"You're right." Shaking my head, so furious inside I thought I might puke, I touched my heated cheek and then looked at my father. "I'm not. And I'm fucking glad that I'm not. You're all just a bunch of shallow hypocrites."

I turned and walked out the door. He called my name, but I ignored him.

When you play the game, you play to win.

Jal lay on his belly, face in the pillow, all but dead to the world. His cornsilk blond hair was mussed, the muscles in his face relaxed. I let my gaze run over the smooth skin and muscles of his back even as my mind ran over what the dream-memory had brought up.

What happened to Bill Rush had gotten to my father more than he'd shown that day. There'd been an announcement in the business section a month after I walked out. Kendrick Hedges had decided on a partial retirement.

Three months after that, the "restructuring" of Rushing, LTD was formalized, and to my surprise, it was actually closer to what I'd heard my father promise Bill Rush. I only knew about that because the news clipping was sent to me along with a letter from my father containing a few specifics not mentioned in the article, and a check for a thousand dollars.

He'd written a lot that first year. Sometimes I wrote back just to acknowledge that I'd received his letters. But I never forgot what he'd said on the day of that meeting.

When you play the game, you play to win.

I walked over to the closet and pulled out one of Jal's shirts. I smiled as the soft cotton slid over my skin, and I took a deep breath, giving myself a moment to appreciate the scent of him.

Out in the living room, I sought out the answering machine and played his message.

In this game, I don't care what I have to do to get the win. I will always come out on top.

Apparently, my father hadn't actually learned his lesson with Bill Rush, because he still treated all of this – treated people's lives – like they were part of a game.

I'd probably played it five times over by the time Jal made his way down and found me. Clad in a pair of jeans and nothing else, he looked good enough to distract me for a moment. He wrapped his arms around my waist and pulled me back against him.

"You can't let this eat you up. It's not your fault," he said softly.

"No, it's not." Resting my head against his shoulder, I closed my eyes and let myself have a minute to bask in the heat of his body, the strength of his arms. Then, I turned so I could look him in the face. "But I'm sure as hell not going to let you suffer for the shit my father and his family have pulled."

Chapter 4

Jal

Allie was hunched over my computer, a determined look on her face as she worked.

And I was seriously considering hiring her. But not because I had some sort of fantasy about bending her over my desk at work...well, not only because of that.

She was fucking brilliant.

"I told you, I don't keep anything on my laptop that could compromise any of my accounts. Too much of a security risk."

Not that it'd stopped her from trying. All morning. Not just searching my accounts. She'd been searching the stock market, looking for something, anything, that could give her a hint about what her father was doing.

Hours of almost non-stop work, and now, she was getting a headache, I could see it.

"I know." She groaned and rubbed at the back of her neck. Shaking her head, she leaned back and pressed the heels of her hands against her eyes for a minute. "I need to access the system from the firm. That's the only way I'll be able to find what I need."

"We can go in tomorrow."

"Today," she insisted.

"Tomorrow," I said firmly. "I'll have one of my top accountants meet you, and you all can start looking for..." I shook my head. "Whatever it is you want to find. Maybe you should give up on styling hair and try your hand at forensic accounting."

She gave me a half-hearted smile. "Yeah, right."

One of these days, she'd accept the fact of how amazing she was.

I leaned over her and reached for they keyboard to close things down. She caught my wrist before I could, her eyes narrowing. "Hey, I'm working."

"No. You're done. I know you're trying to help."

She tugged on my wrist again, and I missed the icon I needed, hitting a folder on the desktop instead.

Bending over her, I kissed her. She bit my lower lip, and my blood raced south. Under my hand, I felt keys clacking, and I shifted my hand away from the keyboard, bracing it. "You're done working for now."

"Maybe…" She smiled against my lips. "Maybe you could distract me, and I'll forget about it."

That sounded good to me.

But as I straightened up, her gaze slid past me and fixed on the screen. For a second, her gaze came back to mine.

Then it went back to the screen, and she kept staring.

"Who…" She licked her lips. I might have bent down and followed the same path with my own tongue, but the expression in her eyes had me pausing. "Jal, that picture. Who is that?"

I was wrong.

We ended up going into the firm after all.

Now, as I stood in the office belonging to one of my execs, I couldn't help but marvel at how much my life had changed in just a few short weeks. I'd gone from being excited about fatherhood while loathing the idea of marriage, to knowing that I did eventually want children, but only with the woman poking around on the computer in hopes of breaking the password.

"I'm not a hacker," Allie finally said, throwing up her hands.

"I can't figure out what to do. I barely knew the guy, other than to say he was tight with Kendrick. Had this stupid poodle. Loved that weird thing. Mistress FiFi."

She looked at me, her eyes widening before she bent back over the computer. A few seconds later, she whooped.

"Don't tell me it was Mistress FiFi." I shook my head. "No dumbass would use that."

"It's Mistress FiFi…backward." She grinned.

"Shit." It occurred to me that maybe I should come down on the guy for being a dumbass, but either we were intruding on his privacy for no reason, or it was a good thing he *was* a dumbass. Still, I made a mental note to send out a company-wide email reminding people about the guidelines for passwords.

"Why exactly are you so sure he's somehow involved in this?" I asked as I moved to stand behind her.

"I've just got a feeling." Her mouth twisted in a sour frown as she navigated the mouse around, clicking on the email. She read a few, shaking her head, then continued, "He used to work with my…with Kendrick. He was let go. I only know about it because Diamond raised hell about him coming over to the house once. There was something shady about the circumstances under which he left the firm, but Kendrick said he had his uses."

"That doesn't make sense." Arms crossed over my chest, I looked around the room. "My background checks are thorough. If there were something that would have caused him to be terminated, it would have shown on a background check."

"Only if he was caught." She glanced up at me. "And this was like fifteen years ago. I just never forgot the man's face. He looks like a rat."

He did.

The office belonged to a Gary Hammerstein, and Hammerstein most definitely looked like a rat, a narrow, sharp face, hair thinning on top and a grayish pink complexion. His eyes were small and beady. I remembered that the few times I'd met him, he'd always had a nervous, jittery sort of air, but I'd been told he was good at what he did. A lot of people who made their living behind computers weren't that socially adept.

My eyes landed on the one personal touch in the office. "Son of a bitch." Scowling, I grabbed the picture and showed it to Allie. "Do you know this guy too?"

Allie glanced at it and shook her head. "No. Should I?"

"He left the company where your dad works a few years ago. I hired him away, actually. Kendrick took it with pretty good humor, but now…" I fought the urge to throw the picture against the wall. "He's the one who recommended Hammerstein."

Allie lapsed into silence when I started to pace, and the only noise was that of her fingers on the keyboard for several minutes.

"He keeps his passwords saved on the computer so I can get into everything, but I'm not finding anything," Allie said finally. "But…"

I turned and looked at her.

She leaned back, her lips pursed as she stared at the computer. "He deletes his internet history. Completely. For somebody who's lazy enough to use his dog's name for a password, and doesn't log out of his work email, that seems a little…odd."

Odd. Yeah. I'd say suspicious.

"I'm calling my tech man in."

Letting her head drop back to rest on the padded, pillowed chair, she studied me. "Is that legal?"

"He signed a contract when he came to work here. As the CEO, if I have any reason to suspect suspicious or possibly illegal activity, I can search the offices, computers, rip up the damn carpet if I want. And he knows it." Phone already in hand, I stared at the computer as though that alone would force it to divulge its secrets. "And the bastard knows it. That's why he's wiping the internet history."

Chapter 5

Allie

Sunshine woke me up.

Lying on my side, I stared at the bright, thin line as it slowly moved along the slit in the carpet.

Jal told me that he expected to get something from Carlo today.

Carlo was his tech man.

I met him last night, and we'd lingered around the office for a while. Jal had called for pizza, and I'd gone to the market on the corner to grab some beer while Carlo tried to coax more information out of the computer.

Nothing ever really disappears, he said. *It just hides really, really well.* Then he'd grinned. *I always rocked at hide and seek.*

Carlo hadn't unearthed too much before we left, but he had managed to find out that Hammerstein was accessing an email account that wasn't work-approved. People could email whoever they wanted if they used their own devices on breaks and at lunch, but anything sent on company time or regarding business in general had to go through the firm's server.

When I'd asked why, Jal was the one who answered, "I don't want any shady deals going on here. The firm's servers are designed to monitor for possible breaches in the firm's ethics, but we can't monitor communications sent through third party platforms. It's all in the contract every employee signs."

"Breaches...like insider tips, that sort of thing."

Jal hadn't responded verbally, but the raised brow had made

it clear enough.

I wondered if Carlo had found anything, specifically something to link Hammerstein to my father.

I wondered if it even mattered because, in my gut, I already knew what was going on.

I didn't know when I'd made the conscious decision, but the plan was already coming together in my head, and I knew what I was going to do even before I really accepted it.

In under twenty minutes, I was out of bed, showered and wearing the last of my clean clothes. I didn't have time to mess with my damp hair, so I just pulled it back into a loose braid and threw it over my shoulder.

I wasn't out to win a beauty contest.

The one thing I hadn't quite planned out was just how I'd get in to see my father. If he kept the same schedule as he had years ago, he'd be working from home this morning, which meant I was going to the house rather than his office. Unfortunately, that left a lot of unknown variables.

It was possible one of the servants would answer the door, and just as possible they'd get my father without mentioning my name to Diamond. Hell, there was a good chance that there weren't any servants left who knew I had any connection to the family at all.

It was also equally possible that Diamond would answer the door. She liked to make a lousy joke – *I occasionally answer the door or even fix meals for Kendrick and myself.* Like that was going to win her a medal.

I had no idea what I would do if Diamond answered the door, although it would probably involve causing a scene because I wasn't leaving without seeing Kendrick. He was going to fix what he'd done, or he wouldn't like the consequences.

I was prepared to do whatever I had to. Prepared for almost

anything.

I had the cab drop me off a quarter of a mile from the house so I could use the time walking to compose myself for what was coming. I walked around the car parked in the big U just as my father and Gary Hammerstein rounded the side of the house. Both of them had big cigars in their mouths, and they were grinning, wide, pleased, smug smiles of satisfaction that made me want to punch them.

When they saw me, my father's smile faltered. Hammerstein didn't recognize me, which wasn't surprising. I'd just been an intern with the wrong shade of skin when he'd met me before.

As Kendrick reached up to tug the cigar from his mouth, I looked from him to Hammerstein, weighing my options. Hammerstein still looked pleased with himself.

For all I knew, he thought I was some reward my father had planned for him. That thought snapped the last of my control.

"How much did Kendrick pay you to set up Jal Lindstrom?"

Hammerstein took a tiny step back, eyes wheeling around for the faintest second. Surprise flashed across his face. It was gone in an instant, but I'd seen it. A hearty laugh escaped him a second later, although my father was still watching me, taking everything in.

"Excuse me?" He smiled at me and then looked over at Kendrick. "Is this new girl working here at the house?"

"No. I'm not a *new girl*," I snapped before my father could respond. "What did you do...send the cops some bullshit tip? No, that couldn't have been it. He got arrested, so there had to be more than that."

"Allie." Finally, Kendrick spoke.

"I'll talk to you in a minute." Lip curled, I stared Hammerstein down. "I hope you did a good job wiping the history on your computer at work. A tech's looking through it as we speak."

All the blood drained from his face, and he shot Kendrick a panicked look.

Now my father looked a little unsettled, his gaze flicking to me before returning to Hammerstein. "She's bluffing. Look, you go on. I'll be in touch, okay?"

Hammerstein didn't wait another second, bumping into me with enough force to half-knock me over as he thundered toward the car parked nearby.

"What a charmer," I said as my father walked toward me. "Long time, no see, *Dad*."

"Allie." Voice stiff, he nodded at me.

"You don't look too thrilled about my dropping in."

I jammed my hands into the pockets of my hoodie. It was one I'd gotten from the school where I'd taken my classes for my aesthetician's license, and I watched as my father's gaze dropped, lingering on the logo. His mouth tightened. He'd told me more than once – in letters, of course – that he couldn't understand why I'd wasted my brain on cutting hair. I hadn't bothered to try to explain my reasoning. He never would've understood.

"It's always lovely to see you, Allie." His voice softened a little, and he took a step closer. "I've missed you. I've told you before, if you'd like to meet for dinner or lunch…"

"Yeah, just don't come around here," I said caustically. He opened his mouth to argue, and I held up a hand. "We've had this talk, and I'm not in the mood to have it again. And it's not why I'm here." Rocking back on my heels, I lifted my chin. "I know what you're doing to Jal."

His eyes widened slightly. "Pardon me?"

"I'm going to assume that Diamond told you that she saw me dancing with Jal. He came and talked to you. I know that, too, so don't try to play dumb. And I know that Paisley pretended to be pregnant to get him to propose."

Now Kendrick's face was an ugly, apoplectic shade of red. "Allie, now listen. I've indulged you quite a bit, but I–"

"Don't." I held up a hand. "Don't you dare start this shit with me. You gave me money every now and then, and you taught me how to play with stocks. But you never walked *me* to school. Matter of fact, you and Diamond went out of your way to keep me out of the schools around here. You claimed it was because I wouldn't be comfortable in any of those places, remember? Christmas time came around? It wasn't *you* who put presents under the tree. That was my mother. When I fell down, Mama was the one who was there. Tyson has been there. You never acted like my dad then, so don't even try to pull that card now."

He sucked in a breath.

"What? Surprised I called you on it?" Giving him a cool look, I let my eyes play over the house, grand as it was. So lovely.

And it had never been anything resembling a home. I'd been nothing but miserable here.

"You're not going to do this to Jal," I said after I'd taken another breath.

"I don't know what you're talking about." Kendrick's voice was stiff, shoulders rigid. As he tugged at the cuffs on his sweater, his eyes drifted past my shoulder, then down the drive as though he was seeking assistance.

"You do." If he thought I would let this go, he really didn't know me at all. "For the record, I wasn't bluffing when I said Hammerstein's computer was being searched. Apparently, your buddy used a third-party email program which is a big no-no at Jal's firm. He'll figure out who he was emailing by the end of the day – and what they were talking about." I wasn't quite sure how accurate that was, but the sweat beading on my father's lip had me feeling reckless. When he looked at me, I shrugged. "Hey, don't glare at me. I'm not the one who pulled this schmuck move. I wasn't *playing the game*."

"Allie, that's enough," he said sharply.

"Is it? Are you going to *win* this time?"

"For fuck's sake, it won't even go to court!" Kendrick snapped. "He just needs to pull his head out of his ass and get back with Paisley, okay?"

"No." Shaking my head, I crossed my arms over my chest. "It's not okay. You can't fuck with people's lives like this. He doesn't love her."

"Love doesn't even come into this. It's a fucking business–" He clamped his mouth shut.

"What?" I barely managed to get the word out. I wasn't even sure he heard me. Taking another step closer, I said it again, but he'd turned away, taking a few erratic steps forward. "What are you talking about?" I shouted at his back.

"It doesn't concern you, Allie!" He turned around and faced me, gesturing to my hoodie. "You cut hair at a shop downtown. If you'd gone to school and made something of yourself, then maybe you could have come to work for me. Maybe *then* I would tell you, but you're just a damn hairdresser!"

I was surprised at how little his comments hurt. In fact, all they did was piss me off.

"You'll tell me what the hell you're talking about, or I'll take

353

a trip to the nearest newspaper office and tell them how you set Jal up. And I'll tell them that you're my father. You know as well as I do, they'll start digging."

"Allie..."

"I'll do it."

He looked defeated. "It would be good for him too. We talked about merging the families – forming our own firm. We've even got backers. But without Paisley and Jal being married, it won't happen. And..." He swallowed, looking pained. "Some of the backers fronted me some money already."

I buried my face in my hands. I wanted to shake him. Hard. Instead, I just took in a couple of deep breaths then lowered my hands and stared at him.

"See?" He gave me a pleading look. "It's a hard place to be in, but the best thing for everybody would be for this marriage to just happen."

"No." Shaking my head, I said, "It's the best thing for *you*. Call off your dogs, Kendrick. I don't know if you've got dirt on somebody at the police department or what, but however you made this happen? Make it *un*-happen."

I cut around him and headed for the driveway. He shouted after me to stop, to not be foolish. In response, I turned around and pulled out the phone I'd kept tucked in the pocket of my hoodie the entire time.

Staring at him, I slid my finger across the screen, then hit the *play* button.

Our voices came rolling out.

The whole fucking conversation.

He was still a few yards away, so I turned up the volume. "Probably not admissible in a real court, but the court of public opinion?" I shrugged. "I'm not sure which your high society buddies would find more distasteful. Framing someone for insider trading, or having a bastard daughter with the black nanny."

His head slumped.

"Call off the dogs," I repeated. "You've only got a few days to fix this before I blow this whole thing wide open."

Without another look at the man whose DNA I carried, I turned and walked away.

354

Chapter 6

Allie

I caught the bus to Tao's rather than getting another taxi. It was longer, and I had to change buses halfway, but the longer ride gave me time to think.

I'd meant every word I said back at my father's house, but if I was going to carry out the threat – no, I corrected myself – the *promise* I had made to him, I needed to talk to my mother. While Tyson knew the circumstances surrounding my conception, no one else did. If I had to follow through and expose Kendrick as my father, it would mean exposing my mother as well.

I hated the thought of doing it. Mom despised drama. The last thing she'd ever wanted in life was to be the other woman. The mistress. My father had played on Mom's emotions when she was young and naïve, and she'd fallen for him. Then he'd gone and fallen for her, too, though I doubt his feelings for her had ever surpassed his own self-love.

I had no doubt Diamond and even my father would tell a different story, but I knew how people in their social circle worked. They'd claim to not believe the rumors, and agree that it all had to be vindictiveness on my part, but they'd talk about it behind closed doors, spread whispers of how they'd always known.

I was counting on that to make sure my father did what I wanted, and while I did have a twinge of guilt about the effect this would have on my mother, I had no such feelings in regards to the Hedges.

The very fact that my father thought it was okay to sit by while his wife and daughter tricked Jal into a marriage showed just what kind of man he was. That he'd framed Jal in an attempt to blackmail desired behavior told me that the years had taught him nothing.

He didn't care that he could ruin an innocent man's life, as long as he got what he wanted. As long as he won.

But I'd had enough. I spent too much of my life walking away from the fight. If anyone was worth fighting for, it was Jal.

He was mine, and I'd be damned if I let my father ruin him.

Mind made up, I walked up the stairs to the front of Tao's building and hit the buzzer. He didn't answer right away, but that didn't surprise me. He'd most likely been out late last night and had probably only been in bed for a couple hours. It took two more attempts before he finally answered, mumbling something completely unintelligible.

Pushing the button again, I said, "It's me. Let me up. I need your help. It's important."

"Good morning to you too, sweetheart," Tao grumbled. He was so not a morning person. "Why yes, I did have a good night. You? Yeah, I'd love some coffee."

I snorted. "Sure, I had a good night. Glad to hear you did too. That means you got laid. So did I. Let me in and we can compare notes while I make you that coffee." I could use some myself.

That woke him up a little bit. "Really? You never want to talk about it."

He buzzed me in, and by the time I got up to his apartment, he was standing at the door wearing a pair of low slung-jeans and rubbing tired eyes. I gave him a quick kiss on the cheek.

He caught one look at my face and shook his head. "I should have known you were bullshitting me." He sighed. "That look on your face is all business. You're not here to compare notes on anything. What do you want? And you're making the damn coffee."

"Yes, I'm making the damn coffee." I offered him a smile as I slid past him on my way into the kitchen. He followed along behind me and dropped down at the table, pillowing his head on his arm. "Don't go back to sleep, Tao. I told you, I need your help. I have to go talk to my mom about something, and I need

356

moral support."

"Your mom is a doll. You don't need moral support from me. Now if I was going to talk to *my* mom? I'd need moral support – an army of it." He mumbled more into the table than anything else, but I didn't let it concern me.

He was upright – mostly – and talking. Once I got some caffeine in him, he'd be good to go.

When I set his *I'm so sexy* mug in front of him, he lifted his head. After a few more seconds, he took a drink and then another. I watched the sleep leave his eyes.

"Moral support, huh?"

"Yeah." I poured myself a cup in my usual leprechaun mug and settled into the seat across from him.

He finished the coffee and poured another cup. "Okay. Give me a few minutes to shower and change." He paused and scrutinized me. "You did get laid. You also look like you're about ready to kick some ass."

"I already did that." Blowing out a breath, I looked away. "Now I need to go tell my mom about it."

"You didn't go and put Paisley in the hospital did you?" He looked both interested and wary. He'd never actually met my half-sister, but he knew enough about her to understand why violence would've been a possibility. "I don't need to go sell my sweet ass to get you bail money, do I?"

"No." A quick laugh escaped me, and I shook my head. "While she might've deserved it, she isn't the one I had a confrontation with."

Tao's eyes widened, and I could see curiosity warring with his desire for a shower.

"Come on," I said as I stood. "I'll tell you all about it while you're showering."

He wiggled his eyebrows at me as he gave me a lecherous look. I smacked his arm.

"This is not a booty call. Let's go."

It was strange, I thought as I followed Tao to his bathroom. The fact that Tao and I wouldn't be having sex again didn't bother me at all. We were back to a normal friendship, and if I had anything to say about it, that's where we'd stay.

My nerves had me practically twitching in my seat during the twenty-minute bus ride from Tao's apartment to my house. Tao reached over and put his hand on top of mine. "You're making me a little nuts, Allie. Calm down."

That was easy for him to say. He wasn't contemplating a move that would most likely humiliate my mother.

Turning my head, I looked out the window as the bus took the corner. Our stop was coming up so I nudged him, but he was already moving. I followed after him, grabbing the handle to steady myself when the bus lurched and jerked.

Once we exited the bus, I took a deep breath. Public transportation was a lot cheaper than trying to manage a car, but sometimes the miasma of too many bodies packed in a small space, combined with those who didn't quite understand basic hygiene made me wish I could afford to drive myself.

We started up the street, and I shoved my hands into my pockets to keep from fidgeting. Neither one of us spoke, and I was glad for that. I didn't need Tao to distract me. I just needed his solid, steadying presence. Sometimes he could come off as a bit flaky, but I knew he was a rock at his center.

We climbed the stairs to the front door, and I stopped for a second to take a breath, steadying myself.

"Hey, if she kills you, can I have dibs on whatever I want from your room?" he asked as I unlocked the door.

"Sure." I rolled my eyes. "You get first crack at my wardrobe."

"That's not fair," he said. "You've got a better figure than I do."

I stuck my tongue out at him, then took his hand and tugged him along with me as I started to search for my mother. She hadn't been scheduled to work today, so I knew she'd most likely be here.

She wasn't anywhere in the house so I headed outside. It wasn't a surprise to find her in the small garden in the backyard. This was her favorite spot to be, and now that the weather didn't totally suck, she was happy to putter around on her days off.

In a hoodie and faded denim capris, she didn't look that much older than me, and when she smiled, she looked even closer to my age. She was one of those women who'd never need cosmetic surgery to have people thinking she was a decade younger than she really was.

"Hey." I sat down cross legged across from her while Tao took one of the nearby lawn chairs.

Mom stripped off her gloves and pushed her hair back from her face. *"Did you two have breakfast?"*

I ignored the question because I was far too nervous to eat. *"I need to talk to you. It's kind of important."* My heart skipped a few beats as her steady gaze raised from my hands to meet my eyes.

She laid the gloves in the garden basket at her side, cocking her head. *"Judging by the look on your face, I would say it's more than kind of important. Is everything okay?"*

"I'm fine." I licked my lips and fought to urge to look at Tao for support. I'd essentially practiced my speech on him, but... *"It's just...well, I went to see Kendrick today."*

Her lips thinned into a flat line. I knew she still had feelings, of a sort, for the man who'd fathered me. I doubted it was love, exactly. It sure as hell wasn't anything founded on respect or admiration. But he was her first love, and for the longest time, he'd been the only man in her life.

Yet I knew as surely as I was sitting there, if Kendrick were to show up right now and promised to divorce Diamond and wanted my mom to go away with him, she'd shut the door in his face.

She'd found what she needed with Tyson. She truly loved him, of that I had no doubt. And yet, I knew, those feelings for Kendrick weren't entirely gone.

"Why?"

It was a simple question, no malice or indignation or anger. Just a simple question.

It was too bad I didn't have a simple answer. Taking a deep breath, I braced myself. *"It's about that guy, Mama. Remember the guy I told you about?"*

She nodded. *"The one who was engaged to Paisley."*

"It's about him," I said. *"Kendrick is...he's..."*

Dammit.

"Just spill it, Allie," Tao said from his spot on the chair.

I shot him a dark look then met Mom's eyes. *"Kendrick had Jal arrested, then said that he'd make the charges go away once Jal got back together with Paisley. He set Jal up, Mom."*

Tao muttered something under his breath that I was sure wasn't complimentary, but Mom's expression wasn't one of surprise. In fact, she looked resigned.

She didn't ask a single question, didn't say a damn thing. All she did was get to her feet and start to pace around the yard, rubbing at her neck. After a few moments, she turned to me, a grim look on her face.

"Tell me what he did this time."

That was when it hit me. She'd seen him do this shit before.

So I told her all of it.

"Why aren't you surprised?" I finally asked her.

Mom sat in a lawn chair, sipping on the lemonade TJ had brought out half-way through my explanation. Tao had saved Mom and me from having to shoo TJ away by immediately challenging my little brother to some sort of video game match. The two of them were inside now, and every so often, I heard Tao shouting at the game.

Mom was silent for so long, I almost thought she hadn't seen me asking her, but finally, she looked over at me.

"I guess for the same reason you approached him to begin with. I've seen him pull this sort of thing before." She took another drink, then put down her glass. *"And so have you."*

She sounded so sure of it that I wondered if my father had told her what happened.

"Yes," I admitted. *"I found some stuff years ago. It was in some of the work he had me looking at. Some things didn't add up back then, and I fought with him about it. Then when all of this*

went down....Jal has somebody working with him that used to work with Kendrick. I had a bad feeling. So I confronted him."

I'd already told her what I threatened him with if he didn't fix things.

Mom nodded. Silence stretched out again, and I listened to the birds calling while she thought. Finally, she looked at me. *"I'll back you up, Allie. Whatever you do. But understand, if you talk, they won't be kind. Are you ready for that?"*

"Yes." I nodded. *"But I don't think it'll come to that. You know how they are. They'll want to save face too much to risk it."* I took a steadying breath. *"Besides, I had to do this. For Jal. I love him."*

She reached up and cupped my cheek. *"I already knew that."*

A noise caught my ears, and I looked up to see Tao studying me. He had a faint smile on his lips, and he nodded at me. I wondered if he'd already known too. Knowing Tao, he'd probably just been sitting around, waiting for me to figure it out myself.

Mom glanced at Tao and then back at me. *"I'm going to make lunch. Are you two staying?"*

I nodded as I stood. *"What do you need me to do to help?"*

"Nothing."

I would've argued, but Mom was giving me that look, the one that said not to bother protesting. It wouldn't do any good. And I knew why she was doing it too. She was reminding me of what she'd told me before. That I needed to stop using the family as an excuse to hold back.

"Come on." Tao reached out a hand and took me back through the house to the front steps. When the weather was nice, it was our favorite place to sit and talk. He waited until we settled in before asking, "Does he know?"

I didn't have to ask him to clarify. I shrugged. "I haven't told him yet. He knows I'm serious about him. I think he feels the same way. But right now…" I grimaced. "I don't think this is the right time. We need to get this mess fixed before we can worry about anything else."

"Or maybe you should let him know why you're pushing so hard to fix it," Tao suggested. He bumped my shoulder with his. "You know this isn't your fault, right? You didn't cause this. But you're working your ass off to fix it, and maybe he should know why."

"Maybe you're right," I agreed.

"Maybe?" Tao threw his arm around my shoulders and kissed my cheek. "Come on, honey, you know I'm always right."

I started to laugh, but the sound died in my throat as I happened to look across the street.

Jal was staring right at us, and the look on his face said he'd seen Tao kiss me.

"Dammit."

Chapter 7

Jal

Jal,
I went to go see my father. I'm not going to let him do this to you. I'll talk to you after.
Allie

After the first few words, they all blurred together, and I had to read it several times through before everything made sense. Then I crumpled the piece of paper into a ball and hurled it on the floor.

"Dammit, Allie! What the fuck." I lifted my face and stared up the ceiling.

She couldn't think this was her fault. Maybe she hadn't written that she blamed herself, but it still came through loud and clear. She felt like she had to fix it, but this wasn't about her. It was about her dad and Paisley. Me and Paisley. Kendrick.

That stupid schmuck.

I should be the one driving over there and talking to him. I was tempted to do just that and then plant my fist in Kendrick's smug face. I still might do it if Allie came back upset.

I checked my phone to see if maybe she had called or texted while I was still sleeping, but she hadn't. I had no way of knowing when she left. It was almost eleven, and I had just climbed out of bed a few minutes ago. I'd left a message for Mrs. Beck, letting her know that I needed a couple days to try to get some personal matters taken care of, so I'd turned off my alarm,

363

but I'd never expected to sleep so late.

I'd been dreaming about Allie, surrounded by blankets that smelled of her and me and what we'd done together, so it made sense that I would've wanted to stay there, in that dream. Except while I'd been thinking about her, she'd gone off to face that jackass.

I picked up the note and read it again. Then I carefully smoothed out the wrinkles and lines and left it on the counter while I forced myself to make breakfast. Maybe she'd be back soon. Then I could shake her and tell her to quit worrying about this. I'd handle it.

But she wasn't back by the time I finished cooking. So I made myself eat to have something to do. But I didn't taste much of it.

And she still hadn't returned.

Okay, so I'd shower. Then if she wasn't back…

"Stop," I muttered out loud.

She'd be back.

But by the time I'd showered and changed, the apartment was still empty, quiet. Too empty. Too quiet.

How long could it take to talk to that arrogant asshole?

I checked my work email, sending off rote answers, filing what needed to be filed. That managed to kill another hour, but my mind wasn't where it needed to be to do anything truly productive. After a quick call to Adam to see where he thought things stood – it was too soon to tell – I couldn't wait any longer.

I almost headed straight for Kendrick and Diamond's estate, but at the last minute, I took a detour. I'd finally gotten her actual address, and something in my gut told me that she might have felt the need to see her mother after having talked to her father.

As soon as I turned the corner, I caught sight of her, and my heart leaped in my chest. I resisted the impulse to leave my car where it was and go to her. I couldn't completely lose my head. Ten minutes later, I finally nosed into a spot barely bigger than a tuna fish can.

Finally.

Feeling self-conscious, I tried not to think about the people eying me – and my car – as I walked up the block and rounded the corner to where I'd seen Allie. The self-consciousness faded quickly enough because I was already getting frustrated. Why

364

hadn't she called to tell me she was going to see her mom too?

In a split second, though, self-consciousness, the lingering worry, and even the frustration faded away, replaced by one simple emotion.

Jealousy.

Allie wasn't alone.

She was with a guy, and after a moment, I realized that I knew him.

The man sitting with her was the same guy who'd come with her to the ball not that long ago. I remembered that his name was Tao, and he'd shook my hand with a smirk on his face.

How long have you been together? I'd asked.

And he'd all but laughed as he said, *Forever*.

Here I'd been worrying about her going to see her father, and she was getting all cozy with this asshole.

He leaned over to say something to her, the intimacy between them undeniable. He put his arm around her shoulder and kissed her cheek. It wasn't her mouth, but it was damn close.

Jealousy exploded into a blistery rage.

They'd been together forever alright.

Something twisted in me, and it took a few seconds to realize what it was. Hurt.

The anger and jealousy were easy to understand, but the *hurt*...I'd never felt that before.

I almost stormed over there, ripped her away from him, demanding to know what she was doing with him – doing to *me*. But one thing stopped me.

I had no right to demand anything of her.

We'd made no commitments to each other.

Not really.

Over the entire course of the time we'd known each other, I'd deceived her, seduced her into sleeping with me when I was engaged, and I couldn't even count the number of times I'd been cruel to her.

Maybe this was what I got for being a self-centered ass.

Maybe I should have walked away then. Maybe I should walk away now.

Before I could decide to do just that, Allie saw me. Her eyes widened, and I backed up, ready to just...disappear. I couldn't be humiliated a second time. Not by someone I actually cared about.

I heard her calling me, but I didn't care. I was opening my car door when she caught up to me.

"Dammit, Jal! Wait!"

Giving her a disinterested look over my shoulder, I asked, "Why?" I managed to shrug even. "It's not like we owe each other anything."

"On the contrary." She stopped and crossed her arms over her chest. "You're about to owe me something. It's called an apology. Tao and I are *friends*. He's my best friend and has been since kindergarten."

Some part of me wanted to take those words at face value and accept them, but I wasn't an idiot. I'd seen the way they were together.

"I wish I had friends that good," I said sourly.

"Stop being an ass, Jal," she snapped.

"You can't tell me there's never been anything but friendship between you two."

She raised an eyebrow. "I never tried to. The term's *friends with benefits*. Yeah, we've slept together. Guys aren't the only ones who get lonely or go looking for a partner at night, Jal. Girls do it too. Tao and I are sexually compatible, but we're not in love, not now, not in the past, not ever."

I snorted. I couldn't look at her, not without thinking about her with *him*, wondering if she'd compared us, wondering what he'd taught her.

"Don't you go giving me that look." She jabbed a finger at me. "Not when I know you've had your fair share of casual sex. Do you have any idea how much easier my life – *his* life – would have been if the two of us *could* just fall in love? I wouldn't have spent the past month going out of my mind over *you*."

This time, she poked me in the chest. Hard. I caught her wrist and yanked her toward me, my body instantly responding to the feel of her curves against me. The band around my chest started to ease. "Friends."

She narrowed her eyes.

"Friends with benefits," I murmured. "You sleep with him."

"I've *slept* with him." She stressed the past tense.

"It stops." I kissed her hard and fast, needing to claim her, to make sure that she knew I wasn't playing around. That she didn't need a friend with benefits. Ever again.

"Well, yeah." She rolled her eyes at me. "I thought that was obvious."

I bent my head to kiss her again, but a movement from just beyond her had me looking up. Tao stood there, leaning against a light post as if he had nothing better to do.

"Don't mind me," he said with an infuriating grin.

I couldn't keep from scowling at him, but he simply laughed. It was an easy sort of laugh, definitely not that smirk I'd seen in his eyes the last time. He approached, holding out a hand.

"Maybe we should try this again," he said. "I'm Tao. Her best friend. And judging by the look I see on both of your faces, that's all I am now."

"Is it?" That snarl in my voice wasn't anything I'd ever expected to hear from myself.

He laughed again. "Seeing as how you finally pulled your head out of your ass? Yeah."

This time, he seemed to be laughing at me, but that was okay. I was pretty sure I deserved it.

Tao winked at Allie before shooting a look back over his shoulder. "Babe, you better take him back to meet your mama. She saw you take off running and came out to see what's up. You know her. I managed to stall her, but it won't work for long."

Take me...wait, what?

Fuck me.

Panic seized me, and it only got worse when Allie gave me an appraising look, and she had the same laughing sort of smile on her face that Tao had.

"It has to happen sometime," she said, her eyes twinkling.

"Sometime? Yeah," I agreed. "Sure. But does sometime have to be today?"

"What's the matter?" Allie winked at me and held out her hand. "Are you chicken?"

I pondered the question before I gave her a completely honest answer, "Well, yes. It's not like I've ever done this before."

"What?" The smile on her face was so bright and happy, so open, I wanted to kiss her again, and not stop. "Meet a girlfriend's mom?"

I wasn't about to tell her that she was probably the first person I could ever really consider...I let the thought trail off. That small, panicked voice inside me didn't want me to finish what I'd been thinking, but it came anyway.

I hadn't ever had a serious relationship with a woman.

That didn't matter, because up until now, I'd never *wanted* to have a serious relationship with a woman.

Hell, half the time, I hadn't really even liked the women I'd slept with. *Friends with benefits* had never been my thing because I didn't really have any female friends.

"Come on, you coward," Allie said with a teasing grin. She took my hand and tugged me along behind her. As we rounded the corner, I looked up, and a cold sweat broke out across my neck.

Her mother was standing on the porch waiting for us.

At least, I assumed it was her mother.

She looked too young, but there were strong similarities.

Allie came to a stop and tugged her hand free of mine. I almost didn't let it go, but she was insistent. She signed to her mother, speaking out loud as she did so, but whether that was out of habit or for me, I didn't know.

"Mom, this is Jal, the guy I've been telling you about." She smiled at me. *"Jal, this is my mom, Malla McCormack."*

For a second, I was so interested in the gestures Allie was making with her hands, I barely heard her words. The signs were fascinating, fluid. Beautiful. I'd caught glimpses of sign language here and there over the years, but I'd never really paid much attention to it, like any other foreign language.

Malla came down the steps, and out of habit, I held out my hand. She shook it while I tried to figure out what I was supposed to do or say next.

Then Malla spoke. I blinked, hoping I didn't look as confused as I felt I instantly felt like an asshole because I *knew* being deaf didn't mean a person couldn't speak.

"Hello, Jal." She glanced at Allie, eyebrow arched and I did the same out of habit.

"She's making sure she's saying your name right," Tao said from behind me, nudging me with his shoulder.

Oh.

Years of business training finally kicked in, and I managed a smile. I handled multi-million dollar deals without blinking, I could handle being introduced to a woman's mother, right?

"Hello, Mrs. McCormack," I said, squeezing her hand politely before starting to let go.

But she held on.

"You're not what I expected," she said, her words a little louder than necessary, but clear and concise.

And her gaze was direct, like she was staring right through me.

I wasn't sure how to respond to that. Finally, I said, "I hope that's a good thing."

"So far, it is." She let my hand go but continued to study me. After a moment, she nodded. "If you hurt my girl, you're going to regret it."

I had no doubt that she meant it.

"Hurting her is the last thing I plan on doing," I said honestly.

She snorted indelicately. "If you two want to make this work, both of you will hurt the other at some point. That's how relationships work. But there's hurt...and then there's *hurt*. You know which one will make me angry."

Tao walked past me and slung an arm around Malla's neck, kissing her cheek. Then he looked at me. "And she's like the Hulk, my man. Trust me, you won't like her when she's angry."

Allie signed for her mother, and Malla rolled her eyes.

"Idiot child," she said, shaking her head. Then she turned and headed up the steps. "Why don't you come inside, Jal? We're having lunch soon."

I looked at Allie, silently pleading for her to say that we had to go.

"You're not getting off that easy," she said as she wrapped her arm around mine. "Consider it your apology."

Chapter 8

Jal

"Dropped." I studied my lawyer over the rim of my crystal glass. "Just like that."

Adam lifted a shoulder. "I wouldn't say just like that. It's a sticky situation, but not for you."

"What do you mean?" Putting the bourbon down, I leaned forward and studied the man across from me. When he didn't answer right away, I felt the tension inside me starting to rise.

He'd called me, told me he had news, asked to meet. It'd been a full fucking week without answers, and now Adam was jerking me around with vague ones.

"Look, are you going to talk to me or–"

"Settle down, Jal." Adam tossed back his bourbon and put his glass down with a distinct click before rising and pacing over to the far wall. "You're clear on this. Clear as day, okay? But it seems that either Kendrick or his idiot associate tugged the wrong tail too many times. One of them is going to hang over this."

"Ahhh…" I looked down at my hands, trying to figure out how I felt about that, how Allie might feel if her dad ended up in trouble.

"Chances are it will be Hammerstein," Adam continued. "He went a little over the line, I think, in his job to frame you. Seems he had some dirt of his own he was trying to hide, and you were a good fall boy."

My hand tightened on the glass. It could have been relief I

felt. Or it could have been something else. I had no idea, and I didn't want to think about it too long either. As pissed off as I was with Kendrick, I didn't want to complicate things between Allie and me, not when we were just getting started.

The old bastard wasn't worth it.

"You can always pursue civil action against both of them," Adam said softly, as if he'd read my mind.

"No." Shaking my head, I looked away. "Asshole should pay for what he tried to do, but maybe he already is."

Adam didn't respond for a moment, and when he did, I wasn't surprised he'd connected Allie to whatever had happened on Kendrick's side. "He's asked for my...legal advice on a few issues. I told him I'd take it into consideration. He's also asked me to pass a message onto you and to Allie. Apparently neither of you are taking calls from anybody with the last name Hedge."

"The entire Hedge family can kiss my ass," I said sourly.

"That seems a bit extreme." Adam tipped his bourbon in my direction. "I've met the younger one – Mallory. She's a nice kid. The black sheep of the family, from what I understand."

I knew what he was talking about. My mother had been scandalized when Diamond had confided in her about the family's shocking secret – Mallory was a lesbian. It was one thing to have some distant relationship involved in an *alternative lifestyle*, as Mom had told my father. Another thing for it to be your own child.

I'd always liked Mallory. I was glad when she moved to Boston and started her own life there. Adam was right. There was one decent member of the Hedges' family.

I didn't count Allie. She wouldn't consider herself one of the Hedges. She was herself.

And I loved who she was.

Allie looked beautiful. She also looked nervous. Dressed in a

371

soft green sheathe that accented her eyes and complimented her skin, she walked next to me as we wound our way through the maze of tables and a gauntlet of servers.

I knew not everybody was staring at us. Most of the people here weren't that rude. But it sure as hell seemed that way. I definitely *felt* like I had a hundred sets of eyes on me, and if I was this uncomfortable I couldn't even imagine how Allie was handling it.

Resting my hand on her spine, I felt the tension there and said, "Breathe. You're better than any ten of these people combined."

"Yeah?" She gave me a slow look. "Including you? Your folks?"

"Well, maybe five of me." I winked at her. "There's only one of my dad though. You'll like him."

Neither of us talked about my mom. We didn't have to. I'd already explained that she was a friend of Diamond's and that pretty much said everything that needed to be said.

The maître d had offered to escort us to my parents' table – they were regulars, after all. But while I didn't come with them as often, I knew where to find them so I'd declined the offer.

As I caught sight of my dad, I reminded Allie once more, "Breathe. I hear it's good for you."

"Ha, ha. Smart ass." She took my hand. "I feel like I'm a guppy being thrown into the shark tank."

"You're not. You put up with Diamond and Paisley for years. If you can handle them, you can handle anybody here. You're no guppy." I raised our hands and kissed her knuckles. "If anything, you're a stingray."

"I'm a what?"

"You ever seen one of them move? Elegant and just as deadly as a shark. But a lot prettier."

She laughed. "Thanks. And FYI, I'd rather be dealing with Paisley and Diamond. Haven't you heard that saying about the evil you know?" Taking a deep breath, she smiled at me then. "Let's do this."

I squeezed her hand as we came to a stop by my parents' table.

My dad was already on his feet, his light blue eyes sparkling. Mom was sitting there, drinking a mimosa, and judging by the glassy, bright look in her emerald-colored eyes, it wasn't her first. Probably not even her third or fourth.

Great.

"Dad. This is Allie Dodds."

Allie held out her hand to Harold Lindstrom, Sr.

He studied it for a moment.

Now we really *were* the center of attention.

My father was laid-back, and for the most part, he was content to let my mother set the course. But Harold Lindstrom, Sr. came from old money. While I'd been the one in the family to increase our wealth, he hadn't done anything to hurt the family name either. He was still the one people looked to as an example.

From the corner of my eye, I saw my mother sit up a little straighter, and I started to feel a little sick. I'd thought for sure that this was something he'd stand up to her about. Was he really going to–?

Dad caught Allie up in a tight hug.

"Hello, Allie." He squeezed her once and then let go. "My boy has told me so much about you…including how you stepped up to deal with that ugly mess a few days back. That prick – excuse my language – takes a lot to stand up to him. I understand you've known him since you were young."

"I…yes, sir." She nodded, giving me a bemused glance.

I gave my head a minute shake. I hadn't told him about her connection to Kendrick. That wasn't my place. If she chose to, she could. Otherwise, it would remain her story. As far as I was concerned, Tyson McCormack was her father.

"Come. Sit." He pulled out the chair where I'd normally sit, putting her right next to him. I took the only other open seat, sitting across from her. "Are you hungry, Allie? We held off ordering because we knew you were on your way."

My mother didn't even look at Allie when she spoke, "Yes, and you know your father doesn't do well if he doesn't eat by a certain time. It was rude of you to ask that we wait so long, Jal. Really."

Allie's cheeks flushed, and my temper flared.

"I'm sorry, Mom. I didn't realize that extra half hour was going to make Dad keel over." I gave my old man an appraising look. "You hanging in there okay or should we call for paramedics?"

One corner of his mouth twitched. "I think I'll do alright, boy." He studied my mother a moment and then leaned back as a white-coated server appeared to refill coffee and offer some to Allie and me. We both accepted, and Allie asked for cream and sugar.

"I detoxed from sugar over a year ago," Mom said loftily. "I've never felt better. It helps a woman remain youthful as well."

"I'll keep that in mind." Allie liberally spooned two helpings of sugar into her coffee – twice as much as normal.

Damn. I already knew it wasn't a good idea to get on her bad side, but this was something else.

"I personally prefer things in life a little sweet, but to each their own." She gave my mom a charming smile.

Dad hid a smile behind his cup. I didn't bother hiding mine.

While my dad peppered Allie with questions, my mom tried to find some way to get under Allie's skin. Each time Mom found a way to take a potshot, I felt my temper growing thinner. Allie handled it all with aplomb.

Right up until my mother said, "I hear your mother used to scrub floors for the Hedges. Among other things. Is that true?"

Allie set her coffee cup down. I was already glaring at my mother. But before either of us could respond, my father cleared his throat.

"Ginny, that's enough."

My mother whipped her head around and stared at him.

I did, too. *Ginny*? I'd never heard *anybody* called my mom *Ginny*. She always insisted on using her full name. Ginnifer. And made sure it was spelled correctly, even if it wasn't being written down.

Then I realized what else he said.

Dad sighed and reached for one of the flaky croissants that had been brought out a few moments earlier. "I'm tired of this game you're playing. I was tired of it a long time ago, but you rarely stooped so low, and never in public. You rarely went against friends or those who mattered to our son, so I stayed quiet. But you're going to stop. This is ridiculous."

He looked at Allie and smiled even as I sat there with my mouth hanging open.

"You're more than welcome in our family, Allie. Don't worry, Ginny will come around. She loves her son just as much as

I do, and in the end, what she wants is for him to be happy." Then he looked at my mother. "And if she'd actually stop sulking and worrying about her petty friends so she could take a good long look at our boy, she'd realize that he *is* happy."

I felt myself going red. Allie's cheeks were a soft, dusky pink, and she busied herself with her napkin as my mother's complexion went from flushed and angry to pale.

Finally, she looked over at me.

After a moment, she took a deep breath. "I...I believe I need to step away for a moment. If you'll excuse me?"

Dad watched her go, and a moment later, he nodded at us and then stepped away as well.

Dad returned before she did.

She stayed gone almost ten more minutes.

The woman who came to our table *looked* like my mother. She talked like her. Hell, she even sounded like her. But the hard sheen I was so used to seemed to have fractured and fallen away.

She talked to me like she hadn't in years. And she talked to Allie too. Their interactions were still stilted, but they spoke nonetheless.

At the end of brunch, I gave my dad a hug, and said softly, just for him to hear, "Thank you."

He chuckled. "Diplomacy comes with the territory, son. You best learn it while you're young." He glanced at Allie, then looked back at me. "And let me give you a piece of advice. Don't let that one go."

I followed his gaze. "Don't worry, Dad. I don't intend to."

Chapter 9

Allie

"Open…"

His voice was like raw silk, rubbing all over my body and my senses too.

I would have moaned, maybe even begged, but my mouth was suddenly full.

I would have reached for him, maybe even clung to him, but my hands were restrained.

I would have whimpered and wiggled and squirmed, done anything to ease the burning ache inside me as Jal fisted his hands in my hair and held my head steady, doing exactly what he'd promised on the drive back to his apartment.

I love your mouth, you know that? And I've had this fantasy…I think it's time I make good on it.

I hadn't realized he was in the mood to play, or I would've been quicker on the upkeep because the rewards were amazing.

He'd ended up with his fingers between my thighs, our bodies angled so the driver couldn't see, but just knowing that someone else was there…it turned me on more than I'd realized possible.

If you can guess the fantasy before we get home, I'll make you come.

It had taken me almost too long because his fingers were really distracting – and clever.

But I'd figured it out. Enough, at least, to have my reward.

And now, I was restrained in a way that I'd never been

before, and I felt more open and vulnerable than I'd ever felt, more exposed, more...*erotic.*

I shivered, and the thin chains that connected the nipple clamps to my bound wrists tugged, a subtle warning of how little I could move.

He let go of my hair and reached one hand down, tugging on the chain that connect my left nipple to the padded cuff around my left wrist. More chains connected the nipple clamps to the collar around my neck.

A spreader bar went between my ankles, and Jal had taken great pleasure in telling me that he could even get chains that connected these nipple clamps to that bar. *But you're not ready yet. I don't want to hurt you and if you move too much...*

He tugged the chain again, and the clamp gave my nipple another delicious bite.

I moaned around the thick shaft in my mouth, a hot dart of heat twisting through my pussy, arching my spine.

He did it again. And again.

Each tug made that heat blaze hotter, brighter until I was moaning endlessly, barely able to breathe as he continued to slide his cock in and out of my mouth.

"Swallow me, baby," he said. Another tug and bolt of pain. "Yeah...that's it. Take more...aw, hell..."

I shivered when he pulled out, coughing and gasping for air. I watched as he fisted his cock like he was going to come all over me. The idea had me licking my lips.

He shoved my hair back from my damp face and asked what I was thinking.

I told him.

He kissed me in the next breath, going to his knees front of me, and kissing me so roughly, it stole the very air out of me. "You want me to come all over you?"

"I want to see you come," I said. "I don't care if you do it on me or not."

"Not good enough." He stood up and came around me, kneeling behind me.

I cried out in frustration as he urged me forward, wrapping his arm around my waist so I didn't fall. I couldn't brace myself, couldn't even fight his hands, thanks to the restraints. "Bastard."

He spanked me, and I yelped in shocked surprise.

"If you wanted to see me come, you should have told me so." He nipped at my ear. "But the first time we're not using condoms, I'm coming inside you."

I groaned, then cried out as he drove into me, hard and fast. I was so ready, I was coming even before he finished filling me. He caught one of the chains and began to tug. Each time, it rippled through me, drawing the climax out longer and longer.

"That's it…you squeeze me, just like that…"

I shuddered and twisted around him, trying to get closer, although how much closer could I get? It was pain and pleasure all wrapped together, overwhelming me until it was too much. I cried out when he withdrew only to surge forward again, and again.

He kept up that slow, steady pace throughout my entire climax, kept on tugging on the nipple clamp chains so I hovered right there on the razor's edge, one orgasm gone, another promising – but he withheld it so easily.

When he stopped moving, I growled my frustration.

"Look up, Allie."

It was a command, not a request, so I did it.

And then I saw the mirror, saw us in the mirror.

"I've never had a woman without a condom before, Allie. I can't begin to tell you how amazing it feels inside you, with nothing between us."

Whimpering, I twisted against him, only to be brought up short by the chains. "Move, please. I need to come again."

He kissed my shoulder. "Beg me."

"Please! Dammit, Jal! Just please…" No other words would come. Then I felt his thumb at my ass, and a shudder ran through me.

"Tell me what you want, baby."

I closed my eyes.

"Open."

I obeyed.

"Tell me what you want."

"I want you to fuck me," I said. "I want you to come inside me."

"And what are you willing to do for me?"

"Anything," I whimpered. I was stuffed so full of him and trying not to rock back against him with the chains tugging and

378

teasing...

"Say it."

"My ass." My eyelids fluttered as the tip of his thumb breached me.

"What do you want?"

"Fingers," I said. "Cock. Something. Anything."

I seemed unable to form coherent sentences. He reached around and pushed two fingers into my mouth.

"Suck."

I did, and his fingers were at my anus again. He pulled back, and as he thrust back into me, he shoved his fingers into my ass.

That knocked a scream out of me.

He did it again...again...again...

Mindless of the nipple clamps and chains, I twisted around him and bore down, trying to take more, more, *more.*

Abruptly, he pulled me up. He'd freed the chains somehow and now had me plastered against his chest, each hand full of a breast, squeezing them as he drove up into me, each stroke enough to lift me off my knees.

I cried out his name as the orgasm slammed into us both. I felt him empty inside me even as my climax made the world go white around me.

It was then that I felt it. The connection, the satisfaction, that I'd never quite been able to manage in other encounters, not even with Tao. There'd always been a little something missing before, but now, I'd found it.

It was him.

Water bubbled and churned around us.

On our left, there was a window that let us see the sprawling panorama that was Philadelphia. A few lights dotted the dark ribbon of a river, marking barges, and maybe a few intrepid boaters who'd been waiting for a true thaw to get back on the water.

"It's a beautiful view," I said, wishing I had the energy to do more than loll against Jal. The day's events, however, had taken it all out of me. It'd gone well, but it'd still been draining.

"Yes, it is."

Something about his voice had me lifting my head, and I caught sight of him in the mirrored wall across from us. The first time I'd seen it, I called him a pervert. He'd laughed.

Now my heart ached, because I could see Jal watching me, and the expression on his face made crazy, weird things dance inside me.

"I love you."

I blinked, thinking I had to have misheard him, that my brain had to be playing tricks on me.

When I didn't respond, Jal said it again, his eyes meeting mine. The emotion shining in their depths told me that it wasn't my imagination.

Tears burned my eyes as I turned around in his arms, ignoring the water splashing over the sides of the tub. Curling my arms around his neck, I pressed my face against his throat. "Jal..." My voice cracked.

"It's not supposed to make you cry when a guy says that." His tone was half-teasing, but I could hear the uncertainty hovering beneath the surface.

"I love you too."

I felt his body relax as I said the words. As I wrapped myself tighter around him, I felt some last little knot of tension give inside me. I wasn't foolish enough to believe that things would be perfect from here on out, but I did know that we'd always work it out. There wasn't anything the two of us couldn't face if we were together.

Chapter 10

Allie

"*Too* many people," I muttered under my breath as I carried my champagne up to where Jal was waiting on the dais.

My family – including Tao and his date – were at a special place up front. Well, technically, dates. Plural. Tony was the guy I'd seen with Tao back in March, and things had gotten serious earlier this summer after Tao explained his polyamorous nature to Tony. To my surprise, Tony hadn't only taken it well, he said he'd been trying to figure out a way to tell Tao the same thing.

Two months ago, they'd added Lyrrie to their relationship.

While Tony's complexion was similar to mine – his father was black and his mother white – Lyrrie was as different as could be. Short and curvy, she had that pale, freckled skin that most redheads possessed. She was sweet and open, the perfect complement to the guys. And she was hard of hearing. Mom had been a bit thrown by the unconventional relationship, but Lyrrie had quickly won her over.

I still didn't know how their relationship worked, but it was their bed to lie in, not mine.

I had a bed I was perfectly happy with, and the man I shared it with was smiling at me from the podium.

All around us, people were talking, a patois of sign and speaking where the hearing sometimes stumbled over their signs, and the deaf and hard of hearing spoke just a little louder than necessary. It could've been chaotic and awkward, but the purpose that had brought us all together made it work.

The kids were up in the atrium, the part of the Philadelphia Family & Community Center for the Deaf that had been solely designed for younger adults and youth. TJ's hands had been all over it, a fact that he had been more than happy to share with anybody and everybody who would listen. He'd been interviewed by the press for it several times over, and the attention had brought him positive attention at school, enough that the bullies he'd been dealing with had backed off. He had a girlfriend now too. She was hearing, but they'd bonded when she found out that he was ahead of her on the waiting list for a book they both wanted.

She ended up buying him the book – and he'd done the same for her – after they'd had an argument over it.

He'd written his argument down since, even though he could speak, he was self-conscious about it. She'd told him she didn't care if he spoke, as long as the two of them could communicate, and that had been that. Since then, she'd been taking sign language classes, and he'd been working on improving his speech.

They were adorable together, and even though Tyson had been wary at first, he'd been unable to deny how good she was for TJ. Carrie was cute, a head taller than TJ. A blonde-haired, blue-eyed princess. Not what either of my parents had expected, but Mom had already told Tyson that most of the time, the best things in life were unexpected.

I thought she was right. After all, the big blue-eyed prince waiting for me was the very *last* thing I'd expected.

He held out a hand, and I accepted, turning my cheek for him to kiss me. He had something else in mind, however. He caught my chin and turned my face back to him, holding me there for a hard, fast kiss that left me breathless.

The crowd went nuts. Some clapped and whistled while the majority had their hands in the air, twisting them back and forth – the sign for applause.

My face was flushed, blood rushing in my ears as he finally broke the kiss. I wasn't exactly opposed to public displays of affection, but that had been a bit much for me. My head was still spinning as Jal began to speak.

"Ladies and gentlemen, may I present Allie Dodds...one of my advisors for the facility. I couldn't have done it without the help of her and her family." Jal nodded to my mom, Tyson, and TJ.

TJ, the little social monster, threw up his hands as he stood, lapping up the attention. Carrie poked at him and signed that he was being a show-off. He bowed to her before Mom managed to get him in his seat, and the crowd roared again. He was a hit.

Then Mom looked at me, a strange, weepy sort of expression on her face. She held up her hand in the widely known shorthand for *I love you*. I returned it, my own eyes burning. We'd always been close, but the events of the past few months had bound us together even more tightly.

The little exchange only took a few seconds, but it distracted me enough that I didn't realize Jal had asked me a question. He touched my shoulder and repeated himself.

"Oh..." Smiling at him, I nodded. I didn't need anyone signing for me, so I moved in front of the podium and began to speak, explaining how the idea for the center had come to be, and applauded the hard work both the hearing and deaf communities had achieved by working together. When I gestured to my family, TJ restrained himself to a single fist pump, and my mom dabbed her eyes with Jal's handkerchief.

I'd been nervous when Jal told me that he wanted me to speak, but I didn't feel any of that now. It had all gone so smoothly that I should've known something was going to happen to catch me completely off guard.

As I finished, I turned to pass the reins back over to Jal.

And froze.

He was down on one knee.

My heart thudded once, hard and fast, then began to race.

Everybody could see him.

I reached out a hand, bracing myself on the podium because the world suddenly went wobbly.

Then he raised his hands and began to sign.

I blinked and everything got all blurry. "I'm sorry," I said. "I missed that."

Everyone laughed, but it was a soft, sweet kind of laughter, the kind that enveloped me, making this moment even more perfect than it already was.

Jal stood and started again.

"Allie, I love you. Will you marry..."

383

I flung myself at him before he finished and whispered my answer in his ear.

Chapter 11

Allie

"My father's out there."

I looked up and met Mallory's eyes.

Mallory was the younger of my half-sisters, still almost four years older than me, and we'd met as sisters for the first time in November. She said she'd always suspected who I was. Considering we had eyes of the same shape and color, that wasn't surprising. She'd never said anything, however, because she'd been dealing with her own family issues and had known asking about me would've only made things worse.

A few months ago, however, she and her girlfriend, Dayna, had come back to Philadelphia for Thanksgiving, and everything had hit the fan. I hadn't been there, but Mallory gave me a play-by-play of what happened when Diamond and Jal's mom, Ginnifer, had gotten into a heated argument.

I have no idea what Mom said to set Ginnifer off, but when I came in, Mom was raging like she'd never done in her life, *and Ginnifer just laughed at her. Then she said it was clear your decent genes must have come from Kendrick, which was bizarre since he clearly had a strange grasp of what decent even* meant. *Then, she saw me and told me that you'd mentioned me once or twice and that if I wanted to see you, just call her. She'd arrange it.*

We'd met two days later. Now, it was May and Mallory was one of my bridesmaids. Tao, of course, was my maid of honor. Jal's parents had been polite about my choice, though it was clear they didn't completely agree. They hadn't argued about it, so I'd given in to some of the more elaborate things Ginnifer had wanted. We seemed to be doing well compromising, even if things between us were still a little stiff.

I was still trying to process what Mallory had said about Kendrick when I heard my name. I jerked my head up and met Ginnifer's cool gaze. She gave me a tentative smile as she reached out to brush a stray tendril of hair back from my face.

"Would you like me to deal with Kendrick? I can get him to leave. Quietly, of course."

"No." I looked over at Mom.

"Kendrick's here?"

I nodded. *"What do you want to do?"*

"This is your wedding. It's your call." She smiled at me and went back to adjusting the train on my wedding dress. Tao's designer friend, Tarja, had been thrilled when I asked her to design my dress. We'd gone through a couple different possibilities before deciding on this one, and I knew it was perfect. She'd also done the dresses and tuxedos for the entire bridal party, and the dresses for both my mom and Ginnifer.

I took a deep breath, smoothed down the front of my dress, then looked up at Ginnifer.

"Why don't you bring him back here? I want to see what he wants."

She nodded and turned to go. Then she paused, looking at Mallory. "It was just Kendrick, right?"

She nodded. "Yes. Mom and Paisley aren't even in town. They left for Italy a couple of days ago. I drove them to the airport." The smile on her face was decidedly strained.

The room had been bright and laughing a few minutes ago, but now it was quiet, too quiet. I had the sudden urge to ask someone to turn on a radio.

Mallory came up behind me. I was standing on a stool while Mom and Tarja were making last minute tweaks, so I towered over my sister. She was already two inches shorter than me, but now I looked like a giant next to her. I grinned at her. "You look like one of those characters from that book you used to sneak to me – *Gulliver's Travels*. The Lilliputians?"

She laughed. "Sometimes I *feel* like a Lilliputian. You're a beautiful bride."

"Yes, you are."

Mom put a steadying hand on my back, but I wasn't sure who was supporting who. Slowly, I shifted my gaze in the mirror to see Kendrick standing in the doorway, Ginnifer at his side, looking like she was standing guard. I felt a rush of affection for her. She was trying so hard to make up for everything she'd put Jal through.

Kendrick looked around the room, his face flushing at the sight of a bunch of women, decked out in their best, surrounding me. Mom had a pin in her hand, and I wondered if she was seriously considering stabbing him with it. I wouldn't stop her.

He nodded at everybody, and when he saw my mom, something softened on his face. "Malla."

She inclined her head. "Hello, Kendrick." Then she looked at me. "*I expect you'd like a moment alone?*"

Panic flooded me. I didn't want to do this alone, but she was already ushering everybody in the sitting room off to the side.

In seconds, everyone else was gone, and it was just us.

"I've already made my apologies to Jal." He shoved his hands into his pockets, ruining the lines of one very expensive suit. If Diamond were here, she'd have scolded him.

I considered stepping off of the stool, but it put me closer to his height and, at the moment, I liked that. "I know. He told me that you'd written to him."

"No." He looked away, then forced his gaze back. "That's not what I meant. I went to see him before I came in here. Considering what I'd done, I figured I should man up and actually apologize, not only have my assistant send him some bullshit half-ass apology."

"Wow." I blinked at him. He actually sounded like something of the man I'd known as a child, the man my mother had fallen in love with. I managed a wobbly smile. "You look like Kendrick Hedges, and you sound like him, but that doesn't sound like something he would say."

"Yeah, well. It's occurred to me that Kendrick Hedges is an asshole." His lips curved up in a partial smile. "And I'm sorry for it."

"Okay."

"Okay?" He looked surprised.

"Yeah. Okay. I can't say I'll forget what you did, but...well, you apologized to Jal. If he can let it go…"

"He said he can." His voice went low and husky. He started to turn to go but then paused. "Allie, you look beautiful."

"Thanks." I didn't want to think about how close I was to crying.

While we had an interpreter for the majority of the ceremony, TJ's girlfriend, Carrie, would be doing the interpreting for the wedding vows. She was a natural, having picked it up quicker than most hearing people did. She'd told us a couple days ago that she was considering going into either education with a focus on those with hearing disabilities, or becoming an interpreter herself.

Her parents sat up front, looking proud enough to burst. They were amazing. They'd liked TJ from moment one and hadn't even blinked over the differences between the two. Now, watching TJ standing at Jal's side, his face glowing as he stared at Carrie, I had a suspicion that these two would be one of the few high school sweethearts who actually made it.

He'd hit a growth spurt over the last few months and was now pushing five-nine. He'd gotten into playing basketball lately. Jal played with him quite a bit at the community center, and TJ had decided to try out for the school team in the fall. When I'd asked him about it, he'd said, "*I can't hear, but my legs and arms and everything works fine. Other deaf people do it. Why can't I?*"

I was so proud of him, I hurt sometimes.

He smiled at me as I walked up the aisle, between both of my fathers.

Mom had come into the room shortly after Kendrick had left and had said that she and Tyson had talked and that if I wanted my biological father to walk me down the aisle, Tyson wouldn't be hurt by it. I'd only thought about it for a few seconds before I said yes, I wanted them both to do it.

388

Weddings were a symbol of new beginnings. Maybe something good would grow from having us all together. Kendrick had never been a perfect father, but he'd never completely abandoned me as many men in his position would have. Tyson had given me the stable father figure at home. It only seemed right that they both give me away.

Then I saw Jal.

His eyes were locked on me like nothing else existed, and my heart skipped a beat. The rest of the world faded away. The vows, the rings, all of it passed by in a blur. It was all formality – a wanted formality of course – but we belonged to each from the moment we first met. We were just making it official.

When he kissed me, the earth finally seemed to stop spinning and everything re-aligned. This was real. It was all real. He was mine, and I was his and we were married.

My head was spinning again when I finally sat down. It could have been from the champagne or the lack of food, but I suspected it was a combination of everything that was making me light-headed.

Somebody pushed a plate into my hands, and I looked up, met Ginnifer's eyes. She gave me another one of her cool smiles. "If you pass out on your wedding day, you'll be sorry. Trust me, I know."

I frowned, wondering if there was a story behind those words, but instead of asking, I popped a bit of toast with brie into my mouth.

"I fainted at my wedding. I hadn't eaten, didn't want to risk having anybody *see* me eat." She glanced around. "It's such a passé thing to do – eat in public. But then again, so is passing out."

She sat in the seat next to me, holding a plate of her own. After I'd eaten a couple of bites, she sampled a crudité.

"You made an excellent choice with the caterer, Allie."

"You recommended him."

"But you chose him." She studied Jal, dancing with my mother. "Just as you chose my son. You have excellent taste."

"I like to think so."

She nodded and rose. "Remember, the car will be here in a half hour. Enjoy the honeymoon. I'm going to find my husband for a dance."

Husband. I had one of those now. I decided to follow my mother-in-law's example.

I spent the rest of my reception in my husband's arms, my head on his chest. It didn't matter if it was a fast song or a slow one, that was where I stayed. I never wanted to leave.

"Are you excited?" he asked, his lips next to my ear.

I looked up at him. "For the trip? Damn straight. I've always wanted to see New Zealand."

His bare fingers tripped across the bare skin of my back. "No, wife. By what I'm going to do to you tonight..."

Chapter 12

Allie

Audrey Anne Lindstrom lay in her crib in her nursery, my perfect little angel.

The whirlwind of activity that started within days of me seeing the little pink *plus* on the pregnancy test hadn't stopped until mid-January.

I loved the house where we'd lived, where I first slept with Jal, but he'd been insistent that his child – his children – have the kind of house that was a home, not a fortress. And he wanted us to pick it out together.

Granted, the place was still huge, but it definitely looked like a place for a family. There was a yard and a playset. And a pool – behind a stone fence with a gate.

All these *ands* – along with others like a family room with an in-home theater – were courtesy of Jal, who simply didn't know the meaning of excess and whose bank account seemed to have no end.

I'd drawn a line at the bowling alley in the basement.

"It's not like you're going to go bowling anytime soon, huh?" I asked her, reaching down to stroke one plump cheek.

She jumped, but it was the touch that had made her move, not my voice.

We'd had her tested as soon as possible since there was a good chance that my mother's hearing loss was genetic. I'd been torn when the news had come back that Audrey was profoundly deaf. It didn't make her any less perfect in my eyes, but I knew how the world worked, how things would be harder for her.

But as my mother had told me a hundred times, *obstacles in life are what makes us strong.*

Audrey would be just fine.

We'd make sure of that.

Arms, warm and strong, came around me, and Jal pressed a kiss to my shoulder. "Hello, my beautiful wife," he said softly.

"Hello, my handsome husband."

We stood there, watching Audrey sleep.

Jal stroked his hands up and down my arms, and I relaxed into the warmth of his body. "I can't believe we have to wait three more weeks," I said.

"After what I saw?" Jal sounded strained. "It might take me six years before I'm ready to put you through that again."

I laughed softly. "Don't worry. I'll help you get over it."

Turning, I slid my arms around his neck, my stomach clenching at the heat in his eyes. We might not be able to have actual sex yet, but there were still plenty of things I enjoyed doing to him in the meantime.

But that wasn't at the front of my mind at the moment. We hadn't talked about certain…things much. After a minute, I pulled away because we needed to talk, which was hard to do it when we were so close.

I twisted my wedding ring as I looked out the window.

"You know, there are changes in medical technology, new breakthroughs," I said. "There are so many options that weren't available for Mom or Tyson, or even TJ. We can–"

Jal cut me off with a soft kiss.

Then, he signed, *"She's perfect. If she wants to look into options when she's older, then we'll support her. But to me, she's already perfect."*

I stepped into his embrace and rested my head on his chest. The steady sound of his heartbeat worked through me, relaxed me. It'd been nearly two years since we'd first met and our lives had been turned upside-down. Getting to where we were had been hard, but it'd been worth it.

I had a tentative, but real, relationship with my biological father now. Mallory was one of my closest friends. Jal's parents were amazing. The last of the chill between Ginnifer and me had thawed when I told her I was pregnant. Tao, Tony, and Lyrrie were still together. Diamond and Paisley were still furious, but word had gotten out about what they'd done – I was pretty sure Ginnifer had been responsible for it – and now it was the two of them that people talked about behind their backs.

"You know," I said softly. "When you first walked into FOCUS, I couldn't have imagined that we'd end up here, like this."

"Me either," Jal admitted. "But I wouldn't change a thing."

As I thought about everything that had happened, the good and the bad alike, I realized I wouldn't either. Those months had been hard, but it'd made the two of us stronger, made our relationship stronger.

"I love you." I pushed myself up on my toes to brush my lips against his.

"I love you too." He brushed my hair out of my face and then grinned. "Now, what do you say we find some creative ways of relieving tension that don't break the doctor's orders."

I laughed and let him pull me from the nursery, down the hall, and into our bedroom.

The End

More from M.S. Parker:

Con Man
Indecent Encounter
The Client
Unlawful Attraction
Chasing Perfection
Blindfold
Club Prive
The Pleasure Series
Exotic Desires
Pure Lust
Casual Encounter
Sinful Desires
Twisted Affair
Serving HIM

Acknowledgement

First, I would like to thank all of my readers. Without you, my books would not exist. I truly appreciate each and every one of you.

A big "thanks" goes out to all the Facebook fans, street team, beta readers, and advanced reviewers. You are a HUGE part of the success of the series.

I have to thank my PA, Shannon Hunt. Without you my life would be a complete and utter mess. Also a big "thank you" goes out to my editor Lynette and my wonderful cover designer, Sinisa. You make my ideas and writing look so good.

About The Author

M. S. Parker is a USA Today Bestselling author and the author of the Erotic Romance series, Club Privè and Chasing Perfection.

Living in Las Vegas, she enjoys sitting by the pool with her laptop writing on her next spicy romance.

Growing up all she wanted to be was a dancer, actor or author. So far only the latter has come true but M. S. Parker hasn't retired her dancing shoes just yet. She is still waiting for the call for her to appear on Dancing With The Stars.

When M. S. isn't writing, she can usually be found reading–oops, scratch that! She is always writing.

Printed in Great Britain
by Amazon